HEALER'S MAGICK
a novel

F. L. Karsner

SeaDog Press, LLC
Ponte Vedra Beach, Florida

Healer's Magick by F. L. Karsner

ISBN: 978-1-943369-00-3

SEADOG PRESS, LLC
830 A1A North Suite 13
Ponte Vedra Beach, Florida 32082

For information about special discounts for bulk purchases, please contact SeaDog Press, LLC, at **business@flkarsner.com**.

Cover Design: Rik Feeney / **www.RickFeeney.com**

Cover Photographs:
© Mousesanya | Dreamstime.com
© Mircea Bezergheanu | Dreamstime.com
© Creative Me | Bigstock Photo
© Bildagentur Zoonar GmbH | Shutterstock
© matthi | Shutterstock

Ship Logo: © Dn Br | Shutterstock
Ouroboros Design: Elizabeth Pampalone / www.JaxComputerChic.com

Dedication

This novel is dedicated to my darling daughters, Taylor and Caroline, who listened to my stories as children and encouraged me to write, and to my dear husband, Garry, who brings magick to my life every day.

The serpent is an ancient symbol of healing and is seen in early drawings wrapped around the caduceus of the Greek god Hermes. Many ancient cultures regarded the serpent as sacred and used it in healing rituals. A serpent devouring its tail is called an ouroboros. It is symbolic of immortality, the eternal unity of all things, the cycle of birth and death. It unites opposites such as the conscious and unconscious mind. It has a meaning of infinity or wholeness and is the Western world equivalent of Yin-Yang.

Acknowledgments

A very special thank you goes to my daughter, Taylor, who plodded through the original, roughly written, book with never a complaint and only encouragement to continue writing. She believed in me, was my constant muse, and often saw the true meaning of the writing more quickly than I.

My content editor, Rik Feeney, was instrumental in keeping me grounded and on track. His editing expertise enabled me to put form to my ideas and cohesion to my work. Nothing less than perfect ever meets his expectations. Without him I would have been stuck in the Highlands somewhere with no way home! His unwavering guidance saw me through to the finish.

My technical editor, daughter Caroline Bowen, graciously saved me from grammatical errors and faulty punctuation that I usually excel at. Her attention to detail is such a talent, and her insightful and learned review and edit of my work made this novel infinitely better. She and Rik are merciless and force you to be better than you are.

My inspirational sister, Dorothy, was constantly in my head as I tried to give meaningful passage to *principles and beliefs that both she and I were taught as children. Her life is a living testament to those.*

And to my very special brother, Jackie. His strength of will and character came blazing through in one of my characters. I almost laughed when I realized who he was! He is a treasure.

This novel would never have been written without the constant encouragement of my dear friends, Dena and Worley Faver, Midge Mercer, Flinn Dallis, Larry Hall, and Linda Zollar and Bess Fleming. Friends and family give purpose to this and any writing. My life is rich with both.

And a very grateful thank you to my Scottish ancestors whose lives I can only wonder about. Knowing them would have been an honor. They are my people — they are my clansmen.

Lastly, and of most importance, a heartfelt thank you to Garry, my dearest husband and soulmate, who held my hand every step of the way. He is priceless, and I cherish him. We will forever walk together.

Chapter 1

"Don't just stand there looking like the idiot louts I know ye ta be! Move yer arse! Hold his arms! Tighter now!" She screamed at them as if they were miles away, rather than right at her elbows. This young man's strength had amazed her, as well as the others, who were engaged in keeping their brother still so she could administer the life-saving interventions that only she could.

The first order of business was to stop the bleeding. Actually, one of the brothers had done a fairly good job of applying a tourniquet as soon as the accident had occurred. But beyond that, they had no clue as to what to do next. The healer meticulously cleaned the wound and knew there was nothing to be done except the one procedure she most disliked to perform, amputation.

"Here, hold his head up so I can pour this down his throat. It will ease the pain greatly and, if we're lucky, he'll lose consciousness and we can get on with this amputation."

"What! Yer going to take his leg off? Ye can't do that! He's just a boy for God's sake!" yelled the huge brother, called Jack.

The oldest brother, a man named Alex, was holding the young lad down. He then reached out and lay his hand on Jack's.

"Jack. The leg's gone man. There's no choice. It's barely hanging on as it is. We need to let this woman help him, brother."

The other brother, called Hector, nodded his agreement and Jack turned away as if he couldn't bear to watch. He was closest in age to the youngest brother lying on the table, and felt great responsibility for him.

Within just a few minutes, the medication began to work its magick and the lad drifted off into oblivion.

"Thanks be to the Creator," whispered Alex.

Even though the lower leg was only hanging on by a few tendons and loose skin, it was a gruesome surgical procedure to totally sever the remaining bits of bone and muscle. The bleeding was under control, and the healer worked diligently to amputate below the knee, which was always a much better choice than above it. But, sometimes the situation would not allow this.

She worked quickly with much experience behind her. Her stitches were even and made with great precision, something she prided herself on.

"Just one more moment. Hold the upper leg straight! Don't let it move! One more second!

Now! There!"

The only thing left was to bandage the wound carefully and watch the young lad. She would pray that infection would not set in, but working in these less-than-desirable conditions, it often did occur.

"There. Rest easy now, young laddie."

They were all exhausted from such a grisly ordeal, more mental and emotional exhaustion than physical, but requiring all their strength and concentration.

The healer spoke as she turned to face the three men, all brothers to the wounded one. She picked up the bottle of vile smelling herbs she had poured down the throat of the wounded boy, then dropped her hands and arms as if they were heavy weights. Exhaustion had set in now. Her mass of fiery, curly hair, usually pinned up when performing this type of surgery, had begun to loose itself, with small tendrils falling at her face and neck. She brushed it back with her hand and looked up again at the three men who had assisted her.

"Well. If he survives the night, then maybe he'll make it."

Those words were spoken in a very deep, harsh voice by Alexander, the leader of the small band of brothers. He had simply spoken them before the healer had the chance. But her thoughts were exactly the same.

Alexander's brogue was so strong the healer had to think a moment before she understood what he had said. In fact, all their brogues took some filtering before the words made sense to her. They were all actually speaking Gaelic, even though they could speak English as well.

Probably a good thing, too, as there were rumors that the Crown would be insisting that all Scots must speak English in future, but that hadn't been declared law just yet. No matter, these brothers spoke their preferred language, Gaelic, as did Caitlin, the healer. She came from the Isle of Skye on the western side of the country, and these men all hailed from the upper Highlands, which was almost a country unto itself in that the brogue was greater, and some of their customs were a bit different than where she came from. Still, countrymen they all were.

The healer turned around and fastened her gaze on Jack.

"Now. For you, big brother. You with the bleeding calf. Come over here. Now." "I'm all right. Don't need no doctoring. I'll be all right," said the big man.

"Yes, and I can grow wings and fly. Stop your blustering and sit in this chair."

The healer took one look at Jack's leg and could see the bullet had gone completely through the calf, which was actually good. If it had lodged, then she would have had to remove it also. But, as it was, she simply cleaned the wound thoroughly and applied ointment and clean bandages.

"You're right. You'll be fine. But change this bandage tomorrow and put some of this ointment on it."

She handed him a tin with some of the medication to take with him.

Jack mumbled something that may have been his way of saying thanks, but she was still having some difficulty understanding their brogue, and his words were more like mutterings.

"Now, all of you. Get back to your business, whatever that may be, and leave me to mine, taking care of your brother."

The healer was quite small in stature, but issued orders as if she were a Captain of the Guards! And, too, the large, black wolf who had not left her side, gave them pause.

"Go, now. He's going to sleep for quite some time. Check with me tomorrow," she said as she ushered them out of the cave entrance.

The looks on their faces said they were not too keen on leaving their brother in this cave with just a woman to look out for him. But, she seemed rather adamant about her orders.

"Remember. Do not tell anyone he is here, and be sure no one follows you when you return. That was our agreement and I'll know if you don't keep it! And, if you don't, I promise I'll let my beast loose on you!"

***

The three brothers left begrudgingly, but knew Ian would be better off with her than with them. In fact, they were almost envious of his being with this woman, this healer, as she was a most interesting woman and none of them had failed to see her beauty, even if she was screaming at them most of the time! When the light struck her hair, the fire it gave off was stunning. And when she turned her aqua gaze directly on you, you felt her energy coming off in waves. Was she indeed the witch some said she was?

"Ye don't think maybe we need to stand guard at the cave entrance?" asked Jack.

This brother was a giant of a man who stood taller than all the others, and tried to use his greater body size to his advantage. His red face indicated he was not at all pleased to be leaving their baby brother, Ian, in the hands of the healer, or witch, or whatever she called herself. All the MacKinnon brothers were very large men, but Jack even more so than the others.

"No matter, witch or no, Ian lives and she's responsible for that. I need no more explanation," this coming from Hector, brother number three.

Hector spent much of his time trying to be the peacemaker amongst the four brothers.

That could be a full-time job if he let it be. Most of the time he was successful in taming tempers and acting as negotiator, but at times like this, stressful times that is, bridling the emotions of this crew was taxing.

"We don't know but what she'll cast a spell on Ian and we'll never know what happened to him! I'm telling ye she can't be trusted!"

Jack was still fuming, his face still glowing as red as his hair. Of the four brothers, he was the only brother with red hair and blue eyes. The others were all dark haired with dark eyes, the same as their father. Nothing pleased these fellows more than to tease their overly-large brother about being the "fair" one. That would get a rise out of him when nothing else would!

Hector realized Jack usually vented his worry and anxiety through angry ranting and threats of violence to someone, anyone! So, as the three of them walked through the trees to where they had hidden their horses, he walked alongside Jack.

"Brother. She could have refused to help him at the outset but she didn't. She's a true healer and that's a rarity about these parts. She's already eased his pain and saved his life. Let that be enough for this day," said Hector, throwing his arm around Jack's shoulder, as he was only just slightly shorter, and giving it a squeeze.

"Pull your bristles back down now, man," he chuckled quietly.

Meanwhile, Alexander, who talked less than the others, but thought more and was known for his ability to plan great strategy, considered their next actions, or maybe inactions. Much thought must be given to their situation, and after he had figured it out, he would discuss it with the others, but not until he had considered all angles. Sometimes he really wished he wasn't the oldest as the burden could be onerous. But, as Da had taught him early on, there were some things in life that simply could not be changed, so make the most of them.

***

Back in the cave, Caitlin carefully looked at her young charge, checking him out from head to toe. She pushed at her hair once again, and mopped at her forehead,

"Oh, my dear boy. However shall I deal with you upon your awakening?"

The healer had treated the wounded far longer than she cared to remember and some of the memories still haunted her. So this wounded young man, boy actually, was just the latest in a long line of young men whose lives had forever been changed because one country or another, one clan or another, had decided they must annihilate each other rather than try to come to terms that would work for both sides. She often thought the male of the species had something within that prevented their being able to reason with one another. At any rate, they had more difficulty than the females did, or so she thought.

Caitlin had carefully bandaged the young warrior's leg, or what was left of it. The lad had sustained a mighty slash from a Lochaber axe that literally took off the lower part of his leg. The brothers had all watched intently as the healer had severed the leg, as if to make sure she did it properly! But no matter how many times she performed that brutal surgery, she always found herself wishing she could do something, anything, to save the limb. However, as any healer knew, saving a life was the most important thing, and sometimes that may require losing a limb in the process.

After the brothers finally left, with a great push from the healer, she was lost in thought, remembering another young man she had tended. It seemed so long ago, but in actuality it wasn't all that long at all. But she remembered it well.

Chapter 2

"What have you done?!"

The tall soldier stood in front of her, his highly decorated uniform informing her of his importance, his face ablaze with anger. He took her by the shoulders, lifted her small frame off the ground, and shook her to the very bone, causing her hair to tumble down her back in a mass of curls.

"He was alive this morning, and now he's dead! What spell did you concoct to bring that about?"

When he had asked for her help with saving his son, he had called her "healer," but when she had been unable to save the young lad, he had called her "witch."

Caitlin had come from a long line of healers. Becoming a healer didn't seem to have been a choice; it was just something that was bred into her very fiber, her very being. Some had thought it was a calling of some sort, but she knew no matter the reason, she was indeed meant to be a healer. But there were those that thought healer was another name for witch!

She had to laugh just a bit when she thought about that word. Just what was a witch anyway? Someone who had extraordinary powers? Someone who could disappear at will? One who could mix up a batch of potions that could harm or cure? Well, she wasn't aware of any extraordinary powers, and she had not disappeared anytime, but she did mix up potions now and then. Well, then perhaps she was a witch, but if so, her powers were always used only for good.

But, even so, using all her powers, she was unable to save this man's young son, as well as the other dozen or so who had contracted a most virulent disease. She had recognized this disease at once, having seen it several times before, and knew perhaps a few of them would survive, but most would go the way of this young one. Something inside, something intuitive, told her there would most certainly be a cure for this devastating illness one day, and she would not stop her efforts to find it. But for now, it still claimed most of its victims. She seemed to be able to fight it off, herself, and that told her there was surely something about being exposed to it as a child, and surviving, that had made her impervious to its clutches.

Learning to administer treatments takes many years, and then figuring out how to battle any new disease was even more challenging, but exciting at the same time. She often had dreams that the future would hold much more information that would bring about cures that now seemed beyond anyone's abilities. Indeed, on occasion, a traveler or bard coming from Edinburgh would tell of the many wonders real physicians in the city were discovering. Caitlin so wished she could learn more and certainly knew there was so much more to learn. But still, her skills had been passed on by those before her and she was confident in her abilities. Generations before her had used these same techniques and many of the sick and wounded had survived because of them.

"I will burn you for this, witch!"

Caitlin had told this officer, Regimental Commander Bernard Campbell, that his son and most of the other young men that he brought with him, had not survived in spite of her efforts, great though they were. The terrible irony of this was that these very brave young men, all members of the many groups fighting for The Bonnie Prince, had survived the Battle of Culloden and were headed back to their homes in the Western Isles of the country, and some would go on as far as the Hebrides. This Commander

Campbell would now be the bearer of this news to the families of the soldiers, an unspeakably difficult task for anyone, even a seasoned soldier such as he.

As he set her back down, he trembled, his grief palpable. Caitlin sensed his anger. It began to grow as he continued his glaring appraisal of her.

However, the Commander was not the only person experiencing emotional disturbance. Caitlin's brain was struggling to keep a balance between the fear that was grasping her, and the anger that she felt building at the same time. Her good sense told her to be very afraid of this man, but her temper was about to get the best of her and she felt it boiling up inside!

"There will be a price to pay for your witchery! We'll exact punishment and you will feel our grief while you burn!"

Campbell grabbed the healer by the shoulders once again, and as he did so, he yelled out in pain!

"Ah, you're burning my hands! Stop it! Look! You've caused blisters! Witch!"

With that, he shoved her back, causing her to land on her backside, and to cry out when she hit the floor. He strode out and quickly jumped on his big mount and galloped away, kicking his horse violently in his flanks.

"Burning his hands?" Is that what he said? What was he talking about?

Caitlin vaguely remembered another incident when someone accused her of burning their hands. She was just a girl, about ten years old and she had come upon Colin Sutherland, a neighbor boy, who had tied a kitten's front feet together and watched as the small kitten cried out in pain.

"Watch Caitlin! He's crippled! Ha! Let's tie the back ones too!"

And Colin proceeded to bring out another piece of string. Caitlin had never witnessed such cruelty to any creature and something inside her glowed red hot! She reached over to Colin and grabbed his hands in hers, all the while staring at him.

"You are so mean, Colin Sutherland! Stop it this minute!"

Colin tried to break away from her, and then started yelling loudly. "You're burning me! Stop it Caitlin! It hurts!"

Caitlin had no idea what he was talking about, but she took her hands away and he fled immediately. Caitlin untied the kitten and held it close.

She had totally forgotten about the incident until now. Had she really burned the Commander and Colin? Then, just as she had done with the first "burning" incident, she tucked the memory of it somewhere back in the recesses of her mind. Perhaps she would think about it again one day. Perhaps not. She shook her head and got on about packing the few items that she would take with her.

Caitlin had indeed seen families, in their grief, react to the loss of a loved one in ways that were always out of character for those involved. Grief drastically alters one's thought processes. Emotions, rather than reason, are riding high at those times. And often, acting on emotions brings even more disaster. In truth, grief seems to have no bounds and cares even less for consequences.

Commander Campbell would report that she was totally to blame, when in actuality, she prevented spread of the disease by insisting the soldiers be left in her care until such time as the disease had spent itself out. Only after that time had passed would they be allowed to leave her and go to their loved ones. Of the eighteen young men, all soldiers, traveling together back to their villages, only four survived, and they had already departed and were on their way home.

And that was only because Caitlin cared for them and did everything within her power to keep them alive. Without her care they, too, would have succumbed to the deadly illness. But, grief has a way of clouding the judgment of almost all families and they most certainly would blame her. And, she knew only too well they would act on their threats. Trust a Scot to avenge a loved one!

Caitlin disliked leaving the last body, the Commander's son, alone. But, she knew the Commander would come back as soon as it was light and take his son home for burial. So, once again, she had to steal away in the dark of night, taking only her medicines with her.

As she left the cottage, the moon had already risen and sent its warm yellow glow over the whole area. She looked about and felt this could have been a wonderful place to make a permanent home.

"Will this never end, this running to escape in order to survive?" she spoke to herself, and perhaps the night owl that sat just above her head in the blackthorn tree. He hooted to her in a mournful tone as if he, too, felt her anguish.

Chapter 3

Caitlin's first escape had happened only a few months ago when she had found it impossible to stay on the Isle of Skye where she had lived all her life. An unlikely event beyond her control had dictated that she leave Uncle Wabi, who was her only family, and her friends behind and make a new life for herself, someplace where she was not known and could not be found. Her roots were in Skye, but now, apparently, her destiny lay elsewhere.

After some long days of walking, she had found this deserted, thatched hut to live in, and thought it was distant enough that she would not be discovered. And, other than being a bit lonely, she was quite enjoying the small hut and had begun creating a home for herself. But now she needed to leave again! But where would she go?

At present, she must just try to escape this mad man. She would forever remember the anger in the soldier's eyes as he held her in his grip. She must lose herself somewhere in the forests and hills or mountains, maybe even go as far as the upper Highlands, across the Grampians, where she had heard many go who wish to be lost to civilization. Apparently, the ruggedness of that countryside deters some from entering such wilderness. But, that just might be what she needed to do, go where others would not.

She had traveled quite a ways, and watched constantly. She hoped no one was following her. Traveling only at night, when moonlight provided enough light, she stayed deep within the forest. It had been almost a fortnight now and she had seen no one, so she was beginning to feel that perhaps she had escaped Commander Campbell at last.

"Well, Caitlin, my girl, what now?" again speaking only to herself, as she did quite often these days.

She knew she was somewhere on the edge of the Grampians as she had struggled to get over the lower mountains and had only passed a few villages along the way. First of all, she must seek shelter in a place that was not easily found even though she truly believed that Commander Campbell had forgotten about her, but no need to be careless. She began to scout the area, and hoped to find another hut, as she did so like the last one.

After several hours of scouring the area, there was not a hut or shanty or lean-to anywhere to be found. She sat down and had a lunch of one of the apples she had picked some way back down the road. She must find shelter, and obviously, she couldn't live on berries and fruit forever. Her packet of food was all but gone as it was.

She gathered up her small sling bag and throwing it across her shoulder, she looked about and listened carefully. What did she hear? What did she smell? It sounded like water maybe. And as she walked over the next small hill covered with heather and short grasses, she could hear the water more clearly. Ah. A river! Well, that was a good find. Rivers meant fresh water, and fish! She was indeed beginning to need more nourishment than fruit could provide. But, still, the problem of shelter had not been solved. As she walked closer to the stream, she got on her knees and leaned over the water, splashing her face and drinking at the same time. The coolness of the water was refreshing after walking such a distance.

"Well, healer. A bath would be a good idea also," more verbal communication with herself and whatever or whomever else may be watching.

She wandered over to a small area of brush and discarded her shoes and clothing, slipping quietly into the water, which was just a small stream at this part of the river, and not very deep.

Still, she immersed herself totally and let the water relieve some of the tension that she had carried with her for such a long time.

She felt much better now, and certainly smelled better, she thought! She saw her reflection in the water and pinned her hair up as well as she could. Then she redressed herself in her ankle length blue dress with long sleeves, and buttoned the many buttons down the front; she put that cumbersome petticoat back on, and slipped her feet into her small leather boots. These boots were made of the softest leather, and they had protected her feet from many cuts and bruises, and kept them warm as well. But, they were beginning to look like they may not have a lot of life left in them. She knew that were she at home, she would take them to old Fergus who would put a new sole on them and make them shine like new leather! But, that was another life, and she wouldn't dwell on that anymore.

Chapter 4

"Well, now, back to the task at hand. Shelter." She saw some large trees up ahead, with lots of brush as well. It was a bit of a struggle to go down the path to reach the trees, and she stopped to catch her breath. As she got up, she heard a sound coming from the brush nearby.

Was it something whimpering? Sounded just like a baby!

"Oh, please, don't let it be a baby!" she said aloud. She knew of several cases where a distraught mother had left her new infant in the woods, hoping someone would find it, and the outcome was not usually a good one.

She stopped again. The crying and whimpering was still coming from the brush. As she bent over and pulled the lower brush limbs aside, she quickly lurched backward with a gasp! It was indeed a baby! And it was definitely crying! And it was so beautiful! Caitlin couldn't resist picking it up. As soon as she cradled it in her arms, the baby stopped its crying and closed its eyes, as if so relieved someone had finally found it. Caitlin smiled at it and stroked the thick hair on its head and looked at its ears, which seemed much too long. And its feet were enormous! She had never been this close to a wolf pup before, but thought this one was a beautiful specimen if ever there was one! Its fur was raven black and its underside a soft, pale, creamy color. And its feet were definitely too large! When she went to reposition the pup in her arms, however, it let out a howl that surprised her.

"What was that about?" she asked the little creature, holding him up under his front paws, letting his small body dangle in the air. After deciding that the cry was one of pain, the healer began to search for the source of the distress. It didn't take much inspection to discover what was ailing this little fellow. She put him down and as he tried to take a few steps, he fell immediately and she could see he was dragging his left hind leg. This small critter had a broken leg, which was usually a death sentence in animals this young.

"Ah, so that's why you were left here," crooned the healer, gently rubbing his injured leg. Caitlin was fairly knowledgeable about the animal world, having lived with her grandparents as a child, then later with Uncle Wabi. Her grandfather had been a woodsman and Uncle Wabi a dog trainer. She had gone on many walkabouts with her uncle and always learned something about an animal on every trip. So, she knew the pup's mother had probably left him as is common practice in the animal world when a newborn pup has a disability. The mother wolf would have had some other pups to care for as well, and would have had to make a choice as to whether they would all be subject to predators, or to leave the small pup to fend for himself. It was not really a choice; it was a reality that all animals have to deal with.

She placed the pup down on a small blanket she kept in her pouch. As she gingerly felt the bone in his leg, she went about positioning it so it was in the proper position to heal. She had done this many times for humans, so doing it for a wolf pup didn't seem too difficult.

The pup whimpered as she continued with her healing process. However, as she tied the bandage up neatly, the pup stopped his crying and licked the back of her hand. In that instant, a bond was formed between the two homeless creatures.

"Well, little one, you'll be as good as new, now!" The healer spoke to the pup as if he could understand every word. And, who knows, perhaps he could. As it was, she picked him up carefully, balancing him in the crook of one arm, and carrying her pouch in the other.

"Looks like we both need shelter, little buddy." So she continued walking to the bottom of the hill where the trees and brush were.

The walk down the hill was even more difficult, what with trying to balance the little pup and carry her pouch. Plus, she was really beginning to tire from such long days of walking and trying to stay hidden in the forests.

As she finally reached the bottom of the long hill, she took one last step and, unexpectedly, found herself falling—falling—falling, and abruptly coming to a halt many feet below the surface. That was quite a hole into which she had dropped! Her backside was smarting, and she was afraid she may have further wounded the pup in the fall. But, there was no noise coming from his direction, so she placed him on the ground next to her.

"Healer, you better check yourself out first," she said to herself, and the pup, too, if he was listening. She stood up, brushed herself off, and other than a good- sized lump on her right elbow, and probably her bottom too if she could see it, she seemed to be in one piece. However, it was very dark and difficult to see.

She reached inside her medicine bag and brought out a small candle she kept for emergencies as sometimes she had to perform surgeries and other healing procedures under circumstances that were not the best. At least a candle helped when more light was not available.

She lit the candle and held it high above her head. Apparently, they were in some sort of cavern with high ceilings and a long narrow passageway. She was a bit unsure about moving farther in, but could see no way of getting back to the top of the opening, so she slowly made her way, still holding the candle high and carrying the pup again. He had awakened from the fall and had perked his ears up and started sniffing the air, looking about from side to side. The floor was sloping ever downward as she continued to walk. Then she had to make a choice as to which path to follow as they had come to a junction. Should she go left or right? Both paths were worn and plenty wide enough to get through, so she went to the left, pausing just long enough to see there were markings on the walls. It was apparent that this cave had been used by someone before her. And maybe they were still here! Her senses heightened a bit and she looked, listened, and put her nose on alert. When all other senses failed her, she knew her nose would not.

Apparently, this was a genetic trait that was passed down the long line of healers. She recalled stories about her healer ancestors who had used this same sense in their time, too. She was glad she also had this trait at her disposal as it had served her well.

The pup was beginning to squirm in her arms, and she stopped to let him down, not sure he was yet able to stand on his own. But, he did stand, and with his broken leg being bound tightly, he dashed off but returned quickly and began to prance around her as if he had use of all his legs. Perhaps having never had use of his hind leg, he didn't know anything different. The healer smiled as she watched him move right along with his ears standing at attention and his nose twitching as he, too, made use of his exceptional sense of smell. Just having another living being with her somehow made her a bit less anxious, but not totally.

"Well, little buddy, there doesn't seem to be anyone else here with us, and I do believe we are well hidden down here. But how are we ever going to get out?"

Her words sounded like they came from a very composed person, but her insides were jittery and she was feeling somewhat fearful.

Caitlin had walked quite a way down the path and presently could smell water, fresh water, somewhere nearby. Perhaps the river they had just left ran underground as well. If so, that was good, as it meant there was an exit somewhere also. She continued walking until she came to a large room-like area. She immediately knew this had been a place where others had lived, for their bones were still here!

"Oh, Holy Rusepheus!" she yelled, grabbing at her throat before she caught herself. The pup started a low growl and she laughed as she saw his fur standing up on his back.

This little wolf was exhibiting signs he would be a great protector if she ever needed one! Unlike most people, Caitlin was not afraid of bones, but she was not expecting to come upon them, so she was taken aback, as it were. And, a quick look at them told her they had been here many decades, and that was somewhat reassuring.

"Well, my friend, looks like we are somewhere close to the Great Glen and we can at least be safe for a bit until we figure out exactly what we're going to do. I suspect we should move on, higher into the Grampians, but for now, we have shelter, and safety and I know how to catch fish!"

The healer continued to wander through the endless cave and found many items that would be of great use to her as she tried to make this place a home until such time as something better presented itself.

The very first task she undertook, however, was to create a resting place for the bones that represented others before her. Something deep within her demanded she treat these bones with respect, and she performed a ritual she was taught years ago. When she went through the ritual, honoring these persons from long ago, there was a feeling of deja vu, as if she had done this before and she had a kinship with these people, but she knew that couldn't be. But, whatever, her spirit rested easy, knowing reverence had been observed for her unknown cave dwellers.

Caitlin had passed a village nearby as they came across the hills, and before they fell into the giant hole that was the opening to the cave. They had been in the cave for an entire day and were still looking for a way out when she came upon a large pool of water, back in the far end of the larger room. Following a well-worn path behind the pool, she found herself going up at a slight angle, then more so, and finally she walked to what looked like a large bush standing in the pathway. With just a little tugging, she was able to pull the bush aside and knew she had discovered the exit! Well, thank goodness for that she thought. Being safe was one thing, but being unable to get out of a cave was another! Apparently, this cave had served many purposes over the years and she and her friend were just the latest inhabitants.

Now that she knew how to come and go, Caitlin felt much relieved and decided the two of them would make their surroundings as pleasant as they could, and then they would venture into the village. Healers have a need to use their skills and all villages are in need of at least one healer. She could possibly exchange her skills for food or, perhaps, even charge for her services if there were any persons of means in the village. Actually, she had little wish for anything other than basic necessities and being allowed to work her magick, as it were. She had found a place to begin building a new life and, hopefully, she would make friends in the village as well. She felt a real need to connect with others.

Caitlin was ever so pleased to find this cave, a place where she could be reasonably comfortable and, for the moment, safe from those men pursuing her. The cave itself had obviously been home to many over the years. She had found indentations in the walls where candles had been placed. There was also a stash of candles, heavy with drippings, and they provided plenty of light. A hole had been created in the ceiling of one room where she could build a fire and the smoke could escape. There was even a small platform that was apparently used as a bed. Plus, there were several large tables where she could deposit her many herbs and medicines that she used in her practice as healer.

She went about cleaning the cave and bringing in heather and flowers from the surrounding countryside. Within just a few days she had made the place actually very appealing. The heather entered your nostrils the moment you entered the cave and wove its lingering scent throughout. She would exchange her healing skills for some items as she found need for them.

Food was not too difficult and the village was nearby.

"Well, little big-footed one. I do believe we can make this place work for us! It's actually not too bad is it?" The pup's expression was one of adoration. This healer had rescued him and now his purpose was to protect her. And he would.

Chapter 5

Many miles south of the cave, down in the borderlands on the English side, another young woman was having her own difficulties as well. But unlike Caitlin, Lady Millicent Sinclair lived in a very large castle with every comfort one could desire. Her windows were covered with brocade drapes, she drank from silver goblets, and servants were at her elbows at all times. But even with all that opulence, it was a most undesirable place to live.

At the very moment Caitlin was struggling to keep a young patient alive, Lady Millie found herself grieving the death of a loved one. She paced the floor of her large bedroom mumbling to herself as she did so. She thought about the conversation she had just had with her father, Lord Sinclair.

"Father! We must go to Scotland and visit Grandmother and Aunt Moira! Grandpa has passed away and they're alone. We're their only family now and they need our help. How will they ever be able to run that huge estate without someone to help them?"

She flung the letter she had received from her aunt at her father's feet. The man was so exasperating she could hardly bear it!

Lord Sinclair stood up, stretching to his full height, which was impressive.

"Millie. Stop your ridiculous tirade. We'll go to Scotland when the estate passes to you and not before! As it is, the estate goes to your grandmother upon your grandfather's death, then to your Aunt Moira as she is the only surviving child. It would have come to your Mother, but as she has already passed away, it will eventually come to you, my dearest daughter, after your Aunt Moira dies."

"The old man was quite a capable old gentleman if I must say so and from my reports he has managed his properties very well. But, those two women won't last long on their own, so I expect you will soon be heir to your Grandpa's lands and castle. What a boon that will be to my holdings! When the old women pass and you inherit the lands is when we will make a trip up to that Godforsaken country!"

Lord Sinclair had a great dislike for anything Scottish, but knew that having holdings in the Highlands would put him in good standing with the other landowners.

"But, we'll not return a day before then! Now, talk no more about it!" And he strode from the room stepping on the letter as he continued on his way.

Millie had fled from his rooms and returned to her own where her friend and nursemaid, Dorothea, was waiting for her.

"Oh, Dorothea. Father says we can't go to Scotland for Grandpa's burial. Whatever will Aunt Moira think? She and Grandmother are the only family I have now that Mother has already left us. Some of my fondest memories are of the times we visited there when I was a child."

"Oh, aye, Lady Millie. Your family in Scotland are special to my kin also. Someone from my family has worked on the estate as long as I can remember. I, too, would wish to go back and pay my respects. But, we both know your father's word is law around here. Your Aunt Moira will understand. She always knew her sister had married a man that was not worthy of her, but your grandfather thought it would be a good match, a Scot and an English lord. Of course, he had no way of knowing he had given his daughter into the hands of a violent man. So, now, we have to survive and make the most of whatever we have. We will do this together, milady."

Millie's mother had given birth to another child just a couple of years before Millie was born. It had been a son, but he had only lived for a few days, a baby born before time, actually. Of course,

Lord Sinclair had blamed his wife, insisting that she did not take proper care of his son!

"What did you do? Did you smother him? You never wanted him to begin with! He is dead because of your carelessness!"

Lord Sinclair's wrath had no limit. He had wanted a son so badly and now his son was dead in just a couple of days.

"But I did not cause his death! He was born two months too early. Most babies do not survive if they are born so early! You must believe me!"

"You insipid fool! You never wanted to have a child! How do I know you didn't cause his death! I must have another son I tell you!"

Then, just a year following the baby's death, Lady Sinclair announced that she was carrying another child.

"Then, you will stay in this bed and my son will survive this time!" Sinclair made his pronouncement and knew it would be followed.

Lady Sinclair wrote to her sister, Moira, as soon as the time neared for the baby to be born.

"Moira. Please find someone in the village to come down and help me with the babe. I dread to think what Sinclair will do if another child dies."

Lady Sinclair's family in Scotland were so thrilled to hear that she, Louise, was well and that a new babe was expected shortly.

She fared well during this pregnancy and went the full term with no complications.

During the final month of her pregnancy, late in the evening in the dead of winter, Lady Sinclair sent her chambermaid for the midwife.

"Hurry, Elspeth! This baby is coming quickly! Bring the midwife. Run now!"

Elspeth, a young girl from the village, streaked down the stairs to the lower level. She stopped at the door to Lord Sinclair's chamber and grabbed the attention of his page who stood guard.

"Keifer! Tell Lord Sinclair the Lady is about to deliver the baby and I'm off to get the midwife! Go now! Quickly!"

The chambermaid knew that Lord Sinclair would dismiss her in a minute if she didn't keep him informed of this impending birth. She was assigned to Lady Sinclair, but she was well aware Lord Sinclair made all decisions in this castle, and she needed to keep her position. Her family depended on her.

When the midwife arrived she hurried upstairs and went directly to Lady Sinclair's chamber.

"Now, milady. All will be well. You've been through this before and know you will survive it."

Lady Sinclair paced the room, perspiration shining on her brow. She halted her movement as a contraction made its way from her abdomen through her body and around to her back.

"Oh, I know. But this baby must live! Sinclair will hold me responsible if it does not!

Please don't let it die!" She wrung her hands and moaned as another contraction grabbed her and she felt its tentacles tighten around her mid-section bringing even greater pain than she remembered. She struggled to keep from screaming, but finally she could no longer refrain.

"Oh! Oh! It's coming nurse! Now! Aieeeeeee!!! "Don't push just yet Lady! Not yet!"

"I must! I have to!" And she did.

The child was born just shortly thereafter and, being full term, had all fingers, toes and limbs. Its head was covered with a cap of thick, dark hair and its rosy skin indicated it was breathing well. Then it let out a cry that would please any new mother and midwife, and most fathers as well. In other words, it was the picture of health.

But, there was one problem that glared them in the face — was evident from the first moment after delivery — the child was a girl.

"Can't you do anything right woman! A daughter is useless. You hear! Useless!"

Lord Sinclair had railed at the top of his voice and left the castle cursing as he walked out the door. Lady Sinclair sobbed in her bed knowing this child would never be cherished by her own father.

Lady Sinclair's sister, Moira, had managed to find a suitable nursemaid, the daughter of a woman who made clothing for the Cameron women. The young girl, Dorothea, had several younger siblings, so had some experience with managing young children. Plus, she was eager to see England as she had never left her home country of Scotland. Going to England to serve in a fine lord's castle sounded like such an adventure and she was anxious to begin her life there.

Lady Sinclair sent a carriage for her and she arrived when the child was but a week old. Dorothea was to become the child's nursemaid, friend and confidante for many years to come.

When Lady Sinclair left her home in Scotland, her family, the Cameron's, had thought she would be well cared for by this English Lord, Sinclair, and bring their two families together, one being Scots and the other English. Apparently, the agreement that was made with her mother's family was done so in order that the English lord would ultimately inherit the Scotland estate as it would pass to his wife upon the death of her last parent. Of course, she had died, so her daughter, Millie, would be the heir apparent now, following the death of her Aunt Moira.

The Cameron's had only the two girls, Louise and Moira. Louise had married Lord Sinclair but Moira had never married and still continued to live with her parents in Scotland and was the one who kept the place going, along with the servants. Her father took care of the business end of the estate, but Moira took on the responsibility of keeping the castle and buildings well cared for. The servants had been there most of their lives.

But, even when Lady Sinclair was getting letters from her family, early in her marriage, her sister spoke of Papa's mind drifting. Sometimes they would have to search for him as he would go missing. That was just a few years ago now, and apparently, recently he had died in his sleep. Aunt Moira had sent a letter telling them of the old man's death, but Millie's father had refused to let her write for some time now, so there had been no communication with her relatives for a long period.

Lord Sinclair never forgave his wife for not providing him a son, but as Millie began to grow up, it was obvious the child was exceedingly bright and quick to learn. The Lord provided tutors, thinking that even if she were not a son, she could at least learn the basics. Well, the tutors saw quickly that mastering the basics was no problem. So, to Millie's delight, she was taught the sciences, mathematics, and languages. She could communicate in French and English, and to a lesser degree, Gaelic. Her mother had insisted that the tutors bring someone from

Scotland to instruct her in that language as well. That was one of the few times she exercised her right as Lady of the Castle.

Dorothea had gone to England and had been given total responsibility for caring for Millie. Later on, when her mother began her downhill slide into ill health, Millie was ever so glad to have Dorothea still with her. It was long past the time she needed a nursemaid, but Dorothea was more than that; she was practically her mother as far as Millie was concerned. Dorothea had been only a young girl when she was charged with caring for an infant. But, she found that Millie was such as easy child. She was rather quiet, and shy with strangers. However, in private, she was a child who loved nature, would much rather be outdoors than in, and was more intelligent than was thought to be becoming in a female.

Millie's quick mind soared during her time with the tutors, and physically, she became someone to take note of as well. She had a most interesting face, heart shaped with sparkling green eyes that twinkled when she laughed. But, her crowning glory was her long, exceptionally thick, black hair. It was as straight as a plank, and hung down her back, having never been cut. And, a fact that could not be overlooked by anyone, she was taller than most men — almost six feet to be exact! Her mother had been a tall woman, and her father well over six feet. So, it was predictable that she might be likewise. However, her father thought her height most unattractive in a woman and chided her about it endlessly.

"How will I ever find a man who wants an Amazon for a wife?"

Lord Sinclair would shout about her unusual height when in one of his tirades. However, Millie had seen several men who looked her way, with smiles on their faces. They had found her most attractive, even if her father did not.

Keeping these thoughts to herself, Millie returned to her conversation with Dorothea. "Yes, Dorothea. I know you're right. We have no choice but to obey Father. I hope Aunt Moira and Grandmother understand my difficult situation. But, one day. One day I'll leave that monstrous man and this pile of stones that have kept me prisoner for my entire life!"

Chapter 6

Having gotten her bearings, Caitlin and the pup she now called Willie, in honor of the first Great Lion of Scotland, William, started to build the foundations of their new lives together. Caitlin thought the pup's name appropriate as he did roar like a lion when he thought she was in danger.

She had been amazed at how quickly this pup grew! She had watched Uncle Wabi with his small puppies, but they didn't seem to grow by leaps and bounds as this wolf pup had. She would really like Uncle Wabi to take a look at him. He'd probably be able to tell her much from his experiences raising other animals, but she didn't recall that he had ever raised a wolf. She felt a definite kinship with this most unusual companion, but still longed for relationships with others. Willie's presence was comforting and she had already discovered he was a great sentry who knew long before she did if anyone approached the cave.

The villagers were glad to have a healer in their midst as many men were returning from the battles that seemed never to end. Caitlin would often take her medicines into the village and try to bring relief to as many as possible. Some, however, needed more care, such as the young man that had been brought to her by his brothers. The villagers knew she lived in the cave, but respected her wishes to keep her whereabouts as quiet as possible. She did not go into detail about why she was here, but they were eager to make her a part of their community as her skills were greatly needed. Furthermore, the cave had a reputation as a sanctuary for many over the years.

Thus it was as she was returning from the village after a long day of caring for the wounded soldiers, most of them returning from the horrors of Culloden, the healer was glad the day was over and was looking forward to a bath and a lie down on her pallet with Willie. It had occurred to her she was going to need a larger pallet soon, as Willie was becoming rather large. Who would have thought the tiny pup with the broken leg would turn into this giant! He slept at her feet and provided a bit of warmth she needed, especially now that winter would soon be upon them.

Just a few yards from where she would turn to go to her cave, she heard riders coming down the path, riding hard and shouting as they rode.

"Just find her! She lives out here somewhere! But beware. Apparently she travels with a wolf, a big black one who protects her!" yelled one of the riders.

"Yeah," said another.

"Well, wolf or no. We'll find her and she'll tend our brother! We'll give her no choice in the matter!" said a deep-voiced one.

Caitlin stopped and quickly looked for some place to hide, but found nowhere she could run to quickly. She managed to get out of the path and waited as the riders came barreling down the hill and were at her feet in a matter of seconds.

"Ye there, woman! Are ye the healer?"

The man shouted at the top of his voice, trying as usual, to intimidate the person to whom he spoke, what with his size, his booming voice and brusque manner. He jumped down from his horse as if his being closer to her would make her even more afraid.

Willie's hackles stood on end, a growl building deep in his throat, and Caitlin spoke in her soft voice.

"Easy Willie. Stay. It's OK. Let's hear them out."

In addition to speaking to Willie, Caitlin made a movement with her hand the wolf understood as well. She had taught him hand signals for the times when one needed to communicate without words, something she learned from Uncle Wabi, who always had one or more dogs in training. He had a most unusual way with animals.

Watching Willie grow was like watching a weed grow! Each day he seemed larger than the day before. And he no longer looked like a young, friendly creature. He was beginning to look like what he was — a ferocious wolf. Now, he moved even closer to Caitlin, rubbing up against her leg as if to say, "I hear you, but I'm not sure about these men."

The man who appeared to be the oldest got off his horse and came to stand between the first, larger man and the healer. He bowed quickly in her direction.

"I'm Alexander MacKinnon, ma'am. Are ye the healer the villagers told us about?"

She certainly didn't look like a healer thought Alexander. He came closer and realized the woman was quite small, not even coming to his shoulders. Why, he could pick her up with one hand if he needed to! But, when she spoke — well now — that was another matter entirely.

Alex watched as the healer walked up to his "big" brother, Jack, and looked him directly in the eyes. He had been the one yelling at her, so she ignored Alex's question and stood in front of the big man. She had to bend her head back in order to make eye contact with him. Alex watched as she gazed at the overly large man. It seemed to Alex that she was assessing Jack and deciding whether to answer him or not. Apparently Jack's "intimidation" technique was not working on her. If this weren't such a disastrous situation, Alex would have laughed at the look on Jack's face!

"Yes. I'm the healer. What's all the ruckus about? I hear very well and don't particularly like being shouted at!"

Jack turned red in the face, unaccustomed as he was to any woman standing her ground in his presence. Usually they tried to stay out of his way as much as possible.

Seeing as how this whole scene was not going well, the remaining brother, Hector, stepped forward. So, now three brothers were standing over her, each one with enough stature to get one's attention.

Hector bowed in her direction and addressed her.

"Good day, madam. Please forgive my brother his poor manners. It is only that we have a desperate situation and require the skills of a healer. I do hope that you'll help us."

Caitlin had actually dismissed the three already and was headed over to take a look at the soldier that had been draped over his horse, apparently wounded from some battle as they all were. Blood dripped from his leg, and he moaned when she touched him. She immediately went into healer mode and could tell this man was indeed in need of her help, and the sooner, the better.

"Quickly! Get him inside my cave. Hurry now!"

The healer had raised her voice also, but was going about her work quickly and with great focus.

It was obvious the most critical wound was the young man's left leg, which was dangling from his knee, barely hanging on by the smallest amount of tendon and a few scraps of skin, and he was bleeding, even through his tourniquet.

"Cut his clothing off. Those pants! Cut them off him now!"

The lad was wearing some sort of pants that gathered just below the knee, very different from the usual plaid and trews the others wore. They were very similar to the ones Uncle Wabi wore. He said he could get about well and still be warmer when wearing them. She quickly laid out her tools and began to gather bandages, medicines, and clean cloths to work with. The injured youngster drifted in and out of consciousness, moaning with pain and trying to get up from the table. That was the point when she was instructing them to move their arse and help her!

Chapter 7

Now, here she was, with the youngest of the MacKinnon brothers, Ian, lying on a table in her cave, and it was her task to keep him alive, something she most assuredly would try to do.

But what if he, like the last young soldier, also died in her care? Would she have to disappear again? It was too unthinkable to even worry about at this moment. She was past exhaustion and needed to rest and keep her wits about her. She made one last inspection of her young patient, then knowing she had done all that was humanly possible, she cleared all her medicines and tools away and began her nightly ritual of food, bath, and rest.

"Something about structure in your life is beneficial." Caitlin could hear the words of her Grandmama. And she was right. Structure provided one a way to get from one thing to another without having to figure everything out every time. She laughed to herself as she thought about this because, as a young girl, she really disliked any structure whatsoever and was usually in some hot water because of her refusal to follow it!

The next morning Caitlin checked on the lad as soon as she awoke. He was still sleeping soundly, which was a good thing because when he did awake, he would likely be screaming in agony. Taking away part of a limb not only causes great physical pain, but the first time one sees a part of their body is missing, there is often more psychological pain, which is even more difficult to overcome.

Caitlin was steeling herself as she had many times before, to help the lad come to grips with his new disability. No doubt, from the looks of the wound this morning, he would recover, but still needed several days of care before she would allow him to leave the cave. So, she contented herself to stay with him and get herself ready to deal with the brothers, not something she was looking forward to. Those three were difficult, probably individually as well as when they presented as a group. Well, she had dealt with worse.

She had each one pegged already, as it were. Alexander, the eldest, was apparently the intellectual one. She recalled his face as he watched her tend his brother. He kept his thoughts to himself and all his actions would come only after careful consideration beforehand. Not bad characteristics, she thought. Even though he was only about an inch or so shorter than Jack, he used his mind rather than his size to influence others.

Jack, the loud talking, stomping bull, was probably the least dangerous one of all. She had seen this sort many times. Giant though they were in size, they really just needed someone with a firm hand and a gentle heart to keep them on an even keel.

Then Hector, the negotiator. Such smooth words. And his manner of speaking! He could talk anyone into anything. She had seen his kind before also. Woe be unto any woman who would believe his drivel! She laughed at this thought.

Then she found her thoughts returning to Alexander. Of them all, she would be most careful with him. Somehow she sensed danger coming from this one, and was aware that her female instincts came alive when he spoke to her.

"Woman! You have been alone in this cave too long!" she chided herself. But being alone was not new to Caitlin. She had led a fairly solitary childhood, having been brought up by her grandparents and an eccentric uncle. As was very common in that time, her mother had died shortly after giving her birth. Her father was unable to care for this infant as his grief kept him in a state of inertia; he barely functioned, and much more was required in caring for a new baby.

Caitlin's grandparents took the child and were glad to do so. Their only daughter-in-law was gone, but this new granddaughter filled an emptiness that no other could have. Her father, still grieving some months later, signed on to a sailing vessel headed for the West Indies. There was no word from him since that time. Caitlin often wished she could have known him. Surely, he must have been a special person for her mother to have created a child with him. Her grandparents assured her he was a fine son, a caring husband and that she had characteristics that were much like him — probably meaning his temper!

Shortly after she had changed the dressings on Ian's leg, Willie ran to the cave entrance, not growling, but announcing there was someone close by. Caitlin spoke softly to him.

"Stay Willie. Let's see who's here."

The healer was expecting to see three brothers, but only one rider came walking down the path, stopping by the trees to tether his horse. It was Alexander — "the thinker that sends out signals of danger," she murmured to herself. She still had not been able to put her finger on what it was about him that warned her to be cautious in her dealings with him. But, whatever it was, Willie did not seem to think he was dangerous as he began wagging his bushy tail the moment the man got to the entry.

"Huh, maybe he knows something about this man that I don't just yet," talking to herself again.

"Good morning, healer," Alexander greeted her, nodding slightly in her direction. He looked a bit more rested today she thought. He was quite a handsome man, with his dark hair curling around the edge of his collar, and the searching dark eyes that seemed to take in everything around him. He was obviously not an extremely young man, but it was difficult to tell what age he really was. Maybe in his thirties, she thought. He was still very muscular, as most soldiers were, but he moved with a grace that was unusual in one his size. He would be even more appealing if he would smile, she thought to herself.

Alexander towered over her and she found herself a bit discomfited being with him without the other brothers.

"I hope I haven't come too early, but we need to get going as soon as possible and make as much time as we can before dark."

He didn't wait for her to direct him, but rather, just started going back to the room where they had taken Ian.

Perhaps because she still sensed some measure of danger from this man, she stepped in front of him, arms akimbo.

"Do you always just barge into someone's home without invitation? This may be a cave, but at the moment it is MY home and I decide who comes through my door!"

Caitlin was surprised at herself as she realized that the tone she had taken could be considered harsh.

Alexander stopped in his tracks. He was at a loss for words suddenly, which was a most unusual occurrence for him as he always knew exactly what to say under most circumstances.

"I . . . uh . . . I beg your pardon, healer. I am anxious to see my brother and I just assumed ye would permit me to do so. I did not intend to 'barge' as ye called it. My apologies to ye," and he nodded again to her.

When Caitlin had raised her voice, Willie was at her side immediately, standing at attention with a brief quivering of his shoulders, waiting for a signal from her either to attack or to stay. She finally gave the non-verbal signal and he relaxed and sat at her feet.

Caitlin nodded to the man and then began to lead the way back to the young boy. She walked over to the lad and touched his brow, finding it still cool.

"He's still sleeping at the moment. But he hasn't developed a fever, so I believe he's escaped infection, at least so far."

"How am I going to put him on a horse if he's sleeping?"

Alexander spoke loudly and looked at her as if she were responsible for Ian still being in this state. And, actually, she was, as she had given him medicine that would relieve pain, but would also make him sleep. But it would wear off shortly now, she knew.

"What was your name again?" she queried. "Alexander. Alexander MacKinnon."

"Well, then, Mr. MacKinnon. Your brother will not be able to leave with you today, even when he does awake, and he will do so shortly. His leg is healing well at this time, but it would only take the smallest amount of jostling on a horse to undo the good that we have done so far.

Amputation of a limb is a most tedious procedure and the recovery is even more so. He will not leave here today, sir!" With that she walked out and headed toward the cooking room.

"I see," he said, following closely behind her, scratching at his several days old beard. Alexander searched for the right response to this news. But, having already offended the healer once, he was still struggling with saying something that would make her understand the seriousness of what he was dealing with.

He followed her a bit farther and asked,

"And should I just continue to call ye healer, or do ye have a name as well?" With a quick jerk of her head, she looked back at the man.

"Of course I have a name. Caitlin. That's enough for the moment. And, you may use that if you wish."

"Caitlin. Somehow I must make ye understand the situation. Our situation that is. What I must do as quickly as possible. He was still stuttering trying to explain this problem, rubbing his hand across the back of his neck, making her wonder if he was in pain.

"Mr. MacKinnon," she began.

"Oh, no. Just Alexander. Or Alex, please. I'm no a formal man, and don't wish to be addressed as one."

45

"I see. Then, Alex, have you had any breakfast yet? No? Good. Then let's go to my 'kitchen,' if you can call it that, and I'll find something for us to eat."

"Yes, yes, I am a bit hungry. We've been traveling with not much time for eating, ye see." She believed him, but also remembered seeing muscles that rippled on his forearms yesterday when he lifted his brother up on her table. Funny. Now, why do I remember that she wondered to herself.

The man's brogue was still strong, but she was beginning to get the cadence of it and wasn't missing every other word as she did yesterday. Strange that people of the same country can have such different ways of saying the same words.

The two of them sat at a small makeshift table she had placed along the side of the cave. There were several candles resting in carved out niches on the wall, and a small bowl with a bit of purple heather she had picked on the moor. Hanging from the ceiling were some herbs she was drying, to be used in cooking, preparation of medicines, and some just for the aroma they gave off. So, it was a pleasant place. As far as a cave goes, that is.

"Here. Sit. I'll find something that will soothe us both."

Caitlin poured some of her herbal tea and passed a large mug of it to Alex, who picked it up immediately and began sipping.

Looking at Alexander across the table, Caitlin was surprised to find small crinkles at the corners of his eyes, a sure sign of one who laughs often. And, she had thought he was too serious for that.

"Well, healer, looks like you might have misread more than you thought," she continued her internal dialogue.

Alex had yet to come across any woman who had held his attention for longer than a night or two. And there hadn't been very many of those either. He usually found women to be just a bit too gabby, or even worse, silly. Having a serious conversation with them didn't seem possible, or at least not to him.

However, this small, fiery-haired healer seemed to capture his imagination and he was having difficulty putting her into one of the categories he usually placed women in, again, silly or too talkative. And then some were just plain out ugly. Well, she certainly wasn't any of those. And, it had registered with him that not only was she not ugly, but she was most attractive. There was something about that flaming hair that always seemed to be coming away from its pinning and falling down her neck.

Bringing his mind back to the present, he continued, "Healer, uh Caitlin, I can think of no other way to make ye understand, so I'll just tell ye the truth. I only hope ye'll not betray us."

He looked at the ceiling as if he would find some assistance up there, then rubbed his neck again and let out a deep breath he apparently had been holding in.

"My brothers, Hector and Jack, are soldiers as am I. We were in the Fourteenth Regiment under the command of Captain Reginald Ferguson. Our regiment's been fighting for many months now, across many different areas of our country, doing our part in trying to return the Bonnie Prince to his proper place. As ye well know, from the soldiers ye've been treating, these battles aren't going well, and there aren't many of us left, especially after Culloden. And the ones of us that are left are exhausted and weary of killing our own countrymen."

"We MacKinnons try to look out for each other, as any brothers would. And, so far, we've managed to escape any dire wounds and we're thankful for that. We've all suffered some minor injuries from firearms and blades, but nothing we couldn't deal with. But, just now, everything has become very difficult. Young Ian, in there on your table, has brought us a new problem we must deal with.

Alex wondered, just for a moment, what was running through the healer's mind as she began to rise from the table and turned herself so she was facing him directly. She put her tea cup down and stood, then put her hands on the table and leaned across into his "space" as it were.

"What is that lad doing fighting with ye anyway? I can't believe ye would put that young man in such danger! Have ye no sense! Any of the three of ye!"

Caitlin's words such as "you" became "ye," a sure holdover from living with Uncle Wabi who sometimes used them, but not always. She had observed Alex also seemed to have that problem. Or maybe he always used them.

"He's only a boy, for heaven's sakes!" She backed away from the table and was practically yelling at him by this point.

With him still seated, they were at eye level and she was staring him down.

"Whoa, healer, er, Caitlin." Alex held his hands up in front of his chest as if to protect himself from this angry woman.

"It's not the way ye think. When we joined the regiment, many months ago now, we left young Ian at home with our Da, which is as it should be. Da needs him to help keep the place up, and Ian was much too young to be a soldier. Of course he pleaded with us to bring him, but we refused. But, as it is, ye see, a few weeks ago he turned up at our regiment's camp, just outside the village where we'd been fighting. We still don't know how he found us, but find us he did. So there wasn't much else to do but keep him with us. Of course, our plan was to send him right back home, but there was a lot of commotion in the area and we were engaged in battle almost full time."

"Well, as ye are aware, the battle at Culloden was a most disastrous day for many, many Scots, on both sides of the argument. His expression changed and his voice drifted off as he remembered that day . . .

***

"The sun was hiding and a thick grey fog was hovering along the ground. Men were moaning and the odor of gunpowder mingled in with the stench of spilled blood, and there were endless bodies everywhere." He looked at her, seeking understanding as he continued.

"It became obvious this battle was lost, and one of us was already wounded. Jack had taken a bullet in his calf, but was able to get on a horse well enough. He's tough as a bull, he is."

"But, just as we were trying to help him to the medical tent some distance away, a Redcoat came charging through our midst, screaming at the top of his voice he was, and striking at any and everything that got in his path! He was swinging an axe as he bent low on his horse. As he got nearer, Ian tried to run, but the Redcoat was too quick, and the axe caught Ian in the leg! Well, I don't need to tell ye anymore about that."

"So, ye see, we had one brother shot and one bleeding to death. We had to have some help! But, the regiment commander had other plans for us, ye see. He yelled to us to return to the battle and continue as long as we could."

"Now, healer, I've seen enough fighting to know when ye need to retreat, and this was one of those times. So, I decided the four of us had done all we could for the Bonnie Prince, and it was time to take care of the MacKinnons! So, with that decision made, we threw Ian over his horse and the four of us left, hoping to find someone to help us. Well, ye see, the commander called us deserters as we rode out. He implied he would send scouts to find us and bring us up on desertion charges."

"Not a pretty story, I know, but there is the truth of it. So, we're trying to get back to our home, which is far up in the Highlands and very remote. If we can just get back, we feel there's a certain amount of safety there. I rather doubt, too, that after Culloden there'll be much appetite for searching for deserters on either side."

Alex watched as comprehension walked across the healer's face. He knew she probably shared Mam's feelings about war — that they were all senseless. But, Alex witnessed that the healer obviously knew her part was to mend those she could, and bring comfort when possible.

After listening to Alex's story, Caitlin could see that even though this soldier had not been wounded, he was suffering nevertheless. The "danger" she had been sensing from him was actually anxiety and fear he felt for his brothers, and it was evident in his every movement.

Caitlin often wished she didn't possess this ability to sense others' distress. She supposed it was helpful when you are a healer, but it could be a hindrance as well.

Alex, being the eldest, probably felt a great amount of responsibility for his brothers' safety. Well, she thought, it's much easier to heal a battle wound than it is to fix this man's situation. About all she could offer was her support and her promise not to "betray" them as he requested.

"Don't you be worried about my betraying you or anyone else as far as that goes. I ask no questions of those I tend, and what I hear, I keep to myself. Your secret is safe with me." With that she stood and went back to Ian's side to take another look at him.

"And just how long have you been awake, young man?" she asked. She could see he was trying to remember who she was and probably wondered if he should know her. Caitlin knew his mind must feel foggy and was pleased when she saw his head turn quickly when he heard a voice that he most certainly did know.

"Alex! Is that ye?" the lad asked, trying to raise up. With this exertion, he let out a loud gasp followed by a mournful cry the healer knew indicated he had realized he was in pain, and why.

"Alex! Alex! My leg! No! No!" Alex quickly ran to Ian and took the boy's hands in his. "Easy brother, easy now. Ye'll be all right. Yer in the best of hands. Lie back now." Alex's voice was deep and very soothing, and Ian responded to his commands.

"Where am I?" the lad asked, avoiding looking down at his leg.

Caitlin stood on the other side and spoke to him. "You're a guest in my home as it turns out," she said with a slight smile on her face. I'm Caitlin, a healer. You're recovering well, Ian, but you must lie still and be as quiet as you can. Your leg will heal, but it'll take some time. I know it's painful, but I'll help you with that as much as possible."

"Where's Jack? And Hector?" asked Ian, trying his best to be as brave about his condition as he was sure his older brothers would be. Being a MacKinnon meant you had to always carry yourself with pride and your actions should always be honorable, showing a certain amount of self-determination and fortitude. So, to give in to his feelings at the moment, of helplessness and self-pity, did not fit this expectation.

"Our brothers are safe, nearby, camped out in the forest. We're just waiting for the healer to let us take ye home. But she says we can't go just yet, so ye just keep quiet as she said. We'll be going home soon, lad, I promise."

Ian was exhausted just from this small exchange and lay back down again without looking at his wounded leg — with the lower part missing. It was too much to take in just yet.

Walking out the cave entrance, Caitlin gave the silent "come" signal to Willie, and he was immediately at her side. Alex came out behind her, and was surprised when the wolf nudged him behind the knee.

"Well, now, I don't believe I've ever met a wolf before." But, he was glad the animal didn't think he was a threat. He WAS a very large wolf and Alex had seen what wolves can do when they are angry. He slowly scratched the wolf behind the ears like he did his own two herding dogs at home, and the beast seemed to like it too.

"Willie seems to approve of you. And he keeps secrets well, also." Caitlin smiled at Alex and walked with him over to the trees where his horse was tethered. Most animals, especially horses, don't want to be in the presence of wolves. But, Willie seemed to have a way of communicating with other animals, and this was amazing to Caitlin. When she first started taking him with her to the village, the people were a bit wary, but somehow none of the other animals seemed to fear him. Uncle Wabi always said that some animals have ways of talking to their fellow creatures. Caitlin was sure that Willie was one of those.

"Did ye know that ye have a 'resident' great horned owl?" asked Alex, smiling down at the healer. He had seen the large bird yesterday when they came, and the gorgeous creature was here again this morning.

Caitlin put her hand up to shelter her eyes, spotting the rather large owl high up in the tree. The owl looked back at her also, his huge eyes never leaving her face.

"Oh, yes, he showed up the same day I found the cave and seems to have made himself at home in that rowan tree. I rather like having him around as he greets me every morning and again in the evening if I venture outside, which I don't do very often. Uncle Wabi says owls are good to have around. He thinks they are most intelligent and have special powers. But then Uncle Wabi thinks everything has special powers!"

"Uncle Wabi? An unusual name, I would think. Don't believe I've heard that one before." "Well, that's not exactly right. After my grandparents passed on, Wabi stepped in and cared for me as well as they had. That seems surprising in a man, you might think, but not for him. Caring for others just seems to be part of his nature. Anyway, his proper name is Rusepheus Rhoden Wabi-Sensu. And, he's not actually my uncle. He was a close friend of my mother and father, and he actually lived next door to my grandparents when I was a child. Apparently the name Wabi has been used for many generations in his family and is the name he prefers. He was always at all family functions and he just became Uncle Wabi to me. He's a most interesting man and I love him dearly."

She grinned just thinking about Uncle Wabi. He was such a special person and she missed him greatly. He had taught her so very much about life, animals, and was a great storyteller. He knew more folklore than anyone. She listened to his stories every night as a child.

Some of them were very interesting and, at times, she felt she had actually known those people by the time he was finished with his story.

"Does your uncle live close by also?" Alex found it most disturbing the healer was alone inside a cave with only a wolf and an owl for companionship.

"Oh. No. He still lives on the Isle of Skye, as I did until rather recently. A very long story I'm afraid," and her voice trailed off and she hoped Alex wouldn't push the issue. Caitlin could tell this man was very perceptive and had probably already figured out there was more to this story than he knew. There were just some things she needed to keep to herself and she hoped he understood that.

"The Isle of Skye, you say? If memory serves me, my people originally came from there, but my memory is not the best! Our bard, Uncle Andrew, will know for sure. His memory is something to behold." He walked up to his horse and adjusted the stirrups on his saddle, twisting them a bit and pulling on the leather.

"So, will we be able to take Ian with us tomorrow, healer?"

"Oh. I don't know, Alex. He's young and strong, but he's been gravely wounded. Let's see how he is tomorrow and then we can make plans for him to go home with you. I know that's what you want, and it's what I want for him. Being home will be the best medicine for him all right."

"I see. Then I'll call tomorrow, with yer permission, of course." He smiled as he thought about Caitlin admonishing him for "barging" in earlier.

"Yes. See you tomorrow. And remember. Tell no one where you're going and be sure no one follows you. Our agreement."

"Yes, Caitlin. I remember." He mounted his horse then and disappeared quickly into the trees beyond.

***

After riding for some time, Alex found his brothers just where he had left them earlier that same morning.

"Ho, Alex! But where's wee Ian?" Jack was on his feet, grabbing at Alex's mount and holding the animal so his brother could climb down.

"He's no with ye? I knew not to trust that woman! What did she do with him! Remember, one of the villagers whispered she might be a witch or a sorcerer!"

The horse was shying to one side trying to get away from the fear he sensed in the loudly speaking brother.

Alex swung his leg over the horse and dismounted.

"Hold on, big brother. Ian does well. The healer's taken great care of him, and he's resting as best he can. I spoke with him for a few minutes, and he's aware of what's happened. 'Twas hard for him, but he's a MacKinnon after all. Made of strong stuff, he is. And if she's a witch, then, that's all right too. She knows her business and our Ian is proof of that."

"So, why is he not with ye?" Hector had joined the other two and, in his usual way, was trying to figure out what was really going on.

Alex took the mug of coffee Hector was holding out and swallowed with a gulp. "Well, the healer says he's doing well, but we can't move him just yet. I'm to return tomorrow and she'll tell me what we must do."

He started pacing slowly, walking between the brothers, sipping the coffee. The warm drink was welcome as it was getting to be a bit chilly the higher up the country they went.

Alex stopped abruptly, "But, I've been thinking on this while riding back here. We need to put our heads together and come up with a plan of our own, just in case we don't like hers!" Alex was unaccustomed to letting others make plans for him or his family. But, this healer, this Caitlin, was a formidable person, no question of that. He was still thinking about her smile, her hair with its many shades of the sunset, and watching her hands as they worked their formidable magick on Ian. Yes, quite formidable.

Chapter 8

Last evening when Caitlin was doing her final check on Ian before retiring, she would have sworn she smelled a scent that she recognized, but could not place. She knew it was from a very long time ago. But even this morning she still couldn't put her finger on it. She had been leaning over Ian, tucking his blankets close to his thin body. Then as she lay her hand on Ian's cheek and stroked it gently, she almost remembered her own cheek being touched — like a mother would stroke a child's cheek. But, she had never known her mother, so that memory couldn't be real, could it? That's so strange, she thought. She was always able to attach a memory to most scents.

The healer had spent a restless night. Whether that was due to the fact she kept checking on her young patient, or found herself thinking far too much about Alexander MacKinnon, she wasn't sure. Whatever the reason, morning came too soon. She draped her plaid over her shoulders and walked out the cave entrance. The dawn was just breaking, with pink streaks of light just at the top of the far away mountains. And, as usual, the great owl was on his perch in the rowan tree and greeted her with a "hoo hoo." He never failed to let her know he was still about. Willie had accompanied her outside and was running about, frisking in the early morning dampness, and there was a definite chill in the air that spoke of much cooler days to come.

Somewhere, not too far off, someone must have started a fire, and the smell of pine resin filled the air.

Would she be warm enough in the cave? She didn't think about that when she took up residence. At the time, it was just a readymade place of safety for her and, so far, she found it to be quite comfortable. Actually, more than comfortable, very pleasant. But, she may have to think about getting another place, but not today.

She returned to her cave and went about her morning ablutions, then tidied her "home" and herself, again pinning up the long tresses so they were out of her way when tending her young man. At present he was resting well, after the early morning brew she insisted on him drinking. Such a very young lad he was. He didn't even have the beginnings of a beard as yet, and he responded eagerly to her comforting touch. Yes. Just a child.

No sooner had she gotten herself ready for the day than Willie went flying out of the cave, announcing their visitor had arrived.

"Some watch wolf you are!" Caitlin called after him.

She could hear a deep voice talking to the animal and shortly they were both standing at the entrance. Willie's bushy, black tail waving from side to side told her he trusted this man, so perhaps she would too.

"And a good morning to ye healer, er Caitlin!" called Alex.

Caitlin noticed a fresh, evergreen aroma wafting in his draft. The scent seemed exactly right for him, clean and fresh, with some remembrance of another time she couldn't quite find a memory for.

"Tis a great morning to be sure and I'm hoping our wee brother fares well?" More of a statement than a question, but she thought he was waiting for an answer.

Alexander MacKinnon filled the entire opening of the cave. She took note of his freshly shaven face, and his thick dark hair had been neatly combed, still curling at his collar. Yes. She had been right yesterday. He was indeed quite handsome, but she didn't think he was aware of it. She somehow had a sense he was not entirely comfortable around women. Interesting, she thought.

"Ah, Alex, come in, please. Yes, Ian is indeed doing well, considering the terrible ordeal he has endured, and is still enduring, I might add." She motioned for him to come forward and walked toward Ian's chamber.

"I'm afraid you'll find him sleeping, yet again. But, he was in considerable pain early this morning, and I felt he needed some relief. My medicines will relieve some pain, but they also bring about drowsiness, and most often, sleep. But, he fares well, Alex."

***

Once again, Alexander found himself having great difficulty finding words, a situation he was beginning to realize happened when in the presence of this small woman. What was it about her that caused his brain to freeze and his tongue to follow suit! But, she just seemed to brighten up this cave when she smiled, and her hair was again arranged up somehow, and again, it was beginning to fall down in wispy tendrils in various places. He felt his fingertips tingle just thinking about touching it.

"Good Lord, man, get a grip on yeself!" he uttered under his breath. He was starting to talk to himself now it seemed!

"Come. We'll make a pot of tea and discuss plans for Ian to return with you to your home."

"Tea. Yes, yes, anything will be better than that bitter brew Hector serves us. He likes being the 'cook,' but some of his dishes could stand a little improvement, so some tea would be most welcome, healer."

***

They sat down at her small table, and Caitlin got a large mug for him, the same one he used yesterday, and put out a smaller cup for herself. Then she poured their tea from the small teapot she kept on a shelf in her kitchen area. She had seen this small pottery teapot at one of the stalls in the village the first day she ventured out of the cave, her first outing to find out what sort of place she had landed in. The small teapot had etchings on the side that made her think of one Uncle Wabi had in his kitchen at home. He had told her the pot was passed down in the family, and it was made by an old potter from generations back. She picked it up carefully, and it fit her hand so well she decided she would ask its price, knowing she had only a very limited amount of funds to her name. Then, on second thought, shaking her head, realizing she couldn't afford it at any price, she put it back down.

Just a few days later Caitlin had set up her medicine station in the village, offering to treat the many soldiers that came through and any locals as well. So, when the old woman from the pottery stall showed up on Caitlin's first treatment day with a very swollen ankle, she had no means of paying, but offered to pay Caitlin in the manner of bartering, most common in remote villages. Apparently, the old woman remembered seeing Caitlin holding the pottery teapot some days ago.

"Madam Healer, I have very little money to pay with, but I can offer you this teapot as payment for your services. Would you consider that?"

Caitlin carefully lifted the teapot and looked at it again. There were etchings of a raven, a wolf, and a young girl with long hair, then a few words in a language unknown to her.

"It is more than enough payment. I will treasure it."

She had smiled at the old woman and carefully packed it inside her medicine bag and brought it home. She used it every day now and found the drawings most interesting.

"So, then, Caitlin. It seems I no can take him today. So what about tomorrow?" asked Alex. He took a swallow of the tea, which was quite a treat for him, and reached for one of the cakes she had placed on the table. It had been some time since he had eaten food this delicious.

"Umm. Can't remember when I've had cake. Certainly not any this good since Mam passed."

"Some of the villagers left it at the entrance to my cave. They seem to appreciate my presence here, and I find their 'gifts' and am grateful for them. Uncle Wabi always says to never question good fortune, but accept that someone cares for you."

Alex wiped his mouth on the back of his hand.

"Healer. I would eat another, but something tells me my Mam is watching and she'd call me a pig or even worse, a Highlander with poor manners. Yep. She'd pin my ears back about that for sure!" He laughed.

The healer talked about how best to get on with taking Ian home. As it was, Alex and his brothers had already made a plan of their own, which entailed some bit of work, but Alex had decided they would proceed with it, hopefully with the healer's agreement as well. But if not, then they would probably do it anyway.

Caitlin looked at the big Highlander sitting across from her. It seemed so natural to have this ease of conversation with this man, one who was so accustomed to being in total charge of most everything around him. He actually seemed to be listening to her and understanding what she had to say, as if it could be important.

"Well, no, I actually think it would be better to wait another day or so, but as you need to be putting some space between yourself and those that might be seeking to find you, then maybe we should try to ready Ian for traveling as best we can. I have some personal understanding of needing to seek a place of safety, as it were, though I wish it were not so."

"Oh, aye, our thoughts exactly. Today, Hector and Jack are making a kind of litter, if ye ken what I'm sayin. It's a kind of litter that we can lay Ian on and then put it up on his horse. That way he can keep his leg, or what's left of it, straight out without bending and maybe that will keep him from jostling so much as ye talked about."

"Yes, a litter of some kind. That might just work, Alexander MacKinnon!" Caitlin certainly understood the feeling of needing to be somewhere else, anywhere, just to stay alive. But, her first concern was for her young patient.

"Alex, you must understand the gravity of Ian's wound. He's a very strong and brave young man. But, if he starts bleeding, it could be disastrous for him and all of you. You'd have to stop, bind the wound tightly, and hope that keeping him still would help. But, there are no guarantees that will work. But, if you don't leave, it may be you all could find yourselves in a most difficult predicament. So, let's plan for you and the others to bring the litter here early tomorrow morning, and with everyone's strength combined, we might be able to rig this litter on the horse and gently ease Ian onto it."

She didn't particularly like this idea, but knew they would most probably do it anyway, even without her agreement. She was quite sure when Alexander MacKinnon made a decision there was no turning back.

"Then, that's what we'll do. I'm also afraid of moving Ian, Caitlin, but we don't have much choice in the matter. If we can just reach the upper Highlands, we can get lost in there from any outsiders. We've lived there our entire lives and know every inch of every glen and hillside. 'Tis our home and we are most anxious to return to it."

Alex almost seemed to be talking to himself as he was staring off in the distance and his last words were spoken almost in a whisper.

"Then, I'll have him ready, early."

Alex was loathe to leave her. He, too, was feeling that conversation with her seemed so natural he wanted to continue it. She certainly was much better company than those two heathen brothers he had to go back to!

"So, if I may be so bold to ask, how is it ye have an understanding of seeking safety?

Are ye in some danger also?"

Alex was reluctant to press her for information, but felt she might need someone to listen also, as had he.

"Ah, well, that's a long story, Alex, and I feel sure you would find it boring."

"Nae, lass, anything is more interesting than going back to spend the day with those louts, Jack and Hector! Besides, they have work to do and if I leave them alone, they'll do a very fine job. When I'm around, they argue and I'm forever having to settle their disputes! So, tell me about your troubles, healer."

Caitlin smiled at him. It was not very often she was offered an ear, usually she was the one who was listening to the sad stories, and there were so many of them it seemed to her.

So, the healer began to tell her tale of woe. Even to herself, it seemed so impossible that she found herself in this position. Up to this point, she had led such a regular, relatively easy life with Uncle Wabi and her friends.

Chapter 9

On the night Caitlin left Skye she had packed the bare necessities, plus her medicine bag. Not knowing where she was going but confident in her decision to do so, she stopped just long enough to write a quick note to Uncle Wabi.

As it was, her mind couldn't stop replaying the scene in the pub, The Wild Boar, in the east end of their village. She had gone there to purchase a bottle of the mulberry wine that Uncle Wabi enjoyed. The pub kept a ready supply of the wine as one of the local women made it and sold it to them. Caitlin sometimes made it for Wabi, but would buy it from the pub owner when she was too busy to make a batch herself. It was simply a concoction made from mulberries, which were allowed to ferment, and infused with a bit of honey in the process. It was quite tasty and Uncle Wabi did prefer it to others.

Caitlin entered the pub, then called out as the bartender was nowhere to be seen. There were only a handful of customers sitting at small tables with a lighted candle on each one. Caitlin knew most of them and nodded at each one as she passed their tables.

Her voice rang out.

"Hello. Thomas, are you here?"

There was no reply so she walked behind the counter and made her way to the quarters located in the rear of the pub. She had been back here before when she needed to tend to Thomas when he had been gored by a wild boar a number of years ago. Actually, that was when he changed the name of the pub from The

Scarlet Rooster to The Wild Boar. He thought it seemed more appropriate and his regulars found it an entertaining name.

Thomas recovered well, but was left with a limp he constantly complained about and prevented him from getting in a hurry about going anywhere. Caitlin had admonished him to be thankful he still lived! A wound from a boar can be rather nasty and she remembered working diligently to keep infection from setting in. Thomas was not one to be thankful for much of anything, however. He was a dour personality for sure.

As she came to a door that was ajar, she was about to knock and enter when she heard voices coming from inside the room. She recognized Thomas' voice and actually the other one as well, Lord Warwick. The lord was a British landowner who owned much of the lands in this area and was a most despicable person in her opinion. Caitlin recalled Uncle Wabi losing his temper when he discovered the lord had swindled several of the local farmers out of their lands because they were behind on their taxes. The Lord had political influence in all the right places and now those farmers had no lands or homes and had left Skye trying to find someplace where they could make a living.

Uncle Wabi still fumed about the incident even today and disliked the man with a passion. Actually he threatened to "turn him into the toad that he is!" Uncle Wabi was forever going on about those who had powers, unknown to them, until such time as they are needed. Caitlin smiled just remembering her uncle's words and his very red face!

As Caitlin stood outside the door, the conversation continued.

"Oh, aye, Your Lordship, there be more than two dozen supporters of the Bonnie Prince, and they be organized too, if you ken my meanin.' They meet regularly too, sir, right here in my pub. I see them puttin' their heads together and then they stop their talkin' if I come by. Give me a minute. Let me check and see if any of 'em are here tonight."

The barkeeper, not aware the door was ajar, pushed it open quickly and ran head long into Caitlin as she was standing immediately on the other side and had heard everything that was said.

Caitlin was trying to decide whether to pretend she hadn't overheard their conversation.

She had never been good at hiding her thoughts and feelings, however.

Thomas, being rather a large, rotund bear of a man, bearded and always in need of a haircut and a bath, stared down at Caitlin. It was obvious from the look on her face that she had heard everything he and the lord had said. So, now Caitlin knew Thomas was working with the British and was a traitor to his own people!

The healer returned his stare and stepped back as he breathed his garlic-laced breath into her face. She returned his stare, and there were no words exchanged between the two of them.

Her expression revealed her thoughts, so she turned quickly about and dashed out the pub door, overturning a chair as she ran past the counter.

She ran as fast as her legs would carry her, and was greatly relieved when she reached Uncle Wabi's property.

"Holy Rusepheus!" she exclaimed to herself as she quickly closed the door of her home that she shared with her uncle.

"Thomas is a traitor to his own people! Oh, that unspeakable wretch!"

She had always known Thomas wasn't a man of particularly high moral character and he had a reputation for bashing women about from time to time. There was even a rumor that suggested he was responsible for the death of a traveler who came into the pub flashing a bit too much coin. The traveler's body was found some months later when the waters receded from the pond at the edge of town. Thomas had been seen plying the man with drink and making conversation with him at the pub. However, there was never any evidence to prove he had committed the crime.

Caitlin, even though she had saved his life, had never liked the man and had never made that a secret. So, she knew without a doubt she was in danger from this loathsome being. In fact, probably anyone associated with her was also in danger.

As far as family, there was only Uncle Wabi, as all the others had passed on long ago. But she had a number of friends, and Thomas would have no compunction about harming them. Of this she was certain. She would leave a note for Uncle Wabi and ask him to explain the situation to her friends so they would watch out for Thomas. Time was of the essence. She must leave at once.

"Well, then, Miss Caitlin, this is a fine mess you've created for yourself!"

She twirled her fingers in the strands of hair that had escaped from her morning pinning. In her bag, Caitlin included a small blanket and a change of clothing. Then, after finishing the note to Uncle Wabi and pushing it under his bedroom door, she reached into the closet in the foyer and took one of his long cloaks that had a hood attached. She was about to leave, then had gone back to the closet and taken a small staff that was kept there also. Wabi had several and used them when walking in the woods with his dogs, so Caitlin thought maybe she might need one also, considering she was going to be walking in the woods for who knew how long. This particular staff was unique in that it had etchings that covered the entire surface of the piece.

Caitlin didn't know if these etchings were a language that she didn't recognize. They weren't Gaelic, and certainly not English. Perhaps they were some sort of hieroglyphics. She would need to ask Uncle Wabi about this one day. Finally, she wrapped her plaid about herself, then put the cloak on, hoping it would hide her mass of bright red hair and help her stay hidden. Then she disappeared into the night. Only the owl in the birch tree was aware of her departure, and he kept that secret to himself.

***

Caitlin looked at Alex to see if he was still listening, as he had not uttered one word since she began her long saga. The look on his face told her he had gotten every word of her story and was ready to hear more!

"Well, to make this long story a bit shorter, after I made my way through several nights of walking and hiding in the day time, I came upon a habitable, small cottage. The thatched roof was in good shape and, from the looks of it; the cottage had been uninhabited for quite some time. So, with nothing better on the horizon, I took up residence in the cottage and began to use my healing skills to help the soldiers coming from the areas nearby. Some were local men who needed tending only slightly but most of them were coming from Culloden, as did you and your brothers. Well, as my wonderful luck would have it, some of these young men had spent time in the bogs and marshes at some point and apparently gotten infected with malaria. I'm sure I don't have to explain to you how disastrous that illness is. Most of us have some personal understanding of it, or know someone who has."

"Most of the young men did not survive, and it broke my heart to see them die off, one by one. But, they were so far gone by the time they got to me there wasn't much I could do, except try to keep them from leaving and possibly infecting others. We still don't know if it's contagious, but until we do, healers will try to keep them apart from others. One of the young men was a soldier whose father was a Regimental Commander, a Commander Campbell, his name was. He had asked me to help these men, and I did everything possible within my power."

"Well, this commander has convinced himself I'm some kind of witch and put a spell on his son and the other young men. He refused to see that nothing could have saved them. In his mind I am totally responsible for the death of his son and he has sworn to see me burn for my witchcraft! So, as soon as I could get away, I left and was once again looking for a place of safety."

"This cave actually has turned out to be such a place, at least so far. But I don't doubt that Commander Campbell will continue to search for me. He's not a man to easily be deterred and will certainly try to find me. And that, my Highland friend, is how I came to be here in this magnificent dwelling!"

She spoke with a smile in her voice, but she knew this Highlander was savvy enough to sense she was more than just a bit disturbed at the circumstances in which she found herself.

"So lass, it would seem that ye are being pursued by an evil English lord, a ruthless barkeep, and a grief-stricken military man. Well, now. That's a bit of trouble I would think, meself."

Alex found himself already trying to figure out how to assist this woman who had saved Ian's life and who was occupying much of his thoughts these days. She had told her story in such a manner that one would have thought she was speaking of another. It was almost as if it were a story about an acquaintance. But, Alex sensed her distress and now had to decide on his reaction to what he had learned. She had been instrumental in helping his family, so maybe he could come up with a plan for her as well. As was known about him, strategy was his greatest strength.

Chapter 10

Wabi rose early, stood up and stretched his long legs and arms, feeling just a bit of arthritis; but all in all he was able to do most everything he wanted. He pulled on his pants and shirt and laced up his old boots as he planned to go hiking through the woods with his latest trainee, one from Mrs. Love's latest litters. Old man Love had died a few years back, but Mrs. Love continued to raise the hunting dogs as had her husband. They were an excellent breed, Gordon Setters, and getting a pup from the Love line meant the dog would be one of the finest hunting dogs. Mr. Love had always engaged Wabi to train the dogs as he seemed to have a fine rapport with animals. Well, both Wabi and the dogs liked this arrangement, so he spent quite a bit of his time outdoors with these beautiful animals.

Wabi reached for his glasses, which he truly needed these days, and sat down to read the note he had found on his bedroom floor, just inside the door. For the second time, he re-read Caitlin's note with a sinking heart, and sat back down on the edge of the bed.

"Why didn't she tell me in person? I could have helped her!"

The old man was so furious that his first thought was to get himself over to The Wild Boar and take care of Thomas.

"That black-hearted devil! He deserves to return to the evil that spawned him! Well, Thomas, my friend, it's been a long time, but I can still manage to create havoc when I need to, and creating something special for you will be a pleasure!"

With that, Wabi walked outside and stood under the blackthorn tree. Immediately, a great horned owl swooped down and sat on his shoulder, just for a moment, then took to the sky and was lost in the darkness.

Uncle Wabi had cared for Caitlin since she was about ten years old. Such a delight she was at that age! She had such curiosity about the natural world, the animals, the flora and fauna, and anything to do with healing. Her quick mind was stimulating for an old man who had seen much in his day and still had much to contribute to others. But, she had never exhibited any interest in that other world, one in which he himself had spent several lifetimes. He knew that his lives were usually spent in conjunction with those who required some tutoring in the "special arts," but so far, Caitlin had not shown any behaviors to indicate she was led in that direction.

Now, however, whether she wished it or not, Wabi may have to resort to his kind of intervention. Caitlin had left, it seemed, in order to avoid his becoming a target for Thomas and Lord Warwick. Well, that probably would not stop Thomas if he were intent on causing harm. But, dealing with Thomas was not much of a task for this old wizard, nor was dealing with the lord, as far as that went. He was just another wealthy idiot!

Wabi had forgotten how satisfying it could be, assisting ones he cared about. Perhaps he was still useful after all! But, he would proceed slowly to prevent Caitlin from experiencing any undue stress. She was a most independent woman and an intelligent one as well. She would not especially thank him for taking over when she already had things well in hand. But did she?

Wabi would ask Owl for regular reports and proceed only when he was truly needed.

Caitlin had been dealt a rather difficult hand from day one, thought Wabi. But, if she had not, it probably would not have been necessary for him to be in her life. Her mother, a delightful woman by anyone's standards, had been so excited when she discovered she was going to have a babe. She had been one of only two children and had so hoped she would have many children and be a part of a family that celebrated occasions, held ceilidhs ,those wonderful gatherings with lots of dancing and celebrating, and which christened babies and carried on traditions that families did. Apparently, that was not to be as she died shortly after Caitlin's birth and then Caitlin's father left the country. The grandparents, her father's parents, did very well with caring for Caitlin for a few years, but as they passed on, it was left to Wabi to take the reins, and he already knew that was his purpose this time around.

This small child kept his mind active, and he reveled in teaching her how animals behave, teaching her about the heavenly bodies, instructing her in mathematics, at which she excelled, and even helped her dabble in the arts such as painting, and a bit of pottery. She moved rapidly through all her studies, but was more interested in taking care of a broken bird's wing, removing a small animal from a trap and tending its wounds than anything else.

Wabi understood his purpose was to help Caitlin develop her special talents, but she never seemed interested when he would suggest she learn some of the basics, such as lighting a candle with a nod of your head, or causing a rainstorm when you were angry, just a few examples of easily learned skills. He had actually performed these particular feats in her presence, but she never even questioned he could do them, and never asked him to teach her how. It was as if she just expected he could do some things others could not.

One thing was evident to him. She was aware of her exceptional sense of smell. That particular trait ran in her family of healers as far back as anyone could remember. Of course, Wabi also knew that most "called ones" carried this trait. He always thought that maybe Caitlin would one day come to realize this was just one of her many talents, and perhaps she would. But, all his students over the many eons had come into their own when the time was right, and he knew Caitlin would also. Sometimes, it took some distressing event or two to jolt them into action. So, he had continued to teach her as much as possible when she was young, and she had blossomed under his tutelage.

When she had requested she be allowed to spend time with Morag, the old village healer, Wabi had no qualms about agreeing to this arrangement. Old Morag had been around a long time, and Wabi recognized her as being of his kind also. It appeared that sometimes the Creator worked in mysterious ways. But, she would be safe with Morag and, perhaps, Caitlin needed some female influence in her life as well. So, between Wabi and Morag, Caitlin had been exposed to some very fine instruction and had become a very knowledgeable healer.

The only problem that occasionally brought the two to loggerheads was Caitlin's temper.

As a young child, she was often catered to by grandparents, and then Wabi, too, indulged her fairly often.

"But, Uncle Wabi! I' don't want to go to bed! It's early still and if I play outside just a while longer, the bull bats will swoop down and chase me! "

"Caitlin. We've been through this already. You've got school tomorrow and that means you've got to be in bed — now!" The schooling being offered was rudimentary, but being with some other children would be good for her in Wabi's opinion.

If he sometimes had to refuse some request she made, she was given to a snit of temper, stomping her foot and turning red in the face. Wabi usually stood his ground, and she learned he could not be budged on some issues. Another learning experience was how Wabi liked to think of it.

Chapter 11

Alex stood up, placing his mug on the table. "I thank ye kindly, Caitlin. Tea and cake will take me quite a ways, I believe! Now I'll be on my way to see that my brothers are completing their tasks. And they will. You can count on them." Caitlin wished he would stay longer, but couldn't seem to think of a reason to keep him here. He walked to the front of the cave, and Willie accompanied him to the door. He reached down and stroked the creature, much like he did Lord and Lady, his own dogs.

Caitlin called out to him, "Bring him some clothes when you come tomorrow. If you remember, we had to cut his pants off, and I don't think he'll like it much if we don't dress him properly before you leave for home!" Alex waved as he mounted and trotted off.

Caitlin smiled as her new friend departed, and she truly felt he was just that. He was a thoughtful, intelligent man and she did so enjoy being with him.

"Well, too bad, lassie. He'll be gone tomorrow and that will be the last you see of him.

Besides, you have much work to do here in this village. They have accepted you here and, so far, you seem to be safe enough." She was saying this to Willie, who looked up at her as if he had understood absolutely every word!

After making sure that Ian was resting, Caitlin gathered her small basket and headed into the village. She managed to survive by trading her skills for food and supplies she needed for tending her patients. She hadn't been to town for several days, however, as she had been busy with the young MacKinnon lad.

73

"Willie. Stay here with Ian. Let no one enter the cave. Stay."

Caitlin watched as her wolf stood up and after getting his instructions, went and lay down on the floor next to Ian's bed. He would stay here until such time as Caitlin "released" him. She was the master, and obey her he would.

As Caitlin entered the village, several people greeted her, asking questions about their various illnesses. Most of them only required some sort of herbal mixture that was easy enough to provide. She was most relieved to see there were no soldiers waiting to be cared for.

Hopefully, that meant that most of the fighting was done, for a while at least. To Caitlin, it seemed that man was forever finding something or the other to disagree about. Such was the curse of mankind.

As she got her needed food and supplies, she began to walk back down the pathway to the cave. She was always careful to make sure she wasn't being followed. And she would take several different paths along the way just in case there was someone she didn't see. Today she saw no one and was truly glad of that.

However, something was happening that she didn't quite understand. As she slowly walked on, she sensed that someone or something was watching her. Almost waiting. A new feeling that was unfamiliar to her. As it was, she could feel the hair on her arms begin to stand up, just a bit, and her hearing became more acute.

She could hear footsteps somewhere behind her and turned quickly. She held her breath as there, not ten feet in front of her, stood a wild boar — probably exactly like the one that had left Thomas with a limp! His body was bulky, and massively built with short and relatively thin legs. His trunk was also short and the region behind his shoulder blades rose into a hump with a mane running along it. His head was very large, and thick mucus oozed from both sides of his snout.

Deep set small eyes and long broad ears made for a really strange looking creature. And he definitely had well- developed canine teeth, several inches long, which protruded from his mouth. All these features together made for one scary looking animal!

Caitlin had the etched staff in her hand, but didn't raise it up — not just yet. The animal stood very still, as if sizing Caitlin up also.

"Huuut!" It had suddenly let out a loud grunt that sent chills up her spine. She might land one lucky hit with her staff, but she'd never be able to win a fight with this wild hog!

For one very long moment in which Caitlin trembled from head to toe, the boar raked his front feet through the dirt, as if getting ready to charge.

"Huuut!" The boar let out another loud grunt that had Caitlin's heart racing! She feared this could be a most brutal way to have her life shortened. She could think of many more palatable ones!

Finally finding her voice, she too let out a loud sound.

"Git! Move it, you hairy beast!" As she screamed, she raised the staff and brought it down.

Her arms quivered as she put as much strength into her swing as she could. Just at the last moment, the boar moved back just inches and she missed him!

"Oh, Holy Rusepheus!"

Caitlin's knees gave ever so slightly and she was not sure she would be able to keep standing. She closed her eyes for a second, not wanting to see what was coming. She felt sure he would be upon her in a heartbeat. Opening her eyes, she watched as the boar stopped in his tracks and looked at her. The air sizzled and Caitlin felt it throughout her body. Abruptly, the hog turned and dashed off into the forest leaving a trail of vile smelling droppings in his wake.

Caitlin's pulse tried to find a regular rhythm, but it struggled to do so. She felt the hair on her arms retreat, and her body stopped shaking. And, as she had experienced several times over the last few days, she was aware of a faint aroma that called to a long ago memory that she just couldn't quite recall. But it always brought a sense of comfort whenever it drifted by. At this particular moment it was most welcome.

But what had just happened with that boar? Why had he fled? Caitlin was too relieved to care why, but was glad he had.

She decided then and there this would be the last trip she made without Willie at her side.

His senses were much keener than hers, although she had always had a most acute sense of smell. Her hearing was also now beginning to pick up sounds she had never heard in the past. As she stood there next to the path, she could see a hummingbird getting nectar from the bluebell bush growing by the wayside, and she could hear its wings fluttering. Strange, but she didn't think she had ever heard that before.

After this incident, she decided to hurry on back to the cave before darkness was upon her. It was already twilight, and with winter on the way, night would come sooner than usual.

Willie heard her coming into the cave, but stayed at his post until she came and "released" him. He then greeted her with a short bark, and she rubbed his head. She still marveled at the size of him. He was much larger than any of the dogs that she had seen Uncle Wabi work with and she thought he was more intelligent also, but maybe she just wanted to think that.

Whatever the case, spending time with her uncle and watching him train his dogs had been time well spent, as she knew how to work with Willie early on.

Chapter 12

Thomas Finlayson and Lord Warwick were more than just a little worried about not being able to find that little red-haired vixen. Thomas had known immediately that Caitlin had heard every word, and being unable to apprehend her at that time, he had waited until after midnight, shortly after he closed the pub, to find his way to the cottage where she lived with her old uncle. The old uncle was a bit strange looking, with his strange pants that only went to his knees, and wearing his hair tied back with a bit of leather string; and he had a scar that ran from his cheek all the way down his face, and across his upper lip. Thomas knew he had nothing to fear from the old man as he was very old and known to be just a bit off — some said eccentric — but Thomas just thought the old man had lost some of his marbles. He was often seen in the village with one of his dogs beside him, and it seemed he was talking to the dog, or maybe himself. It was just another example of his feeble state of mind, Thomas figured.

Thomas, being the whale of a man that he was, and struggling with his limp, had great difficulty climbing over the fence that surrounded Wabi's place. It was out of the village a ways, so he wasn't worried about being seen. He peeked through every window he could and that woman, that healer, wasn't to be found anywhere. Well, he would just come back tomorrow night and take care of her then. He quietly went back to the fence and was trying his best to get back over it when out of the blue came a loud growl, followed by the loudest barking he had ever heard! Then, something grabbed his foot and gnawed on it at the same time! He shook and shook his foot until the dog fell off, but in doing so, a large chunk of his calf came with it!

"Jesus! Let go you varmint!" What pain!

Then he heard the old man calling out, "Who's out there? Get off my property before I turn you into a toad, you miserable excuse for a man!"

Thomas was so relieved to get over the fence that he didn't even think of looking back. The old man didn't seem to have a gun or weapon of any sort, so Thomas thought maybe he was going to get away... but damn that dog!

"Well, I'll take care of him, too, before long," he said, still struggling to get his breath as he ran down into the woods trying to find his way through the forest. Just as he reached the edge of the woods, thinking he had reached safety, something hit him smack in the back of his head, causing him to topple over onto the ground.

"Almighty God! What was that?" he saw nothing, but just then a large owl flew up in front of his face and startled Thomas, then headed to the tree tops. Thomas had never known an owl to attack.

"Just let me get out of this place!" He mumbled. Finally getting back to his feet, he was still muttering to himself.

"Maybe I didn't find you tonight, but I will, my nosey little healer," he promised himself. It never crossed his mind to recall that it was this woman who had saved his life some years ago, and even if he had, he would still need to be rid of her. She could cause great trouble for himself and Lord Warwick.

Chapter 13

Caitlin rose early and went to check on Ian. He was lying there awake, but making no sound. She walked over to his table, where he had been lying for several days now. Caitlin sensed this young lad had need of someone to listen to his concerns, but, being very young was reluctant to say much.

"And good morning to you, Ian. Did you sleep any at all?" Caitlin touched his head, and then changed the dressing on his leg.

"This will do, I believe!" She said it with some authority as she knew that usually went a long way in reassuring a patient they were on the mend.

"No, not much, I think. Do ye think I can go with Alex today?"

"Yes, my good lad, I do think we can arrange that! Your wound is really healing well, and I have no doubt Alex and your other brothers will be able to care for you. It's a great thing to have so many looking out for you. Not everyone is so fortunate."

"Oh, aye. They do look out for me, as ye say. But, still that's not the same as when my Mam was with us. She kept everyone on their toes, and everything was done properly and at the right time." He smiled

"Ye kinda remind me of her when ye start giving orders. She could get the four of us moving faster than a hive of bees coming after us!"

"Well, then. She must have been quite a woman if she could keep the four of you in line! I don't envy her that task." Caitlin smiled back at the boy, who looked so forlorn that she fought a need to enfold him in an embrace and soothe him with words. She was quite sure he might need that, but now was not the time. Perhaps she needed it also. Now, once again, she smelled that same aroma. It was related to her past, but what was it? And, again it left her with a feeling of warmth and comfort, as if being cared for.

"So, now, let's get you dressed so you are quite ready when Alexander calls for you. He brought some clothing in this bag, I believe," she said, picking up a satchel that had been tied on one end. She reached down inside and pulled out another pair of those unusual pants, as well as a shirt, and there was a plaid there also.

"Looks like these are what we'll use today. There's another pair also, but you can only wear one pair at a time."

"My Mam made those for me. She thought they would keep me warmer as I was sickly much of the time. I got to liking them so I just kept on wearing them after she died. But, they're beginning to be just a bit tight, so I guess I'll go back to the plaid and trews again."

"Yeah, I'm sure you miss your mother, Ian. There's never anyone to take her place, but memories can be called up whenever you wish." Caitlin observed the look on the young lad's face. He liked that thought.

Getting Ian dressed was quite an ordeal. He cried out in pain when she moved him just the smallest bit. Caitlin certainly had second thoughts about letting Alexander take him today. But, she knew he would anyway, and certainly he had reason.

"You'll make it alright, Ian. It may be difficult, but I know you four men have faced more difficult challenges than this one. You'll come through this one too, I do believe."

Willie darted to the front of the cave in order to properly greet their arriving guests. Caitlin smiled to herself. Willie was quite taken with Alex, and he wasn't the only one, she ventured to admit to herself.

She walked outside, and the three brothers were all there walking toward her. These three men, each with his own confident stride, would make one think twice about crossing them. She had already decided not to do so in the matter of Ian, and it was just as well. Taking on one of them was one thing, but all three was something else entirely. Caitlin was certainly glad they had become friends, rather than enemies.

"Ah, the Highland Brigade, I see!" Caitlin tried to make light of their arrival, but immediately realized they probably did not find the humor in her remark. They had done their share of fighting and wanted no more, and that was something she did agree with.

"Caitlin. You seem to be in fine spirits today." Alexander came closer and bowed slightly. His scent came before him, an evergreen freshness she would always associate with him. Hector and Jack greeted her as well. "Good morning, Healer."

"So, is the laddie ready for riding, do ye think?" Jack was about to walk on back but Alex caught his arm. "Hold a moment, brother. Caitlin will tell ye when ye can go back."

Caitlin laughed aloud. "Thank you, Alex. Come, all of you. He's as ready as I can make him. And he'll do, he'll do. Quite a fine young man he is."

"You two go on; I need to speak with Caitlin for a few moments." Alex wandered back outside and went over to the horses, fiddling with the straps on his saddle, which were already just right. Caitlin could see he was working up to saying something, but she had no idea what it could be.

"Alex. Come out with it. I see something is bothering you, so tell me what it is." Caitlin long ago learned to get her patients to confide in her. Sharing a problem often made it seem just a wee bit smaller.

"Ye be right, Caitlin. Something is disturbing me. Well, actually, all of us. We spent a great deal of time working on this problem last night and now I need to make ye understand our plan." Ever the strategist!

"We're all anxious to take Ian and depart from this area. We have a ways to go, but when we get there, chances are we'll all be safe and can return to our home back in the mountains, where we have lived all our lives. Our Da still keeps the place up, but with Ian having been gone these weeks, he's probably having a bit of a time just keeping the animals fed and the sheep in their pastures. So, we need to get back to him." He stopped rearranging the saddle straps and turned to face Caitlin. His face showed a look of determination that was not lost on the healer.

"But, just listening to your story, yesterday, it seems to me ye are actually in a worse predicament than we find ourselves. So, we've all agreed we should take ye with us, to safety that is. We have a crofter's hut ye would find a bit more comfortable than this cave, and we would be around if ye needed any protection. And, certainly, a healer in our area would be most welcome. Mam used to help a bit with the villagers, but she certainly wasn't a healer like ye.

Still, her help has been missed."

"I see. You want me to go to the upper Highlands with you all, to a place of safety." Caitlin was never so shocked! She was having difficulty finding the right words to say to him.

"Aye, that's it exactly."

Caitlin shook her head as if in disbelief.

"Oh, Alex. I thank you kindly, but I believe I'm pretty safe here. I've made a few friends in the village, and my skills are needed here as well. Plus, this isn't so far from Skye. Perhaps I might even see Uncle Wabi again if I don't stray too far away. He's getting on in years now and I would hope some of my problems will work themselves out and I might even return to my home one day."

"Caitlin. We're able to take care of ourselves, and there are four of us. Ye are alone, with yer protector, of course, and a fine one he is. But, with three different men looking for ye, one of them is bound to find ye sooner or later. It would pain me to think something might happen to ye, lass. It would truly be better if you came with us."

Caitlin hardly knew how to reply. She found this man most intriguing, and being with him felt so right. But, to just leave and go with him? She walked closer to him, looking up so he might see the resoluteness in her face.

"No, Alex. I must stay here. If I must leave this place for some reason, then perhaps I'll come to the upper Highlands and find you four. Some of my relatives were from that region, but I've never been that far. For now, staying here is what I must do."

That decision did not sit well with Alex. It showed in his drawn face and tight lips. He pretty much made the decisions regarding his family, and he had expected any sane person would see this was a most reasonable plan. But, Alex was good at reading people also. He saw the set of Caitlin's jaw and chin when she said her piece. She wouldn't be changing her mind, not just yet anyway. But, he disliked not being able to persuade her to do what would keep her safe and close to him. He found this woman very much to his liking.

His voice got louder. "So that's the way of it then? Ye'll no listen to reason, but stay here and become prey for any one of the three out to get ye!" His worry had now turned into anger and exasperation.

By then Caitlin's temper was simmering a bit too. She turned to him, hands on her hips, face flushing.

"Again. I thank ye. But I'll be staying here!"

Caitlin had been making her own decisions for quite some time now. Uncle Wabi had encouraged her to think long and hard before coming to any decisions about most anything. She accepted that most times she had made good ones, but she wasn't so sure about the latest ones.

Did she really need to leave Skye? "Of course you did. You had to protect Uncle Wabi and your friends," she murmured under her breath.

"And then, leaving the thatched hut? Was that really necessary? Yes, absolutely."

She feared Commander Campbell much more than she did Thomas and Lord Warwick.

Thomas was too lazy to give much pursuit and the Lord didn't even know her on sight.

Caitlin turned her back on Alex and marched inside the cave. Alex was following closely behind her, frowning and still fuming about her decision. He watched as she swirled about, the blue dress swinging around and her petticoat flashing in the process.

"Damn, woman. She ought to listen to reason for once!" he spoke to Willie, apparently, as Caitlin had walked on ahead of him.

***

Hector and Jack had indeed built a "traveling bed" for Ian. They had spent the entire day yesterday making sure it wouldn't fall off once they had it secured on Ian's horse. Ian was a very thin young man, so weight didn't present much of a problem. Now they were both ready to see how this would work. And it must.

Jack carefully picked the young lad up and carried him outside. He nodded to Caitlin as he passed her. He still wasn't sure about her, but was thankful to have Ian back with them. And, he wasn't so sure Alex's thinking was clear where the healer was concerned. Jack had never known Alex to care for any woman, especially one like this one, prone to speaking her mind.

Alex and Hector helped hand Ian up onto the litter bed on the horse's back. Ian grimaced but tried to keep his groans to a minimum. He was ready to go home also and had to endure this in order to get moving.

"Now then. I do believe this will work fairly well."

Caitlin was impressed with the "traveling" bed. It would certainly make the boy much more comfortable than trying to ride a horse. She just hoped that he didn't begin to bleed. She had spent time yesterday instructing Alex on what to do if that occurred. Alex was experienced in tending wounds, but listened just the same. This healer had a wealth of knowledge he welcomed.

Ian seemed as comfortable as he might be. He felt secure in this contraption and smiled down to Caitlin. She took that as his way of saying thank you and returned a smile to him as well.

"Do what your brothers tell you now, young Ian. They care for you, lad."

Hector and Jack mounted and waited as Alex walked back over to where Caitlin and Willie were standing at the cave entrance.

"Caitlin. If ye ever need us, just head north, past the Black Isle. After ye cross Cromarty Firth, travel on, always north, and go on across Dornock Firth. Ask any crofter and they'll know where to find us. We live far up in the forest and it will take ye some days, but if ye ask anyone in the area, they'll know where the MacKinnon land starts, and word will get to us that ye be looking for us. Then we'll find ye. I'm indebted to ye, healer, and I like to pay my debts."

He quickly turned away from her, mounted up, and they all started down the long path toward home. Ian waved and Caitlin smiled again, calling Willie to come as he was trotting beside the group, maybe hoping he could go too.

Chapter 14

Commander Bernard Campbell rode hard — until his poor horse was about to collapse, as was he. His mind would not stop replaying the sight of his son, Bradford, lying on his bed, his life having ended before his father could get to him. And the others were already buried, because the bodies were deteriorating and some local men had helped her complete the task.

"They can't be dead! They survived worse than this! What did you do to them?" He ran from one bed to the other, as if he must convince himself they all were indeed dead. He could still remember her voice, so soothing.

"Please, Commander, come with me," said the healer as she pulled him away from the last bedside, that of his son, Bradford.

"This disease, this fever, leaves few alive in its wake. It's a most terrible illness and one that has no treatment that seems to make much difference. As it is, it appears these soldiers all picked it up in the bogs and some even before them had already died in some of the local villages.

But now, after riding all night, consumed with his grief, the commander could not accept this fever had killed them all and as he lay on his cot, covered only with a light blanket, waiting for morning to come, he spoke to the empty room.

"I know she must be some kind of shaman or witch. She worked her evil on all these young men, and she will pay for this!"

He had ridden all night, stopping only briefly to rest his horse. He was now in his home village, and he was calling on the families of the dead soldiers, trying to explain to them their sons would not be coming home.

"And she buried them also!" The families were most distressed to learn they could not even retrieve the bodies of their loved ones and bury them properly.

"She said it was done in order to keep the disease from spreading, but I don't believe her. I tell you she's a witch and I'll make sure she burns for this!"

At the home of the Frasers, he told his sad tale and, as he was leaving, Mrs. Fraser touched him on his sleeve.

"Commander Campbell, sir, we've already had the fever here in the village, just a short time ago. And it did bring much death with it just as the healer told you. We've already buried a number of our village folk and now the sickness seems to have gone. I don't believe it to be the work of a witch, ye ken, for a few of us that are older have seen it before and we believe it to be the same disease, that malaria. It is a most dreadful illness, I fear. Don't let your grief keep you from seeing the truth of it."

But Commander Campbell jerked his arm away, stomped down the steps and left, as he had several more stops to make. His grief was the only thing that was keeping him going at this time, and he would hold onto it and he would see that witch punished.

After delivering the last of his frightful news to all the families, he started out immediately, back the way he had come.

He mumbled to himself, "Call it malaria. Well, they can call it whatever pleases them, but I know her to be evil, what with that head of fiery hair and soothing voice of hers. I know she is a witch, and her days are numbered!"

With that, he lashed his horse with his whip and sped off with even greater urgency. He was sure he would be able to find her. He needed some purpose to keep going, and she was it.

Chapter 15

Caitlin had not realized how quiet and desolate her cave was without the young lad being here. He was a quiet one, but his presence offered her a chance to understand she needed to get herself more acquainted with others in the village. She had pretty much kept to herself, believing to stay in the cave as much as possible would prevent her three "enemies" from discovering her.

But, her skills were welcomed, and she did go to the village to tend the ones who were in need. She was also concerned that she wasn't able to check on Uncle Wabi. They always kept up with each other's events, as it were, and she missed talking with him. He had, jokingly, always told her that all she had to do was think about him and he would know it. Leave it to Uncle Wabi to be so fanciful! Yes, he was eccentric, which she found delightful.

She walked back outside as somehow the cave was too lonely just now. It was twilight, more quickly now this time of year and she heard the great owl "hoo hoo" at her as she looked up in the tree. She liked knowing he was there. He and Willie were about the only permanent things she had at the moment. Willie had been with her since she arrived here, as had the owl. Something about the owl was comforting as he made her think of the old owl that had always resided in the hawthorn tree at Uncle Wabi's. Uncle Wabi appreciated nature more than most people and had passed on his beliefs about the animals to Caitlin.

Lately, she had dreamed of Uncle Wabi, and it was always the same dream. He was walking in the woods with one of his dogs, which is probably exactly what he would be doing.

She hoped he didn't worry about her and knew she would return one day when some of this confusion worked itself out.

But, was it a dream really? She had awakened in the night several times and felt a presence in the room. Almost as if Uncle Wabi were right there with her. She could actually smell that scent she associated with him - leather and some cinnamon with oranges. But, she had to have been groggy and still dreaming. But the feeling was something she couldn't quite shake.

Chapter 16

The MacKinnon brothers had been traveling for most of two days now, headed north, and young Ian had managed to stay in his bed and kept his complaints to himself. After all, MacKinnon men didn't whine, or at least that's what Jack told him. Jack took a bullet on the same day that Ian had been slashed, but Ian never once heard him complain about his pain. But it surely must be there, thought Ian. In his opinion, his three older brothers were fine men, and he so wanted to be like them, except that sometimes he wanted nothing more than to strangle Jack! Sometimes he started stomping and ranting about something when Ian knew that, if he would just listen for a moment, he would understand what was happening. Jack was the closest in age to Ian, but even so, there were ten years between them. Ian had been a "late life" baby for Mam. She would always say "he might be late, but he's my fine baby boy, he is." Ian missed her, as he knew the others did also. All their lives were different without her. It seemed that a bright ray of sunlight had gone out of their lives when she died.

***

Hector, the negotiator, had been watching Alexander most of the day. Alex was never one to be excessively talkative, but Hector found this brooding for two days a bit unusual. This amount of time was even more than Alex usually took when he was trying to figure out some problem or another. He had a suspicion as to what was on Alex's mind, but decided to engage his older brother if he could. He brought his horse up next to Alex and walked alongside him.

"So, Alex, what is it that has ye so wrapped up yer not even giving us orders or shouting as usual?"

"Humph. Giving orders to the bunch of ye is like trying to herd kittens. Useless. But, when I resort to shouting that seems to get yer attention." Alex rubbed the back of his neck.

"Ah, I don't know what to tell ye. I didn't like it then, and I still don't like it now." "What is it you don't like, brother?"

"Eh? Oh. Well. Leaving Caitlin, the healer, back there in the cave all by herself." "Well, if I remember rightly, she made it pretty clear she preferred to stay there, and it seemed she meant what she said. She didn't beat about the bush, I don't believe. It seems to me she was getting along very well, actually. It was a cave, but somehow she had managed to make it a bit of a comfortable place, candles, flowers, and it was really clean! Did you notice that?"

"Yes, she had put some womanly touches on it, I give her that. But there's more to her story than you three know."

"Then, dear brother, tell us all!" Hector grinned at his older brother. He figured this might be an interesting story and getting Alex to open up with his worries might be good for all of them.

"As it is, ye see, Caitlin is in a situation much like our own. Someone, really three people, is trying to catch up with her. And, these three, all men, would like nothing better than to get rid of her permanently. And one of them is particularly worrisome.

"What! Why would someone, a woman, be running from three men? Did she promise to wed them and then run off?" Hector laughed, but Alex didn't.

"Nae, I wish it was just that simple. Nae, it seems she overheard a local innkeeper, a bar owner, and an English lord discussing which villagers were working for the prince. These two were turning their names in to the Redcoats for rounding up and taking in. Knowing that Caitlin had heard them talking and knew what they were planning, they need to silence her. But, now after Culloden, perhaps that information isn't as important as it might have been beforehand. I'm no so concerned about those two."

"But. Now the other. That's the one that causes me to worry. This man, a Commander Bernard Campbell, has accused Caitlin of being a witch. It seems there were a number of soldiers, returning from battle, who were stricken with the fever and who came by her cottage for treatment as she was known to heal many illnesses. Caitlin thought it was malaria. Well, as it stands, most of them died, including the son of this Commander Campbell. Naturally, he wants to blame someone for his pain, grieving as he rightly is, and has decided that Caitlin is the person responsible. And he has labeled her a witch, ye see. So, there's a reason for my worry, and as yet, I haven't quite decided what to do about relieving my worry, and her danger."

"She didn't let on that she was in any danger, or not that I could tell. She seemed to have made some sort of home and is allowed to practice her skills in the village. On the outside, it seemed like a fair arrangement for everyone there. But, as you say, she is all alone," Hector responded.

Hector backed off as he knew Alex would ponder on this until such time as he was ready to share his thoughts with his brothers. Then, as they were brothers, they usually tried to help each other with whatever the problem was.

"Well, ye know we stand with ye, Alex, even Jack. He's very glad to have Ian back, and he knows who's responsible for that. He may mumble and complain about her, but he feels the healer has done this family a great service. He'll do his part, whatever that needs to be."

Alex walked his horse away from his brother, coming to a halt just at the top of a ridge where they were to camp for the evening. Looking out over the countryside, he couldn't quite remember feeling this way about any woman, witch, or healer, or local village woman, not one.

He could still see her smiling as they rode away, throwing up her hand as they left. He had looked back just at the last moment and saw her bend down and put her arms around the wolf's neck.

"What woman in her right mind would have a wolf for a companion? And an owl who lives in a tree close by?" he asked himself. He decided to think on it a bit more, but he had an inkling what he would do in the end. Just convincing his brothers, however, would be a monumental task.

Chapter 17

Caitlin had only been outside a few moments when the wind began to pick up. The moon had risen brightly in the east and the sky was littered with thousands of stars, lighting up the darkened canopy. Caitlin pulled her plaid closer to her body and stood there thinking about the four MacKinnon brothers. What a special family that must be. So many of them! Having been an only child, raised by older grandparents and an eccentric uncle, Caitlin wondered how that would feel, to have so many family members to share a life with, to lean on, and to be with.

Turning to go back inside, Caitlin heard a rustling behind the trees some distance away. In the past, she would never have heard this, but with this new ability she seemed to have, this acute hearing, she stopped and listened again. Suddenly, as if someone were standing next to her, she heard a voice.

"Get inside, hide! Run inside! Hide deep down in the cave! Now!" She hardly knew what to think. She could see no one, but her intuition insisted that she obey the voice, wherever it was coming from.

Just before she ran through the cave entrance, the owl zipped past her as if leading the way. He had never come inside before! Having no other thoughts that made any better sense, she followed the owl far into the cave, back to one of the chambers where she hardly ever went. That being the case, she had no candles there either, so it was very dark.

"Now be very quiet! Don't move a muscle!" The voice was there in the cave also! Caitlin knew no one else was in the cave, only she and the owl. She hadn't seen Willie in the last few minutes but he hadn't come in with them. So where was the voice coming from? As she was still pondering this question, feeling her heartbeat with every breath, she heard a noise coming from the front of the cave. Apparently, she was wrong. Someone else WAS in the cave. Whoever it was must be in the kitchen. She could hear them. They must have bumped the edge of her table for they let out a short groan and a curse. It was obviously a man. The voice told her that much. She wished now she hadn't run back here as there was no way out. She was a sitting duck just waiting to be discovered.

"Quiet, I tell you! He will leave if you remain quiet!" That voice again!

"Who are you? Where are you?" Caitlin whispered loudly and hoped the man up front couldn't hear her. She had to know who was speaking to her! She knocked over some bottles of herbs on a table and gasped at how loud the noise was. He would surely find her now! Shortly after she heard the cursing, she could actually feel him coming closer. Her skin began to tingle and her hair felt like it was lifting off her head. Her breath was coming in short bursts and she tried to look about for some kind of weapon. She didn't have a gun or a sword, but as she got to the corner of the room, against the wall, she felt about. This was where she stored things she didn't use very often, some extra bandages, herbs for ointments, and feeling still behind her, this was where she kept her hooded cape. Next to that she felt the crooked staff she had taken from Uncle Wabi's closet. The one with the etchings on it.

Suddenly, the quietness was shattered by a deep, male voice.

"Well, well. So I've finally found you, little witch. Did you really think you could hide in this cave?" He laughed at her, a loud echoing sound in the cave.

"He must have better night vision that I do," she said inwardly.

The silhouette of the man finally came into view as he got closer and he was holding a lighted candle up high. Actually, she knew the voice, but even if she hadn't, she would have remembered the smell she associated with this man, henbane, an herb that she used in creating one of her more vile smelling concoctions. It had a most offensive odor! And, he was wearing that most imposing uniform, again, as though he never took it off. She remained quiet and tried not to move.

He kept coming, slowly.

"Thought I would forget about you? Not likely. I will say you have given me quite a bit of a chase though. You would have made a good soldier. But, then I am a better one it seems. So, now you will pay the price all witches must pay when they are found out. They all eventually become ashes! I always keep my promises, wicked lady, and this one I have looked forward to.

My son was the only person I have ever cared for! Not his spiteful, hideous mother. But him! He was my life and you took him from me! Burning you will bring me great satisfaction!"

With that statement, he took a large step forward and grabbed her by her hair, pulling her up close to him, her toes barely touching the floor. She was so frightened she was trembling and desperately trying not to call out, letting him know how scared she was.

Just as he was yanking on her hair, bringing her to her knees, she felt every fiber of her body was on fire! Something or someone was coming; she could feel it. With one giant leap, Willie came flying through the air and with a hair-raising growl, grabbed Commander Campbell by the throat, his great bicuspids digging deeply into tissue and bone! The soldier dropped Caitlin, causing her to fall on all fours. He then let go of her hair and desperately tried to pry the wolf from his throat. He struggled to breathe. He reached for the knife that he wore on his belted uniform, pulled it out of its sheath and began to strike at Willie. Caitlin heard Willie let out a cry and yelp, but still he did not let go of the soldier's throat. The instant she heard Willie's cry was when she lifted her staff and brought it down on the commander's head, with all the strength she had. She hit him with such a thud that it sent ripples of pain up her arms. She never knew she had so much strength! She quickly gave a command to Willie to release the solider, which he did, but not readily. He was still growling as he let go of the man, every muscle still taut, hackles standing tall and baring his great teeth.

"Let him go, Willie. He can't hurt us now. I understand you want to finish him off, but let's just get away from her. Come." Willie held on for another minute, then finally responded to his master's command, but continued to stand over the man's crumpled body.

Caitlin was shaking, but quickly felt for the commander's pulse. It was there, so he was unconscious, but not dead. A part of her wanted to finish him right there, but the healer had a most difficult time killing anyone, even this man who was her enemy.

She knew she would have to flee, once again. She called to her wolf and he came to her side. As she reached down to him, hugging him closely, she felt a wetness on his underside.

"No! He's wounded you! Come, Willie!"

She quickly ran to the large room where her supplies and medicines were. She tried to pick Willie up, but he had gotten so heavy that she couldn't. At that point, she just laid him on the floor and made a quick assessment of his wound. It appeared he had only been cut once, but it was quite a deep, long gash that required stitches, which she made short order of as she knew they must leave as quickly as possible. Willie laid on his side without a whimper as she bound him up and grabbed her staff, her medicine bag, a small packet of food and took the long, hooded cloak with her. At the last minute, she picked up the bag of clothing that had belonged to Ian and opened it. Inside there was still a pair of pants, a shirt and thick woolen leggings as well. She made a rash decision, Uncle Wabi would have said. But, time was of the essence, so she made her decision and got on about it. She quickly removed her dress, her petticoat and thin stockings. She kept her camisole on and then she put on the warm stockings. Over the camisole, she pulled on the warm shirt belonging to the young lad. Then she donned the woolen leggings and pants and, lastly, put her boots back on. She didn't have a full-length looking glass, but she knew if she had one she would have seen a young lad, looking back at her, which is exactly what she hoped for. She fashioned her hair into one long braid, falling down her back, and pulled on the beret she had found in the bottom of Ian's bag. All the clothing was a dark brown, including the beret, which should help keep her hidden in the dark, along with the long, dark, hooded cloak. She grabbed her staff and medicine bag. Then lastly, she grabbed the soldier's pistol and stuck it in her bag and made a quick exit from the cave. Once again homeless and on the run.

"This is becoming quite a habit, and one that needs to be broken!"

She spoke to the wolf who was so close to her she could hardly walk. He still sensed danger and would stick to her like glue until they were in a place of safety. Caitlin was again so grateful to have this most competent protector and stopped long enough to put her arms around his neck, her forehead on his, and sent thanks to whomever had sent him her way. As they passed the rowan tree, she looked up and the owl was nowhere to be seen. Caitlin hoped he was able to find his way out of the cave.

Chapter 18

Lady Millie had reached the end of her very long rope. No longer could she stay in this place, Warwick Castle. Her husband's castle. Not even one more night! Having survived her entire life living with a beast of a man for a father, one would think that living with a husband who was cut from the same cloth would be easy enough. However, Millie knew she must get away from the man, and quickly. His rages and fits of anger were becoming unbearable and, had she only to think of herself, perhaps she would just continue on as she had for the past three years.

She had been given to Lord Warwick by her father, as payment for lands that Lord Sinclair wanted in order to increase his holdings. Neither of these men ever considered asking her for her consent. Her father had thought no more of this exchange, his daughter, than trading for a horse. This hardly surprised her, however, as she had seen early on that her mother, the former Louise Cameron, probably had no say in her marriage either. It was most definitely a joining of families for political purposes that worked in her father's favor.

However, as it was, her situation had changed some months ago when, to her surprise, she discovered that she was with child.

"Oh, dear God! No!" she had exclaimed to her reflection in the looking glass. "This can't be."

So, now with more than just herself to consider, she had been making plans to escape from both these men, her father and her husband. At the moment, they were both traveling to

London for a great meeting of other landowners, lords, and probably the king himself! She knew that if she was going to go through with her plan, then it must be now. But, it was a bit more complicated than just sneaking away in the dark. Millie was not far from delivery time, and she moved rather slowly and was unwieldy to say the least. One of her serving ladies would certainly help her if Millie asked. But after thinking on it a bit, she decided that she would not involve anyone in her scheme. Then, when she was found to be missing, no one could accuse her serving women of helping her escape.

But, of course, that meant she would have to do everything for herself, pack food, a wrap for warmth. And yes, she thought, I will take one of my husband's horses.

"He'll not care that I'm gone, but he will be most angry that I have taken one of his horses," she spoke again to her reflection. The irony of this was almost too painful to give much thought to. She turned away from the mirror to avoid seeing any tears that might have trickled down her cheek.

She had been living in Warwick Castle for the past three years, the three longest years of her life. Living with her husband, Edward, a man some years older than she, was even more difficult than she had imagined it would be. When he imbibed too much of his fermented mead, he was a physical brute, just as her father had been. But even without the drink, he was a mentally cruel man, given to unexpected bouts of depression, followed by periods of unbridled exuberance when he was almost unbearable. But, even in those times, he seemed to delight in stomping about the castle, yelling at the servants, and belittling her, convincing her that no other man would ever have looked at her, much less have wanted her as a wife. She had been used as payment for land, and that had positioned him as son-in-law to one of the wealthiest lords in the country. Lord Warwick had never truly wanted her as a wife, and he forever reminded her of that fact.

She never wondered that he would be distraught over her leaving him. He cared nothing for her, and only wanted this unborn child because even more properties would come his way upon the birth of his first-born son. Again, the child would be used as just another pawn as she had been.

"Well, I so hope that it's a girl and then you will not get more of your precious land!" The chamber maid had walked in and turned to her.

"Beg pardon, milady?" Millie just shook her head, not really wanting to speak to anyone.

The maid went on, and Millie returned to thinking this situation through. She must be prepared to travel many days, alone, heavy with child, and with winter about to set in. She knew exactly where she would go, but had never traveled there alone, so was not exactly sure how to proceed. But, she had an exceptional sense of direction, having learned from her father as a child how to watch the sun, look for mountain ranges, and to pay attention to the landscape and trees. She had gone with him many, many times when he would fly his beloved falcons. Watching them soar high into the sky, she often wished she could do that too. She loved watching these marvelous birds as they climbed higher, and higher, and always got their prey. Of course, they returned to Lord Sinclair's hand and he covered their heads, limiting their view of the world, much as he had hers.

The most exciting part of going out with him came at the end of the day. He would allow her to find her way back to their castle, which she loved to do, and not once had she failed to do so. She had no idea this would be invaluable training at the time. It would certainly help her as she undertook this escape, and finding her way to her destination may not be as trying for her as it might be for some.

Millie wandered about her chamber and then went downstairs and out into her garden. This was the only place where she had felt she could be at peace. Warwick had scoffed at the idea of her planting a flower garden, but in the end had not made a fuss about it. So, she had turned her green thumb loose and as a result, there was usually something blooming at most every season. The English winters, however, would put a screeching halt to that, but she would keep her seedlings and place them in the room she used as her hothouse along with her most treasured flowers, her orchids. Even through the winter, she would keep them, along with the help of her gardener, Robbie, whose thumb was almost as green as hers. She would miss this one place of solitude.

As she wandered about, she thought about Dorothea and how she wished she were here with her right now.

When her father had informed her she would wed Lord Warwick, Millie was at a loss for words. Apparently, the decision had been made by her father and Edward, Lord Warwick, without her agreement, and she was to have no say in the matter. These two conniving men made their deal and informed Millie of it just a day before the ceremony was to take place. Knowing she had no choice but to marry Lord Warwick, she thought at least to have some say in how the event took place.

"But Father! I want a real wedding, with a beautiful dress, and relatives from Scotland!

Every girl wants her wedding to be special!"

But, there was no celebration, no dress, no bridesmaids, and no relatives to come to visit. Instead, the ceremony was conducted by a local vicar, and she was to be taken away immediately to live in Warwick Castle.

***

As Dorothea packed Millie's clothing and items that she would need in her new home, she hoped her mistress would find life a bit more enjoyable with her new husband, but somehow she had great doubts about that happening. Lady Millie's new lord was a sullen man with few words for anyone, and certainly none for someone of her station, a nursemaid. She had learned to stay out of his way, just as she had Millie's father. The two men had many like characteristics, and Dorothea wished that were not so. But, no matter, she would take care of Lady Millie as she always had, and she would be content to do so.

Lord Warwick had sent a coach from his castle to collect Millie and her personal belongings. So, she and Dorothea had everything ready and stood outside, Millie ever scanning the air for whatever creatures may be soaring the area. She could recognize a hawk, a falcon, a kestrel, an eagle, or even an owl from a far distance. Each bird had its own way of gliding or soaring, or flapping its wings. And, most interesting of all, each had its own call, or as Millie thought of it as a child, its own language. She delighted in learning to make the various sounds of all the birds and would call to them when she went riding through the woods around the estate.

Millie heard the coach coming around the gate, as it crossed over the cobblestones that led up to the front of the castle. She was still angry over what had transpired, but knew that she, a woman, had no choice but to obey and do her best to make a life as best she could, given her circumstances. Dorothea was quiet, but she stood next to Millie, looking up at her and smiling.

Dorothea was quite small, especially standing next to Millie. They had made it through many struggles over the years, living in this home, so they would survive this move also. Dorothea made a short quick nod as if to say, "Yes, my Lady Millie, together we will make it work," which was what she always said when faced with a difficult situation.

The coach pulled up with the horses snorting and pulling at the reins. The coachman jumped down and loaded several trunks onto the top of the vehicle. As he opened the door of the coach, holding out his hand to assist Lady Warwick, he gently lifted her arm and helped her settle into the seat. He turned back to Dorothea then and announced,

"I am told that Lady Warwick will travel alone. Another coach will be sent to take you back to Scotland and your family." With a quick nod and jerk of his chin, he closed the door and began to climb back up on his seat atop the coach.

Millie, unable to hear the coachman, looked out and saw Dorothea with a stricken look on her face.

"Whatever is it, Dorothea? Come, we must be going."

"Oh, milady. It seems I am not to go with you. The coachman says I am to return to my family in Scotland. Lord Warwick is sending a coach for me." Tears were streaming down her cheeks, and her entire body was beginning to tremble

"No! Of course you will come!" Millie tried to stand up and, just as she did, the coachman cracked his whip causing the coach to lurch forward with a giant leap, the horses pulling with all their might to get away from the sting of the awful whip. She was thrown back into the seat and felt her heart beginning to ache as it never had before, not even when her mother died. Dorothea was truly the only person that she had ever loved and one who had certainly loved her in return.

That seemed so long ago now, thought Millie. She had written to Dorothea at her family's place in Scotland, but had never had any return letters. At least she had never seen them if they were indeed sent. Her life had been totally managed Lord Warwick and now she had decided he would NOT control her for even another minute.

Chapter 19

"Whadda ye mean yer going back? We just got here and now ye want to go all the way back down the mountains to check on that witch!" Jack was beside himself listening to Alex's plan that he had sprung on them within just a few hours of them reaching their home.

"I'll thank ye not to refer to her that way ever again!"

Alex stood up and looked Jack in the eye. Jack may be a little taller, but Alex knew how to use his voice to command when he needed. He never had particularly liked being the eldest, but when he needed to, he would exercise his right of first born.

"She's the reason young Ian here is still with us and mighty glad of that we all are, even ye, ye big oaf!"

With that, he gave Jack a quick slap on the back of the head, smiling as he did so. Jack was just a bit ashamed of himself then as what Alex had said was right, the healer was responsible for keeping their young brother alive.

A bit taken aback, Jack began to speak.

"Aye, brother. I'll not repeat it again and I'm glad that she made our Ian well enough to travel. He'll mend now that we're home again."

"Then I'll start out early morning and head back to her cave. Something tells me she can get herself into a whole lot of trouble without even trying. As it is, she has no one to help her and we most certainly have a debt to her. I aim to pay it whether she likes it or no."

***

Hector was busy in the kitchen, doing what he liked best, cooking. At the moment he was making a big pot of stew. The large room was very comfy mostly because of the big fire Jack had made the minute they got here, and the warmth of the fire, plus just the pleasure of being home had everyone in a good mood, even Jack.

During the several weeks since Ian had left the home place, Da had taken a spill trying to catch one of the new lambs that had just been born. He could see the small kid was not nursing much and wanted to bring it back to the house so he could hand feed it. That was a common enough way to handle the situation on a sheep farm, and usually the little one would eat well and grow up to be just as large as the others. But, when he went to catch the small kid he stumbled over a large limb that had fallen during a storm a few days earlier. He had been meaning to clear it away, but what with having only old Jamie to help him, he was just a bit behind on a number of tasks that needed to be done.

As he picked himself up, he seemed to be pretty much alright, until he started to lift the small animal. Then, pain in his right shoulder shot through his entire arm, causing him to almost drop the wee lamb. What now! He began to feel around his arm and shoulder and when he touched the bone coming from his neck and going out to the edge of his shoulder he yelped in pain and knew he had most probably broken his collarbone.

"Well, now, this I could do without!"

So, doing what he thought was the proper thing, he put it in a sling and went about his business as best he could. But, glory! It was painful! Mam would have known how to take care of this, but she wasn't here anymore, so this would have to do. But, it greatly hampered his ability to get things done and was still very painful.

***

As he was closing the gate on the pasture near the house, Da heard what sounded like a herd of horses thundering down the lane. He walked out into the path to see what was going on. It was getting on to being almost dark, so he had to strain his eyes a bit to see what was causing such a racket. The sight he saw was a most welcome one. His sons. All of his sons. Safe they were. And lifting his eyes to the heavens, he murmured quietly,

"And thanks be for their safety" — a prayer he had uttered every day since they left.

When he had discovered Ian was gone, he knew immediately where the boy would be off to. That lad so disliked being left at home while his brothers went to fight for the "cause."

"Fighting for the cause . . . my arse!" Da said to himself.

As long as he could remember, there were wars for one reason or another, and he was certainly at the stage of life where he wanted no more. With the death of their mother, his sons were even more important to him. And, proud of them he was, but now it was time they were home for good.

There had been a reunion, MacKinnon style, with a lot of loud talking, laughing, and hugging all around. Da, and old Jamie, the farm hand that had lived on the MacKinnon land as long as anyone could remember, were there to greet them. Uncle Andrew was usually there, but had gone down to Edinburgh to research records in the kirks and government offices. Jack had built a roaring fire the moment they came into the house. Winter had come early to the Highlands, and the fire was welcome. Then Hector, taking over the kitchen again, was in his element. Some hearty food would be welcome. They had sustained themselves fairly well on the trip home, but they were all ready for something that would stick to their bones a little better and fill their bellies better than brose and oatmeal had.

They set up a place for Ian and his "bed" next to the fire. He was too exhausted to carry on much of a conversation, but just seeing Da and smelling the scents that were still left there by his mother's numerous dried flowers and pots of potpourri, he smiled and went right to sleep.

Da, still nursing his broken collarbone, was distraught when he saw what had happened to Ian. But, living in the Highlands, you always had more than enough difficulties to deal with, and he would deal with this one as well. He was glad that his Alice had been spared this tragedy. Ian had been her baby boy, no doubt. He smiled just remembering how excited she was, even at her advanced age, to have another bairn on the way!

Hector stirred his stew, listening to his brother's plan to go back to the cave. However, as he was listening to the brothers discussing Alex's intentions, he heard what Alex was telling Jack... "paying our debt..." and knowing he might be doing that; but, Hector knew, most of all Alex needed to see the healer, Caitlin, was safe. There was no doubt in Hector's mind Alex was very taken with this woman. And, she was about as hard-headed as Alex, so this might prove to be interesting! He laughed aloud remembering her ordering them all about. She would indeed be a challenge for Alex and something about that just tickled him. Just thinking about it. That small woman telling "big brother" to get back to his business! Ha!

Chapter 20

Caitlin, so frightened she could hardly move, eased up to the horse tied in the trees. He had actually snorted to her when she came out of the cave. It had been her plan to keep to the woods, along with Willie, wearing her disguise of boy's clothing and the cloak. She hoped to escape being seen by anyone, most especially a soldier intent on doing her harm.

But, as she walked past the trees, a horse made a neighing sound and snorted at her as well. She stopped, thinking again.

"Caitlin, my girl, you can make a lot more time on horseback." She hadn't been on a horse since she was a child, so was unsure how this might turn out. She had a pony when she lived with her grandparents, but as she got older, she preferred to walk as that way she could gather her herbs and plants when she went about the forest and countryside.

Giving Willie the "stay" command, she eased up closer to the animal. She was afraid Willie might spook the horse, and now that she had access to him, she wanted to make sure he didn't dash away.

She walked slowly and quietly towards the animal. "Hey, gorgeous man."

She hoped he was a gelding, but feared he may be a stallion as that would probably suit Commander Campbell better; it certainly would be in keeping with his personality. But, the horse just shook his withers and lowered his head for her to stroke his face.

"Well, now, maybe you and I could become friends. You can be sure I will treat you better than that soldier did." She could see lash marks on his hind quarters, and rubbed them gently, speaking softly to him. The horse leaned even closer to her, as if enjoying her soothing touch.

"Well then. Now let's bring Willie over. He's a good friend to have around, so don't let him frighten you." She was speaking to the animal as if he were a person. And, so far, all was well. Caitlin was well aware of the fact that horses and wolves don't usually get along very well, but she had seen how Willie was able to get close to other animals without spooking them. She knew Uncle Wabi would say that Willie "talked" to them.

"Willie, come." The wolf trotted over and stood close to Caitlin.

"Willie, this fine fellow is going to go with us. So, you make him welcome, and let's get going here."

Willie nudged the horse behind his knees and the horse stamped his feet, but not in anger, just acknowledgment. Caitlin was just a bit taken with this behavior. Well, Uncle Wabi may have known what he was talking about. They did seem to understand each other.

"Gees! I'm beginning to sound like him!" Caitlin said aloud.

She adjusted the stirrups as best she could and climbed on, noting it seemed a lot farther up when she looked down.

He was indeed a rather large horse, very muscular, and a beautiful red color. She smiled when she thought about that. So, with some help from the horse, she felt she might get to the higher part of the Grampians before being found by Commander Campbell.

Off they went, with Caitlin trying to find a rhythm with the horse. She could remember a few things about riding, something about going with the horse, finding his gait, changing lead, and giving him his head. At the moment, she was just content to not fall off.

Still staying with her original plan of keeping to the woods, Caitlin wasn't sure exactly which way to go. She recalled what Alex had said, "Go north and ask where the MacKinnon land is, and we'll find you." Well, she could tell which way was north and headed that direction. She rode all day, staying away from any villages she came close to. There was enough food in her bag for a couple of days, and she found the Commander had also brought some supplies with him, something an experienced soldier would do. She wouldn't allow herself to even think about how angry he would be, finding his horse gone, and her as well.

"Well, he'll have quite a headache to deal with first, and I'm quite sure he's not going to enjoy getting his throat stitched up!"

After two full days of keeping on a northerly path, Caitlin had seen no one and heard no one. This ability to hear well was really paying off and she was sure she would know if anyone was following her. But what had changed her hearing? She had always been aware of her keen sense of smell, but now, having this extraordinary hearing too? Why? She wished Uncle Wabi were about as he would have an explanation. He had an explanation for everything. She was sure he would mumble something like,

"Caitlin, my girl, don't look a gift horse in the mouth... just be thankful." How many times had she heard him come out with something along those lines?

On the evening of the second day, Caitlin found a place to water her horse and let him graze in the grass nearby. Willie had taken off into the woods looking for his supper, which she probably didn't want to see. But, he always managed to eat well and she was glad to see him still running about, letting her know the wound the Commander had given him had not left any long-lasting effects. She cringed every time she thought about that man. How could he be so obtuse in his thinking? She knew if she could just get out of his reach for some time, then his grief would subside enough for him to come to his senses.

"Why can't I get you out of my mind? You don't deserve this much attention from anyone! Especially from one who detests you as much as I!" Caitlin exclaimed.

Suddenly it hit her. "Oh! That smell! Why do you think he would smell like henbane, Willie?" She had taken to talking aloud to her companion, probably as a way to forget about how alone she really was.

"Henbane is a type of poison, an herb that has been around for many, many eons. It doesn't grow everywhere, but it can be found if one searches diligently. Most healers know about it and know to be careful when using it. It can relieve toothache, arthritis, gout and a number of other ailments. But, it's not to be used lightly. I've made a tincture out of it as it can help relieve pain, especially surgical pain, and help one to sleep. But, it would be used as a last resort, only if I had nothing else to give. It's been known to create some serious mental problems if one takes too much. But, for the Commander to reek of it? That means he must have some ailment that he thinks to treat with henbane, but it can kill him. The healer that gave it to him told him that, surely." Her companion listened, his ears flicking about, but made no comment.

Caitlin had settled down for the night, if you could call it that. She had only her cloak to lie on, and her plaid to keep her warm, plus Willie, who brought a great deal of warmth to her feet. Another thing she found amusing was wearing these "pants" that had belonged to Ian. What a surprise! Riding a horse wearing these was so easy. There were no petticoats to wrestle with, no skirts billowing up, and they were very warm to boot.

She realized she could pass for a boy, so she was hopeful that if a situation presented itself, she could do just that. As it was, she was planning to go to the edge of the next village and ask about traveling to the MacKinnon lands. Perhaps she was getting closer.

"And just what will you do when you get there, Miss Caitlin?" she asked herself. She actually didn't have a clue about that, but refused to think about that issue just now.

"Take one problem at a time, Caitlin." Uncle Wabi did have some good sayings sometimes. She wished she could talk to him, just to let him know she was all right, well, sort of. But, that thinking could wait, too. Right now, she laid back and looked up at the trees, trying to calm her mind and drift off to sleep. Just as she began to feel drowsy, she heard a "hoo hoo," and there, just above her head, in a large pine tree, an owl sat looking down at her.

"I swear that is the same owl that was at the cave!" Knowing that was impossible, Caitlin closed her eyes and drifted off, knowing Willie would stand guard all night and alert her to any danger.

Chapter 21

It had been two days ago that Millie had made her decision and left Warwick Castle. She had packed her provisions and waited until darkness had settled over the land. She quietly walked to the stables and spoke to the young stable lad who bowed quickly.

"I'm just out for a stroll, Malcolm; you need not wait up for me," Millie said to the young man. He was relieved to hear that and off he ran to the front of the stables where he slept in the loft.

Millie saddled one of the older geldings, an Arabian named Dillon, who was sure-footed and large enough to carry her and her babe. Together they were a bit of weight for any animal. But this horse was dependable, and she had been on his back many times. He neighed to her as she approached him.

"Hey, old man. How goes it? Huh? Think you can carry the two of us for a ways?" He shook his withers and stamped his left front foot. "Yeah, I'm sure you can." She led him out the back door of the stable and found the bundle she had hidden there in the edge of the woods. She brought Dillon up next to a tree stump in order that she might get on a bit easier. She eased herself up and settled into the saddle without difficulty.

"Well, then. Let's get moving. It will take some time to get to my grandmother's home in Scotland, but we will get there and we'll be most welcome." She talked to Dillon as if to keep him informed of her plans. The night was dark, with not even a slice of moon to show the way. But, Millie could hear numerous birds about, calling to each other in the darkness. "It's almost like having a candle to light the way," she said to herself.

Chapter 22

The only person left in the cave the next morning was one lone soldier, one with a most painful headache. Commander Campbell tried to lift himself up from the floor, but fell back down rather quickly. The pain that was taking his head off seemed to know no bounds. Jesus! What had happened? And, as his vision cleared somewhat, he realized he was in a small room that was very dim. As his brain tried to make sense of his surroundings, he slowly tried to get up again and was successful this time. But, my God, how his head hurt! Even more painful than his head, his throat felt like someone had poured hot oil down it. He put his hands up to his neck and felt a thick, sticky substance still seeping from the wound. He had seen enough wounds in battle to realize this was no small problem and he must get help.

As he started to move back toward the cave entrance, he began to recall some of the events from the night before.

He remembered finding the witch, huddled back in a corner of the cave. But after that it was all just a blur of fuzzy shapes, sounds and memory of terrible pain — at his throat! He walked a bit farther toward the light. The dog! Yes, the dog. In his mind's eye the animal came out of nowhere and was the biggest dog he had ever seen! But wait. That was no dog. That was a wolf! What was the witch doing with a wolf? To Campbell, that was just more evidence of her connection to the wicked ones. "So, she travels with a wolf does she? Well, then he'll burn too!"

He slowly ambled back through the cave, picking up his knife that was lying on the floor.

He was thinking how quiet it was and figured out the healer was no longer here.

"No matter. I'll chase her until I find her again. She's just a woman and not a very smart one at that. If she were smart, she would have killed me!"

He looked about the cave trying to find something to bandage his neck. There were a few scraps of cloth, but he could find no medicines anywhere, which meant she was not planning to return. Well, she can't have gotten very far, walking through the woods, trying to hide, and keeping company with a wolf.

Then he discovered his pistol was missing. "Damn her! I need that gun!"

And, he had one more surprise waiting for him. When he came outside into the bright sunlight, it was almost blinding. He closed his eyes again, waiting for them to become adjusted to the brightness. As he looked about, seeing no one and hearing nothing, he tried to remember something. Where had he tied his horse? Ah, yes, he had hidden him well, back behind that rowan tree, when he came and waited for the witch to come home. And he had indeed seen her and his plan should have worked well. How was he to know she had a wolf protector? Well, he did know now, so he would be prepared for that this time. He stooped, going under the limbs of the tree and walked around behind it, but the animal was nowhere to be seen. This was surely where he left his horse. He was positive.

When it dawned on him what had transpired, he cursed vehemently and shook his fist at no one in particular. No one was watching anyway

"That witch will not get away with this! She's pushed me way beyond my limits!" He stomped around a bit, and then realizing he had no choice, began walking toward the nearest village. He would get another horse there, have someone tend his wounds, and then he would resume his search for her.

Just as he walked back under the rowan tree, something smacked him on the back of his head causing him to stumble and lose his balance. He watched in disbelief as a great horned owl soared straight toward the sky and screeched to bloody heaven.

Chapter 23

Uncle Wabi was not happy with the latest report from Owl. But, all in all, Caitlin was coming into her own. When time was of the essence, Owl and Wabi communicated through mental images sent to each other across a vacuum of time and space that Owl did not especially enjoy. But, there were times when this was the only way.

"Master. I know you want information about Caitlin, but I can only be in one place at a time!" Owl had stated to Wabi.

"So, if we must, then we'll use this method, but please keep it brief for my sake. It ruffles my feathers, Master!"

"I was beginning to think she was never going to find her power." said Owl.

"She thinks too much and tries to figure things out, rather than just trusting her intuition and going with it."

Uncle Wabi also thought too much, sometimes. He had always known Caitlin was a "called one," or else he wouldn't be here. But, she always kept her thoughts pretty much to herself and, even though he could, he had never entered her mind to see what was going on in there.

"Yes, my wise old friend, she has been taking quite a long time to exercise her special talents. But, she's slowly coming along. Let us continue to be patient. I must say, she has been quite resourceful so far. She stole his horse! Hee hee! What a shock that must have been to him."

He threw his head back and laughed aloud, then walked away with his dog following behind headed to the forest for more training.

Owl had made his report so went back to his station, keeping his eyes and ears open.

Chapter 24

Alex took the morning to ride about the farm. Sheep farming took a lot of hard work, and the more hands, the better. But with the three older brothers having been off fighting for the last months, and then young Ian being gone the last few weeks, the entire place was beginning to look a bit run down. It was just too much for Da, even with Uncle Andrew and old Jamie doing what they could. Those two were even older than Da, and both were sound in mind, but age had a way of taking a toll on even the best of men. This land had been in MacKinnon hands for decades now, having been passed from one generation to the next, each building on the accomplishments of the ones before. It was good land, even in the Highlands, but sheep farming was not the easiest way of making a living. When lambing season came, every available hand was needed, plus some. He could always take on some local hands, as he often did, if things got to be too much for them. Of course, Da always got steamed up when Alex resorted to this measure. But, he would keep it in mind.

Stopping at the small stone wall, and dismounting, he sat on the wall for a moment, looking out over the land. Alex thought about Mam, how she so loved tending the new lambs, especially the ones who were too wee to even suckle from their mothers. She would make a straw bed for them in a small pen and place it just outside her kitchen door. That way she could keep an eye on them and go about her business of feeding a house full of hungry men. Quite a full time job it was.

Alex recalled hurrying through the kitchen door on a cold afternoon, the wind ushering him through the door with a blast, and he forgot to wipe his feet.

"Alexander MacKinnon! Don't ye dare bring any sheep shite into me kitchen! Out with ye and wipe yer boots!" This memory brought a smile to his face. And, now, Hector had stepped in and was doing a fairly good job of the cooking himself. Their Mam would be proud to see him so at ease in her kitchen.

He stood back up, stretching his back. Somehow though, some of the joy had gone out of all their lives when Mam died. "I suppose some things just can't be replaced," Alex said to his two dogs. These two, Lord and Lady, were some of the best herding dogs he had ever had. They were brother and sister, coming from the same litter, with both their sire and mother being Border Collies. He still had old Tess, but she had gotten too old to chase after the sheep, and was blind in one eye. As it was, she was free to walk about the place, but seemed to understand that her herding days were over. But, she still got attention from all the brothers as she could often be found lying at the feet of one of them, warming herself by the fire, both of them enjoying the crackling logs and perhaps snoozing a bit.

Climbing back on his horse, Alex trotted off, whistling for the dogs to come along with him. "Lady! Lord! Here now!" Alex called to the two first-class herding dogs. They liked nothing better than for him to send them off to chase a few sheep who had wandered too far.

Herding was in their blood, just as sheep farming was in Alex's. These black-faced sheep had a long lineage too.

As quickly as Alex whistled, the two dogs brought three rams and a ewe back into the pasture and had them scurrying to the front of the herd. Sheep aren't very smart, but didn't especially enjoy their heels being nipped at by these two. Alex saw the whole place was in need of attention, and the sooner the better. But, first things first.

Having made his decision, Alex mounted up early the next morning as planned. He had taken a moment to speak with Ian, who was recovering well now that he was back home.

"Ye stay right here on this bed. We need ye to be back up and able to help us, ye hear?

We all have a job to do to keep this place going, and having an accident, such as ye did, will only get you a little sympathy. But, know that I'm counting on ye to figure out how ye are going to handle this. Mam always thought you were the best MacKinnon of all, so let's see ye making her words ring true." Alex knew the young man needed to be a part of this place, and he would be.

Then a quick hug and out the door he went.

Jack and Hector were waiting just outside.

"Jack, I know 'tis not to yer liking, me going back to the cave. But I must do what my conscience says is the right thing."

Jack walked a bit closer, pulling himself up to his full height and looking only slightly down at Alex.

"Yer conscience or yer heart, brother? It's no secret that the witch, er healer, took your fancy. Just don't be blind to her is all I ask."

"Aye. No pretty skirt has caused me blindness just yet, but I'll keep yer words in mind," he was smiling as he spoke.

"And Jack. If I'm no back in a fortnight, come looking for me. I'm no fool, and I realize there could be some trouble, but that makes it even more urgent that I go."

"Aye, brother, that I will."

Alex slapped the horse on the rump and tore off down the road, planning on making as much time as possible. The longer he had waited, the more anxious he had become thinking about what could be happening to Caitlin.

As he had said to Jack, he was no fool, not even when it came to women. There had been several, but only one he remembered with any fondness. It was during the time he had traveled down to Edinburgh, to study, as Mam had wanted. Mam had come from a family who placed great importance on education. She, herself, had had tutors at home and was to have gone on for more schooling in England. But, as happens when two young people meet and are "thunderstruck" as Da was so fond of saying, those plans all go by the wayside. So, when she had met that strapping, handsome Highlander at the MacDonald's ceilidh, that was the end of any more education, and she went with him when he returned to the Highlands. And, she had never regretted it a day of her life, or so she said. But she still wanted her sons to be educated if at all possible. So it was that Alex tried his best to please her and took himself down to Edinburgh and began an education in earnest.

About a year into his schooling, he was assigned to a class with a female instructor, an English woman she was, who taught the Greek classics. Alex particularly enjoyed reading about early times in other parts of the world, and found this woman to be especially interesting. She was attractive, a true English rose, and intelligent as well. As it was, he started to develop a relationship with his instructor. He figured this was probably not a very good idea, but nevertheless, he did.

The chemistry between the two was strong from the very beginning. She was just a few years older than Alex, and more than ready for a long-term romance. Alex, on the other hand, was not exactly looking for anything that meant taking on more responsibility such as a wife or children. But, the physical side of the relationship was quite dynamic.

This beautiful English rose, Fiona, walked up to Alex and placed her arms around his waist, pulling him closer.

"So, just how long do you think we will continue in this manner? I'm not getting any younger, you know," she said to Alex after one of their more "steamy" evenings.

Alex had known this was coming for some time now, but had hoped it would take place much later.

"Well, then. I'm no ready to make any promises just now, ye ken. I've got my schooling to complete, and then I'm back to the Highlands to my family and the sheep."

"What? After an education you can do more than be a sheep farmer! You don't have to be like the rest of your Scots, an uneducated heathen idiot!" With that, Fiona dropped her hands to her sides and strode out of the room, slamming the door behind her.

Chapter 25

Morning had broken at Warwick Castle, and Lord Warwick was ranting and raving, which wasn't unusual for him. But this morning Lady Warwick had failed to show for breakfast, as she was required to do. Early in the marriage, Lord Warwick had insisted that they start the day with breakfast in the very large dining hall — as his family had done. Somehow he thought that if they had the appearance of a happy couple, then perhaps he would be the great Lord his father had been. Now, after waiting a short time for Millie to arrive, he began yelling.

"Elspeth! Get yourself in here!"

The young girl who had been assigned as lady's maid to Lady Warwick trembled as she ran into the dining hall.

"Yessir, Lord Warwick. I'm here, sir."

"Where's Lady Warwick? Why isn't she here already?"

"Oh, milord. I went to wake her like I always do, but she's not in her bed! I don't know where she is sir. I've looked about everywhere but she's not anywhere! I even looked in her garden where she sometimes goes, but she's not there either, sir." She wrung her hands and pulled at the hem of her apron. The girl was beside herself just thinking about what he might do to her if she couldn't find Lady Millie.

"Well. Have everyone get about finding her!" And he pushed away from the table, causing china and silver to tumble in his wake.

He strode out to the stable, intending to have his horse saddled. His morning routine included a short ride about his property. This went a long way in reassuring himself that he was indeed an important landowner and one to be honored. He had not yet figured out that honor comes from within, not from material holdings. He called for the stable lad, Malcolm.

"Malcolm! Where are you, boy?"

The young boy came running at the sound of Lord Warwick's voice. He had been on the estate for some time now and had learned to stay away from his master as much as he could. But, Lady Warwick was another matter. He found just being in her presence made him feel worthy. She had a way of expressing her appreciation, no matter how small the job he might have done for her.

"Malcolm! Have you seen Lady Warwick this morning?"

"No, your Lordship. Not this morning. I spoke with her jest last evening when she was out for her walk."

"What! You saw her last evening?"

"Yessir. She come down here, but said I was to go on to bed. Said she wouldn't be needin' me anymore. Was out for a walk, she said."

Warwick's brain as on full alert. He knew their relationship had disintegrated drastically in the past months, and he chalked it up to her "condition." But it had just dawned on him that she may have taken measures that he would not have thought her capable of.

"Malcolm. Are all my horses still in the barn?"

"Uh. Well. No, sir. Actually one of the Arabians is missing — the big one, sir. The one called Dillon. I wonder if maybe he jest was left out in the pasture. I was jest about to go down there and look for him." Malcolm had hoped to find the horse without ever having to let the lord know he was ever missing. These horses were of great importance to Lord Warwick. And Malcolm had witnessed the lord's temper more times than he liked to recall.

"You imbecile! Have you no sense at all? Why didn't you stop her? Boy, you'll not forget this day!"

Lord Warwick had been angry when he discovered his wife was gone, but absolutely furious when he discovered the stable boy had seen Lady Warwick the night before and let her leave without telling him. Now he had the boy by the shoulders and pulled him up close to his face.

"But, Lord Warwick! Lady Millie said she was jest out for a short walk. She never said she was leavin'! I woulda stopped her if I thought she was leavin'! She takes a walk sometimes in the early evening, sir! Wasn't my place to ask her no questions, sir!"

"Anyone with an ounce of sense would know she shouldn't travel in her condition! If she harms my son, I'll show her no mercy! As for you, you stupid boy, you need a lesson that you won't soon forget!"

With that he grabbed the horsewhip hanging on the wall next to the stall. He brought his arm down and with all his strength, struck the young boy's face, flaying the skin from his upper cheek, going down the entire side of his face and through his upper lip. The blood flowed freely, and the boy screamed in pain.

"Ah! Lord Warwick! I would never let the lady leave if I knew!"

"Shut up, boy!"

And another lashing of the whip laid open another, even deeper, layer of skin right next to the first one. The bone was visible with its milky whiteness showing clearly. It had been some time since Warwick had taken a whip to one of his servants, but it still brought him a feeling he enjoyed – one of power — yes — he was all powerful! And this young man would never fail him again, of that he was sure.

"And you let her take one of my prize horses!" Warwick snapped the whip once again and delivered one final blow across the other cheek. The small boy collapsed and lay there, hoping that the lord had spent himself and would just leave now.

"How dare she steal something that belongs to me!" She would receive retribution for this, he promised himself that. He flung the whip at the boy and stomped out of the stable. It never occurred to him to send someone to help the boy.

***

Warwick was reasonably sure she would have gone to Scotland, but decided to call at Lord Sinclair's place and discuss the matter with him.

"So you think she probably fled to Scotland, then?"

"Yes. Stupid woman! She's got less sense than my hunting dogs! At least they know how to obey commands!" Sinclair retorted.

"Well, then. Looks like I'll just have to make a trip up to that heathen country and bring her back. She's due to have my son any day now, so she can't have traveled very far."

"Yes. She would have no other place to flee to. She spent a lot of time up there when she was a child and always wanted to keep going back. What she likes about that place is beyond me! The estate is certainly impressive, but beyond that there is no appeal for me. "

"I refused to take her up there for her grandfather's burial some years back, and she threatened to go up there then, but of course she didn't. But, in her condition, I'm surprised she would even attempt it. Did you two quarrel?"

"Nothing more than the usual. She's not exactly been pleased to be my wife and live at Warwick Castle. But, you and I knew that would be the case. Actually, it doesn't matter a lot what she wants."

"Her mother never liked living in England either. But, her father was anxious for the two of us to wed as I convinced him she would become a lady held in the highest regard within the nobility of England. I told him this marriage would unite a Scottish family with an English one and how we could serve as examples to others to help bring these two countries together. The old laird had a reputation for being very high-minded and spent a lifetime trying to bring peace wherever he could."

"Sounds like an old fool to me."

"Yes. He was certainly a fool. He believed every word I told him and handed his daughter over with nothing more than a promise from me that she would be well taken care of and would be Lady Sinclair! He was too honorable to ever go back on his promise, so even if he suspected she wasn't happy living here, he never changed his will. So, rest assured, Millie will return with you and the holdings will become hers, and ultimately yours and mine, of course."

"Well, Sinclair, we made an agreement and I expect you to stick to it. Millie will inherit the lands and estate in Scotland and with those combined with yours and mine, we will both be the wealthiest land barons in these parts." The two men clinked their wine glasses in a toast that spoke of their many like weaknesses.

***

Later that same evening, Lord Warwick strolled about the lush gardens that his wife, Millie, had planted at his castle. He had thought it was a ridiculous idea, but made no fuss when she called the gardeners and supervised their planting of numerous flowers, plants and vines.

Millie had a green thumb certainly and working in the garden kept her out of his hair. Now, with her gone, he had hours with nothing to do but think about his situation.

"That old woman just needs to die!" Warwick uttered the words aloud as if verbalizing them would justify them and his plans to see them come true.

"And then that old maid daughter will inherit; but then, how much longer before she will die!"

These thoughts ran around and around in Warwick's alcohol-laced head. Having been born a second son himself, and only coming into an inheritance at the unexpected death of his older brother, he needed this estate and the Scottish lands to add to his own. It was well known the English crown would be taking over much of the Scottish holdings, following the Scots' defeat at Culloden. Warwick saw this as a chance for him to be well placed in the aristocracy.

Marrying Millie Sinclair was certainly a strategic move on his part, but he needed to add considerably to his lands as quickly as possible, and he could only see one way to do this. He and Lord Sinclair had conspired to usurp holdings of others, those unable to oppose them, on several occasions. So, he had broached an idea to Sinclair while on his visit to his place right after Millie disappeared.

"It would be easy enough for the old woman and aunt to meet with an accident, Sinclair.

There are a number of people that I know who would help us with this problem."

"What! You don't mean kill them, do you?" Sinclair stood up and walked over to where Warwick was pouring another glass of his very finest wine.

"We might stoop low enough to rob others of their belongings, but family is another matter altogether! No. These women are on their last legs already. Have a little patience Warwick. Time will take care of this matter for us. Now, go. Go back to your place and prepare to fetch Millie."

Somehow, some of Sinclair's mother's teachings regarding ethical behavior and dedication to family still remained in his otherwise devious heart. That being the case, Warwick knew the plot he was drawing up presently would have to be done alone as Sinclair would not participate in doing away with family, even if they were Scots. He began to make plans that only he and one other person would know about. And that would not be Sinclair.

Chapter 26

Commander Campbell found the trip into the village a bit more taxing than he might have wished. Being accustomed to riding, rather than walking, he had plenty of time to think about his situation. If that red-haired witch thought he would let her get the upper hand, she had another think coming. He had many years of experience dealing with men who needed to be taught a lesson, and when he had finished with them, they were glad to have survived whatever punishments he had dreamed up. Whipping a man, or causing him pain in any way, had no effect on Campbell. In fact, he found it quite pleasant. And he looked on this characteristic as one to be proud of, thought it made him an even better soldier. So now, the task at hand was to find someone to help him get this wound bandaged and then to find a horse.

"Damn you, witch! I've killed men for less offense than that!" Stealing his horse was the most deceitful act he could think of.

Upon entering the village, he saw a number of people milling about, going about their daily business. He had thought he would find a healer readily enough, but there didn't seem to be one about.

"Hey! You there, man. You hear me? Where might I find the healer?" Commander Campbell had spoken to one of the men loading a wagon with supplies. When he called to him, the man stopped and looked at the soldier.

The man took one look at the man and could see that he was in need of help. But he didn't particularly like the way the soldier had demanded attention. The soldier's uniform told him he was an officer, his chest full of medals and such. That was still no excuse to be rude.

"She only comes around on occasion, not every day. She lives out of town somewhere, but I don't know exactly where. But she's a fine healer, I tell ye."

Campbell immediately understood he was speaking of the witch. "Where is she?" "I don't rightly know. She said she were going north, looking for a friend's place." "Well, surely there's another one somewhere!" Raising his voice even louder, the commander grabbed the man by the collar. "I need one now, you imbecile!"

The man pushed away, looked at the soldier, and walked off without looking back.

Commander Campbell thought about just shooting the man in the back, having bought another pistol in the last village as the witch had stolen his along with his horse. Several other men were staring at him, almost daring him to do so.

"There's another village just down the road, maybe about another three miles or so. Ye might find one there," offered one of the villagers. Then they all turned away, too, and the commander stood there seething at their refusal to help him.

The soldier walked on, not knowing what else to do. When he came to a stream just out of town, he stopped and did what he could to clean his throat and used his handkerchief to bind it. Yelling, as he had at the men in the village, had caused the bleeding to start up again, and the pain was returning with a vengeance.

"That wolf will get his punishment also!" he yelled at the emptiness all around him. He was most unaccustomed to having others ignore him. He demanded those around him cater to his every whim, and thus he was groping for a way to deal with his present problem.

After walking another couple of miles, he came to a very small village, much smaller than the last one. There were only a few cottages, huts actually, with thatched roofs, and he stopped at the first one. He rapped harshly on the door and called out.

"Hey! Who lives here? I need some help!" Some minutes passed and he beat on the door again. Finally a voice answered his call.

"Who's there? I'm coming."

Eventually, an old, old woman opened the door and a fuzzy white cat, almost as old as the woman, darted out, startling Campbell. The old woman wore a full-length homespun dress that had seen better days, and her ragged shawl was pulled tightly around her thin shoulders. The solider saw the old woman's eyes were clouded over with a fine sheath of tissue, obviously limiting her eyesight. Campbell took one look at the old woman and could tell she was not only old, but was probably feeble in mind as well. Just what he needed!

"I require a healer, old woman. Do you know where I might find one?" Campbell's bleeding was becoming more profuse, and he had only a small amount of henbane left in his jacket pocket. The medication helped greatly with the pain, so he must get more somewhere.

This old woman, even with very poor eyesight, could smell and feel Campbell's distress. She had treated many a soldier in her day and her nose, still quite adept at detecting odors, could smell the mixture of blood, and something else. She kept sniffing and then nodded to herself. Ah, henbane. A very dangerous combination that was, blood and henbane.

"Aye. I'm a healer. Ye've come to the right place." Commander Campbell pulled away from the old woman as she reached out her wrinkled, bony hand to touch his arm.

"Wait a minute, old woman. How do I know you can treat me? You're too old and almost blind. I don't think you'll be of much good to me." He pushed at her arms.

"Get your hands off me. I'll take my chances somewhere else." At that juncture, he stepped back, intent on moving on to the next village.

The old woman, stooped as she was, raised up as best she could and looked at him.

"I am, indeed, almost blind. But even a blind healer could tell what ails ye, young sir. Ye are bleeding from some wound that needs tending, and ye reek of henbane, probably what ye are using to control the pain. So, if ye wish me to help ye, then ye'll have to come inside here. There mostly likely will be another healer in the next village, but ye may not make it that far."

Campbell thought for a moment. His bleeding had soaked his uniform jacket already, and he was so tired. The henbane was no longer making the pain go away. Plus, he seemed to drift off to sleep if he even stopped for a moment. Then, when sleeping, his dreams were disturbing. He couldn't make heads nor tails about them. In them, he was running and running, but his legs refused to move!

Ultimately, he decided that he had no choice. The blind old woman was probably right. It could be he might not make it to the next village. So, he let out a sigh and went inside her cottage and followed her to a small room next to the kitchen. The room had no furnishings except for a small cot with a blanket on the foot of it. Next to the bed was a rectangular table that held a lighted candle. He sat down, waiting for her to begin whatever treatment she thought he needed. Shortly, however, he found he could not stay awake, and he fell over on the bed. Exhaustion had finally claimed him.

The old healer was actually glad to see him succumb to the tiredness; that, along with his bleeding and pain, had caused him to collapse on her bed, and now she could treat this man. As the healer was preparing her medications, the white cat came back in and jumped up on the bed, walking slowly around the soldier, sniffing him, then jumped back down and went over to where the old woman was stirring her ointments and herbs. The cat walked between the old woman's feet and rubbed up against her. They had been together a very long time. The old healer spoke to the cat as she continued her rubbing against the woman's feet.

"Oh, aye, Regina, I know. He's indeed an evil one, but my heart will no allow me to refuse to treat him. But I can keep him quiet for a while. Something tells me he'll create disaster wherever he goes, so we'll detain him just a bit." The cat rubbed against her again, and purred as if she agreed with the woman.

Chapter 27

Caitlin awoke from a night filled with dreams in which Uncle Wabi was a central character. Not surprising, she thought, as he was a key person in her life for as long as she could remember. Being a confirmed bachelor, he was always available to her for any purpose where she might have need of him. He taught her so many things. She hardly knew how she could have had such a full life without him. But why was she having these dreams of him now?

And, what was most on her mind as she lay there, not moving a muscle, was remembering the voice that was in the cave, trying to help her hide from Commander Campbell. She had heard the voice. It sounded like a person was right next to her — talking to her! It was almost like Uncle Wabi himself had been talking to her, but with an English accent. And, why had her scalp started to sting? And her hair had felt as if it was rising from her head! She had purposely put all these remembrances aside, which was something she had always been able to do, until now, when no one was chasing her, and she felt relatively safe.

"I didn't just imagine that voice, Willie. It was real! And it had a very British accent!" Willie was still lying at her feet, awaiting the minute when she would call him to get underway again.

"There was no one else in the cave. It was just me, by myself."

Then, she remembered something else. Just as she had looked up in the tree outside the cave, the great horned owl was there, looking down as her, and then he flew into the cave.

Following that event, she started hearing the voice urging her to hide.

"Oh, Willie, what is happening to me?" As she spoke, she stood up, stretching her arms above her head trying to straighten out the kinks from sleeping on the ground. As she stretched, she was greeted with a "hoo hoo" just above her head.

***

The owl looked down at the woman and decided he would give it one more try, talking to her that is. Wabi had told Owl he believed Caitlin would slowly begin to find her place in their special world, but it must be in her time, when she was ready. But, the owl was ready for Caitlin to exercise her talents, or at least be open to learning how.

"Well, my girl, it's about time you looked up here." The owl watched as Caitlin's head jerked up, then she turned her entire body around, reaching for her staff for protection.

"Willie!" she shouted, and the wolf stood at attention and waited for more instruction. "Who said that? Where are you?" Caitlin could feel her heart racing and her knees were like quivering jelly, a feeling that she didn't care for.

The owl groaned inwardly.

"Oh, please, calm down and follow your intuition. It will not lead you astray. Where do you think the voice is coming from?" asked the owl.

Caitlin looked at her wolf. He did not seem to be anxious, nor was he in his attack mode.

Rather, he just seemed to be waiting for her to decide what to do. "So, if he's not uneasy, then why am I?" she asked herself.

Speaking loudly, Caitlin demanded. "Show yourself! Come out into the open where I can see you!" She still held the crooked staff, ready to swing it if she needed to. She remembered the thud it made when she had hit the commander on the head with it. It was a good weapon if you used it right. The owl then gently flew down to stand on the ground next to Willie, who paid him no mind whatsoever.

"I'm right here, standing next to Willie," said the owl.

Caitlin looked at Willie, seeing no one else, and Willie would always alert her if someone came near.

"Where? I don't see you. Come out!" she said, turning first one way, then the other, her eyes growing bigger.

The owl fluttered his large wings, trying to get her attention that way. "Caitlin, I am right here, fluttering my wings at you!"

Caitlin remembered there were times she had sworn Uncle Wabi was talking to some of his dogs, but dismissed it as just some of his eccentric mannerisms. As she thought further, however, she could recall him "chatting" to himself, or so she had thought, when the geese flew by on a chilly morning. And, again, she had seen him caressing an eagle with a broken wing that he mended and murmuring to the bird. But each time, she just accepted that Uncle Wabi was different than most other men, and she liked that about him. But, now, as she looked into the owl's very large eyes, she found herself wishing Uncle Wabi were here with her. She was totally out of her depth and she knew it. Uncle Wabi had always told her that if nothing else seems possible, then you must consider the impossible. And she just knew it was impossible for an owl to speak to her. But that was exactly what seemed to be happening!

With her scalp stinging and her brain on fire, she could think of nothing to do but test her theory, hoping it to be wrong, for she really did not know how to handle this just yet.

"I'm going to ask you once more to show yourself," said Caitlin, not knowing where to look for someone to appear.

"And I'm going to tell you once more that I am here, next to your friend, Willie, who certainly knows that I am here."

Caitlin looked at Willie and the owl. Both of them were looking up at her with large eyes.

"Owls don't talk," she said, shaking her head from side to side.

"This one does, as you can see, if you WILL see," replied Owl.

Caitlin gasped and tried to retain her composure. "Oh, Holy Rusepheus! I must be so tired from traveling I'm hallucinating!"

But, somewhere deep inside she was receiving confirmation of any number of unexplained happenings over the years, all having to do with Uncle Wabi. He was forever telling her to "be open to new experiences," and "you don't need to question everything you don't understand, just go with your intuition," and endless more instances of the same nature.

One really telling experience was when she climbed out on a limb, high up in the hawthorn tree, to get a peek at the new sparrow hatchlings. The limb gave way and she screamed, then found herself falling. Suddenly, she felt as if arms had reached out there, cradling her, and she landed softly, on a pile of leaves. But the tree limb had been very high up and she should have been hurt; now she wondered.

"Uncle Wabi?" She knew very little about her ancestors, but there were many tales in her family's history of some family members who had been thought to be eccentric, even a couple who had been labeled witch or shaman. Both, of course, had only been healers, as Caitlin was, and Wabi was just another eccentric one. Hmm. Maybe those tales had been more than just folklore.

"Oh, Uncle Wabi. If only you were here!" She would ask him a thousand questions.

"Well, he is not here, but I am. So, let's get past this and figure out where to go from here."

That same clipped British accent again! Caitlin sat back down, breathing deeply, trying to stay calm and figure this out.

She held her head between her hands.

"All right. All right. This owl can talk and Uncle Wabi is some sort of wizard or whatever, and he is my uncle, and he is most unusual, apparently."

She felt like she had entered some sort of dream world and she would surely wake up any moment now.

"I would prefer you say he is very special, which he most definitely is!" replied Owl, bristling at Caitlin's semi-derogatory remark regarding his master.

"Does Uncle Wabi talk to you, also?" she questioned.

"We have been conversing for many years, Caitlin. It is only you that have been slow to come to grips with your talents, given by the Creator, I might add."

"Talents given by the Creator, you mean some sort of Supreme Being?"

"If it suits you to call it that, then that will do. What term you use is not important, but that you have been selected by the Creator, that is what is relevant."

"Selected. But why me? And for what purpose?"

"Ah. Some things even I do not understand, Caitlin. But as you accept these facts as truth, more will be explained to you, and your understanding will increase as your acceptance grows.

Wabi would tell you, "Patience, dear girl, patience," replied Owl.

"Yes, that is exactly what he would say. But I need more than patience. I need Uncle Wabi to make some sense of this to me!"

"And he will, my dear, when the time is right. However, at this moment, you seem to be in the middle of a dangerous hornet's nest, and you should be making plans for what comes next. And, now that you know I am here with you, mayhap you will rest just a bit easier. I cannot change the situation, but I can be of assistance in some unique ways if needed."

Not sure what else to do, Caitlin gathered her cloak and bags together and climbed back up on the horse. When she thought about it, she wondered that the horse was not alarmed either. Animals have their own alarm systems, she decided. She had learned long ago to trust Willie's.

What had Alexander told her? "Travel north, past the Black Isle, then something about going over the Cromarty Firth and on past Dornock Firth," and "ask anyone, they will know where the MacKinnon lands start." Well, something like that anyway. So, she would head north, and would have to trust her intuition now as she had no way of finding him otherwise. But, Alex had seemed to think she would be safe there. It certainly sounded like a good place to get lost.

Caitlin and her horse had made friends, the horse most likely understanding very quickly this woman was a much more caring rider than his previous one. And, she was much lighter to carry also. Caitlin was ever so glad she had taken the horse. Of course, she was now a horse thief as well as a witch!

Still heading north, traveling to the Black Isle, she was exhausted, but tried to continue moving as long as there was light. She decided to not think any more about the "talking owl," as she was having some difficulty digesting this strange phenomenon.

"Oh, Uncle Wabi, why didn't you tell me about this 'calling,' or whatever it is. Right now I could use some extra help from anyone or anything!"

She was aware the owl was flying above her head, keeping pace with her. She wasn't sure what help the bird could be, but obviously there were some things she knew nothing about, and this worried her to some degree. She had thought she was an intelligent, mature woman who had a good head on her shoulders. But, this latest development, talking birds, a Creator, and a tingling scalp. What did it all mean?

Chapter 28

Wabi walked along, deep in the woods, listening to the birds calling to one another. He was followed by his small, four-legged companion. Darkness was coming early and he liked the sound of leaves crunching under his feet. His nose told him someone had built a bonfire and the scent of toasty leaves permeated the air. Wabi was talking to himself; actually he was talking to his latest trainee, a young Beagle pup who had the makings of a remarkable hunting dog. Beagles were not common here in Scotland, but the British had used them for many years. Wabi called his little friend Maximo, as he was small, but had just the greatest attitude and already showed he would work hard.

"Maximo. Your name is exactly right for you! I do believe you must be the finest beagle I have ever had the pleasure of teaching. Why, you'll run as long as I ask you to. And that fox you cornered! Why he was never so glad to get away from your ferocious bark!"

The pup looked up at Wabi, his tail curled over his back, his shoulders squared and he pranced even more than usual. Wabi laughed. Perhaps the little dog had understood everything he had said to him — and agreed with him.

The young pup was learning to obey hand signals and, even though he still broke a command occasionally, Wabi was pleased with his progress. As with people, size usually had little to do with ability, and this little pup was really coming along. The only thing Wabi didn't like about training the dogs was he always got attached to them and, of course, they moved on to their owners eventually. But, in his special way, Wabi communicated with all of them and that brought pleasure to him, and made them better companions for their masters.

The training was over for the day, and Wabi and Max were headed back to his cottage, both of them satisfied with their day's work. Wabi had been at this work for a lifetime and was proud of his abilities as a trainer.

As soon as the two got near the cottage, Wabi's nose picked up a most familiar and pleasing aroma. Shepherd's pie! Mrs. Fav.e, Aned, his nearest neighbor, was gracious enough that she brought one over about once a week and left it for him, or sometimes, stayed and shared it with him. Mrs. Favre, a widow for some years now, was French, and was quite a proficient cook. She, too, took pride in her endeavors. Not only was she a culinary expert, she was a very beautiful woman, even in her advanced years. Her silver hair and her ready smile went a long way to convincing you she was much more beautiful than she truly may have been, and she still dressed as she did when she lived in Paris. She and Wabi enjoyed each other's company, so they sometimes shared some of his mulberry wine and her delicious creations. Each preferred their own space, however, so they parted at the end of their evenings, and that was an arrangement that suited both.

This time of year, just before winter set in, Wabi always opened up the windows of his house and let nature enter, wherever she so wished. Of course, many winged critters wandered through, namely butterflies, mosquitoes, and midges. But, the breeze blowing through the trees also brought the smell of greenery such as spruce, cedar, evergreens of all kinds, and his favorite, pine. These smells carried over from all his travels, throughout time, and lent just a touch of continuity to his many lives. He was at home with all these aromas, and was thankful he had been called to this life. He had lived many lives, but didn't actually remember all of them, but rather, certain events in each one. Most assuredly, however, he knew the Creator had called him to serve as mentor to any number of "called" ones who needed guidance in order for them to learn how to use their special talents for the betterment of mankind. Wabi had spent this lifetime with Caitlin, providing her with incidents that would have allowed her to exercise her special talents; but, so far, she seemed unaware of her unique abilities. Perhaps, because she was so involved with her healing, she had not allowed herself to listen in the way that is required for those talents to manifest themselves.

But, now, apparently, Caitlin was beginning to open her mind and discover her talents and her purpose in life as well. Wabi smiled to himself, then picked Max up and placed him in his lap.

Scratching the pup behind his ears, he talked to the small pup.

"Well, my brave little beast, you know we all have the same purpose, to serve mankind and do our part to bring peace and harmony to this wonderful world of ours. If we can achieve even a small measure of this, then we shall have accomplished much. But, for all those who would undertake to work toward this end, there are even more who will strive to undermine our works. Ah, such a waste of effort that could be put to productive use."

Max kept still, flicked an ear, listening as always, but made no comment, preferring to close his eyes and take a little nap.

"Well, maybe this is just too much information for one so young, then," said Wabi as he placed Max in his basket by the hearth.

Wabi poured himself a glass of mulberry wine and was looking forward to his shepherd's pie dinner. He would stop by tomorrow to thank Aned for this most appreciated gesture. He was a very good cook also, but having someone else prepare a dish and deliver it to your doorstep was a treat. So, he laid his place on his scrubbed pine table and put out his finest dishes, some colorful pottery ones that had been passed down through several generations. He then served the steaming food onto his plate. Wabi believed that one should dine, not just eat.

As he began to dip his fork into the scrumptious smelling pie, the steam was rising up indicating it was extremely hot. But, the steam began to climb higher and higher, in front of his face, then expanded to cover the table entirely. He felt the familiar tingling of his scalp and knew someone was trying to reach him, but who? And why was it happening this way, through the steam? There are several much more direct ways of calling to another, thought Wabi. Then, another familiar aspect was present — lavender with a touch of mint. He would know that particular scent anywhere. Caitlin! Caitlin was trying to call him!

Opening his mind and allowing access to his center, he waited to hear what she had to say. But, he could barely hear her.

"Yes, Caitlin, I am here. I hear you." Wabi waited and waited, but the steam finally dissipated and he no longer felt the connection with Caitlin.

He took a sip of his wine and thought for a few moments.

"Ah, she doesn't quite know how to do this just yet and is probably just thinking about me, very hard, and some of her thoughts are escaping. She hasn't yet learned she must let down all barriers in order to get across time and place. But, if that is the case, then what is happening with her?"

Verbalizing his thoughts was habit with Wabi. It seemed to help him organize his thinking, somehow. After a bit more thought, he took his wine and walked back outside, where the wind was whistling through the tall pines, and he listened carefully. Nothing there. Looking up, thinking that he might find Owl, there was nothing there either. What could be happening that would create an opening for him to know she was calling?

Like being hit by a bolt of lightning, Wabi stopped and stared at the ground, watching the small frisky squirrels chasing through the leaves that had fallen.

"Of course! The only thing that would cause this 'partial communication' would be that Caitlin is in distress! She really doesn't understand what is happening, this new experience of using her newly found abilities. So, when she's worried, or distressed, the barriers lose some of their cohesive structure." Wabi spoke to himself again.

It had been so long since Wabi had first experienced his "awakening" and learned these skills that he had forgotten what a frightening experience it could be. He had been much younger than Caitlin when his powers first began to manifest and, as he recalled, it was a most unsettling time. Like Caitlin, he was by himself when it all started happening. Over the years, he had tried so hard to help Caitlin realize these special talents, but she walked away from them every time they tried to appear. But, now, for some reason, she was receptive and in the throes of something that was distressing her. He knew he could call for Owl, but also knew Owl would contact him if he were truly needed. So, after considering several options, he decided to stay put. At least for the moment.

After completing his washing up in the kitchen, Wabi went outside to make sure all gates were closed, all windows shuttered. Maximo was snug in his basket. All was ready for the evening. As he was about to close the stable door, who should make a flying dip down and land on his shoulder but Owl.

"Well, my wise old friend. I was just thinking about you, but then you knew that I am sure. We can use 'cerebral communication,' you know. It might keep you from making such long flights, my friend."

Wabi waited for Owl to respond, enjoying the clipped, very British, accent Owl had "adopted." Apparently Owl, too, had lived several lives, and one was most certainly in the company of a very proper Englishman. And to think he was now keeping company with a rather gruff, old Scot with a Gaelic brogue. That must be trying for him.

Owl turned his head, almost all the way around, something that still bothered Wabi. "Master Wabi. I did, indeed, feel you thinking about me and Caitlin. And, you know how I detest cerebral communication!" Now. Back to Caitlin. At the moment she is well enough, but engaged in a very disturbing journey, it would seem. At present, she is running from an innkeeper, someone from here in this village, as well as a lord and, even more worrisome, a soldier, one who is sure she is a witch and seeks to dispose of her."

"Good heavens! That girl has a penchant for getting herself into tight places, and it has always been thus. But, when she was a child, it usually didn't take much 'special' attention to retrieve her. But now, she has really brought on a challenge for herself and maybe me as well!"

Wabi shook his head, "I don't know Owl. I might be getting a bit too old for this nonsense. But, if need be, I'll go to her aid. But unless you tell me otherwise, I'll assume she is dealing with this in her own way, which is all any of us can do. All challenges bring about growth, and Caitlin still has need of that."

"She is still struggling to come to terms with communicating with others, meaning me at the moment. That was a bit uncomfortable for both of us. Why she finds it difficult I can't understand. But, she is accepting that I am traveling with her. Of course, Willie, that's her wolf, knows she is special, so hopefully, he will play a part in her understanding of abilities that she has let lay dormant for her entire life."

"Oh. She travels with a wolf, you say. Interesting." Wabi stroked his beard, trying to remember.

"Yes, of course. Family folklore tells of an ancestor of hers who also traveled with a wolf. I wonder if Caitlin has heard this tale. This could be interesting. I'm glad he's with her. A wolf can be a great protector, if need be."

"Ah, yes, he has already saved her from the soldier, and the soldier has not forgotten, it I am sure."

"Well, then. Let's just see how she does. Keep me up to date, please, my friend." Wabi watched Owl as he soared high to the treetops and heard his soft "hoo hoo" as he was lost in the darkness.

Chapter 29

Alex was not sure what he would say to Caitlin to convince her to leave the cave and go back north with him. As Hector had reminded him, she seemed to have made up her mind and that could present some difficulty for him. His Mam had usually gone along with whatever Da had decided, but on the few occasions when she didn't agree, then you couldn't pull her off her decision with a team of mules.

"Woman! Ye've got a lot in common with me mules sometimes, I tell ye! A stubborn streak as wide as Loch Ness!" Da was just a bit put out with her on that day. Alex remembered it clearly, and it was a fond memory.

"So, Alex, old man, ye got some more thinking ta do," he said to himself, pulling his horse to a halt and dismounting. He knew the path to take to get back to the cave, but it was not an easy ride. He had been on the road for some time now and needed to rest, and he was concerned about his horse as well. Caring for animals was something that Da had instilled in him early on. "If you take care of your animals, then they'll take care of you," his Da had said many times over the years. People might learn from the animals also, thought Alex. The MacKinnons did care for their animals very well, and this same caring attitude was evident in how they cared for their kin as well.

Some of their folk they took care of was old Jamie, some distant cousin of sorts, who had worked on the farm all his life. Being the oldest of the men, he couldn't do as much as when he was a young man, but he still contributed what he could and was very much a part of their family. Then Uncle Andrew, also an oldster, was perhaps THE most important member, as he was their bard, and that was a position that was well respected in any clan. As bard, he knew the history of the MacKinnon clan and could recite their lineage with nary a mistake. It had occurred to Alex that it would be good to get this information down on paper, as none of them knew it like Uncle Andrew did. So, recently he had asked Uncle Andrew to give some thought to "putting it down on paper" as Alex called it.

"Uncle Andrew. Nothing pleases this bunch more than listening to your stories in the evening. But, it occurs to me that none of us will probably remember who is who and what was what. But, when ye be gone — sometime in the next century, as I see it — then our history will be lost."

"Aw, Alex. Ye won't be forgetting it. But, if it makes you more easy, then I'll give a try at "putting it down on paper" as ye say. 'Course, I may have to check some records down in Edinburgh, at a few kirks around here, and maybe even some over on the west side, around Skye. We got cousins all over the place!"

Alex wrapped himself tightly in his plaid and settled in for the night, and a chilly one it would be. Winter seemed to be right around the corner, and the air was crisp with a fine mist blowing about. He would like to finish this task quickly and head back north before the snows got heavy and hindered his progress.

As he lay there, under a tall pine tree, he heard a number of sounds he recognized, birds, squirrels, some critter digging in the leaves, and the quiet "hoo-hoo" of an owl. At least at this time of year the midges wouldn't carry him off. Then he drifted off to sleep within a few minutes, tired from his traveling.

Sometime in the wee hours of the morning, he raised up on an elbow and listened. What had awakened him? His Mam would have said someone "walked over your grave," but Alex had sensed a presence, and thought he heard the whimpering of an animal.

But, perhaps he was just dreaming. He lay back down and was fast asleep once again and never realized that the noise and presence were indeed near, just beyond the ridge he had crossed a short while earlier, a horse and a rider, being trailed by a wolf. As they passed in the dark of night, each of these travelers was thinking of the other and wondering if they would meet again.

The next morning, very early, Alex stood up and tried to stretch out some of the kinks from sleeping on the ground. Up above him, an owl greeted him with a hardy "hoo hoo" and Alex was reminded of the owl that lived in the tree at Caitlin's cave. He saddled up and started out again, renewed after some rest. The ground was covered with a fine frost, a sure indication winter was about to make its appearance. He heard the crunching of the icy leaves as his mount began to walk briskly himself, finding the cool air to his liking. Shortly, he would be warm enough as Alex would ask him to run at a fast pace in order to make good time. The horse sensed his master's anxiety and would respond when asked to move quickly as this animal recognized a good master and was eager to please.

Horse and rider went cantering along the downhill side of the mountain and headed directly to the village just south of Inverness where he had met the healer. Not far now. But what would he find when he got there? He was just hoping Caitlin would listen to reason this time, otherwise, he had actually considered kidnapping her.

"Good Lord man! Yer beginning to sound like Jack and one of his crazy schemes!" But he was convinced that Caitlin was in real danger, whether she could see it or not.

As the sun began to sink into the western sky, Alex moved over the moor, skirted the village, and went directly in the direction of the cave. He wanted to keep his presence unknown until he could see what the situation was before he went inside. He had no doubt she would be aware of his presence as that giant wolf would announce his arrival. He hoped the animal was as friendly to him this time as he had been when he was here last. That had to be the largest wolf he had ever seen! And how in heaven had she trained him to be her companion? He had killed any number of them in his time, mostly to keep them from attacking his sheep and scattering them to kingdom come. Wolves and sheep didn't go together. That thought had not occurred to him until now. Even if he did talk her into coming, she would never leave her wolf behind. That was something else to think about. Well, for right now, he had enough to dwell on.

He tied his horse well away from the cave entrance, back in the trees, just as before. There was a crescent moon brightening the sky that provided enough light for him to move about. He was half expecting something or someone to jump out and grab him, most probably a wolf. But, the closer he got to the cave, he could hear nothing, not even birds or scurrying animals. It was as if the entire area was uninhabited by man or beast.

He poked his head in the entrance to the cave, and there was total blackness. No light could be seen anywhere. But, something was still there. The scent of lavender and mint. Caitlin's scent. Unique to her. He was not good at determining smells, but this one he recognized and it brought memories of a smiling face, lots of red, curly hair, and a will of iron. Whatever, just smelling it made him more determined than ever to find her.

He found a candle near the entrance up on a small ledge that had been carved into the cave wall. He lighted it and then lifted it high in order to find his way back to the larger room and the kitchen area. It was obvious no one was here, certainly not Caitlin or her wolf, and the cave had a feeling of having been deserted for a while now. As he looked about the large room, there on the small table, where they had enjoyed tea and conversation, was the teapot she was so fond of.

"Now, why on earth would she leave without taking her teapot?" he questioned. She had felt this teapot was special and was meant for her. He remembered her telling him the story about how she came by it.

At this juncture, he lighted several more candles along the wall of the large room and walked farther back, farther than he had gone before. As he continued to light even more candles, the room actually was very bright and as he looked around, he could see Caitlin's touch everywhere. There were bunches of herbs hanging from the ceiling, and pots of heather all about. Yes, she had turned a cave into an inviting home.

Just as he was about to return to the large room, he walked around one more corner and saw a chair had been overturned and a broken bowl lay on the floor. Some white powder was strewn about on the floor also, and as he stooped down and touched it with his fingers, sniffing them; he could tell it was one of her medicines. Caitlin would never have left this mess, unless she had left in a hurry.

As he started to get back up, he spotted something of interest — several dark spots on the floor. Again he put his fingers in the spots and smelled them. He shuttered as he knew immediately what it was — blood! The blood was old and congealed, and there was actually quite a bit of it. Whoever the blood belonged to must have received a sizeable wound of some sort.

Maybe a patient? But, no, Caitlin would never have left this mess on the floor. Something had happened that caused her to leave in a hurry. Alex didn't even want to think about what it could be.

After looking about for another moment, he saw Caitlin's medicine bag was not here, and certainly the wolf was not either. She would never willingly leave either behind and he hoped this meant she had left of her own choosing. But, now what was he to do? He still had to find her. And he so hoped the blood was not Caitlin's!

Alex decided he would stay in the cave for the evening, and the next morning would wander into the village and see if, perhaps, Caitlin had moved to a new dwelling. Maybe she thought the cave would be too cold in the winter. At least he could ask around the village, and maybe even hear something about Commander Campbell, but he would have to be very cautious.

Getting up early, and finding some of Caitlin's delicious tea, he had a cup and tried to make a plan of some sort. If he didn't find her in the village, then he would slowly make his way back home, asking along the way about the red-haired healer. Looking about the cave for the last time, he started to go and, at the last moment, for some strange reason, picked up the teapot, wrapped it tightly in some bits of cloth, and put it in his travel bag. It was very small, but seemed to mean a lot to the healer.

This village was like most others in the area. The people were desperately trying to get by, doing whatever they could to feed their families, and provide a shelter over their heads.

Many of them were either hoping for their loved ones to return from the fighting, or more probably, were grieving the death of them.

He walked slowly around the watering trough where he had tied his horse. There were several other horses there also, drinking their fill. He nodded to a few villagers, then finally, walked up to an older woman, rather rotund and wearing some sort of apron over her tattered dress. She was placing her vegetables on a table, no doubt hoping to sell some of them before they rotted. He picked up one of the apples, paid her for it, and then began to ask her about a healer in the area.

"Oh, aye. We had one. And a fine one she was. A young woman, with that fiery hair of hers!" She laughed. "But, mind ye, she knew her business fer sure. She tended many of the soldiers returning from Culloden, and pleased we was to have her."

"Is she still about here?" asked Alex.

"Oh, now, that I can't answer, ye see. She usually came in a day or two a week, but we no have seen her for a couple of weeks now, and we haven't seen her friend either, the black wolf." She laughed again, revealing the few teeth she had left.

"You shoulda seen the look on the soldiers' faces when the healer would come to their beds with that wolf by her side. They would agree to anything she said! Ha ha! But, they learnt quickly she could ease their pain and help them get back to their people. Yes, a fine healer she was."

Alex ambled back over to the trough, untying his horse, ready to move on. As he was about to mount up, a frail old gentlemen, moving along with the help of a walking stick, came up to him and nodded in his direction. "I hear ye asking about the healer. Ye ain't a soldier are ye? Ye ain't wearing no uniform, I see."

"Nae, my soldiering days are over. I'm just a sheep farmer headed back north to my home."

"Be ye a friend of the healer?"

"Well, yes, ye might say that. She tended my young brother and now he's doing well, thanks to her. But I can't seem to find her anywhere."

"There was another man looking for her too, some days ago, now. A soldier it was, with a lot of ribbons an' such on his uniform. He was certainly in need of a healer, what with blood dripping from his neck and covering the top of his uniform. He asked about the healer, the one with the red hair. Seems he wanted her to treat him. But, we didn't much like the looks of him, so we sent him on, told him to look for a healer in the next village. Not a pleasant one, that man."

"Do you know which way he might have gone?" asked Alex.

"Let me see, now." The old man removed his old tam, scratched his head, and then placed it back on his sparsely sprigged head.

"As I recollect, he left here headed north as it was, same as the healer. She said she was headed north looking fer a friend of hers. But, more than that, I can't tell ye. But, back to that soldier. It could be he may not have made it very far, ye ken. He was in pretty bad shape."

"Oh, she be riding a very fine horse, too. Red it was, just like her hair! Hee!" He slapped his knee with his worn tam, laughing at his own bit of humor.

"Thank ye, friend. I'll keep looking for her then. But, if she should return here, tell her MacKinnon is looking for her. She'll know who that is." With that he mounted and started out at a fast pace, thinking to get on to the next village and see what he might discover there.

Chapter 30

With Millie gone, Warwick spent his evenings sipping his wine or mead, and remembering scenes from his childhood, some of which were better not remembered.

"You're not worth very much, dear brother. The first son gets everything, so you'll end up a pauper!" These words were etched in Warwick's mind as if they were written in stone. His older brother had spoken them when Warwick was just a young boy, but he had not forgotten them.

Warwick's retort was etched there as well.

"Come on, you bully! You think you can push everyone around, but I'll find a way to send you to hell and laugh when you get there!" Warwick stood with his blade drawn, having placed the point of it in his brother's cheek.

"Put that blade away, you imbecile!" Their father had shown up at that point and shoved Warwick down the hall.

"And stay in your quarters until I say you can leave!"

Warwick had learned early how to fend for himself, seeing as the older brother had indeed inherited most everything. Even when his brother died and Warwick was next in line, he continued to feel he never had enough, no matter what it was.

"Well, so much for childhood memories," Warwick uttered and poured the last of the wine into his cup. He sat down before a blazing fire and watched as the cinders drifted up the overly large chimney. He had thought that if everything was bigger in his castle, then that meant it was better. He had grown used to the unending nightmares that had haunted him since his brother's death. Why couldn't his brother be satisfied that he had made Warwick's life miserable when he was alive! Must he continue to invade his dreams too?

Gazing into the fire, he pondered how he was going to take care of his little problem up in Scotland. He had managed more difficult situations than this.

A very large looking glass had been mounted on one of the walls in Warwick's castle. In his drunken state, he looked into the glass and addressed the face that returned his stare. Was that his face? Somehow it looked a lot like his dead brother! Why, the face even had the scar on the cheek where Warwick had nicked him with his epee, just shortly before their father had stopped him from more damage. Well, then. It had been some time since he had talked to that pompous ass!

"So, now, dear brother, just who is here and has more holdings than you ever thought about! And now, I'm about to have a grand estate in Scotland! Too bad you can't be here to see it."

The face remained still — never even moved an inch.

"Well. Just as well you remain silent. Wouldn't listen to you anyway."

Well, whoever it was, it was better than just talking to himself. So, he addressed this image once again, knowing he would have the last word.

"Ha! It'll be so easy! I'll have someone sneak into the castle during dead of night and see to it that those two women never wake again! It will need to be done very quietly, of course, and after it's done, then I'll insist that Millie go visit her family. Once the babe is born, that'll be a good excuse. Of course, when we arrive, we'll be told of the unfortunate deaths of the old woman and the aunt. Millie will be heartbroken, and I'll pretend that I am distressed over the losses, too.

The story will be that both apparently had been smothered to death by an unknown person, most probably a highwayman who sneaked into their rooms looking for jewels or money!"

"Why, I do believe this story is plausible, don't you brother!" Warwick lifted his glass to his image and toasted himself.

"And then the estate and lands will come to Millie and ultimately to me. Yes. This is a good plan." Now he needed to find someone to execute this diabolical scheme.

***

The next evening, Warwick found his way down to the shipping docks where the odor of rotting fish and old, dried up seaweed greeted him. He was familiar with the odors as he came down to this end of town occasionally, especially when in one of his depressed states. He placed his handkerchief over his nose and mouth for a moment, then walked inside the tavern that still stood in spite of the rotten timbers that held it up. The smoke was so thick in the room that he could hardly see, and he walked over to the bar.

"Looking for Henri. Is he here?"

Warwick had addressed the bartender. The lord's face was known here, and the locals knew him to spend some coin and drink a lot of whiskey. So, they were more than happy to accommodate him if possible.

"Gimme a minute. See if I can find him. He was here earlier."

Warwick wound his way to a small table at the back of the tavern and brought a bottle of whiskey with him. Certainly wasn't what he was used to at home, but would suffice for this event. No sooner had he poured his first glass than he was greeted.

"Lord Warwick. At your service, sir."

The small man removed his beret and bowed from the waist. Henri's English was heavily accented but understandable. He had hurriedly left France some years earlier in order to escape some rather unpleasant issues that seemed to forever hound him. He was always just one step ahead of authorities whatever country he was in.

Henri was a very slight man, on the short side, with arms that seemed just a tad too long for the rest of his body. But, the muscles of these long, hairy arms revealed that he had done some manual labor sometime in his life. He was always dressed in dark clothing, scruffy boots and his ever-present black beret. His greasy, lank hair was pulled back and tied with a snip of leather. Bathing or shaving should be done on occasion, Henri thought, but certainly not very often, and his daily intake of alcohol helped camouflage his personal odor.

The Frenchman put his beret back on and pulled out a chair from the table, then had a seat. He was always pleased to see Warwick as that meant his pockets would be jingling more than usual.

"Ah, Henri. Glad I found you. Like a drink?" "Can't say no to that, milord."

Warwick poured the liquid and watched as Henri tossed it back in one large gulp. "Another?"

"Well, if you insist, sir." And he polished off the second one.

Knowing he must get down to business before Henri was totally addled, Warwick leaned back in his chair and sipped his whiskey.

"I need your services—again. It's not much of a job, but one that you can handle easily." "What did you have in mind, sir?"

"Well. There's a small problem up in Scotland that needs to be handled immediately. It's important to me, and I expect to pay you well to make it go away."

After another couple of drinks, Warwick had made his deal with Henri and left the dingy tavern to return to his castle. He would almost rather stay at the tavern than return home to that empty edifice. He found it irritating to realize he actually missed his wife, and wasn't sure what to make of those feelings.

***

Warwick was anxious to get his plan underway, so made his way back to the docks the next morning. Certainly, his head ached, so he knew Henri would be in even worse condition. He could care less about Henri's head, but he wanted this job done now.

Henri slept above the tavern in a room that was barely more than a closet where the bartender kept his supplies. The Frenchman was rudely awakened this morning by two men who forced their way through his door, which never had a lock anyway. They burst into his room and jerked him from his bed, causing him to land on the floor with a thump.

"Well, Henri. I see you're still able to find enough coin to drink yourself into oblivion!

Then, you must be able to pay back what you owe us also, huh?"

That pronouncement was followed by the two men throwing Henri up against the wall and jamming a pistol just beneath his chin.

"So. Where's our money? Huh ,Henri?"

"I can get some of it today! Just give me a couple of hours! I promise!" Henri had planned to be long gone before these men caught up with him. Leaving town was his usual way of repaying his debts. When excited or angry, Henri's English became mixed with French and no one could understand him.

Just as the men were about to convince Henri that they meant business, a loud voice rang out.

"I wouldn't do that if I were you, gentlemen." Lord Warwick stepped inside the room with his own pistol pointing in their direction.

"What does this man owe you? Ten pounds, twenty, what?"

"He owed us twenty-five pound and was to have paid it last week. But, he had some lame excuse for not paying. And now he's in debt even more after last evening. He should learn not to gamble after a couple of drinks. He's not a very good gambler when sober, and even worse when drinking. So now that twenty- five has become thirty pound! And we mean to get it from him or if not, then take it out of his hide!"

"Hold on. Here Take this. It's more than enough to pay his debts." And he tossed over a bag of coins — whose weight satisfied the two men. They let go of Henri and he dropped, instantly, to the floor. Then they slipped out leaving the door wide open.

Warwick walked over to where Henri had fallen to the floor.

"Oh. Lord Warwick. You saved my life, sir." Henri took a deep breath and tried to regain his composure.

"Yes. I probably did, Henri. But then you and I made a deal, and I expect you to complete your part of it. I want you to leave today and get this business we discussed finished. It's important to me."

"Yessir. I'll leave right now. Just let me get my horse and I'll be on my way."

Warwick walked out and had no doubt the man would do what he had asked. Henri might be a drunk, but he had done a few other jobs for Warwick, and they understood each other. Henri always thought of these events as "jobs", and this was how he survived. Not once had he thought of himself as an "assassin," but that was precisely what he was.

Chapter 31

Jack had kept himself busy, which was easy to do on a working sheep farm. Da, Uncle Andrew, and Old Jamie still carried as much of the workload as they could. But this was a large farm, and caring for it was a constant job for many hands.

But, farm or not, Jack was not comfortable with letting Alex go back down the mountain looking for that red-haired healer. Heaven knows she had brought Ian back from a sure death.

But Jack could not ignore his feelings about Alex going alone to find her.

So, after much gut-wrenching thought, he informed Hector and the others that he would leave in the morning. He was also going back down. For all they knew, Alex could be in trouble and there was no one at his back. Of course, Alex had said to wait a fortnight, but Jack was not planning on waiting another day.

Very early, the moon still giving off a soft light, Jack went to the stables and brought out his favorite steed, Goliath, the largest gelding in the entire stable. His dark brown coat was beginning to thicken, anticipating the coming of winter, and he was full of energy, ready to go. Jack was a tall, heavy load, so it took a horse with some bulk and stamina to carry him. And these two had been friends for a long time. Goliath lowered his head to receive a pat on the forehead. He actually preferred being out of the stable and being of use around the farm. He was bred for this job, carrying a heavy load, and Jack used him often.

Traveling alone gave one a great deal of time for thinking, something that Jack preferred to leave to Alex. However, he certainly was capable of some deep thought himself, and found himself thinking about Mam. She had been such a unique woman, always finding the best in everyone, it seemed. Her greatest joy had been raising her sons, and never did she complain about the work it took to keep them all fed, clothed, and in line. She was soft spoken, but they all knew when she said jump, then, you best ask how high! She ran the house with an iron fist, and sometimes her voice made you think perhaps she was soft, as she was when caring for small animals or babes. But, she expected her sons to make her and Da proud of them, and so they had. Still, there was such a void in their home, and no one to fill it.

"Ah, git on with ye, ye maudlin man!" he said to himself. "Mam would kick yer arse and tell ye to find something useful to do!"

After traveling several days, Jack knew he was close to the Black Isle. From there he would move further south and through the village to Caitlin's cave. In another day or so he should be there. But, for tonight, he and Goliath both needed to rest. Goliath was tied to a tree, with enough rope to allow him to graze on the plentiful reindeer moss that grew at the base of the trees. There was also some grass, not quite brown yet, that he could nibble on. Jack had some of Hector's brew, or what Hector called coffee, but Jack was not sure you could call it that. Still, he was glad to have that and a couple of oat cakes and bannocks. That would fill his belly for a while, and he would feel like moving on tomorrow. The earlier, the better.

Chapter 32

Commander Campbell tried to open his eyes, but they didn't want to respond to his wishes. He was so, so sleepy, and drifted back to sleep again.

The old healer watched him from the rocking chair where she was sitting, stroking Regina and continuing with her knitting.

"A most evil one, Regina. But, I've kept him as long as I dare. He'll no be pleased to know he's been here for three days. But, he's alive and maybe he'll consider that fact when he realizes his difficult situation."

The old woman had stitched his neck and cleaned several other cuts on his hand. She was sure his neck wound had been caused by an animal of some sort, but she didn't know exactly what.

"He's lucky to have made it this far. He had lost a lot of blood," she said to Regina. The fuzzy white cat enjoyed the stroking and rubbed her head against the healer's hand.

She, too, sensed the blackness in this man and would be glad to see him leave. She thought that a good swipe of her claws would be just the thing!

"No, my pretty one. Let him be. He'll bring about his own demise in his own time."

***

When next he opened his eyes, Commander Campbell looked around the room and had to think a moment. He tried to remember where he was. And why was he here in this room?

Suddenly, his memory came into sharp focus, and he quickly started to get up, but was somewhat dizzy. He slowed his movements and sat on the side of the bed. His throat was throbbing, but he could tell the bleeding had stopped.

"Hey! Old woman! Where are you! Where are my clothes! Bring them to me!"

The old healer entered the small room and placed the commander's uniform on the end of the bed. She had done what she could to clean it, but blood stains were most difficult to remove.

"Here they be. I've repaired a couple of ripped places and cleaned it the best I could, but it's seen better days." Regina hopped up on the bed and sniffed at the man.

"Get off here, you mangy cat! " He struck out at Regina, but she quickly leapt off the bed and disappeared from the room.

"How long have I been here? What day is it? What did you give me?" The soldier stood up and held on to the bed for support until the dizziness passed. He began to pull his uniform on and then reached for his boots. The uniform now smelled of various herbs, apparently ones she used in cleaning it. He observed that his boots had been cleaned also. Reaching into the inside pocket of his uniform, feeling for the packet of henbane that he kept there, he found nothing. He knew there had only been a small amount left, but he wanted it. Needed it.

"Where is my packet? It was in my uniform!"

"Sir, that medicine is poison and is only used when there is no other available. Ye've used so much of it that yer body has suffered greatly. You would do well to let it recover on its own, and it will, if you allow it to."

"Old woman! Get me my packet! Now!" he yelled at her and started to walk from the room. She went to her cabinet and removed the packet, handing it to him, and he promptly stuck it inside his jacket.

Stomping his feet, trying to get them further down into his boots, he grabbed his sword laying on the table and walked out the front door.

"I need a horse. Where can I find one?"

"Oh, that I can't tell ye. Mayhap ye can find a farmer down the way that may have one, but I can no promise ye that."

Without another word, and certainly no thanks to her for her help, he walked a few steps, then looked out into a side field next to the healer's cottage. Far out in the field he spied an old horse.

Turning back to her he yelled, "There's a horse out there. Who does it belong to? I want it." The soldier was demanding as always.

"That's old Bellboy, but he's too old to ride anymore. He's barely able to stand on his feet and he's almost as blind as I am," she said.

With that information, the commander walked to the field and, pulling the old horse by his mane, brought him back to the small shelter behind the cottage. There he found a bridle, reins, and a very old, deteriorated saddle, with leather so old and stiff it would hardly bend enough to buckle beneath the horse's belly.

"I tell ye he's too old! It'll kill him!" The old woman had hobbled out to the stable. She was beside herself with fear for the old horse. He had been such a good old plow horse for many years when her husband was living. But, he was so old now that arthritis had all but frozen his joints, and just ambling about to graze was all he could do.

"Get out of my way, old woman! He's no good to you, and I need him now!"

After securing the saddle after a fashion, he climbed up on old Bellboy's back and kicked him sharply in the sides.

"Get on now!" And the old horse tried to trot, but was limping on his right, front leg. The rider paid no attention to the animal's distress and continued kicking him trying to get him to move faster.

When they got to the edge of the path leading to the next village, a screaming yowl caused Commander Campbell to jerk his head around. Just at that moment, Regina came flying off the ground and landed on his chest, then raked her claws across his freshly stitched neck! The soldier screamed to high heaven and plucked the cat away, throwing her to the ground. He felt to see if his neck was bleeding again. But it was alright for now.

"I'll kill you yet, you four legged demon!" He looked about, hoping to see where the cat had gone. She ran into the woods, and the soldier cursed at her and kicked the old horse even harder.

Commander Campbell had soldiering in his blood. The men in his family had always been military men, and he was proud to carry on the tradition. He had two older brothers who had entered the military service as young men, and had advanced in rank quickly. Their father had thought the sun set on his first born, and Campbell and his other brother were in constant battle for their father's attentions. The older brother had one large character flaw, in Commander Campbell's opinion. He cared about others and conducted himself in an honorable manner, as his father had taught him. As fate would have it, several years ago the older brother lost his life when he returned to a burning barracks to try to help some fellow soldiers escape. Someone had apparently not put out the campfire, and a spark had ignited the roof and began to burn as the soldiers were sleeping. As Campbell's brother went back for the second time, to carry a wounded soldier out, the roof collapsed on them, and both were killed instantly.

"Serves you right, you fool!" thought Campbell. So, now, that left Campbell and one brother. Perhaps he would prove to his father that he, too, was every bit as worthy as his older brother had been. But, their father grieved for his son, and Commander Campbell felt resentment toward his brother even more so. Even in death, his brother was still his rival.

Campbell had married well, or at least he had married a woman who came with a sizeable dowry. He thought his father would be pleased with that accomplishment, but if so, he never voiced it to Campbell. But the woman was stupid, insipid, and given to coddling their son, Bradford. He would forever blame her for trying to lead his son astray from what should have been his true calling, a military career as all Campbell men had aspired to. And, now, having lost his son, he was beginning to understand how his father must have felt when Campbell's brother had died. He well recalled the day they learned of his brother's death and how his father had fallen to his knees as if he could no longer stand.

***

"I'll show him now what a real son can be! You were always the one to get his attention, but I'll outrank you very soon and Father will have to acknowledge that he was wrong all along. I've always been the best! You were just older and he could only see your accomplishments.

Well. Mine will outshine you, dear brother. Let him grieve for a while. Then he'll come seeking my good graces."

Campbell had stood over the coffin and recited this sentiment to the corpse of his brother.

This scene he remembered well also.

But, unlike his father, who had resorted to remembering his son, grieving appropriately, and moving on with his life, Campbell would never be satisfied until he made that witch pay for killing his son. He didn't believe for one minute her story about it being a fever of some sort. She had put some wicked spell on all those men, and he would see to it she paid for her actions.

Campbell had actually been a caring father when his son was young. He often took him riding across the moors and taught him to shoot. At times, he struggled to keep the boy's interest, but stayed with his instructions and exhibited a great amount of patience with the young boy.

"Now. Here. Just slowly lift the rifle, bring it to your cheek, then make sure there's no space between your cheek and the gun. That'll help you maintain your steadiness. And make sure your feet are well planted — not too far apart, mind you — then put a bit more of your weight on your left foot. Bring it forward just slightly. Keep both eyes open now. None of that closing one eye business. You'll learn to focus better with both eyes."

"Yes, Father. I'll try."

"No! Don't tell me you'll try! Tell me you'll do it!" He realized he had raised his voice, then immediately returned to a quieter, soothing manner. He had already learned his son responded favorably to instruction that was calm and deliberate. And Commander Campbell wanted this son to succeed as he had.

"There. That's good, Bradford, very good."

The boy actually was beginning to become quite a fine marksman and Campbell was ecstatic.

"Bradford, you've come a long way my boy. By the time the military academy opens its doors to you, you'll be leading the way, showing the other new recruits how its done!"

"Yes, Father."

Of course, it suited Campbell not to remember that his son had never wanted to be a soldier and had told his father that on numerous occasions. Campbell had spent much time and money trying to secure a place for his son in a military school that would prepare him for being a leader of men, a military strategist, or a regimental commander at least.

"But I'm an artist. Painting is what I do best! It's the only thing I want to do!" Bradford had wailed.

Campbell cringed just remembering his son's remarks to him. That was the result of his wife's interfering in the boy's upbringing. That detestable woman! She had presented the young boy with a special Christmas gift when he was ten years old — an easel and some oil paints.

Bradford had taken to painting with a passion, and from that time on, he had no wish to do anything else. Painting was his life. And the ridiculous woman arranged for him to study with an artist who was well known in their social circle. With some instruction from the artist, Bradford's artistic talent had grown quickly, and he had begun to produce very fine work. He then began to talk of going to Italy to study with other artists, and was encouraged by his mother to do so.

"That will never happen! Do you hear me! You will do as I say and go where I tell you!"

And, threatening to send the young man to an uncle who lived in a fishing village far over on the east coast, with no contact with his family, the boy was forced to enter the military, following the path his father had chosen for him.

Refusing to dwell on the past and unpleasant memories, Commander Campbell turned his thoughts to his present. He was feeling much better after having his neck tended to and, now, with a horse to carry him, he would find her, no matter how long it took.

He reached up and felt the new scratch that Regina had delivered to him. That wretched cat! If he hadn't been in such a hurry, he would have gone back and taken care of her. Still, that old woman had apparently known her business as his neck was healing very nicely.

After another day's ride, Campbell was near the Black Isle and made inquiries in the villages trying to find out if they knew anything about a red-haired healer. There were only two or three trails that led north, so she must have taken one of them. And this was where he knew his soldier's training would be of help. He could track as well as any bloodhound and would not stop until he caught her.

It was late afternoon and the sun had long ago disappeared, with the leaden color of the sky suggesting that snow was on its way. Campbell mounted up, hoping to make a few more miles this day in order to catch up with the healer. Of course, she had his horse, damn her hide! This old nag didn't move quickly at all, and he was frustrated with his slow progress. As he took the reins in his hand and kicked the old horse in both sides, the animal groaned and then stumbled. This infuriated Campbell, and he lashed at the horse with his whip.

"Get a move on, you stupid beast!" And he kicked even harder.

With that last kick, old Bellboy fell to his knees, then on down to the ground, letting out one long breath and groan. His eyes closed and, with a shudder, he expired. Campbell stood, looking down at the animal, then kicked him once more in his side.

"I'll kill you. You old nag!"

But, then, as he looked again, he realized that he would not need to kill the horse. He was dead already. He kicked him once more in frustration. So, now, he was back to no horse and still had not found the healer. But, he was close. He could feel it. Some intuition told him to be patient. He would find her.

He felt inside his coat pocket for the henbane, which was almost gone. But, he knew just a taste of it would render him relief, so he threw his head back and downed another bit of the poison. He felt more relaxed immediately and began to walk in the direction that would bring him to the Black Isle.

Chapter 33

Warwick had paid handsomely to have Henri make his way to Scotland and the Cameron holding. Finding the estate was not difficult, as it was very large and most of the villagers nearby knew of it. So, the Frenchman went on the path that led to the rear of the stables and waited for the castle to be put to bed, meaning all the animals had been stabled, the old hands had gone to their crofter huts in the field, and the serving ladies had returned to their families nearby. Of course, Henri was aware there were sometimes a few servants who remained in the castle and had quarters usually somewhere close by the kitchen in case they were needed in the night. He would need to be especially quiet.

Henri tied his horse at the stall that was farthest away from the doors and crept up silently. So good so far. But as he rounded the last stall, he ran headlong into a young stable lad carrying a pail of water. The young boy dropped his pail and exclaimed,

"Oh, good Lord! You scared me near to death! Weren't expecting to meet anyone here tonight. You must be the new gardener the missus said was coming. Well, she does like her flowers and the old gardener is just too old to keep up her gardens, so I reckon you'll be needed. I be Archie. I work with the horses and keep the stalls clean."

"Oh, yes. I'm the gardener," replied Henri, struggling to understand the lad's heavy brogue.

"I just need a place to put my horse and sleep tonight. Then tomorrow morning I'll see the mistress and get my orders, I expect." Henri was quick on his feet, mostly from learning to be so any number of times.

"Aye. The last stall there is empty. And up above, there in the loft, there's another cot up there. Ye can stay there tonight. I'm off to see my lass now, Debra. That is if her Da will let me. He's right strict about anyone talking to his daughter. But, I'll keep trying. It might be late before I'm back, but the loft is not too bad. There are blankets and a lantern if ye need. Just be careful, don't need a fire in here for sure!"

"That's a real different voice ye have there. Not from around here, I guess. One of the upstairs maids sounds just like that when she talks, too. Huh." And the lad went quickly on his way.

Henri breathed a long sigh of relief.

"Damnation! Hadn't counted on anyone seeing me. I might have to take care of that boy before this night is over." Henri muttered under his breath. This was not going exactly as he had planned.

As soon as the stable boy was out of sight, Henri slowly ventured a little closer to the back side of the castle. The only sound he heard was an owl, somewhere close, with his constant "hoo hoo" call which seemed to never stop. Drat that bird! The night air was chilly, and he wanted to be done with this job. Inching his way to the far side of the bailey and climbing a tree close by, he entered the grounds, and found a door cracked open at the rear of the castle. The door squeaked when he pushed it, just enough to squeeze his thin body through. He felt around in the dark and quickly realized he was in a wine cellar.

"Well. Now this is what I call a first class place. This looks like very fine wine. French wine at that!"

His first thought was to take some of the wine, but he dared not stop for anything just now; he needed to get this finished. Climbing the cellar stairs slowly, he got to the top and cautiously opened the door. The stairs led up to the kitchen, which was filled with smells of freshly made bread and some kind of fruit pies. Those smells made him wish he had time to stay awhile.

He had just started across the expanse of the large kitchen when a young girl came strolling in. She was rather thin and had her hair tied up with some kind of kerchief. She walked over to the oven and opened it. The aroma coming from the oven made Henri's stomach come to life as it had been some time since he had eaten. Then, turning back to the larder, the young lass started over in Henri's direction, carrying a candle before her to light her way. Henri hoped she would not notice him, but the girl stopped in her tracks and looked directly at him.

"Oh! Who are you? What are you doing in here?" The girl started to back away. Then she held the candle higher and the Frenchman's face was clearly shown in the light. Henri knew a scream was imminent and had no choice but to clamp his hand over her mouth. Now there was yet another person who had seen him!

Henri was no stranger to killing, but she was so very young. But, she would certainly alert others if he didn't take care of her.

"Ah. It's not what I wanted, chéri."

The girl never had a chance to even think of screaming. Within just a short few moments, Henri had grabbed the kerchief on her head, pulled it down, and tightened in around her neck.

There was no sound from her. But now he had to do away with her body.

He easily lifted her thin body and deposited it in the corner of the larder. It would at least be out of the way until someone came to start breakfast tomorrow morning.

Now, he had to find the bedrooms. Warwick had said the women would most likely be upstairs as that was the usual place for family quarters. He crossed the kitchen and went out into the great hall. The remnants of a fire were smoldering in the giant fireplace, the small embers still giving off red flickers of light, and the warmth felt good to him. The sheer size of this place was amazing to Henri, but a flight of stairs to his left seemed to be the logical place to start.

He could hear every creak of the stairs as he climbed. He just hoped no one else could hear them as well. Reaching the top, he looked about. All was quiet. There were several rooms on either side of a wide hallway. Which ones did the women sleep in? He had not thought of this, but made short work of looking quickly into the first one he came to. This room was vacant, and was probably a guest room when needed. He proceeded on to the next one on the right, and it, too, was empty. He was beginning to wonder if there was another flight of stairs and he had taken the wrong one.

He walked to the other side of the hallway and turned the knob on the first door. Clearly he had had found one of the women, as a most pleasant aroma filled the large room. Flowers. Ah, definitely a woman's room! He knew nothing about flowers, but found this scent pleasing to his nostrils. Tiptoeing over to the bed, he looked only briefly at the very old woman, lying on her side, facing the wall. When he reached the edge of the bed, he looked down and was taken aback as the old woman was awake and staring at him! He jumped back, not sure what his next move should be.

"Who's there? Is that you, Moira?" Henri held his breath and remained perfectly quiet.

"Moira?" He quickly discerned that the old woman had her eyes open, but in the dark she was having great difficulty making out who it was. Then, in one long stride he was back at the bedside. It took only a moment to complete his assignment as she offered practically no resistance to his great strength.

Henri had felt absolutely nothing as he taken this woman's life. He left the room and pulled the door closed behind him. The next door was also closed, so he turned the knob slowly and stepped inside. Again, he was met with the scent of flowers and some kind of herb. The bed in this room was over by the window, which was cracked just slightly, to allow some fresh air into the room, he thought. He could still hear that noisy owl calling "hoo hoo" as he came closer to the bed. Did that bird never sleep?

As he crept closer to the bed, the woman suddenly turned over in her sleep! His heart began to pound so loudly he was sure she could hear it. He waited, barely breathing, until she settled back into her blankets again. She sighed deeply and then he looked at her. This woman was probably no more than fifty years of age, not young certainly, but she probably had some years left, and she had such a kind expression on her face.

Henri jerked the pillow from beneath the woman's head and placed it over her face. "Whaa . . . wh . . . No!" This movement had awakened the woman, and she tried to push

Henri away. After a brief struggle, he had to get up on the bed and straddle her body.

"Hel. . . help!" She managed to get the words out, but there was no one around to hear. Unable to think of anything else, Henri struck her on the chin and she ceased any movement. He hesitated briefly, then put the pillow over her face and held tightly. He didn't like to hit a woman, but he had no choice. She was still now, and quiet — for all time.

Henri was glad to have this job over with, and he would start his trip back to Warwick Castle to claim the remainder of his payment. As it was, Warwick had just paid his most recent debts, so Henri had no choice but to do this job. He didn't particularly like Warwick personally, but did like his coin.

He started back down the stairs intending to leave the same way he came in, when he heard some commotion coming from the kitchen.

"Malcolm! Leave that bread alone. The missus will blame me if there's not enough for breakfast!"

Henri halted his step on the stairs, trying to figure out what to do now. There were more people moving about in the middle of the night than he would ever have expected. Jesus! They would find that girl's body any minute now!

"Ah, Miss Ethel! She'll not miss a couple of slices!" And off the lad went smiling and taking two thick slices of the still-warm bread. The cook had come to work much earlier than usual as she had extra cooking to do for a gathering of local folk to be held at the kirk. Just a couple of days ago, she had been in her usual place, the kitchen, when her mistress walked in.

"Good morning, Ethel. We'll be needing some cakes and sweets for the gathering at the kirk on Sunday. I promised the vicar you would prepare some of your wonderful currant scones and maybe one of your special custards. Do you think you could do that?" asked Mistress Cameron.

"Of course, milady. 'Twould be me pleasure. The vicar has a sweet tooth hisself, so I'll be sure to make a couple of extras for him personally!" laughed Ethel.

Malcolm, too, had come early as it was his job to keep the fireplaces going, and he needed to bring wood in early before the household awoke.

Henri had thought he would have plenty of time to do his work and then leave, but he had apparently misjudged these early risers. Now he had to find a way to leave this place and right now! He watched as the young lad left and the cook went out another door that took her into the garden.

Moving with purpose, Henri fled through the kitchen, halting long enough to grab a loaf of the freshly baked bread sitting on the counter. This was one of the loaves the lass had just taken out of the oven when he had encountered her in the kitchen. He then continued down the cellar steps, stopping to take a bottle of wine also.

"Now that's what I call luck! Bread and wine for my trip home." At least he would have something to eat and something to keep him warm on his return trip back down to England, he reasoned. And he left, with never a moment's regret at having snuffed out three lives on this dreadful evening.

He headed directly to the stable, hoping not to run into anyone else. There were a lot of people at this one household. Warwick hadn't exactly told him what he might encounter, but this was more than he bargained for. He was now responsible for three deaths, and there was still the stable boy who could identify him.

"Well. He'll have to find me first, and that'll be difficult to do. England is quite a ways from here, and I've gotten away from many others who are still looking for me." He spoke to himself which was not unusual for him. Most of his job required that he work alone, so muttering to himself had become part of his ritual.

Practically running to the stable, he turned the corner at the last stall. Then he heard that blasted owl again! "Hoo hoo. Hoo hoo." Henri felt chills running up his back. That owl seemed to be everywhere.

"Will you stop that noise! I can feel you looking at me, bird!"

He knew it couldn't be, but he mounted up and fairly flew out of the stable slapping his horse with his whip. He needed to put a lot of territory between himself and this estate. He saw no one, but couldn't be sure that no one had seen him.

In just a few days, he was back in England and made his way to Warwick Castle. He reported to Lord Warwick he had completed his task and no one had seen him nor heard him. And, he was correct, no one had seen him, nor heard him — except the owl, that is, whose mournful cry could be heard all across the moor surrounding the estate.

Chapter 34

Caitlin readied herself for another day of riding, after a strange night filled with disturbing dreams. She couldn't quite recall it clearly, but she had heard Willie whimpering and raised up to listen. She heard nothing, but for just a moment, she caught a scent that always raised the hair on her arms — like Alex's scent. Of course, she knew he wasn't here. But Willie continued to whimper and stand until she told him to lie back down. If there had been any danger, he would have been much more alarmed. She immediately returned to the dream world and gave Willie's whimpering no mind.

Caitlin liked this horse, but was ready for a real bed, some real food, and ready to walk on her own two feet. But, for now, this big guy was a life saver for her. She still smiled when she remembered that she had stolen him. Riding was certainly a lot better than walking. But she did get off his back frequently in order to give him a break.

"Caitlin. You must care for your animals the same way you care for your family. They will return your care in more ways than you know." Uncle Wabi had taught her to do this when she was very small and learning to feed her new puppy.

More often than not, she found herself thinking about Uncle Wabi, and now the dreams were a nightly ritual. Uncle Wabi was calling her, from deep in the forest somewhere and it looked familiar to her. But, where was it? As she tried to follow a path that seemed to be going north, she hoped she would get to the Black

Isle soon. Maybe then it wouldn't be too much farther to MacKinnon land.

"If only Uncle Wabi were here! He would know what to do." Caitlin addressed Willie, who just wagged his tail and let his tongue hang out. Just at that instant, the owl flew in front of her face, flapping his wings and "standing still" it seemed to her.

"If you want to talk to him, then just call for him! It's as simple as that, you ninny!" The owl's eyes looked even larger than ever.

Caitlin, jolted back to her senses, just shook her head. That owl had spoken to her again! Just like yesterday, and it's the same voice that was in the cave. Obviously the "impossible" was no longer "impossible!"

It was late, all was dark, and Caitlin stopped for the evening. Frustrated beyond words, she lashed out at the owl.

"Just call him . . . just like that! Well, should I just yell to the top of my voice calling Uncle Wabi, Uncle Wabi?" she asked. For a woman who had always prided herself on being level headed and intelligent, she felt most foolish and, truth be known, just a little afraid.

"No, of course you don't yell! How ridiculous!" said Owl, clipping his words in a truly English fashion. Realizing the girl was most uncomfortable, Owl decided to calm down, get his feathers back together, and try to help her.

"Dear girl. Get off that horse and let's sit down here under the trees and discuss the matter at hand." He sounded so very British and so very proper that Caitlin didn't know whether to laugh or scream.

Pulling the reins back gently, something the animal was not used to, but liked, she stopped and got off. Her backside was too sore to contemplate, and sitting on the ground was a great relief.

"Now, dear girl, just relax. That is required to learn this most essential skill. I, too, wish that Wabi were here. He is much more adept at this sort of undertaking than I. But, if you will listen, I am quite sure that we may accomplish our goal of learning to communicate with other species. It's child's play, actually. Relax . . . just relax," said the owl.

Caitlin peered over at Willie as if he may have some explanation that could be helpful.

But her wolf was just lying at her feet, enjoying this whole experience, or so it seemed.

So, lying back on the soft grass, she tried to relax.

"Start with your feet and work up to the top of your head," said Owl.

So, Caitlin, well experienced at teaching patients to relax their muscles in order to help with the healing process, mentally went through the process of starting with her toes, up to her ankles, then the calves, feeling each muscle becoming more relaxed. Then she moved to the upper thighs, the abdomen, muscles along the spinal column, which she knew could create backaches, and even higher to the shoulders. She felt completely relaxed and could almost have gone on to sleep, a thought that was very enticing.

"Yes, that's right. Now, just picture Master Wabi in your mind . . . remember how his voice sounds . . . and open your mind to receiving a message from him."

"Open your mind, Caitlin. Open your mind, Caitlin." She whispered the words to herself.

Then, she did indeed see Uncle Wabi in her mind. He was in the same woods she saw in her dreams, but this time, she recognized where he was. He was walking along the edge of the water, picking his way through the ruins of an old castle that had been there since the Vikings, along his property line in Skye, the place where he did a lot of the training with his dogs. She could see the small inlet that led from the sea to a rocky area farther inland. It actually seemed that she could hear the wind whistling through the tall trees on the bank! And the water became a stream and made a tinkling sound as the water cascaded down the rocks and came to rest in the larger pool of water.

Just at that moment, her scalp began to tingle, just as it had in the cave when the commander was coming for her. She panicked! Immediately, the tingling stopped and she could no longer hear the water. What had happened?

"Oh, Owl! I could hear the water and see Uncle Wabi in my mind. But my scalp began tingling and it scared the daylights out of me! That's what happened in the cave! Does that mean the commander is near? We must leave!" And she started to jump up.

"Hold on, dear girl! The commander is not near. You know that Willie would tell you if he were. No, no, my dear. The tingling scalp is apparently the way your body tells you someone is trying to communicate with you, or you with them. It is exactly what should be happening.

Now, no fear. All is well."

"Try again, dear girl, just once more."

After a brief moment, Caitlin went through the relaxation process once again, having been assured by Owl that this tingling was to be expected. Once her muscles were all at ease, the tingling came back, but stronger this time.

She closed her eyes and almost instantly she was aware of a strong scent of leather, cinnamon and oranges. Uncle Wabi was near! She knew that scent as it always permeated his very being and was something she knew from childhood.

"Uncle Wabi? Can you hear me?" she whispered very softly, as if afraid that he might just hear her. And then what?

A momentary roar of wind filled her ears and she put her hands up to them as if to block the sound.

"Caitlin? Yes, Cait. I can hear you! Splendid my girl, splendid! I was beginning to think you were never going to answer the calling. But, for reasons known only to the Creator, you have embraced your destiny, and I am glad!"

185

"Uncle Wabi! I can hear you too! However can we be doing this? I don't understand any of this. Why did you not explain this to me when I was younger? What is the purpose of my 'calling?' What does it mean?"

"Oh, well, that would take some time, explaining, and we'll discuss all at a later time. But, for now, just know there is a line of communication available to you. But only in times of great distress. Trust your instincts and intuition, Caitlin, for they will not lead you astray. Know that I am here and always within your reach."

Very quickly, the roar returned briefly and then total silence. She could feel Uncle Wabi was no longer there. But, my, what an experience!

Owl had kept himself mute during this exchange, but then hopped closer to Caitlin, waiting for her to gather her wits. He could see this was a very moving experience for her and he knew it could leave one a bit disoriented. But, he could see she was very excited and her eyes were sparkling.

"Ah, I see you no longer fear the power, but wonder what else lays in store for you.

That's a step in the right direction," Owl offered.

"Owl. I'm glad you're here. Having you close somehow makes me feel Uncle Wabi is near, and I'm not as alone as I thought."

"Yes, Caitlin, I am here."

"Well, then, let's continue. We should pass through the Black Isle by nightfall and that's a major accomplishment as it will mean we are getting closer to MacKinnon land. Hopefully,

Commander Campbell will have sorted through his grief enough to know I'm not to blame for his son's death, but I'll feel safer when we get farther north."

Chapter 35

Jack tried to figure out what he would do if he were wearing Alex's boots. It was no secret that Alex was going to some great lengths to ensure this healer came to no harm. But, after that? What then? She certainly had a mind of her own, and he laughed when he remembered her putting Alex in his place when he suggested she should come with them. Well, now, Alex may be in charge on the farm, but Jack was not so sure the healer would feel that way about him.

It was way past time for Alex, actually all three of them, to find a woman and wed. Their Mam had taught them manners, how to treat women, and had told them to "listen to ye heart as it will no lead ye astray," and they had believed her. But, up in the Highlands, as far up as they were, there weren't a lot of occasions in which a man could meet a woman, especially one that would agree to live on a sheep farm with a whole house full of men and not another woman in sight. Mam never complained, but just caring for a house full of men was quite an undertaking. But, when he thought about it, just remembering her face, almost always smiling, he realized that to Mam it wasn't a chore. She accepted her place and took as much pride in her work as they did in raising the finest sheep in the country. Mam was special. Yes indeed.

Alex had, a long time ago, sort of taken up a little bit of time with a woman, a few years older than he. He had met her when he had gone down to Edinburgh to "study" as Mam had wanted.

"Ah, Jack. You shoulda seen her! There was certainly some physical chemistry between the two of us and I thought maybe she was the one for me. 'Course, this woman was an

Englishwoman, a real English rose who could take her pick of men. So, we began a courtship which, initially, had seemed amenable to both of us. She was keenly intelligent, brother, and I actually liked that in her. Oh, you wouldn't believe the discussions we had relating to cultures, beliefs, and philosophy. Now, as it was, we often disagreed about some issues, but that was alright, too, kept things more interesting! As you know, I hadn't had much experience with women, and finding one who had an opinion on many things was exciting. The one thing we most disagreed on, however, was the differences between us Scottish folk and the English folk. Well, after some time, these differences began to surface more often, and we didn't just discuss them now. We actually had begun arguing about most everything. The final straw was when my English rose constantly referred to Scots as 'all a bunch of heathen, unschooled barbarians.' Well, I was gentleman enough not to point out to her that she had received her education in Edinburgh from some of these very Scots that she so disliked!"

Alex was proud of his Scottish heritage, and even if most Scots were not educated as this English rose had been, he was well aware that most of them were very intelligent and able to survive and thrive when others could not. That alone was enough for all the MacKinnon men to wear their heritage with pride.

"Well, in the end, I realized she would never see me as anything other than heathen, even if I was pursuing an education. As it turned out, it was just as well we parted. But, ye ken, I found that even though I enjoyed many of the discussions by the masters, particularly the Greek classics and learning more of the geography of the world, the classroom was just too confining for my likes. I needed to be outside, feeling the wind on my face, listening to the calls of the birds and animals, and smelling the peat fires on a chilly evening."

Alex needed to be surrounded by his family. So, he ended his relationship with the English woman and shortly returned to his home where his heart was.

"And what about you?" Jack spoke aloud to himself, and maybe Goliath if he was listening.

Jack had grown up in these mountains, surrounded by a beauty he was still aware of every time he looked around himself. There was never any doubt in his mind this was where he belonged. He had never wanted to go to Edinburgh for any reason, well, maybe just to see the sights, but never to stay very long. He worshipped his older brothers and had never resented them. There had never been time for much bickering about family position. Everybody knew they were loved and needed, and that was enough for Jack.

As for women, he had danced with a few girls at a local ceilidh now and then, but never had found one he thought fit in with his idea of living, which was staying on the sheep farm and being around family. Plus, the biggest obstacle in his pursuit of any woman was his size. They all seemed to think he was some sort of giant and were usually afraid of him.

"So, you might as well accept you will be a loner, my boy." Jack said to himself. "So leave the next generation to Alex and Hector."

So, what would he do if he got to the village and the cave and Alex was nowhere to be found? Well, then he would ask around to see if anyone had seen Alex, or the healer, or maybe the soldier. He was a bit reluctant to ask too much about the soldier as he might just be as wretched as he sounded. Jack would like nothing more than to clobber any man who would talk of hurting a woman, even if she was a witch! Actually, Jack had decided the healer was just that, a healer, someone who had taken great care of Ian, and now it was his time to be of help to her. But, first, he had to find her.

How had she been able to care for herself anyway? She must be some strong woman, thought Jack. She didn't seem to be afraid when they met her on the path, and as he recalled, feeling rather sheepish, she hadn't cowed at his presence either. So, anyone willing to go after this woman should think twice before doing something stupid. He hoped Alex had thought about that.

Chapter 36

Now, stopping to rest for a few minutes and have some of his tasty treats he had packed, Wabi spoke aloud.

"Alright wizard. You've avoided thinking about this situation long enough! Get down to business and concentrate on what may be causing your awareness to be heightened lately. It might be more than Caitlin."

Wabi's audience was likely the trees he sat under. His first experiences with learning about his powers had happened under a banyan tree in a country far, far away from Scotland. He was just a young lad, resting against this tree with its many roots that ran out many feet from its trunk. The roots were gnarled but smooth, and Wabi liked to rub his hands over the twisted tentacles. One day, he had felt a stirring in his blood when he took a nap under this tree. He awakened and felt vibrations coming from within the tree, so he placed his ear close to the trunk and found he could hear whispering, and felt a presence, a spirit. Soft and continuous. It was his first attempt at connecting with the plant world, and he still communed with them to this day. So, as was the case, he was actually never alone.

Verbalizing his thoughts aloud had always helped Wabi get focused. So, he sat down, leaned against a large hickory tree and closed his eyes. Eliminating any visual distractions was a necessary step in his structured process. Within just a few seconds, a large swarm of Monarch butterflies began to circle about his head. They swarmed as if he were one of their favorite places to find nectar. "Ah, my multi-winged friends! Thank you for joining me. Now, with your help I may be able to get where I need to go."

The butterflies started a slow dance, round and round Wabi's head. Then they began to go faster and faster, and Wabi's spirit flew to a distant place where he could sense the essence of one that he recognized immediately, but had not visited for many years — Caitlin's mother! Flinn!

"Flinn! What an unexpected surprise! It's been so long since I've taken this level of journey but, my, what a pleasure it is to find you!"

"My dearest Wabi! I felt someone pulling at me, but for a moment I couldn't figure out who it was, so I tried to ignore it. But, finally, the pull was so strong that I had no choice but to come. Whatever do you need from me? You have every power, perhaps more, that I have. Is there something we need to do together?"

"Ah, well. Perhaps that's why I'm here. I wasn't sure whom I was seeking, but I'm glad that it's you. And yes, maybe we need to put our spirits and minds together and see what we can do. As it is, I keep getting certain vibrations that seem to tell me Caitlin needs my help."

"I've tried over the years to tutor her and make her aware of her special abilities. Until just recently, however, she has never responded to any of my suggestions. And, now that she is beginning to get just a glimpse into this world, she keeps shying away. My friend, Owl, tells me Caitlin could be headed for some trouble. I never thought the child would need much protection, but it looks like she's made a true enemy who is intent on causing her harm, maybe even death. I'm most concerned about her, but according to Owl, she travels with a wolf who serves as a companion and a protector, so that's some comfort."

"Yes. My darling Caitlin. Oh, she travels with a wolf, you say. Well, of course she does! Her grandmother, Ci-Cero, did also. Some things just never change, I guess. But, when I came along, I wanted nothing to do with the "other world" either, and never did join. It is only now that I see I might have done better to embrace it, but I had so wanted to make my own way and be my own person! But, the choice is always ours, and I made mine. But, it seems that my Caitlin may be making a different choice, thanks to your mentoring, Wabi."

"Ah, Wabi. I was not there for her childhood as you were, but she is my daughter and it is only right that I intervene if necessary. Along with you, of course."

"Well, perhaps if you were to stay close by, within her mental reach, she might sense that she has some feminine wisdom at her disposal. She's just learning to communicate and it may take her some time before she can do it readily." Wabi said.

"Oh, that's easy enough. My spirit has always resided within her, she's just never realized it. So, I'll make it a bit more apparent to her, that way she'll feel she's not alone. Most times all we need is someone who understands our problems, not someone to fix them. She's quite capable. I have been able to sense that over the years. Maybe a bit head strong, however!" Then she laughed as if she knew where that particular trait may have come from.

"Yes, my dear Flinn. You could certainly say that! Then I'll continue my walkabout and pay close attention to any vibrations from Caitlin, as will you. My notion is just to head north as Owl tells me Caitlin is traveling that way, but exactly where I am not sure. But I know to follow wherever I am led. My intuition has proven to be a most trustworthy asset."

"I see. Then, no doubt I'll keep up with you along the way. Surely two spirits are better than one. Maybe I'll get to know her now that she's trying to come to this world as well. What a treasure that would be for me."

Wabi felt Flinn's spirit drift away and found himself back under the hickory tree. The butterflies were slowly making their way back to seeking nectar from the flowers along the trail.

Wabi was comforted knowing that Caitlin's mother would hover close. But he also knew that once Caitlin started exercising her powers of communication, sometimes dark spirits could be residing in the spaces between where her present world and the other one joined. There was certainly danger that she could be prey to any number of less-than-desirable entities that would take advantage of a young, frightened one making headway into their world. Some of them were just waiting for the opportunity to attach themselves to an unsuspecting, naïve one and take up residence. Caitlin had a good head on her shoulders, but she was young and inexperienced.

"Why didn't I make her do this sooner?" Wabi was exasperated with himself.

Worry over Caitlin's vulnerability had him in a tizzy. But, he knew that no amount of badgering would have made her more receptive. It was only when one was ready that the leap was made, and even then some of the chosen, like Flinn, never made the leap. But, the fact remained that Caitlin may be in danger, so he must move on now and be there if needed.

Another thought bothered Wabi. What if Flinn does get "closer" and Caitlin senses her but can't understand it and is even more frightened? Caitlin never knew her mother, but Wabi also knew that a bond from mother to child was begun long before birth. Perhaps Caitlin's spirit would recognize her mother even if her brain did not. Wabi was in a quandary, and an element of fear had a hold on him. A most unusual experience for this wizard.

Chapter 37

After traveling some distance, much later, far into the night, Caitlin decided to dismount and walk alongside her horse with Willie next to her, brushing her leg as they walked. Stretching her legs seemed a good thing and she had donned her long cape. She pulled up the hood as well, trying to ward off some of the chill of the night air. Each day seemed to be getting colder now, and she would really like to complete this journey without having to deal with snow. They didn't receive a lot of it in Skye, but up here she knew that was probably a different story.

The night was unusually quiet. She listened with her new auditory awareness. She could hear the wind, a raven calling somewhere far off, and something else, like an animal grunting, or perhaps a wild hog rooting around the woods. She really would rather not have to face that, again, but wasn't too concerned as Willie would take care of that event should it arise. The moon was giving off brilliant light, and she could see well all about, so she continued walking and she smiled to herself.

"That is a waxing gibbous moon!" Uncle Wabi would have explained details about it if he were here, she thought to herself.

She spoke to whomever might have been listening, probably Willie and Owl, but they made no comment in return. Why had she never understood about Uncle Wabi's special talents? They had been right in front of her nose, but, as children will, she accepted them and never even thought to question him about them.

Walking on, she heard the grunting sound again, so she stopped, as did Willie. He made no sound, no growl, and nothing to indicate that she was in danger. She tied her horse and listened, trying to locate the exact spot where the sound was coming from. The sound was getting slightly louder, and she found herself moving off to the right, going down a slight incline toward some brush farther down the hill.

Using a hand signal, she called for Willie to accompany her as she followed the sounds to the bottom, where she believed they were coming from. As she got just a few feet from the brush, she could hear the grunting again, and some moaning as well. Stooping down in order to get a better look, as the bushes were blocking her view, she carefully looked behind the larger brush.

Lying just under the brush was a body — a large body.

"Oh, dear Lord! Another soldier needing care!" Caitlin was speaking to Willie, and Owl, who had alighted in the yew tree above them. He "hoo hooed" his agreement, but stayed put.

Willie began to sniff the ground, but there was still no growling coming from him. Caitlin ran back to get her medicine bag, and then returned and made her way down the incline once again.

"He must have fallen from his horse and rolled down here," she thought to herself. He was a large man, wrapped in a dark blanket and lying on his side. As she got closer, she began to speak softly to him.

"Hey, now. Rest easy. I'm a healer. I'll help you. Just be easy."

Still, no words from the man, but another groan escaped his lips and then an anguished cry, meaning he was in great pain. Caitlin reached for his shoulder and slowly turned him over in order to see how extensive his wounds were.

As she pulled the man's shoulder back, lying him on his back, two large eyes stared up at her. Then he let out another agonizing cry that had Caitlin holding her breath!

She just stared at him for another moment. Even in this unlit brush, she could tell she had made a mistake. This was no man.

This very large body belonged to a woman. And this woman had a very large stomach. Caitlin gasped when she realized what she was seeing. This woman was about to have a babe any moment now!

"Oh, Holy Rusepheus!" she wailed. This woman was in the throes of birthing a baby and Caitlin knew it was going to be any second now! When you've delivered a large number of babies, you can tell by the cry of the mother what stage of delivery she's in. Caitlin's reactions were quick. She began giving instructions to the woman, just as if they'd planned this event. It never occurred to her to not assist the woman and the child.

Taking the woman's face between her hands, Caitlin got her to focus on her every word. "Hold on now. I'm a healer and have done this many times. The pain is great, I know, but it won't last forever. So, just now, try to slow your breathing down if you can. There, slower, slower. Yes. Slower still. That's good. Very good. This baby is ready to come any second now, so, when I tell you to push, you must give it all you can in order to help him be born!"

The woman still had not spoken, but nodded her head as if to say she understood. Then she screamed once more, and her breathing was erratic again.

Caitlin had placed the woman's legs as far apart as possible, and one quick glance, even in this moonlight, showed the baby's head was crowning. Birth was imminent and Caitlin was glad. A long delivery is most difficult for the mother and the child.

"Now! Push now! Hard!"

The woman strained with all her might and screamed as she did so. The pain was unbearable and it never seemed to end! To her, this baby was taking forever to be born.

"Good — good — now take a deep breath — slowly now — now push again — hard!"

The woman raised up on her elbows and grabbed her knees, letting out one blood curdling scream. "Aieeeeeeeeeeeeeeeeeeeee!"

And, as the woman took another breath, Caitlin put her hands under her hips and helped ease the baby's head out.

"That's perfect! Easy now. Relax for just a moment. Easy now. Now just one more push!"

"I can't push anymore! The pain! Make it go away! Help me!"

But, then, another contraction swept through her body and she raised up once again and screamed loudly, groaning with the effort.

Caitlin watched as the baby's shoulders escaped their confines and she knew the rest of the work would be easy. Promptly, the baby was totally out of his wet, warm, safe haven, and had entered into a cold, strange, unfamiliar environment with two women, a wolf, and an owl.

Following the most wonderful sound, a piercing cry from this new little one, Caitlin cleaned the babe up enough to be sure it was breathing properly and then placed it up on its mother's abdomen. She proceeded to tie the umbilical cord, then snipped it properly and was relieved there had been no complications with the birth.

She gently placed the baby up higher, on its mother's breast now, and the mother put her arms around the small infant. As soon as she felt the soft skin and plump rounded bottom, the mother began to cry softly, stroking the child's backside. But, the baby didn't stay still very long, and began to let out some wails of its own.

Folding her cloak and placing it beneath the woman's head, Caitlin propped her up in order that she could do what all new mothers do. She took the child to her breast and started a most important process, that of bonding between mother and child. The little one had no trouble rooting around and finding a nipple that would work just fine. She sounded just like a little piglet.

"Well, I do say you have a most beautiful daughter, Madam," said Caitlin, sitting down next to the two. She was a bit exhausted herself. Having a baby had been work for all three of them.

The woman looked at Caitlin, and the most wonderful smile broke out on her face. "Oh, aye, I do believe she is the most beautiful baby ever!" Caitlin noted that even though the woman had replied in Gaelic, and certainly with a Scottish "aye," it was said with an English accent.

Caitlin smiled in return and began to gather her medical items together. She needed to think for a few minutes about her next move. This development was certainly unexpected, but then everything in her life seemed to have turned upside down in the last few weeks. So, she supposed coming upon a woman about to give birth was just as reasonable as any of the other happenings had been. But, what a strange new life she seemed to be living.

Chapter 38

Wabi's senses were sizzling even more than usual. He never paid a whole lot of attention until one or the other of them screamed loudly enough for him to truly take notice. In his life, he had become accustomed to filtering out stimuli that he always picked up from others.

It had only been yesterday that Wabi had been busy with the never ending chores about his home, training with Max and feeding several other animals that he kept around the barn, when he felt a tingling about his scalp again. Caitlin? He turned his attention to this and opened his center, waiting for her to come through. But the tingling stopped. And did not return. Now today, he was again getting an exceptionally irritating sizzle from several areas.

"Well, then. Alright!" Wabi spoke to Max who walked along beside him. The dog looked up as if waiting for some further explanation, which never came.

So, that meant Wabi had to put up a defensive wall on his feelings and dwell on what was trying to get his attention. He had learned long ago the best way to do that was to go "walkabout."

Over the years, he had found that going "walkabout" was one sure way to clear his mind when it seemed too full. It was a good thing, getting back to nature in its truest form. He truly loved being among all the forest creatures that he had such a special connection with. These creatures could be all about him, and always were, but they accepted him as one of them and that allowed him to become part of the scenery without disturbing anything in his surroundings.

When Caitlin was small, Wabi would often take her with him on some of his jaunts, usually to some new place they had never been. But, on occasion, he went alone. The quiet private time renewed his energies, and he always returned with some new project to work on. Mother Nature seemed to have a way of recharging lives if one would but spend time with her. That was one belief Wabi had instilled in Caitlin, and she had taken it to heart. Even when she was practicing her healing, it was often done outside where she thought nature provided a perfect setting.

So, after spending a little time packing his backpack with necessary items for his walkabout, Wabi set off on the trail. He had a very old, crooked staff that he always carried with him, so he picked it up as he left his cottage. He didn't usually go on these journeys when winter was about to be upon him, but with these latest scalp irritations and something niggling at his brain, he knew this was the time. So, never one to question his intuition, he listened to it and usually was glad to have done so.

Wabi and Owl kept in constant contact, sometimes through cerebral communication, by far the easiest way, but not one that Owl liked very much. Owl always preferred taking to the skies and enjoyed moving at lightning speed when he needed to. So, recently, he had made a quick flight to discuss Caitlin's situation with Wabi.

When the "hoo-hoo" call came, Wabi smiled and Owl came flying over his head, circling and diving like a young owl might.

"Ah, hello dear friend," said Wabi as the large creature alighted on his shoulder. "And where might you be off to, Master?" asked Owl.

"Well, after much thought, I believe it's time for a walkabout. My old legs could use some stretching, and breathing some fresh air will be good for me. Don't you agree?"

"And just where do you think this walkabout will take you?"

"I've not decided just yet, Owl. I keep getting sensations and vibrations that I feel are coming from Caitlin, but I can't be sure. Somehow it worries me enough that I feel a need to catch up with her. She may need my help, but I had hoped she would call me directly."

"Well, Master. Your senses are working well. Caitlin has been rather a busy girl the past few days and I have tried to stay close by. You have probably felt her vibrations as she has been struggling with a number of situations that are new to her. She's handled them well, but a great amount of anxiety fills the very air she breathes."

"At the moment she has a new companion, an English woman, I do believe. This woman speaks Gaelic, but there is definitely an English accent, and a most proper one I might add! "Tis music to my ears, Master. And, not only that, but this woman has just given birth to a child that Caitlin delivered in the dead of night." Owl delivered this news as he always did, trying to just present the facts and not imposing his feelings on the matter.

"Well then, she's been busy. I've taken care of Thomas, the innkeeper. He'll no longer be after her, but what about the soldier? Is he still pursuing Caitlin?"

"Oh, yes, Master, I fear he is still coming for her. I haven't spotted him anywhere, but this man is obsessed with finding our Caitlin, so he's still out there somewhere."

"Owl, I must make myself more available to Caitlin, I think. I'll avoid time and place- weaving if I possibly can. It may be the fastest way for me to get from one place to another, but this mode of travel takes a toll on me at this age and I won't resort to that unless it's absolutely necessary. And, I'm trying to give her room to call on her newly-found powers. They are there. She just must learn how to access them."

"When she was young, Caitlin was forever getting herself into many difficult predicaments. The child had been stung by bees so many times one would have thought she would stop robbing the hive! But, that never seemed to occur to her. Rather, that just provided her with a reason to "tend" to her own wounds." Wabi laughed aloud, remembering how the child had kept him on his toes. He could remember a few of his other students well, but Caitlin was more determined than most, which could be an asset eventually.

Owl departed with a most eloquent maneuver, wheeling high into the air, just to show that he could still perform. Wabi waved his hand and laughed at the great bird's gesture. Owl was such a fine specimen of his species, that thick tuft of feathers between his huge luminous eyes. One had to wonder at such fine workmanship from the Creator.

As he walked deeper into the forest, Wabi found himself grinning at his latest accomplishment. Of course he had known it was Thomas, the innkeeper, prowling around his house looking for Caitlin. He had hoped Thomas would keep out of his way after the dogs had taken a chunk out of his leg and Owl had given him a tumble. He realized the man was not exceptionally bright, but that didn't give him license to go after Caitlin.

Shortly after Thomas had prowled around his place, Wabi had occasion to be in the village picking up some of his mulberry wine at the Wild Boar and Thomas was there, as expected. Wabi never let on he had known Thomas had been out to the cottage, and casually asked for his usual bottle of wine. Thomas went to the store room and brought it out. Handing it to Wabi, he had the audacity to ask Wabi a question.

"So, where's your niece, the healer? I haven't seen her around for a while. I could use some of her medicine as my gout is killing me."

"Oh, Thomas, I'm sorry to hear that. I understand gout can be most painful, or so Caitlin tells me. She's gone visiting some family, but I'll tell her to call on you as soon as she returns."

"Yeah, you do that. Tell her I have a gift for her. Something to thank her for helping me way back with my leg infection."

"Certainly. She always likes gifts."

Wabi stopped, but then turned back to Thomas with a question.

"Oh, by the way Thomas, I haven't seen that English lord about for a while. Does he still stop by?" asked Wabi as if just curious.

"Uh, uh, no. He's gone back to England — for good. His wife's expecting a baby any day now, and his business is finished here," replied Thomas under his breath.

That little exchange was just enough to get Wabi's anger fired up. Did that ignoramus really think he would let him harm Caitlin? Idiot man! As he was paying Thomas for the wine, Wabi lightly touched Thomas' fingers and sent a stream of fire that raced from the man's fingertips to his brain. In an instant, the man was bowing and smiling and offering to help Wabi.

"Here, sir. Let me carry the bottle of wine for you. I can take it out to your cottage for you if you like. It would be my pleasure!"Wabi thanked him and left laughing as he did so. He had been so angry at Thomas for trying to harm Caitlin he spent some time dreaming up a very special treatment for him. In the end, he had decided the very best treatment would be to turn Thomas into a kind, gentle giant, something he would have never been in this lifetime. But, for those around him, this would indeed be a welcome change. Wabi's little streak of fire would take care of any thoughts of ever harming Caitlin. This was an easy task for Wabi and one he especially enjoyed. Plus, he really did prefer to make changes for the better, rather than turning Thomas into the toad he had almost done.

Chapter 39

Wabi had traveled some time when the first snowflakes began to fall. The crisp, wet sprinkling was most refreshing, and when you looked closely at just one snowflake, it was a wonder to behold. Just another example of Mother Nature's perfection thought Wabi.

Wabi was familiar with the geography of Scotland, having lived here in several lives. He had never traveled through the Black Isle, but he recognized this was where his walkabout was taking him. The Black Isle was not really an island, but a peninsula surrounded on three sides by water; the Cromarty Firth was to the north, the Beauly Firth to the south, and the Moray Firth to the east. On its western side, its boundary was marked by rivers.

If Wabi's memory served correctly, the Black Isle was originally called Ardmeanach, and there were several castles in the area. Redcastle, Castlecraig, and Cromarty Castle came to mind as he rummaged around in the many recesses of his mind. Some of these were still in use, but some had been deserted many years ago and were beginning to fall into ruin.

But why was he being brought to the Black Isle? It seemed a most unlikely place to go walkabout but, again, he would trust his intuition.

As the snow continued to fall, gently at the moment, Wabi was enjoying his outdoor adventure. But, he felt he might better look for a warmer place to spend the evening as the temperature was beginning to drop rapidly. He listened to see if there was anything in the wind to direct him, it usually did if he would just pay attention. He had been walking a path that led him through the woods, but as he came out from the forest, looking across a heath-covered knoll, some distance ahead he could just barely make out the outline of a building, a castle perhaps. But, whatever it was, it would take him some time to reach it.

Wabi was hopeful this dwelling or castle would be one that was a home to people and someone there would give him shelter for the evening, and tomorrow he would continue on his journey. His concern for Caitlin was mounting as was the snow.

Chapter 40

Alex was still trying to find Caitlin, still heading back north. He hoped he could find shelter from the snowstorm, but, so far, he hadn't seen anything that would provide any cover. After tying his horse and nestling up under a group of small trees, he wrapped himself in his plaid and took cover as best he could under some low limbs, close to the ground. He was still cold, however, so he built a small fire. Lying back on the ground, he watched the flames reach upward while the smoke was being tugged in every direction as the wind couldn't seem to make up its mind about which direction it wanted to blow. It was whistling through the taller pines, and the faint sound of rushing water was somewhere in the background. Then there was the "hoo hoo" of an owl, also close by. These were all sounds Alex associated with these woods, his woods, and they were soothing to him.

As he was trying to settle himself for the night, he heard a sound, a bit far off, but he heard it nevertheless. Shortly it became clear to his ears. A coach was coming. He could hear the driver cracking his whip and calling out to the horses.

"On with you . . . you laz . . .Lazy . . . scags!" And Alex heard the whip crack once again.'

Then he heard the horses snorting as the man called out again, "Ho now! Ho he . . . here . . You whoa …now..whoa..now." And the wheels slowed down and came to a halt just a few yards from where Alex was sitting by his fire. He heard the drive talking again to someone . . . or maybe to the horses.

"Hol…hold here…stop…"

Alex walked out to the clearing where the coach had stopped and watched as a very large man climbed down. He was dressed with a great black cape covering his shoulders and a fur hat of some kind, both expensive items of clothing. What was someone who could dress like that doing out here in the cold, in the middle of the night? And what was he doing driving the coach? Where was his coachman?

As a matter of personal safety, Alex drew his pistol and had it held up close to his body.

"Hold on!" the man yelled. "I've got money! Here!" The man quickly began to reach into his coat.

Stepping out into the firelight now, Alex held his gun steady and pointed it directly at the stranger.

"I don't want yer money. What are ye doing here? Where's your coachman? he asked. Alex knew this was not the soldier he was searching for, but couldn't help wonder what this "gentleman" was doing out here during the storm.

"I'm headed no...no...north, goin to wife's family home ...Black Isle. She ....there and...a babe.....about to have babe any.....any day...tryin' to get there....in time....birth of son.......but storm....storm slowed me.....trying to find shelter."

"I said. Who are ye?" said Alex, still brandishing his pistol near the man's face. He was generally a good judge of character, and this man had alook about him that set Alex's hackles on end.

The man looked straight across to Alex, both men being about the same height. "I'm Lord...Lord E..ward Warwick.....Warwick Castle....in Englan...England." He said this as if Alex should be impressed, perhaps even bow. But Alex had spent enough time in the presence of lords and ladies to know a true gentleman when he met one, and this man might have resources, but he was no gentleman.

"Where's your coachman?"

Coach...coachman deserted...deserted me ....last....stopped in village....he ...never came back....blast him! Never any....no good....anyway. Good rid....riddance...to him."

Still, Alex had no reason to question him further and put his pistol back in his belt. Mayhap the man was doing just what he said, going to visit his wife's family in the Black Isle.

Seeing the pistol was put away, the man then began to question Alex.

"And.....an...why you.....out in weather...may.....may ask?"

"I'm heading home, back to the upper Highlands. Didn't count on having to deal with an early snowstorm, however, so I'm camping under the trees until the morning."

"Then, perhaps....I can...warm...warm...by fire...you fire....few minutes?" asked the man, still staring at Alex.

"Aye, I reckon that could be all right," returned Alex. Far be it from him to begrudge someone seeking a little warmth before moving on in this weather.

So, the "gentleman" walked over closer to the fire. Alex watched him as he took off his gloves and held his hands out to the flames. After a few moments he reached inside his coat and brought out a flask, took a large swig, and held it out to Alex.

"Would...you care...a...a small...taste? It does help....keep the....insides...a bit....bit warmer," he offered.

Alex declined the offer. First of all, he knew that alcohol and cold weather don't mix very well. The alcohol might send fire to the stomach, but it actually takes heat away from the core of the body. This was something anyone who spent a lifetime up in the Highlands learned early on. And, this "gentleman" had already consumed more than his share. Alex could see that well enough.

"Suit . . . self, but it help . . . helps on a night.... like this." And that statement was followed by yet another gulp of the brew. This last gulp was, apparently, the one that crossed that very fine line between enough and too much.

"So, ye are about to become a father then, it would seem," said Alex, tossing another small limb on the fire.

With the last bit of alcohol beginning to take its toll, the man's words were really beginning to slur.

"Hhrrmp . . . yes, sus . . . suppose I am. Every man needs at least one son . . . or actually, ONLY one son . . . a second one is . . . not much needed . . . as I see it."

"So, hopefully, ye'll be there for the happy occasion. And a new babe can bring much happiness to a family. It did to ours."

"I'm not concerned with . . . with . . . happiness . . . just wanna son . . . to carry on name. . . bring more wealth . . . me when . . . comes." The man was obviously inebriated, and his speech was getting more difficult to understand. He was obviously not thinking straight, Alex realized. However, he kept his thoughts to himself.

"What's your wife's family name in the Black Isle?" asked Alex. After getting no response, he continued.

"My mam originally came from there, and I believe there may be some cousins or kin of some sort still about the area. But, we stay in the higher regions pretty much, and don't get down there very often."

"Cam . . . cam . . . eroom . . . Cameroom." Really slurring his words now, the man began to walk toward the coach.

"Are you sure ye won't stay awhile, ye may not be in the best condition to drive a coach, especially in this storm," offered Alex. He didn't much care for the man, but certainly didn't think he needed to be moving on.

"I thank you to keep pinio . . . your opinions to yourself . . . my condition no . . . is . . . none . . . concern of yours." He climbed up on the coach and picked up the reins.

"Then I'll bi . . . bid . . . you g'night . . . be . . . be moving on . . . it's no far to the Bla . . . Black Isle now . . . will be shelter . . . me there."

Alex nodded to the man, then watched him as he struggled to climb up the coach. As soon as he was seated, he lashed out with the whip and had the horses pulling the heavy coach forward. Alex thought for a moment. Something about this whole encounter felt uncomfortable to him.

First, the man was obviously under the influence of some kind of alcoholic beverage, and smelled like a brewery. Second, why would a "gentleman" be traveling in this weather? And, third, a true "gentleman" would have offered Alex to come with him and get shelter at the family's home in the Black Isle. There was more to this story than the man was telling. But, Alex was not one to put his nose into anyone else's business, unless she happened to be a small, fiery-haired healer. He finally closed his eyes and wrapped himself tightly in his plaid, his one piece of travel gear he was never without. It offered protection when nothing else would.

Sometime, in the wee hours of the morning, Alex had a moment when he raised up on his elbows to listen. What had awakened him? It reminded him of what Mam always called "someone walking on your grave." He was sure he felt the presence of someone, and maybe he heard the whimper of an animal. But, he fell back to sleep immediately and didn't even remember it the next morning.

Alex was concerned he had yet to find Caitlin. He'd talked with an old healer in one of the villages, and she told him of treating a soldier with an injured neck. She felt it had been caused by an animal, not a wound from fighting, and she was very upset as she told him the man had stolen her old horse and was seeking some woman who had killed his son. She also said the man was not in his right mind and she feared for anyone who had any dealings with him. Alex was even more afraid for Caitlin. If only he could find her! That woman could certainly be most exasperating! He had decided she was coming back to the upper highlands with him whether she wished to or not! Well. At least he hoped so.

Morning finally came, and Alex was glad to have this night over with. He had kept the fire going for a long while, but it died down, and by morning there were just a few embers with wisps of smoke lifting into the cold, crisp morning. He was intent on making the Black Isle today, assuming the path was clear. There were only three major paths that led to the north country, and sometimes one of them was almost impassable in bad weather. He had used this one many times and was familiar with every village along the way.

He had lain awake for quite some time after Lord Warwick made his departure. Alex kept thinking of what the man had said. "Camer….oom, Camer, er, Cameroom," when Alex had asked him his wife's family name. Alex realized the drunken man most probably was saying "Cameron." That was a name he was most familiar with. Just a few years ago he and Jack had come down to the Isle to pick up a flock of sheep from Laird Cameron's estate. The old Laird had passed away, and the mistress was needing to sell off the stock as she had decided they could no longer operate as a sheep farm. So, Alex and Jack came down, purchased the sheep and herded them back to the farm. Since that time, he had stayed in the stables at the Cameron estate several times when passing through. Mistress Cameron offered most anyone use of her stables for their horses and, of course, the men could take shelter there also. In fact, Alex was thinking he might stay there tonight if he could make it before nightfall. Even a bed of straw in a stable was better than freezing in this weather.

It had crossed Alex's mind that, being as these three paths were the only ones the soldier could have traveled, he surely would have come across Commander Campbell by now. The old healer had expressed concern that the man was a danger to anyone in his way, and she remarked the soldier repeated several times he would find "that red haired witch." That phrase kept running through Alex's mind.

So, he was off again, stopping in every village asking if anyone had seen the healer or the soldier. At least the storm had abated, and Alex always liked traveling through the first snow of the year. But, he well knew this breathtaking beauty would become slush and make traveling more difficult as the day wore on. So, with new determination he moved along quickly.

Chapter 41

Caitlin had never been so exhausted in her life. No matter how many babies she had helped into the world, it was always an awe-inspiring experience. But, this particular birth was even more special. As she was trying to reassure the poor woman in the throes of childbirth, she felt as if she were being directed by a presence, certainly an unseen one, but there nevertheless. This presence was warm, caring, and brought a scent that had been buried in Caitlin's brain long, long ago. And it had brought some kind of golden light that helped Caitlin as she struggled to deliver this baby. She had thought the moon was producing it, but as she sat here now, she recalled how it had only covered the place where she and the woman were. It had been very dark when she had discovered the body and started to help this woman. Where had the light come from? And that scent? So soft. So embracing.

"I know that scent. But how? Why can't I remember?" Caitlin had spoken aloud and the new mother had heard her.

"What scent? I don't smell anything." The woman's voice was very soft and Caitlin looked in her direction. The two of them, mother and child, were sharing a moment that only they could. Caitlin had never had this experience.

"What? Oh, it's nothing. I just have a very keen sense of smell. I'm always smelling something that isn't really there!" She brushed the question off, but that scent was still running around in her brain — searching — and in her heart as well.

"I don't know how to thank you. I don't know what I would have done if you hadn't come along. I will forever be in your debt. " The new mother was in tears.

"I'm Caitlin. And I'm a healer. Aye. I'm glad I came along too. Of course, nature would have taken its course and you would have managed on your own, but it really does help to have someone around in these situations! I think you will both be fine, but we must get going now and try to find some shelter for ourselves. There'll be snow before morning I do believe."

"And I'm Millie, Millie Sinclair." The woman offered Caitlin her hand, as was the custom for proper ladies when introduced to someone new to their acquaintance.

"Where are you going? Is it close by?" asked the woman.

"Well, actually, no. I'm traveling to the home of a family, the MacKinnons, who live in the upper Highlands. I've no idea how far it is, but I must be moving on. It's rather difficult to explain, but I must go quickly.

"Then, let's try to get to my family's place in the Black Isle. I don't think it's too much farther, and they'll be delighted to shelter us."

"Seeing as I have no better idea, we'll do just that," responded Caitlin, ever so glad to have a place to wait out the storm.

The healer helped Millie get on her horse and handed the baby up to her. The strength of will that this required was unspeakable. Caitlin marveled at the woman's stoic response to sitting on a horse having just given birth.

"Are you sure you can do this?" asked the healer. She didn't know which was worse, trying to weather the storm out here in the open, or watching this woman climb on that horse. Either choice was not one she liked.

"Yes. I'll make it. Let's just go, please."

Caitlin made sure Millie was settled, then got on her horse and started out, holding the reins of both horses. The band of misfits moved on slowly always in a northerly direction.

Millie had not complained once, but Caitlin knew the woman must be in great pain.

Having a baby is a natural event, certainly, but leaves one with considerable discomfort and pain, even after the blessed event is over. But, they had no choice; they must get to shelter somehow.

"How am I ever going to find the MacKinnon lands now, traveling with a very tired, new mother, and a baby a few hours old?" Caitlin had spoken aloud, and even she could hear the desperation in her voice.

Millie explained to Caitlin she was trying to get to the home of her family, actually a grandmother and elderly aunt, in the Black Isle. Millie had not heard from them for several years now. This was her mother's side of the family. Millie remembered them well and knew they would welcome her. Millie did not tell Caitlin that these relatives had no idea she was coming to visit.

According to Millie, they had just a short way to go to reach her family's holdings. "But, how will we know when we have reached their lands?" Caitlin asked.

"Well, actually, it'll be easy to find," Millie hesitated before continuing. "It's rather a large place, Cameron Castle, you see. And my grandmother and aunt will be most pleased to have us as guests."

"Ah. Well. Yes. A castle. Then let's get moving and get out of this weather." Caitlin was worried about the woman and baby, both subject to catching pneumonia, and hoped this place wasn't far. But a castle?

Caitlin and Millie gingerly asked questions of each other, and both cautiously answered them. They both had secrets the other one didn't necessarily need to know, or so they both thought.

But, as both were females in distress, there was an unspoken bond being formed. Caitlin was aware that it really was simply the fact they probably sensed a kindred spirit in the other and each was alone without any other.

Without going into great detail, Millie told Caitlin enough of her story to make her understand the difficulty the new mother was facing.

"Oh, aye. He's a beast and more. He never wanted me for the person I am. He wanted me because I came with a sizeable inheritance. He and my father are so alike that it's almost laughable. It's like they must have been brothers or something. And, when I told him a child was to be born, he was more excited than ever as he will now inherit even more from his family. You know, that first son business they all so dwell on. But, I've made up my mind that no man will ever control me again and seeing as how our child is a daughter, my husband will never even care to see her. So, 'tis a sad tale, but I'll figure out how to make this situation work for me and my daughter." The only small detail that she consciously left out was her full name, Lady Millicent Sinclair Warwick. She just told Caitlin to call her Millie and let it go at that.

"My, oh my. And I thought I had problems! Well, I mean, a crazed soldier chasing you is not too much fun either. But so far, I've only had the best of treatment from the men in my life. First my grandfather, and then Uncle Wabi. I never knew my father, but it appears that he was quite a fine man. And apparently inherited his temper!"

"So, he was a well-mannered gentleman with a bit of a temper, perhaps red hair and sparkling eyes?" Millie tried to lighten the conversation just a bit.

"I believe the hair is from my mother." Caitlin smiled at the woman and they kept going. Each felt a new friendship could come from this unexpected situation.

Caitlin had learned long ago to let Willie lead the way and to trust his instincts. Suddenly, he stopped. His hackles were raised, and a deep growl rumbled louder by the second. Caitlin felt the hair on her arms rise, and she was aware of an odor she had smelled before, but could not place it. Willie walked to the edge of the woods, next to the path where they were walking and began an even deeper growl.

Caitlin climbed down from her mount, then tied the reins to a young yew tree. She put a finger to her lips, indicating that Millie was to be very quiet.

"Shh! Let me see what's spooking Willie." "Willie. Stay here with these ladies."

Willie growled deeply, not wanting to obey this command. He was still in attack mode, hackles still standing on end, ears straight, and baring his tremendously large teeth.

"Stay Willie."

Caitlin had a pistol, actually another item she had relieved Campbell of, but hoped not to have to use it. Shooting wasn't something she was very good at. She reached into her saddle bag and pulled it out. Just as she reached her arm out, pointing it at the brush ahead, she received a whack on her wrist and the gun went flying from her hand.

"Ah. No!" she yelled as she was flattened to the ground.

She looked up into the face of one she had hoped to never see again — Commander Campbell! Now she remembered the smell — henbane — and he still reeked of it! He had straddled her body and had a very firm grip on her left hand, and her right one was trapped behind her back.

"So. We meet at last, witch! And, I see you are without your wolf. I had hoped to find him too and take care of both of you. He'll also pay for his part in your little game!" His left hand held his gun and his right one went to her throat. He squeezed, but only slightly so far.

"Campbell! What do you want from me?"

"Why, nothing, little witch. I just want to make your punishment last as long as possible and then, just when you think it's over, then I will strike the match and laugh as you burn!"

"You're insane! I did not cause your son's death! He died from malaria as did all the others. You must see that!"

"No. All I see is that you are responsible, and I will watch you suffer! "

Caitlin could not move. All she could do was stare at the crazed man. As he began to put even more pressure on her throat, she felt more fear than she could ever remember having experienced before. She saw that someone had bandaged his throat, but it was still continuing to seep blood, and he had strength that was unbelievable in his condition. Suddenly, Caitlin went rigid and saw a red flash before her eyes, then a blinding light that had her squeezing her eyes in an effort to shield them. Once again, she managed to push her fear aside and let anger take over. She was only just beginning to understand how to access this power of hers.

"No! No! Ohhhhhhhhhhhhhhhhhhh!" screamed Campbell.

The soldier went flying through the air and only stopped when a huge tree trunk met with his back. He fell to the ground in a crumpled heap. Caitlin stood up slowly, unsure what had happened just then. And most unsure about what might happen next! Had she done that? Thrown the commander into the air?

"No. Surely not. I couldn't have done that!" she spoke to herself.

Then, in a matter of seconds, her nose alerted her to another scent and one that was most welcomed — Alex! As she turned around, she was never so glad to see anyone. Alex was standing just a few behind her and looked as if he had lost his ability to speak. His face registered a look that spoke volumes about what he had just witnessed. How had Alex found her?

Neither of them said a word for a very long moment. Then Caitlin rushed to Alex and his arms went around her of their own accord, without a conscious thought from him, as if they knew that was their proper response to this woman.

"Oh, Alex! How did you find me? I've been trying to get to your farm, but it's taking so long! And so much has happened!"

"Aye, lass. Finding you was part determination and part luck. There are only three paths for getting to the upper regions, and this one is used most often, so I hoped maybe you would take it too. But, there've been a few who have taken the other paths. They all finally lead to the same place, so I would have caught up with you eventually.

"Alex. I have so much to tell you. But first, you must meet Millie."

"Oh, good God! What do I do now?!" A voice Alex was unfamiliar with rang out in the night.

Millie had not moved a muscle for what seemed like an eternity. But, finally she could stand it no longer and walked her horse over and managed to dismount, moving toward Caitlin. Willie had stayed when Caitlin had told him to, but when Millie started to go, he trailed along behind her, trying to keep her safe as he assumed Caitlin had wanted.

"Oh, heavens! What's happened?" She stood staring at the man lying at the base of the the tree.

"That's a very long story, Millie. This man is crazed and thinks I caused the death of his son. Of course I didn't, but he won't listen to reason. But now? I can't just leave him here to die, can I?"

"Well. I don't know why not, if he's trying to kill you!"

Caitlin was familiar with observing a new mother's protective instincts, and this mother's were working overtime. Protecting her infant was number one priority on her list.

"If he's crazed, then he might still try to hurt you, or all of us!"

"Yes, you're right, Millie. Let's think for a moment. Oh, where is Uncle Wabi when I need him!'"

Alex stood listening to the two women and they seemed to have forgotten he was there. Finally, as Willie ran to Alex as a "welcome committee" might, and was rewarded with a quick ruffing of his neck, Caitlin realized that an introduction needed to be made.

"Oh, Alex. This is Millie. She's traveling with me and we're trying to get to her family's estate, where we can get shelter. It's difficult to explain everything just now, but trust me when I say we need to get moving."

Alex came forward and offered his hand to the striking woman standing next to Caitlin. Two women could not look more different! One was barely five feet tall with fair skin and red hair, and the other was six feet with a dark mane that ran down her back.

"I'm Alex MacKinnon. It's my pleasure, I'm sure." Millie smiled at the man, then walked a short distance away as the babe had begun to make her presence known also. The new mother was learning about crying babies and how a short little snack would quiet one. Millie put the infant to her breast, and both of them rested quietly.

Alex turned to Caitlin and her expression was one that he had never seen her exhibit before, one of fear. Even in the cave when she was alone except for Willie, the healer had not shown this amount of anxiety.

"Oh, Alex! What should I do! Should I, the healer, help him or should I let him lie here and die?" Caitlin looked at Alex and then at Willie, wishing he could speak to her. Alex drew her close and held her for a moment. Caitlin relished the moment and nothing had ever felt so right!

"Well. It looks like we have to make a rather quick decision and get out of this storm.

But, I don't think we can leave the man out here. We'll tie his hands and feet and put him over his horse. Then, once we get to our destination, we'll figure out what to do with him."

Caitlin was glad to have Alex here with her. But, still she felt the whole situation was out of control. Why had her life become so unmanageable?

"I'll walk back into the forest and see if I can find the soldier's horse. He can't be very far away." Alex began to walk away and to his surprise, Willie went with him. Meanwhile, Caitlin paced back and forth, mumbling to herself.

"Oh, Uncle Wabi! Where are you when I need you?" Caitlin had not truly tried to contact him since her initial failure, but she certainly wished he were here now.

So, what was it the owl said? "Relax . . . every muscle . . . and open your mind . . . be receptive to hearing Uncle Wabi's voice . . ."

"Relax . . . relax . . . every muscle." And, much more quickly than the first time, Caitlin felt the now familiar tingling of her scalp. But this time it was more than a slight tingle. In fact, it felt as if her entire head was being singed with some sort of torch. Not painful, but certainly sizzling.

"Uncle Wabi. Please hear me. I need you. Please hear me!" Caitlin was sobbing at this point and didn't hear him when he first responded. So, he answered once again.

"Yes, Cait. I hear you."

"Uncle Wabi! Oh, please help me. I'm in real trouble this time and don't know what to do! I so wish you were here!"

"Easy my girl, easy. Just continue to think about me and hear my voice. I'll be there shortly. Just keep calling me so I can find you more readily. I'll only be a moment now."

***

Wabi took a second to look about himself. He stood very still, facing north, and raised his hands to the sky, palms upward. He began to chant in an old, forgotten language that his kind had spoken for millennia. All at once, a great roll of thunder rumbled across the entire region, and the snow began swirling around his body, from his upraised arms down to his feet. And the earth began to quiver, then shake violently. The snow turned into a whirlwind that felt more like a tornado than a snowstorm. The sky lit up with a thousand stars that seemed to shine a path for the tornado to follow and, instantly, Wabi and the storm disappeared into the stars above. The sky changed colors — from blue to pink — then to green — like a wave of colored lights moving across the sky. Even the Aurora Borealis couldn't compete with this event! Were they having a tornado and an earthquake at the same time?

An instant later, the whirling snow stopped and the trees reached for the sky again. The earth ceased to shake, but still quivered and the stars drifted away. The colors faded and they were left with only the stars that made up the Milky Way still shining down on them.

Caitlin looked up and standing just a few feet in front of her was Uncle Wabi, his hair standing on end and a light covering of snow still clinging to his shoulders. And he was grinning from ear to ear!

"Heavens! I had forgotten how thrilling time and place weaving can be! The sheer excitement of moving from one place to another or one time to another is truly remarkable!" Leaning on his crooked staff, Wabi spoke to Caitlin.

"Uncle Wabi? How did you get here?" Caitlin looked at the man that had raised her for most of her life. She just shook her head. Finally, maybe, she was beginning to understand he was indeed a special person, just as Owl had said.

"Uncle Wabi. Did you come on the tornado snowstorm?" She looked quizzically at him, not sure what she was hoping to hear as an explanation.

"Yes, Caitlin, I did indeed. Place 'weaving' is a method of travel that I only use when nothing else will suffice — in a time of great need. At the moment it seemed the most logical way to travel as it sounded as if you may be in a dangerous situation."

He was so calm Caitlin found herself remaining calm also, even in the presence of one who could "weave" from one place to another.

Caitlin rubbed her temples with her fingers and looked about.

"Oh, Uncle Wabi, I hardly know where to start! I left Skye hoping to keep you safe from Thomas and his friend, that awful lord. And then I took care of some soldiers who had malaria, but most of them died. And the father of one of them, a Commander Campbell, accused me of witchcraft and threatened to burn me! So, I left there and moved to a cave just south of Inverness, and started caring for the wounded there. Uncle Wabi, there were so many of them! All coming from Culloden. It was a blood bath for both sides, I do believe." She stopped just long enough to get another breath and started again, rattling off information so rapidly that Wabi had trouble keeping up.

"Then the commander found me in my cave and attacked me. Willie, my wolf, held him off and I fled as fast as I could! Willie gave him quite a wound and he's bound to be most angry about that. And, I'm trying to get to the MacKinnon lands, in the upper Highlands. They've offered to help me and I couldn't think of anywhere else to go!"

Taking her hands, Wabi tried to comfort her.

"Ah, Cait, dear girl. I've always been at your fingertips, you just never would see it.

Hopefully you can see there are some things that are possible even though we may not understand them. I know I have taught you that and repeatedly so over the years. However, we all come to our understandings in our own good time. Your time is now."

Millie didn't know whether to run or try to sneak away quietly. Who were these strange people? This old man appeared out of a blinding snowstorm that had come upon them, or was it a tornado? She had pulled the baby as close to her bosom as possible and stood staring at the young woman who had helped her through a most trying experience. Was this woman a witch as the soldier had thought?

Millie decided to address the situation straightforward.

"Caitlin! What's happening here? Who is this old man? And, for that matter, who are you?" she exclaimed. Too many unexplained events were beginning to frighten her.

Caitlin saw the stricken look on Millie's face and understood exactly how she felt. She, too, was reeling with coming to grips with this whole situation that was unfolding. The only thing she knew that Millie didn't was that Uncle Wabi's purpose on this earth, as he had explained it to her early on, was to care for others and do what he could for the betterment of mankind. So, even though she may not have expected him to have these particular powers, she was unafraid and trusted him implicitly. Somehow she must reassure Millie they were all safe.

"Millie. Please don't be afraid. Uncle Wabi will help us and he has never harmed anyone in his life. Please just trust that he will know what we must do. You and I, and your babe, are safe with him."

"Come, Millie, come over here and meet Uncle Wabi."

Caitlin watched as Wabi stepped forward and touched Millie's shoulders with both hands, sending an instant outpouring of warmth. She saw Millie's expression of relief.

"Madam. It is with pleasure that I meet you. Please do not be alarmed. All will be well, and we'll find shelter. Come. Let's put our heads together and see what choices we may have."

As he removed his hands, Caitlin knew that Millie's fears had been allayed, probably as Uncle Wabi had planned, she guessed. She could see Millie was almost sorry to lose his touch.

***

Alex heard voices through the woods, one of which sounded like a male's voice. He listened for a moment then started back to the clearing where he had left Caitlin. He decided the commander's horse must have run off as he could not find him. When he got back to the clearing, he was surprised to see her talking to an old man. He walked a little closer, Willie still by his side. Alex was aware the wolf had not sent out any warnings, so the old man must not be a danger to them. So, he came to stand next to Caitlin. Was this old man a friend? Or was he going to have to do battle with a very old man who might be after Caitlin also?

"Alex. This is Uncle Wabi. Uncle Wabi, this is Alex MacKinnon. He has offered to take me to his home in the upper Highlands as he feels there is greater safety for me there."

The two men shook hands, and a look of understanding passed between them, a look that said "she's important to me."

***

So, this was the gentleman Owl had told him about, thought Wabi. Quite a large fellow. And, according to Owl, he was intent on making Caitlin a part of his life. Well, then. I must get to know him better.

The only member of the party that Wabi hadn't met was Willie. Wabi got on his knees and Willie walked over to him. The old wizard put his hands under the jaws of the creature and looked at him, and the two recognized each other for what they both were,

226

travelers from many times and places. Willie quickly licked Wabi's hand and lay at his feet.

"Whatever is that about?" Caitlin asked. "He acts like he has known you forever!"

"Well, yes. Maybe he has." The old one straightened up and walked along beside Caitlin. "Owl has told me a bit about your troubles, but not everything."

"Owl told you? How?"

Wabi smiled and took Caitlin's hand.

"So now. Tell me about this soldier." Wabi saw the man's body lying on the ground and could see that he was unconscious. However, someone had applied fresh bandages, and Wabi was sure a healer had done that.

"This is Commander Campbell I told you about, the soldier who accused me of killing his son. He was wounded by Willie. Apparently he found a healer to help him, and he's tracked me. I don't see a horse, but I don't think he could have walked very far with his wound. But, of course, I stole his own horse when I fled the cave. It seemed the only way to get away from him as quickly as I could. So, that probably infuriated him even further. And, what a fine horse he is!"

"Well, he found me earlier today, and after a frightening ordeal with him, he's lost consciousness. But I'm so afraid when he regains consciousness he may harm one of us! But we can't just leave him here to die, can we?"

Wabi walked over to the man, bent down on one knee and put both his hands on the man's head, almost like a priest "laying on hands." The old wizard bowed his head and murmured some words that Caitlin couldn't understand. In just a few moments he released the man's head and stood back up.

He walked over to where Caitlin had sat down near Millie. He looked at her with his riveting eyes and began,

"Caitlin. This man cannot be saved. Perhaps in body, but his soul is as black as night. He's pure evil through and through. I know it's difficult for a healer to understand, but some people are not worth saving, and this man is one of those."

"But I must try, Uncle Wabi. You taught me to preserve life, even in those we may think are unworthy of saving. I clearly remember you saying 'the Creator believes all people have self-worth and should be treated accordingly.' I don't recall you saying 'except for some.' I must try to help him."

"Yes. I did teach you that. But, just know your efforts could well be in vain. We'll take him with us, but you must understand he'll still wish to dispose of you, so we must watch him at all times."

Alex had remained quiet. Where had the old man come from? How did he get here? He wasn't here when Alex went to find the horse. Obviously he's Caitlin's uncle and the wolf is at ease with him, but being Alex MacKinnon, he would get more facts before he formed an opinion. So, for now, he would watch and listen.

Wabi and Alex lifted the soldier and draped him over the horse, his own horse actually.

The horse shied away as if he would rather not carry this load.

Animals have a very good memory and Wabi sensed this animal was afraid of the soldier. Stroking the horse gently, Wabi whispered, "Hey, handsome man. Just carry him for a short way, then we'll relieve you of him."

"And, which way are you all headed?"

"Oh. Millie has family in this area. She thinks it isn't too far now and we should get there by nightfall."

"Do you think your family will mind that we come with you? And what about this soldier? He may prove to be a real problem for all of us before this is over."

"My family will welcome me and anyone I bring with me. As for the soldier, let's just keep him tied up on his horse and when we get there the local law enforcers can have him." Millie was not sure that was the right thing to do, but she wanted to be on their way again. She must take care of her babe at all costs.

"I agree. We'll secure him on his horse, maybe tie him up, although from the looks of him, that's probably not necessary." Wabi responded.

Chapter 42

The moon provided some small amount of light, and they could see their destination was a short distance away.

"Are you sure this is the right place?" Caitlin asked.

"Yes. There's a moat. It was one of my favorite places to play when we visited them. I would place flowers in it and watch them float down the stream."

Wabi rode Caitlin's horse with Campbell draped over the back. Caitlin doubled with Alex and Willie walked along beside them, and occasionally ran off to the woods briefly, but always returned when Caitlin whistled for him. Millie had fashioned a sort of carrier for the babe. It was a blanket that tied across her breast and went up around her neck. It certainly made the ride much more comfortable than trying to hold the child in her arms. But uncomfortable hardly described her feelings.

Caitlin's arms were wrapped around Alex, and she felt safer than she had in such a long time. Here she was with an old man whom she had loved all her life, and another one she thought may be important in her future.

They eventually found the drawbridge. And, lucky for them, it was down. Of course, the days of using drawbridges were pretty much over. Most of these estates had been in the same families for generations and were not used as fortresses anymore.

As they entered the bailey, it was eerily quiet. There were no night sounds, no birds, no critters moving about, and certainly no sign of people. The entire area looked as if everyone had just dropped what they were doing and left. Tools were about on the ground, baskets of grain were turned over and upended, and fruit was left in heaps on the steps, as if every person had left in a hurry.

"Are you sure this is the right place, Millie?" asked Caitlin once again, looking about and feeling something was not quite right.

Wabi helped Millie down and she stood upright slowly.

"Yes, this is the place. I've been here many times, but it looks deserted. I haven't heard from Aunt Moira for several years now, and both she and Grandmother would be getting on in years. But surely some of the servants would be about."

Alex and Wabi told the ladies to stay outside with Willie while they went up the steps to the main entrance. The large doors were heavy, but with some real effort, Alex was able to pull one of them open. Why had they not been locked? Looking around and listening closely, he heard nothing. Again — that same deafening silence was in the castle as well.

Wabi could feel in his bones something had happened here, but he didn't know what. He walked through the great room then went up a flight of stairs that led to the upper chambers where the family would have slept. At the top of the stairs, he came into a large hallway with rooms off either side. All the doors were open to the rooms except one toward the rear of the castle. Wabi turned the handle on the door, which was not difficult, then leaned his weight into the door causing it to come open. It apparently had been stuck awhile, but just a little push opened it readily.

Looking about the room, Wabi noted a feminine touch throughout the room. The linens were of a very fine fabric, and there were silver-backed brushes on the dressing table. Clearly, this was a woman's or girl's bedroom. As he was about to leave the room, he caught glimpse of movement in his peripheral vision. He turned just in time to observe a peregrine falcon land in a window that had been left slightly open. Below the window was a window seat, one that had been appealing to the falcon, apparently, as she had created a wide, but shallow nest on it. She looked at Wabi briefly, standing very still, and decided there was no danger from this man. So, she went about her business of scratching around the edges of the nest, getting it just right then settling down and ruffling her feathers in the process. Wabi knew falcons were territorial, especially when they were incubating eggs. He walked over just a bit closer. She was such a beautiful creature, thought Wabi. And, he knew that falcons, like owls and several other birds, mated for life. So, he was fairly sure another falcon, a male, was probably close by as well. As he left the room, he closed the door again. No need to bother this beauty as she went about her work.

Across the hallway was another room, just a bit larger and with a small fireplace in the far wall. The fireplace was laid with logs and kindling, as if ready to be lighted at any moment. Wabi nodded in the direction of the fireplace and flames immediately raced up the chimney. This would keep some of them warm for the evening at least. There were two beds in this room, and both had very nice linens also, but not as eloquent as the first room. He went back downstairs to the great hall, looked about the enormous room, and saw the rear wall held a very large fireplace. It, too, was ready for use with several large logs already laid. Another nod to this one and the flames were licking at the logs within moments.

***

Alex went through the rooms downstairs, and he heard Caitlin as she entered the castle.

Or maybe he just sensed her.

Wabi instructed Caitlin to take Millie and the baby upstairs to the room where he had started the fire. He had asked Caitlin to stay outside, but just smiled when he saw her.

Meanwhile, he and Alex went back outside and carried the commander up the steps to the great hall and laid him on some blankets close to the fire. The room was large and cold at the moment. The soldier was still unconscious and lay unmoving on the blankets. Wabi tried to make him as comfortable as possible, but the man was not aware of anyone or anything at this time. Alex loosened his wrist ties, just slightly, as the man's hands had swollen considerably from hanging over the horse for so long. Wabi covered him with another blanket and went about exploring more of the building.

Wabi entered another room behind the great hall. Apparently, this was the kitchen. And, again, the room seemed to have been deserted. There was a basket filled with dried apples, another with pears, wheat that had been ground but not put in containers, and potatoes, carrots and some dried beans had been sorted and left lying on the counter. At the rear of the kitchen was a shorter door. Wabi opened the door and had to bend down to enter the space. He found himself looking down into a cellar of some sort. He lit a candle and held it aloft to light the way, carefully taking the steps one at a time.

"Bless the Creator! A wine cellar!" Wabi exclaimed. He did enjoy fine wines, which were not always easy to come by. And this cellar was rather large and well stocked. So, he chose a wine he recognized and particularly liked, and went back up the steps whistling as he went.

As Wabi was trying to come up with vittles for everyone, Millie went upstairs and entered the room with the fire going where she and the baby could rest and stay warm. She was past exhaustion, and only wanted to lie down before she fell down. The bed linens were beautiful, and the bed felt like heaven to her. She snuggled under the blankets with the babe, holding her close against her breast, and watched as the little one started rooting, looking for her next feeding.

Meanwhile, Alex had taken the horses to the stables where he had spent several nights over the years. The Cameron mistresses were generous to any travelers and often allowed one to sleep in the stable if they needed to rest before moving on. Shortly, Caitlin came in behind him and helped him find stalls for the tired horses.

There was a large open-mouthed well inside the stable, and someone had used it recently as all the stalls had a pail of water. There were a few other horses here, and all the stalls had an abundance of hay, and a bucket of oats was already hung at each one.

Caitlin took the time, even though exhausted, to brush the horses. Commander Campbell's horse was quite a beauty and Caitlin never regretted stealing him.

Alex found blankets for the horses and helped Caitlin wrap the animals. The night would be cold and the animals would likely be glad to have them. They worked side by side, and after Alex finished securing the last ties on the blankets, he turned and took Caitlin's chin in his hand, gently, sending a quick streak of shivers up her arm.

"Caitlin. I'm not asking for explanations. But there's a lot I don't understand. I've looked for ye for such a long time, and ye must feel how much I wish to be with ye. Is it just my imagination, or are ye feeling anything close to the same?"

Without any words, and certainly no explanations, Caitlin put her arms up around his neck. She had to stand on her tiptoes and even then, it was almost impossible to reach him.

"Alex MacKinnon. You have become more important to me than you can ever know. I have felt you in my dreams, and I knew you would find me. I don't understand a lot of what is happening either. But, somehow, when you are with me, it feels like I have come home, that all is as it should be." Then no more words were necessary as Alex pulled her closer and bent down and kissed her. The kiss was ever so gentle — not demanding — but with promise of delights that she had no understanding of as yet.

"Yes. Yes. This is what I want. This is WHO I want," she whispered. Alex made no other remarks, but was slow to break their embrace.

After they finished with the horses, Alex and Caitlin went back to the castle and returned to the great hall to warm by the fire for a moment. Caitlin headed upstairs to check on Millie.

After she assured herself that Millie and the baby were comfortable, she came back down the stairs, and the aroma filling the great hall made her mouth water. Uncle Wabi was known for creating the tastiest meals ever, even when he had very little to work with. She found him in the kitchen, whistling some tune she had heard before, and stirring a pot he assured her would be delicious potato soup. And, she could smell bread baking in the oven. How had he ever gotten all this going in such a short time? There was also another aroma which really grabbed her nose, some sort of fruit, or maybe more than one fruit?

Caitlin lifted her nose. "Wabi. What's that wonderful smell?"

"Ah, yes, that would be the apple and pear tarts that will be ready in just a few more minutes," replied Wabi to her question.

His energy never ceased to amaze Caitlin. Personally, she was about to expire any moment now. A bath would be wonderful, followed by a bed with blankets to snuggle under. But, first, she would have a meal with Wabi and Alex and try to make some sense out of their situation.

***

Following a most scrumptious meal, the three of them felt half human again.

"Uncle Wabi. You never tell anyone your recipes, but maybe one day you'll teach me how to cook like this," Caitlin commented.

"I don't know much about cooking, but maybe you could teach Hector too. He does our cooking and we've learned not to complain, but I believe you could teach him a thing or two," said Alex.

Caitlin stood up from the table, "I'll take a tray up to Millie. She's bound to be even more tired than we all are."

However, Millie was covered from head to toe, and Caitlin decided just to leave the tray on the bedside table and Millie would find it if she awakened.

After a quick washing up, Wabi, Alex, and Caitlin went to sit by the fire in the great hall. Wabi had poured them both a goblet of the wine and had given himself a generous portion also. So after Caitlin checked once again on Commander Campbell and found him still unconscious, she, Alex, and Wabi gathered their thoughts. But, in just a few seconds, Alex was nodding in his chair. Rousing himself, he stood slowly.

"If ye'll excuse me, I believe I'll find a bed somewhere. It's been several nights with not much sleep, and it's caught up with me," said Alex, trying to stifle a yawn. He actually felt that Caitlin may need some personal, private time with her uncle. And, Alex was still not sure what to think about the old man.

"Of course, Alex." Wabi nodded to him.

"Yes. Off to bed with you. I'll sleep in with Millie. There are several rooms upstairs. Just find one and lay your head down," said Caitlin. Then she rose and gave him a kiss on his cheek as he got up from his chair. He simply smiled and started up the stairs.

Twisting her goblet in her hands, first one way, then the other, Caitlin peered across at Wabi. She had debated with herself whether to have this conversation or not.

"Uncle Wabi. Did I see you nod your head to start a fire in the fireplace?" she asked.

"Well, yes, as a matter of fact you did. But Caitlin, you have seen me do this many times when you were a child. You just never questioned it then. Children have no trouble believing the seemingly impossible, unlike adults. And, Caitlin, you too, have the power to do this. All you must do is think about it and know that it will happen. Most of your powers need only be accepted and they will be at your fingertips."

"This wizard weaving . . . or place weaving . . . time weaving . . . lighting fires . . . why me . . . what am I to do with these powers?"

"Oh, Cait. There is a destiny determined for you long ago. You will find what that destiny is as your life proceeds, but you must not continue to disbelieve or these gifts will never manifest themselves for the purpose the Creator intended. I do not know what this entity had in mind, but it will be for mankind's good, and you are being called to serve in some capacity, it seems. This calling can seem a burden at times, but ultimately, you will understand how you are to take your place in the universe. I will not be surprised that your destiny was designed to include the gift you have always had . . . healing others. Of course, there are many kinds of healing. You may be called on to administer more than one."

"Don't worry so, dear girl. We will talk more of this once we have sorted through our present situation. Now, to bed with you, too. Tomorrow will take care of itself, so let's not think about that tonight. I've been running on leftover energy from the 'weaving,' but tomorrow I'll feel like I have the biggest hangover ever. 'Weaving' has a way of catching up with you, both physically and mentally. So, it may be that you'll have to wake me in the morning. But, please be gentle with me, I am an old man, you see." He laughed as he bade her goodnight.

Wabi made himself a pallet near the soldier. His personal code of ethics never allowed him to kill unless there was no other solution. But this soldier could only bring disaster wherever he went. Wabi hoped he would just continue to sleep, and may it be forever.

"I will sleep down here tonight, just to keep an eye on our 'friend.' I'll call you if you're needed."

She started to walk away when Wabi called to her. "Oh, Cait. I did want to ask you a question, if I may." "Of course, Uncle Wabi, anything."

"Well, these, uh, uh, pants you're wearing. Much like mine that gather just below the knee. And your hair braided down your back. I actually thought you were a young lad when I first saw you. This look is most unusual you must admit — on a young woman that is."

Caitlin laughed at her uncle. "Well, I was trying to figure out how to escape from the commander, so I thought maybe if I disguised myself as a lad, he wouldn't recognize me if he ever caught up with me. I thought getting about would be much easier without having to deal with petticoats and long dresses. And, I must say, these pants and stockings do work very well!"

"Yes, I can see that. So, does that mean I should get use to seeing you in this attire in the future?"

"Oh, I don't know. I'm not sure a healer would be well received dressed like this. But the outfit may come in handy again. Think I'll hang on to it for a while."

"Your inner beauty will always show, Caitlin, no matter what you wear." She kissed his cheek and walked on.

Caitlin slowly climbed the stairs thinking what a magnificent place this must have been to grow up in, or even visit, as Millie had apparently done. And, remembering Millie as she had walked up the stairs, carrying her babe and murmuring to her, Caitlin thought to herself, there was such an elegance about this woman. She had a regal bearing and when she spoke her voice was quiet, gentle, and made you want to listen to her. At almost six feet tall, Millie towered over Caitlin, who barely made five feet. But, a camaraderie was developing between them. They didn't know each other at all, or only briefly, but each recognized some characteristic in the other they felt missing in themselves. Maybe a friendship would be a good thing. Not something that Caitlin had given much thought to before.

When Caitlin got to the top of the stairs, she looked back down and could see Wabi and the commander both sleeping by the fire. If the soldier did awaken, she felt sure Wabi would be able to handle the situation.

Entering the hall at the top of the stairs, Caitlin saw the open door where Millie was sleeping. She also saw several other rooms farther back, and one with a closed door. Curiosity got the better of her, even in her tired state, and she gently opened the door and looked about. Was Alex in this room? She didn't wish to wake him if so. But just knowing he was near had her heart wishing for something more in life, and she hadn't even known something was missing until he came along!

Her brain quickly registered this was a bedroom where a woman had slept. The linens were exceptionally fine with hand tatted lace on the sheets and pillowcases. The window was adorned with curtains that reached the floor and made from a soft fabric her fingers wanted to touch. As she walked closer to the window, however, she heard a soft fluttering sound. She stopped and looked in amazement as a falcon moved about on a large nest on the window seat. The falcon stood up, turned in the other direction, scratched around the edge of the nest, and reseated herself. Caitlin smiled, just watching the bird. Did falcons make nests in windows? She thought they only liked high ledges in nature. Apparently she was content to use whatever was at hand. Caitlin wondered why mankind couldn't be so content, just to do what we were put here to do. She walked away and quietly closed the door. Alex was not there, but she didn't look into any more rooms.

Caitlin went into the small dressing room attached to the bedroom where Millie slept.

The fire had warmed the room and the light from it flickered on the highly polished floors. There was a ewer with water and a bowl waiting, again as if ready for use. And, there was a bar of chamomile soap! Oh, what a treat! The water was cold, but just removing some of the grime from her body was most refreshing. She had to put the same clothing back on, however, as she had nothing else to wear. But, she really liked these pants and the shirt she "borrowed" from Ian. She lay down on the other bed, relishing the feel of the fine linen and soft bedding. Such a luxury, and she didn't count any black-faced sheep before she drifted off into a deep sleep with no dreams this night.

Chapter 43

Hours later, in the deepest, darkest part of the night, Caitlin heard something as did Willie, who was on his feet and waiting for a signal from her — a signal to attack!

As Caitlin and Willie quietly walked down the staircase and reached the bottom, she tripped over a large object of some kind at the foot of the stairs. She picked herself up and listened, trying to see and hear. As she looked about, the object she had stumbled over had come to life and was reaching for her. It was a giant of a man and he was holding her by her shoulders, lifting her off her feet. He was enormous! But Willie did not growl, and Caitlin held her breath as the giant continued to hold her by her shoulders and squeeze her. She had awakened him and he was about to cause her great bodily harm. Why had Willie not attacked him?

"Who goes there?" he called out, still holding her tightly, lifting her even higher, her legs dangling in the air.

"Let me go this minute!" Caitlin screamed in his face, all the while kicking him in the shins with her small feet. He held her farther away in order to see her face more clearly.

"Jesus!" The man didn't need to see her face, he would have known that voice anywhere.

The healer! Whatever was she doing in this castle?

"Caitlin? What are ye doing here? Is Alex with ye? Are ye alright?"

As the giant lowered her to the floor, Caitlin caught her breath and looked carefully at the man. It was one of the MacKinnon brothers. Jack or Hector? Yes. Jack MacKinnon! What was he doing here?

"Jack!" she gasped, thankful to be back on the floor and released from his terrifying grip. "It's a long story, but we're here trying to keep out of the storm. And, yes, Alex is with me. He caught up with us today." At least she now understood why Willie had not attacked him. He had found the MacKinnon brothers to his liking from the very beginning.

Jack was breathing heavily as he was certainly awakened abruptly and not expecting to find the healer here.

"Alex left some days ago headed back down to the cave to try and talk some sense into ye. He felt the soldier would not cease looking for ye and ye were in danger. So, after he hadn't come back in another few days, I came down to look for him. Thank goodness. He's all right, then?"

"Yes, Jack. He's fine. A bit too tired, but all right. He's upstairs asleep." "Good. I'll go up then and talk with him."

"Oh, Jack. Let it wait 'til the morning. We're all past going another minute. He'll feel better with some uninterrupted sleep." The healer was forever trying to get folk to understand the body needed to rest in order to keep going. But, trying to tell that to a sheep man was like talking to the wind!

"Ah. Well then. Ye've got a point there. I'm a bit tuckered meself."

"Oh, what a complicated mess," said Caitlin. "We all need to put our heads together, as Uncle Wabi would say, and sort this one out."

"We all? It's just the three of us, Caitlin."

"Well. Not exactly. Uncle Wabi is here, as is Millie and her newborn babe, and the soldier, too."

"Who is Uncle Wabi? And a woman with a baby? What is she doing here? And a soldier?

Rubbing her eyes with the back of her hands, Caitlin could hardly explain the situation. "Jack. Some of these events I don't even begin to know how to explain, but, nonetheless, they have happened. But, first things first."

"But, Caitlin, where are ye and the others headed? This storm is likely to last a while.

What about food and water?"

"Well. I was trying to get to your land and hoping you might allow me to stay there until this soldier comes to his senses. But, that plan has changed a bit, so I'm not really sure what I'll do now." She hesitated before adding more to her story.

"As it is, rather than running from him now, I've brought him here with me." "What! Have ye lost yer mind, bringing in the man who wants to burn ye!"

"That's not exactly what happened, you see. I was just coming north on my own, with Willie of course, and then I came upon this woman in labor, and then I delivered the baby, and it started to snow and . . . and then I was attacked by the soldier, but Willie took care of that . . . and then I called for Uncle Wabi . . . and he came and . . . Owl was there . . ."

Even to her own ears, Caitlin knew this story sounded utterly ridiculous.

Jack stared at the woman. He had long ago decided she was not a witch, and was indeed a most skilled healer, and he acknowledged that Alex was taken with her. But, my goodness, she did seem to be spinning a really unbelievable yarn. Maybe he had made too hasty a decision.

Maybe she was a witch!

As they continued their conversation, Uncle Wabi awoke and stood up holding his blanket about himself, just listening, wondering who this giant of a man was and what action he might need to take to protect them all. He noted Willie was not alarmed and understood there must not be any danger at the moment. Well enough, but who was he? Apparently, they were discussing Alex. Wabi pulled at his beard and took a deep breath. He had forgotten how complicated Caitlin could make one's life. He just hoped this would turn out well, but, at the moment, he was not so sure.

Walking closer to the two, he cleared his throat, "Ahem, uh. Whatever it is that you two are discussing, I believe it can wait until tomorrow. I must sleep now." He promptly lay back down, and the snoring commenced immediately.

"But what about the soldier? Where is he right now?" Jack whispered loudly.

"He's tied up, down by the fire. He's been unconscious all day and still remains so. I don't think we need to worry too much about him. Uncle Wabi will take care of any problems from him."

"Caitlin. That soldier could overpower that old man in a minute! He's dangerous!"

"Don't count Wabi out so easily. He's got more on the ball than you know. He can handle the soldier."

Jack was not happy with that conversation and thought Caitlin was making a big mistake bringing a mad man into the house with them.

"Caitlin. Alex will tear me apart if I let anything happen to you. You're putting all of us in danger!"

Caitlin could see there was no changing Jack's mind, so she just shook her head and started asking her own questions.

"Why are you here, in this castle?" Caitlin whispered, looking at Jack as if he had two heads.

"Well, you see, I've been here before, several years ago, when the old laird passed on. The estate was looking to rid themselves of a large number of their sheep, so we, me and Alex, came down and made our agreement with the old woman, Mistress Cameron, I believe it was, to herd them back up to our place. She felt she wouldn't be able to run the sheep farm without the laird, so she was pleased that we wanted to make the purchase."

"So, what with the storm, I thought perhaps they would allow me to stay in the stables, so I came to the door to inquire about that. I knocked, but no one answered. But, the door was unlocked, and I could see a fire. So, I came in quietly and saw there were some other travelers as well who seemed to be resting here out of the weather. So, I just bedded down at the bottom of the stairs, out of the way of the other two. It was quite a dreadful storm. But where is the mistress?"

"Oh, that's a good question and one I can't answer. But maybe Millie can explain more to us in the morning. Right now, let's get back to bed and try to get some sleep"

Caitlin found some blankets for Jack, and he settled back at the foot of the stairs. He tried to sleep, but was still fuming about the soldier, and Wabi made enough noise to wake the dead! After some time, tired of listening to the ever-snoring Wabi, Jack got up, blankets and all, and ascended the stairs, hoping to find someplace to sleep. Someplace with no snoring!

At the top of the stairs, he saw the door open to a room on the right. A quick peek in there and he saw Caitlin in one bed, and another person in the other, totally covered from head to toe. They were both sleeping soundly, and he walked on across the hallway to the room with the closed door.

As he went inside, he never noticed the falcon in the window. He only saw a most inviting bed with what looked like warm blankets, and he made a beeline for it. He collapsed immediately, and the bed groaned under his weight.

Chapter 44

Caitlin awoke feeling more rested than she had since leaving the Isle of Skye. The fine linens and blankets on the bed had felt like heaven. And, now, she was ready to go down and talk with Uncle Wabi, Alex, and Jack and see what kind of plan they could come up with. She put her boots back on, casting a critical eye at them briefly. To look at them now, you'd never know they had been a Christmas gift from Uncle Wabi last year, crafted from the softest leather and handmade by the leather maker in their village. They had served her well and had kept her feet warm and dry, so she was glad to have them and hoped they would last a little longer.

One look at the other bed and she could see Millie and her babe were still enjoying their rest. Millie never complained about any discomfort, but Caitlin knew the woman must have been in agony just sitting on that horse for hours following delivery of a baby. This woman was most unique, of that she was certain. Just before Caitlin left the room, Willie sat up, ears ready for any instruction. She decided he, too, needed to rest while he could, so she gave him a "stay" hand signal, and he settled back down on the rug next to the bed.

As she got to the bottom of the stairs, Wabi was still wrapped in his blanket. His rhythmic snoring indicated he was dead to the world. The commander was still near the fire, covered from head to toe. She decided to check his status hoping he would be in a better state of health, and that his senses had returned to him. Surely, by now he would have figured out she was not a witch and his pursuit of her was ridiculous. Alex must still be sleeping, too, which was probably a good thing.

She gently turned back the covers from the soldier's face and gasped. The blanket was empty and the soldier was gone! Oh great glory! Where could he be? She felt panicky just wondering where he might be hiding. But, she also knew he was in poor physical condition and not likely to have gone very far. She prayed he had realized this mission, trying to find and do away with her, was not one he should continue. Why else would he have left? But, when she had found him yesterday, he had not been aware of anything, and had shortly become unconscious. He had not regained consciousness before she retired last evening, so she didn't think he could know she was here with him. Maybe he had left, still thinking to chase after her, still unaware he had been in her care.

She thought it might be a good idea to check on the horses. And, he may have taken one of them, most likely his own. They, too, must have had a better night, with plenty of water, fresh oats, and a blanket on their backs. She was still glad she had stolen the soldier's horse and she would do it again.

She stopped and looked across the fields beyond the stables. The sky was announcing a new day, and the sun was just peeking over the mountains. The snowstorm had subsided and as far as she could see, all across the distant moor, the ground was covered in a white sheet of crystals that winked at her when the light struck them. There was not a sound anywhere. It was truly Mother Nature at her most beautiful, calm and peaceful. Caitlin wondered why the inhabitants of the world couldn't find this same tranquility, for surely it was available.

She made her way to the stables and could see tracks left by Jack when he had brought his horse in last night. It was still amazing they had crossed paths in this unlikely place. The stable doors were unlocked, and slightly open. She remembered closing them completely herself, but Jack must have left them ajar in his rush to get inside to a warm fire. She had to use both hands to pull the large doors open, as they were built of very thick, heavy wood, and had been here for ages. Stepping inside and again seeing the large well, she thought whomever had come up with that idea had been quite a resourceful person. At least you would be inside, out of the weather, when you needed to get water for the household or for the livestock. She peeked over the edge of the well and could see water far below. The particular smell of the water told her it must be some sort of underground spring. She would bring up one of the several buckets that were hung over the side, and take water to the horses and maybe take a bucket full to the house as well. Maybe she could make a pot of tea or coffee if they could find any.

She reached down, grabbed the rope and began to pull the bucket up. As she leaned over, something lunged at her from behind. In a flash, a large, muscular arm was around her neck, cutting off her oxygen.

"Well, now, my lovely little witch, when I make a promise, I keep it!" Commander Campbell, even in his condition, had more strength than she could imagine. She felt her heart racing, and a fear she had only experienced once before was threatening to overwhelm her ability to think.

Trying to keep her mind working, she tried to recall what Wabi had told her. "You can always call me, Caitlin. When in a dire circumstance, just think about me and call me, in your mind."

Caitlin was far past relaxing as Wabi had instructed, but her scalp began to sizzle and in her mind she screamed, "Uncle Wabi! Help me! Wabi!"

But, no sound came from her lips as there was no oxygen left for her to breathe. She felt herself fading away and desperately tried to stay conscious.

Then she called once more. And this time she screamed, "Alex! Help me!"

***

Jack had also awakened early, as was his usual routine. He was hesitant to leave this warm cocoon and was enjoying the smells in this room. He hadn't noticed any of these details last evening, as he was far too exhausted. But, in this early morning light, he knew he was in a female's bedroom. The lustrous drapes at the window, and lace on the linens, and something that smelled like Mam's heather or some of her herbs. And, across the room was a most unexpected sight. A window seat appeared to be home for a falcon. She was sitting quietly on her large nest, as if not aware of his presence. Now that was an unusual sight, a falcon nesting in a window. He had seen them many times before, but always up high on a ledge of some kind. He smiled and got up, put his boots on and walked out of the room, taking time to close the door. He was anxious to talk with Alex, but would go downstairs and wait until his brother came down. Alex was not exactly at his best early, and Jack knew to hand him a cup of coffee before trying to talk to him.

As he came out into the hallway, he heard a small animal mewing, like a small kitten seeking its breakfast. But, looking about the hallway, he found nothing.

He walked across the hall to another room, one with the door cracked just a little. A quick glance told him that Caitlin must also be an early riser as her bed was empty. But in the other one, the woman was still asleep — but her bed partner was not. Jack could see the small infant flailing its arms and legs about, totally out of the covers. This was where the sound of a small animal was coming from. And it was most definitely a small animal.

He went over to the bed and gently picked the small babe up and held it close to his chest, fully supporting the head, just as Mam had taught him. He, Alex, and Hector had learned much when Ian was born. Ian was a change-of-life baby for Mam, and these three older brothers found this baby even more exciting than a new puppy. Mam had taught them all how to care for him, change him, feed him, and most of all, how to love him. Of the brothers, Jack had most enjoyed taking care of the little brother and so holding this new infant felt natural.

"Why, you're no bigger than a little midge!" whispered Jack. Of course, midges could be irritating, as could some babies.

Taking a small blanket lying on the table next to the bed, he wrapped the infant in it, then decided to go downstairs with her so the new mother could rest. He couldn't imagine what an ordeal this woman must have gone through. Having a baby under the best of circumstances was one thing, but to have one in the middle of a snowstorm and outdoors was another. Willie watched as the big Highlander picked the child up, but knew this child was in no danger from this man.

Jack cautiously walked down the stairs and headed for the kitchen, hoping to find the makings of breakfast, or at least coffee. As he held the infant closely, the babe rooted up to Jack's neck seeking some breakfast too, but finding nothing, made some little animal sounds and drifted back to sleep. Jack continued to talk soothingly to the babe, holding her easily in one hand. He found some baked goods, but they were very old and had been here a long time. He puttered about some more hoping to find coffee or tea.

As he opened a cabinet door, still searching for coffee, he felt a tremendous vibration, and it was shaking the entire room. Then the whole place reeled with the screaming of a woman! He ran back to the great hall and the walls fairly echoed with the same voice calling out.

"Uncle Wabi! Alex!"

Jack watched in awe as the old man with the beard jumped straight up and held his head between his hands, then fairly ran from the room. Just moments later, coming from somewhere upstairs, Alex flew down the stairs and dashed out the door, just a few seconds behind the old man.

"Caitlin! I'm coming! Hold on!" yelled Alex.

Then the old wizard ran down the steep stairs. Jack tried to think what he must do. He started toward the stairs intending to return the infant and follow the old man outside. But, as he looked up to the top of the stairs, another scream — from a different female — met him head on.

"What are you doing? What are you doing with my baby? Give her to me!"

Suddenly this woman flew down the stairs with her long, black hair billowing out behind her and such fury in her face that Jack found himself backing up! He knew trouble when he saw it.

"Whoa! Hold on! She's fine! I was just holding her so ye could rest!" "Give her to me! Get away!"

The woman plucked the infant from Jack's arms, shoving him back as she did so. In a moment, Jack had regained his footing, and stood still for a brief second. He could still feel the warmth left by the baby and it felt like such an emptiness now. How strange, he thought.

But, he had no time to dwell on this incident as the room was still vibrating, and he dashed out to see where the old man and Alex had gone. There were several sets of footprints in the snow, all leading to the stables, so he headed that way quickly.

Wabi had flown through the stable door without a thought as to what or who might be on the other side. He needed to find Caitlin, and then he would proceed from there. Once inside, however, he stopped in his tracks.

Commander Campbell was holding Caitlin at the edge of the well, his arm around her neck, threatening to break it if Wabi came any closer.

"Stop, old man. Nothing would please me more than to kill her now. And I will if you don't stop right where you are."

Wabi considered sending a bolt of lightning into that sinister man's insides, incinerating him completely. But, there was a chance Caitlin could be harmed as well, so he tried to reason with the soldier, all the while trying to get closer to them.

A few moments later, Jack reached the stable doors. He decided not to rush in, as he could hear voices being raised in anger. Hurriedly, he ran to the back side of the stable and entered the small door that the stable boys used. He crouched down behind one of the stalls and listened. He froze when he saw there was a confrontation going on and Caitlin was in trouble. He had enough experience to quickly drop down on his knees and find his way along the back side of the stalls. He listened for a moment and jumped straight up when someone touched him on the shoulder.

"Alex! Jesus, brother! You scared me to death!" Jack whispered.

Alex motioned to Jack to creep along the walls and come up behind them. Alex would very quietly climb to the loft and see from above. He had his pistol and knew how to use it. Jack nodded that he understood and began to move along the walls. That would bring him up behind the two at the well. Jack wasn't sure what he would do, but didn't figure the old man could help much. He listened as Wabi tried to reason with the soldier.

"Let her go, Commander. She's not a witch. She's only a healer without a wicked bone in her body. She can help you, still. Come. Let's go inside and have her tend you."

"She killed my son! My only son! She will pay, I tell you!" and he increased the pressure on Caitlin's neck causing her to gasp.

Hearing Caitlin's sound of distress, Wabi prepared to send his solution to this frightening situation and prayed Caitlin would break away, as the commander would not be able to hold on to her once the powerful surge entered his body.

Wabi lifted both his hands high in the air, muttering under his breath and watched helplessly as Caitlin's eyes closed, indicating she was close to losing consciousness.

The big Highlander watched as the old man started raising his hands, muttering. Jack was only about one foot behind the soldier and stepped forward, pulling the commander off his feet with one arm around the man's chest. The soldier abruptly dropped Caitlin as he tried to remove the enormous hand that was pulling him away from the witch!

Jack put his other arm around the man's neck, just as the soldier had held Caitlin, and began to squeeze slowly, causing excruciating pain to the already severely wounded neck. Jack hoped to cause the man to black out and then they would deal with him.

Just as he felt the man begin to struggle, he heard an ear-piercing sound, then the wind began to roar, and that was followed by a blinding light that filled the entire stable. At once Jack found himself thrown across the room, having dropped the soldier and landing rather unceremoniously on his arse in a pile of hay. There was a flash of animal fur flying through the air, then a loud growl as the wolf's fangs made contact with the soldier's neck. There was another agonizing scream, and a final whimper. And both came from the soldier.

"Jesus Christ!" yelled Jack. He felt like his brain was on fire and his hands burned as if he had stuck them into the flames of a brushfire.

***

As the soldier dropped Caitlin, the healer saw only blackness and then felt herself falling. . . falling . . . falling . . . and she screamed as pain came searing through her body. She had slipped over the edge of the well and landed on the buckets down below, with her left leg dipping down into the water. On the verge of passing out, she controlled her anguish long enough to call out.

"Uncle Wabi! Alex!"

***

Wabi lowered his arms, looked across the floor, and saw Jack sitting there, almost looking comical, as if in a stupor. Hopefully, he will snap to attention momentarily, prayed Wabi. But where was Caitlin?

"Caitlin!" he yelled and started for the well. Before he could get there, however, Alex was at the edge peering over the side. Caitlin had landed at the bottom of the well and was suspended on some of the buckets. And she was sobbing.

"Ah. She's crying, Alex. That's beautiful music to my old ears!" stated Wabi.

Alex made no comment, but continued climbing down the side of the well. Reaching the bottom, he called out to Wabi.

"Throw me a rope! I'll put it around her waist!" So, the old man dropped one of the ropes from the nearest bucket down to Alex.

"Ok. Now. Pull us up. Slowly!" Alex yelled.

Wabi had to think for a second. What was that big man's name? He had just met him last evening, or actually in the middle of the night, but that was all a bit blurry. Ah, yes, he thought, I remember now.

"Jack! Come help me pull them up!"

Wabi was aware that Jack was struggling to get up and probably still trembling as he had to have absorbed some of that bolt Wabi had sent to the soldier. Plus, Wabi knew the man didn't understand what he had just witnessed, so there would probably be some difficult questions to answer later. As for himself, Wabi was always weakened immensely after using his power. He needed Jack's help.

"I'm coming!" Jack called out as he got up and hurried to the well.

His knees were weak, but he began pulling the rope slowly, knowing if he and Wabi pulled too quickly Caitlin might be hurt even more. Jack was a strong man, but it took great effort on his part to pull Caitlin and Alex up from so far below. Wabi wasn't much help at this point.

Finally, they managed to get both to the top of the well. And both men were thoroughly exhausted. Alex climbed out and reached for Caitlin. He was again reminded how small she was. She was very much alive and reached out to him with both arms. Alex picked her up and wrapped his arms around her as if she were a precious package he never wanted to let go. She continued to sob and he held her closely all the while whispering softly to her.

"Ah, Cait. You're alright. You gave me a fright, my girl." Wabi sighed.

He stroked her cheek and relief could be seen on his face. He helped Alex lay her down on the stable floor and began to take inventory of possible injuries. After a quick assessment of Caitlin, Wabi decided she was in great pain, but not irreparably harmed. Now he needed to see about Jack as that man had to be in pain also.

"Jack. Here. Let's have a look at you, man. Where are you hurting? Let me see your hands. Can you speak?"

Wabi had felt he had no choice but to send the flaming bolt to force the soldier to release Caitlin. But he wished Jack had not grabbed the man at the same time. But, he had. So now Wabi must do whatever he could to help Jack.

Jack nodded.

"Well, yeah. Looks like I can talk. My hands are burning and stinging a bit, but nothing awful. But, I do believe my heart is working overtime!"

"Here. Let me see you hands. Open them."

Wabi took both Jack's hands in his and rubbed them slowly between his palms.

Immediately they began to lose the burning sensation and the stinging stopped.

"Your heart is just responding to the circumstance, Jack. It will get back to normal shortly."

***

Jack looked at the three of them, Alex, Caitlin and Wabi. He didn't begin to understand what he had just seen. Actually been a part of! But, he decided there were just some things he didn't want to know about, and would ask no questions. But, good Lord he hoped Alex knew what he was getting into if he continued chasing this woman. His life would never be the same again.

***

Wabi was thankful that Jack hadn't suffered any worse consequences from his experience. Now they needed to look at the soldier and see what was left to do with him.

One look at Commander Campbell, crumpled in a heap next to the well, told Wabi the man had finally gone on to whatever resting place his soul deserved. The wizard was certain it would be a lonely, desolate eternity for this one. Wabi touched Willie and gave him a signal to "release." All this while, Willie had kept the man's throat pinned in his jaws and would have stayed there as long as he possibly could have. For another minute or so, Willie still held on. "It's all right, Willie, he's done for. Let him go. You've finished him off this time."

Wabi stroked the great beast's head, and then the wolf let him go, reluctantly.

Alex sighed a breath of relief now that the soldier was no longer a threat to Caitlin. And Jack, too, began to feel better. But just as his heart had almost returned to its regular rhythm, he found it racing again in one quick moment. For out of the blue a loud voice shattered the quiet that had followed the events in the stable.

"Caitlin! Where are you? Answer me!"

Millie had taken her baby from the giant man and watched him as he rushed out of the castle. She, too, felt the vibration in the room and was frightened for her infant, as well as herself. But, never one to run from confrontation, but rather, always ran toward it, she found herself wrapping the babe and herself in a blanket and running toward the stables to see what was happening.

"Ah, Millie," said Wabi. "Do come here, child. All is well. Don't be afraid."

Wabi had an understanding of new mothers that came from observing animals in the wild. He had learned quickly you should NEVER interfere with a new mother and especially not her new pup, or fledgling, or kitten. It didn't seem to matter what the species, new mothers were just not to be tinkered with.

Millie came to Caitlin's side and kneeled down to look at her. Then, her voice changed, and it was almost a whisper. She looked at Alex.

"What is happening? I thought I heard a tornado, and a woman screaming, and there was a blinding light." Her cheeks were rosy from the cold, and her eyes flashed as she looked at the two men.

Jack could not take his eyes off the woman that had just entered the stable. He remembered the fire in her eyes as she came tearing down the stairs screaming like a banshee. There was so much determination in her face he thought she was going to attack him with all her might. But, of course, all she wanted was her child.

He looked at her still and could not stop staring. She was certainly beautiful and her voice belied the rest of her. The voice was soft, unlike the one she used when she screamed at him to give her babe to her.

He finally got to his feet as this vision came in his direction. He was not sure whether to run or stand his ground. Their last encounter was still fresh in his mind. She gently lay a hand on his arm and looked up at him. And her eyes were only a few inches below his.

"I do apologize. I do not usually behave in such an ill manner, but I thought you were taking my child. But, obviously, you are a friend of Caitlin's, so you are a friend of mine."

He had told Wabi he could talk, but at the moment his tongue didn't behave in its usual manner. Maybe the old man had fried it. Whatever, it didn't seem to have any connection to his brain, so he was mute for the moment. It was the first time he had ever met a woman who could look him in the eye without tilting her head at some great angle. And all six feet of her were breathtaking. Still unable to make any coherent response, he just nodded and looked back to Caitlin and Wabi.

Wabi had decided the first order of business would be to get Caitlin inside to find out what, exactly, her wounds might be. At the moment, she was being brave and only making the smallest noises that would indicate she was in pain. But, Wabi knew this woman. She always downplayed any illness or difficult predicament that befell her. It seemed to be a lifetime pattern with her.

Alex and Jack, too, could see Caitlin was in a bad way.

These men had seen enough wounds in battle to know she had a broken leg and maybe more issues than that, but of that they were certain. Alex very slowly lifted her and, with one look at Wabi, they had a moment of non-verbal communication. Wabi also saw the angle from which her left leg was jutting out. So, with a nod of his head, Alex lifted her body and Wabi tried to hold the leg up and keep it from falling below the level of her body. Even with their combined efforts, however, Caitlin let out a loud cry of anguish that was painful to everyone's ears. Millie was leading the way, trying to keep the baby covered and opening the door for the two men to come through, carrying their most precious cargo.

"Here, Alex. Let's put her here by the fire for the moment," Jack called.

They placed Caitlin on blankets in front of the fireplace in the great hall. At some point, however, it appeared Caitlin had lost consciousness and was as limp as a rag doll.

"Ah. She's out. That's good. Now we can set her leg without her being in such agony.

Alex, you hold her, tightly, and I'll give the leg a proper jerk. If we don't, it'll never heal properly, and she'll have limited use of it."

In another moment of silent communication, Wabi and Alex agreed this was a welcome event. This positioning of the leg was an extremely painful procedure for the patient. Wabi had set many legs for his animals over the years, and began at once to go about making sure Caitlin would have full use of her leg once the healing had completed. It was at moments like this he was so tempted to use some of his extraordinary powers. But, he knew nature would take care of this problem. He never used his powers unless there was no other solution. It was an agreement he had with the Creator.

Chapter 45

Lord Warwick had lost track of time.

"Good God! Did I lose a day somewhere? What day is this? Am I going the right way?"

The snow was still falling, and Lord Warwick wrapped his blanket tightly around his shoulders. His greatcoat was of the finest wool to be found in all of England. His Hessians were especially handmade for him; even his undergarments were of the best quality. In addition to his greatcoat, he had a woolen cape that reached to the ground and, presently, he was wrapped in it trying to stay warm. He was hoping to reach Millie's family soon as it was getting bloody cold out here and his backside was tired of sitting on this animal.

He had left his coach in a tiny village some ways back as one of the wheels had gotten stuck in a large rut and he, in his inebriated state, couldn't quite figure out how to manage it. So, with a few coins he was able to buy a decent horse from the farmer just across the bridge from where his coach sat stuck. Damn that coachman anyway! Just leaving him without a word! He'd take care of him when he got back to England. But, most probably the man would never show his face at Warwick Castle again. So be it. So, he had been on horseback for some time now and was ready for a rest.

He didn't know exactly what he might find when he arrived at the castle. Henri had reported to him the two women were taken care of, and he had not seen another soul when he was there. But, that didn't mean the place would be vacant when Lord Warwick arrived. For certainly, the morning after the women were "dealt with" as he thought of it, the household staff would come early to prepare food and run the household as usual. What would they think when they found the two bodies? Would the local law enforcement, whatever they might have, be looking into the matter? After all, two women smothered to death would cause quite a stir in a small village, and the entire populace would likely be afraid themselves.

"Well. Good. Let them be afraid. When the property is mine, they'll learn to be afraid of me as well." He believed if your servants and workers feared you, then they would never be stupid enough to cross you. Of course, it usually took at least one example of his punishment to make an impression on the staff. His father had tried to teach him you could gain loyalty by treating servants with respect and by being fair in your dealings with them. Warwick disregarded this advice as he had all other such ridiculous ideas his father had passed on to him. He had no doubt that a few whippings with the lash or a few days locked in the lower chambers, with only water, would gain him all the loyalty he required. Plus, he found these events to be quite pleasurable. But, of course, his stupid wife accused him of being an animal with no compassion for others.

"Well, I've had enough of her whining also. Once she has had my son, and I have possession of her lands and estate in Scotland, then I'll have her taken care of also. I wonder what old Sinclair will have to say about that!" He laughed a hollow laugh that lingered in the quiet of his surroundings, where no other person was to be found. Traveling alone was at least better than sitting in his vacant castle. Since Millie had left, the servants stayed as far away from him as possible, leaving him quite alone in the empty, hollow castle.

Warwick Castle was rather medium-sized, as far as castles go, but Lord Sinclair had led him to believe the Scottish estate was very large and the lands extensive. But, then of course, old Sinclair could well be bluffing about those holdings also. He had been known to exaggerate when speaking about his own personal wealth. Warwick had plenty of cash, but land was what was important in order to be recognized as a great lord.

Stopping and dismounting for a short while, just to give his back and legs a break, he broke out his flask and had several more gulps of his brew. His mind became even more clouded than usual. He felt sure he would find Millie at the Cameron castle, grieving for her grandmother and aunt. And, he would be understanding and promise to find whomever it was that had caused the deaths of her family. Certainly, she would realize she couldn't take care of herself and his son alone, so would be glad to see him and be ready to return to England and Warwick Castle. After all, she was only a woman and most dependent on him for her every bit of sustenance.

"Well, I'll be there shortly and have the necessary papers drawn up, and we'll be on our way home." He was not even aware he was speaking aloud and no one was listening, except the owl that had been following along the entire way.

Chapter 46

Millie was learning rather quickly how to take care of her bundle of joy. And this child did bring joy to Millie. Here was something that was hers, something that belonged to her. And she cherished this babe like all new mothers do.

She started back down the stairs after feeding the baby and making herself a bit more presentable. Of course, this was difficult as she only had a few items of clothing in her bag. But, she would make do. Sleep had done wonders for her, and she felt light as air. Even though she knew that was really not true, but being pregnant had made her feel so unwieldy and clumsy. It was heaven just to be able to bend over and lace her shoes. And, Caitlin and Wabi had been so kind to her. How would she ever repay them?

As she started down the stairs, with the babe sleeping on her shoulder, she stopped, remembering just earlier this morning when she discovered her child was gone. She had absolutely flown down these same stairs and screeched at the man holding her infant. As she saw in her mind's eye the same scene playing over again, she recalled that the giant was holding the babe in one large hand, and was saying something, something very soothing, and the small babe was snuggled up to his neck as if perfectly satisfied and at home. She smiled at the thought of this giant of a man, obviously at home with a babe in his arms. She was embarrassed when she remembered her actions at the time. Well, all seemed to have worked itself out, so she would try to keep her emotions on a tight rein after that incident.

Jack was a most capable man, apparently. He had taken care of the soldier and had helped Wabi set Caitlin's leg. Never once did he behave as if it were anything but usual for him. She must learn more about him. He was quite a man, now that she thought about it. His height alone would make him stand out in a crowd. And he certainly had an arrogance to that sharply chiseled jaw and nostrils that flared when he was excited, as well as blue eyes that had narrowed when she screamed at him. And his hair was almost as red as Caitlin's, and in need of a trim. And, had he blushed when he had seen her in the stable? What was that about?

Chapter 47

Wabi, Millie, Alex and Jack had all had their turn caring for Caitlin. As soon as she regained consciousness, Caitlin became the worst patient ever.

"Why did you not wait until I got back to my senses? I could have instructed you as to what needed to be done!"

The four of them just looked at each other and smiled indulgently, as they all knew she could not have done any better than they had, and so did Caitlin.

Wabi grinned, leaned down and kissed her on top of her head. Caitlin's behavior following any kind of ailment had not changed from the time she was a child. She had so disliked being cared for when she was small. Even then, she knew she was to be a healer and being on the receiving end of these ministrations was not to her liking.

"Ah, Caitlin. 'Tis great to see you feeling better," laughed Wabi.

He couldn't recall when he was so relieved. Just knowing the infernal soldier was no longer a threat to his niece brought peace to the old man. Now, perhaps, her life would get back to some sort of normalcy again.

After assuring himself that Caitlin was as comfortable as she could be, Wabi called a meeting of the five of them. They brought up chairs and made a circle around her in order that they could have a much needed meeting of the minds. Wabi watched quietly as Caitlin administered her own pain medication, and he saw that she was careful not to take too much. If he knew Caitlin, he knew she would actually rather have some pain than be totally addled on medication. As it was, he was glad she was alert and almost back to herself.

Leaning forward with his arms resting on his knees, his hands held together in a prayer- like fashion, Wabi started the conversation.

"It is most regrettable that a man lost his life today. I believe if one looks hard enough, one can usually find at least one redeeming quality about another to justify their being on this earth. And I have no doubt this man must have been given some worthwhile attributes at one time; however, it appears that life had taken much from him also and he had become unhinged, I do believe. Let us pray he is at peace."

With that, Wabi bowed his head momentarily, and then looked at the others. Then, he started up again.

"Let us also give thanks that you, Caitlin, no longer have to worry over some mad man pursuing you across the countryside. This ordeal is over and, perhaps, now you can get your life back on track and live it in peace. You must heal first, of course, but time will take care of that. So, where do we go from here? Back to Skye, I presume?" Wabi looked at the others hoping they may have some suggestions.

Wabi looked at the two brothers, Alex and Jack. They remained silent. Next he turned to Caitlin, who hesitated a moment, but finally responded.

"Oh. I haven't had time to give it much thought," she stammered, looking to Alex who was sitting next to her.

"But, Uncle Wabi, I'm not sure I should return to Skye, at least not just yet. I'm most grateful that Commander Campbell will no longer be at my heels, but there were numerous other young men that died also, all to malaria just as the commander's son. Might not some of them also think I was responsible? There is so much grief in this entire area, what with Culloden having happened so recently. It takes a long time for families to accept their loss, and some never do. I feel I should stay away for a while longer. Plus, if I return to Skye, Thomas will most certainly be searching for me. And probably that lord also. With those worries still out there, I think I'll move on to higher land. And, there is always need for a healer, so I know I can be of service somewhere."

Wabi looked at his very dear niece. For some reason, she had always felt she should serve mankind. This was surely the Creator's work. Wabi had cared for Caitlin most of her life and felt honored to have been chosen for that purpose. He had waited so long for her to come into her own, realizing her special status, and now it was time to allow her to do so, with only a little help from him. Yes, she could move along now, and he would fade into the background, but always be available.

"Caitlin. Always one to think rationally. Of course, I believe you should follow your intuition, as always. But, as to Thomas, when you see him next, I believe you will find a much changed man, and one more to everyone's liking."

Wabi looked next at Millie, who couldn't seem to stay seated. Wabi had watched as she had gotten up and down several times in the last few minutes. Saying she was anxious would be an understatement. She pulled at a long strand of hair that fell over her shoulder. It had curled slightly from her constantly wrapping it around her finger. And, the more anxious she got, the more the baby seemed to squirm in her arms. Obviously, the babe could sense the unrest in her mother.

The wizard was not surprised when Jack stepped in, and was actually pleased to watch the interactions between the two.

"Here, Millie." Jack looked directly into her eyes and held out both hands, in supplication maybe, and she returned his look. Wabi knew Millie was not sure what he was asking. Was he asking to hold the babe? Jack nodded to her.

"May I hold that little midge again?" Millie smiled at him and handed the small, squirming body over to him. Jack brought the child up to his neck, again, and by the look on his face it was obvious to Wabi that the Highlander had taken in the scent that was unique to babes. The wizard had seen this same reaction in the animal world also. Mother Nature had a way of creating a smell that makes all infants alluring to others, but he found it especially interesting that Jack was taken in so easily. The female will almost always respond, but the male sometimes takes longer. But not this time. Jack obviously was more than just a large physical man; he apparently was rather special also. The child let out a sigh and snuggled closer to Jack's neck.

Wabi understood, whether anyone else did or not, that these three were destined for many more interactions.

Wabi had to keep himself from getting up and coming to Millie's assistance. She began to pace again, and Wabi smiled as Jack found a way to help her without being obvious. The big man went to the stove and brought over a pot of tea and poured everyone a cup, easily holding the little lass with one very large hand on her back and pouring the tea with the other.

"My mam thought a 'cuppa' would soothe anyone's nerves," said Jack, and Wabi thought that may just be the thing now. He studied Millie as she sat down and held the cup in both hands. How many times had he done the same thing? He watched as the warmth from the cup seeped into her body, easing some of the tension. Ah, Jack to the rescue again, thought Wabi.

***

Millie looked at Caitlin, Wabi, Alex and finally to Jack. He nodded to her, and she understood he was trying to help her put words to her feelings.

"I hardly know where to start," she began.

"As it is, I appear to have put you all in a very precarious position, and I would never have done so willingly." Her voice was beginning to crack, and she feared she might break down into tears at any moment.

"This castle and estate belong to my mother's family, members of the Cameron clan. It is a place I visited many times when I was a child. But, in the last three years, I have had no correspondence from my grandmother or my aunt, the only ones that were living when I last heard from them. My grandfather, Laird Cameron, passed away several years ago, and Aunt Moira, my mother's sister, was running the estate with the help of some workers and ladies who have been here most of their lives. But, when I married, some three years ago, I lost contact with them. I have written, many times, but I never had a reply. Only recently has it finally dawned on me that my husband Edward, Lord Edward Warwick, probably disposed of any letters from them."

"It's a very complicated predicament, but, you see, I am fleeing my husband, an abusive man, whom I will no longer tolerate. I was coming here in hopes that I might find safety away from him and have a place to live with my child."

Taking a deep breath she continued, "But, I don't know what to make of what we find here. The whole place has apparently been deserted for some weeks, perhaps. Where has everyone gone? Where are Grandmother and Aunt Moira? Why is there no one here at all?"

"And does your husband know you have come to your family's home?" Alex asked. He had kept silent as long as he could. The longer he listened to Millie, the more he feared for Caitlin as well as Millie.

"I left in the middle of the night while he was gone to London for a meeting, along with my father. He didn't know I was leaving, but certainly he knows how unhappy I've been. He sees me only as a possession and one who can bring him more lands and an estate in Scotland. Once he returns and finds I'm gone, he'll either send some of his men to look for me, or maybe even come himself, although I'm not sure he would put that much personal effort into the task. But, he thinks that a son will bring him even more riches, so he'll be seeking me for that reason if nothing more."

"He would use his child as a pawn?" inquired Jack.

"What kind of man would be so callous as to do such a thing?"

"He'll do anything to increase his wealth, even use his child. But, in that respect he is in for an unwelcome surprise, for he does not have a son; rather, he has a daughter, which to his thinking will mean another useless female to care for. He won't be interested in her whatsoever." She smiled when she delivered this news.

***

Wabi saw Caitlin sit up straighter, clearly concerned, and with a quizzical look on her face.

"Millie. Did you say your husband's name is Warwick? Lord Warwick?"

"Yes, Caitlin. Lord Edward Warwick. Someone I never wish to see again! He's a very despicable person, and I will not live with him any longer."

Wabi had been listening and had already realized who this gentleman was, the same lord that was in league with Thomas back on Skye. The same lord that may well be after Caitlin still!

Wabi decided to take over as Caitlin was reeling from this latest news.

"Well. We've got a new problem, I'm afraid. Millie, Lord Warwick may also be seeking to find Caitlin, so we must come up with some plan. What if his men or even he comes here? What will he do? Would he harm you or the child?" asked Wabi.

Millie started pacing again. "Why would he seek Caitlin?"

"It's a very long story Millie, but it seems that Lord Warwick made some deals with an innkeeper in Skye and Caitlin overheard their plans regarding capturing Jacobite sympathizers and seizing their properties. So, the innkeeper and the lord have been searching for her. I've taken care of the innkeeper, Thomas, but Lord Warwick seems to still be looking for her. So, you see, even though Commander Campbell is no longer a threat, your husband still is."

"No! Oh, I've been such a fool! Coming here would only have put my family in danger. I wasn't thinking straight, obviously, but I had nowhere else to go. My father was as bad as Edward, so I couldn't go back there. And now, you all have taken care of me and my child and you're in danger too. What have I done?"

Chapter 48

Wabi's first inclination was to take them all to the Isle of Skye where he could keep an eye on them. But, again, he must let Caitlin walk her path, wherever it might take her.

The old man walked over to stand next to Jack at a large window that looked out onto the moor. There were a few crofter's huts and a dozen or so sheep ambling about. The snow was deep and the sheep burrowed their black faces into the ground, hoping to find anything that might be edible underneath the frozen snow. Wabi could almost feel Jack's mind working as the man struggled to come to a decision.

"Da, Hector, Uncle Andrew and old Jamie are all keeping the place going while me and Alex are away. And I know they have their hands full. But they wouldn't even think of leaving two women and a child to fend for themselves, and neither will we."

Some of Jack's earliest memories were of Mam and Da, sitting with them outside on the porch and listening to them talk about a neighbor, Mrs. Finlayson, an old woman who lived alone. She was unable to care for herself anymore, and no relations seemed to come to her aid. Mam brought the woman into their home and cared for her until she passed away. It was "what any caring person should do," Mam had said, then Da had chimed in, "We should treat family like friends, and friends like family."

The two Highlanders knew exactly what they must do. They would never leave two defenseless women to fend for themselves. Well, maybe not totally defenseless, Jack thought, remembering

Caitlin's wolf, and Millie's temper. But, it was time for them to get these women to safety.

Usually Alex made most decisions related to family affairs. But, just now, walking around the room, rubbing the baby's back gently, Jack began.

"Well, I don't know if ye want my ideas, but if I may offer one suggestion?"

"It seems to me Caitlin has been given a reprieve from the soldier, but both she and Millie are in some danger from Warwick still. I don't want to be presumptuous, but it could be a good move on our part to get ourselves together quickly and head on to MacKinnon land. It's not so far now, only a day or so if we stay with it. Once there, there are plenty of farm hands and family to come to our aide if we need. Plus, it's pretty difficult to find our place, which is an advantage."

Wabi liked Jack's idea very much. This way, Caitlin would be protected as well as Millie. And, according to Owl, this man called Alex was intent on making Caitlin a part of his life. And from Owl's account, he was a most decent man, one that honored family above all else, as did Wabi. What more could he want for Caitlin? More gossip from Owl indicated there was great chemistry between the two. But Wabi knew from personal experience that such chemistry could also make for fireworks in other areas as well.

Wabi still stood next to Jack. The scene outside was one of peace and calm, very unlike the one inside.

"Jack. As for me, I think that your idea is a very fine one. If you and Alex are willing to take on two women, or three as it is, then I would be most agreeable and personally thankful. If you need me, then I will gladly accompany you. But if not, then I believe I might be of more assistance if I continue my walkabout and go back to Skye. As it is, you never know who I might meet along the way."

Jack was still unsure what this old man truly was. But, no matter, he took care of his niece and finished off a most despicable soldier, something Jack was glad of. He had not forgotten the sparks flying through the air, and the noise, and the sizzle that went through his brain. But, his heart knew the old man was a good soul. So, accepting that some things were beyond his comprehension, he accepted all this and put any more thought of it aside. As for being concerned about the old man going back to Skye alone, Jack pitied anyone who might try to do battle with him.

Millie looked at her new friends.

"Jack, I'm aware that my concern for my babe may be clouding my judgment. But you all owe me nothing. And I'll only bring danger to you and your family. You are too generous for your own good. But, I can only speak for myself, Caitlin may not feel the same way. Surely, I can get away from Warwick some way without involving so many others."

Jack handed the babe back to Millie. He just looked at her, standing there with her small infant, both of them just pawns in some horrid lord's diabolical plan. He would take care of them and would listen to no more protestations from any of them. Taking Millie by the shoulders he began to speak, slowly and calmly.

"Millie, danger is a constant when you live in the Highlands. You learn to accept its challenges, and you become stronger each time you face it. This is something I must do. Please help me with this task."

Alex stood there, having weighed as much information as he could. He coughed, a sure way to get attention.

"Jack, I like your plan as well. But I'd like to make one small change. It seems to be that none of us are safe as long as Warwick is out there. Now, there are only three paths that lead from the Culloden area up this way, and the same ones continue up to our place. I'm thinking that if Wabi travels one of those and I go back on the other, one of us is bound to run across Warwick."

"You could take the ladies north while Wabi and I go back down. Then I'll catch up with you all at the crofter's hut on the edge of our property. I'll move much faster than you'll be able to, so I might be there shortly after you are. Wait overnight, and if I'm not back, then you go on home. But, I'm tired of running from this idiot. It's time we changed the situation." Everyone nodded their agreement with Alex's addition to the plan.

Wabi spoke with Caitlin, alone, for some time, then gathered his belongings and his crooked staff and started down the path, with Owl following along overhead. The two old friends conversed for a few minutes, then the owl took wing and headed back in the direction of the castle. Wabi was willing to let Caitlin make her own decisions, but he still wanted to be aware of any happenings that might warrant his attention.

Chapter 49

The goings on at the castle last night and this morning had not gone unnoticed. Old Clint still lived in one of the crofter's huts located on the back side of the moor and, as had always been his habit, he walked to the crest of the moor overlooking the estate and took in the scenery every evening before he retired. He may have never owned any part of this land, but his soul was embedded in it as surely as if he were the owner. And, the old Laird and the Mistress had always treated Clint and all their workers as part of the Cameron family. So, anything that happened here didn't just affect the Cameron's, but all those attached to this place. His mind went immediately to the terrible event of late. He supposed his memory of that day would never leave him.

***

When the two young parlor maids arrived at the castle that morning, they went up to the bed chambers to awaken the ladies before bringing the early morning tea. They knocked lightly, as always, and entered the bedroom of Mistress Cameron and Mistress Moira, like all other days. Upon discovering the women dead in their respective beds, the two of them dissolved into hysterics. They had run down the stairs and out into the bailey, screaming to the top of their lungs. The two old farm hands came running, and found the girls crying uncontrollably and not making much sense, or so it seemed to them.

Old Clint got there first and took one of them by her shoulders, forcing her to be still and look at him. "Hold now, Susie. Gwendolyn! Hold now. Quiet. What's happened?" he asked, being the older of the two farmhands.

"Oh, Mister Clint, they be lying perfectly still! Neither of them is breathin', I tell ye! And, the Mistress Moira! She still has a pillow over her face! Someone has done taken they lives!"

Leaving the girls in the capable hands of Winston, Old Clint slowly walked up the stairs to see for himself. Susie and Gwendolyn had been here for some time now, but they were both very young and tended to have emotional bouts over just about anything. So, he thought to find they had probably exaggerated the entire event.

But, having seen much in his time, Clint could feel the emptiness even before he entered the bedroom where he knew the older Mistress Cameron slept. Somehow, when there is life in a room, one can feel the energy — that is, if one pays attention. And, there was no energy at all in this room. He looked about, saw the Mistress' body on the bed and then retreated, quietly closing her door. Walking to the next door, Mistress Moira's room, he paused before turning the knob.

When the door was just slightly open, the same emptiness hit him in the face again. "Oh, dear Lord, why would someone harm these ladies?" he asked himself.

One quick glance told him that the girls had seen the unbelievable calamity as it truly was, a most gruesome scene. He hung his head and sent a prayer to whomever might be listening.

Coming back down the stairs, he looked over to Winston, the other farmhand, with a quick nod of his head.

"Winston, take them to the kitchen and have Ethel make some tea. That'll do more for them than about anything else."

Winston then took the young girls and started to lead them to the kitchen. Tea would soothe them, he thought, when nothing else would. Some traditions serve well when they are needed.

The cook took one look at the girls and Winston, then quickly got about the tea. "Whatever has happened, Winston?" She, a rather hefty woman who kept her kitchen staff on their toes, wiped her hands on her apron and poured the liquid into the cups. She had been cooking for the Cameron family for many years now and was about to get the breakfast ready for the ladies upstairs.

"Oh, Ethel, 'tis a very sad day, I'm a thinkin," he replied.

As he explained what was happening, Ethel sat down at her kitchen chair and covered her face with her hands. She must not let tears start just yet, she knew. Likely, the others would be looking to her to keep her wits about herself and help them all get through this terrible ordeal.

She would save her tears for later, and there would be many of them no doubt. So, with that thought, she straightened her cap and her apron and gathered herself together.

Taking a deep breath and rising from her chair, she spoke to Winston. "Then, there's work for me to do. Vittles will need to be prepared."

There would need to be food for a crowd and she must get busy with her task of having it all ready. She walked over to the larder to gather her ingredients and all but fell over the body of the young girl lying in the floor.

"Oh. No! No! Clint! No!" Ethel ran from the larder and ran directly into Winston. "They've gone and kilt Mariah too! She's in there. In me larder! Oh, what should we do?" Ethel was not one given to dramatic scenes, but even she was shaken by the latest discovery.

Clint came running when he heard Ethel screaming.

"What's wrong, Ethel?"

"Clint. In the larder. Mariah. They've done kilt her too!"

She was sobbing loudly and finally sat down in her kitchen chair. This morning would forever be remembered by all who were there.

Of course the local law enforcement, which was just the parish constable, made an official inquiry, but was unable to discover any clues that would help him learn who had committed these atrocities. With nowhere else to turn, they tried to find out if there was more family to be notified of the untimely deaths of the Cameron ladies. They all racked their brains trying to figure out who they should contact. Surely there was family left somewhere!

As it turned out, old Clint remembered a local girl, Dorothea, had gone to England to serve as nursemaid to old Laird Cameron's oldest daughter, Louise, who married Lord Sinclair of England. When Louise had given birth to a daughter, she sent word to her family here in Scotland to please send her someone to help her with the baby. And, so, Dorothea went south and stayed for many years, long after the time a nursemaid would have been needed. Then, just a few years ago, she had returned to the village without much explanation as to why she had come home. Perhaps she could help them locate any remaining family.

The constable was pleased to have found Dorothea and now, after he had brought her up to date with the latest events, he needed her help.

"Dorothea. Would you please write once more? I can't tell you how important it is that we find Lady Millie."

"Yessir. I'll write. But don't expect anything in return. I've written many times in the past three years, but never had a response from Lady Millie. That husband of hers most likely destroys all mail addressed to milady. He's a right awful man, ye ken!"

Chapter 50

Dorothea had written the letter to Lady Millie as she had promised the constable she would. Just thinking about the day Lady Millie was separated from her was still a painful memory for her. She could remember every detail of it still . . . . .

***

Dorothea stood watching as the coach carrying Lady Warwick started down the path, the driver lashing out again and again at the team of horses that were given the task of pulling the weight of a large coach and going as fast as they could. The faster they went, hopefully, the less the blistering lash would be used on them.

She stood there long after the coach was out of sight and her charge taken away from her.

Certainly she knew that Lady Millicent Sinclair Warwick didn't need a nursemaid, but she had taken care of her since she was a small baby, and the bond they shared could never be broken, no matter how far apart they might find themselves. Lady Millicent had loved her mother, Lady Sinclair, but the closeness she shared with Dorothea was uncommon. Millie never thought of Dorothea as a servant, but rather, as a loving person who always brought out the very best in others and one who had spent a lifetime in the service of this family. Never once had Millie heard her complain about having no life of her own outside the castle. Dorothea still had family in Scotland, had visited them numerous times over the years, but she was most happy when she was caring for Millie.

Of course, Dorothea was totally at the mercy of Lord Warwick now that Millie was gone.

So, she was greatly relieved when he wasted no time in telling her to pack her bags. The very next day after Millie was taken, Dorothea was roughly thrown inside a coach, much like the one that had taken Millie, and transported back to her own country, Scotland. The trip took some time as the roads were merely paths, and the coach lumbered across the moors as if it could feel the reluctance of its occupant to return to her home. It wasn't that she didn't want to see her family, but Millie was more like a daughter than a charge, and Dorothea had such an emptiness inside now that she could not fathom ever being able to fill.

Of course, time passed and the world went on, whether Dorothea wished it or not. And, as it was, Dorothea was content presently, for she had found herself in demand once again. She was needed to help care for another child. The local vicar had known about Dorothea returning, and just shortly after her return, he had petitioned her to care for an orphaned child.

***

Upon entering the sanctuary early one morning, preparing for morning prayers, the vicar discovered, to his amazement, a small child sitting on the floor, its thumb stuck in its mouth and seemingly taken with the sunbeams of light that were coming through the stained glass window above the crucifix. He picked the child up and took it back inside where the warmth from the fireplace could bring some comfort to this child who was wearing only a long dress, almost like he would expect to see at a christening. The child was not wearing any shoes, and the vicar held his hands around the small little toes, which felt like small shards of ice attached to feet that were just as cold. But, the child made no sounds to indicate it was uncomfortable in any way. It just smiled up at the vicar and drooled down the front of its dress.

The vicar was accustomed to caring for people in need, but an infant was totally beyond his scope. Being unmarried himself, he needed to find a caregiver for the child, and immediately thought of Dorothea.

Yes, Dorothea could remember every detail vividly — even today.

Chapter 51

Now, on this bitter, cold morning, Clint was up early as always, making his usual trek around the property, when he saw smoke coming from two chimneys at the castle. After watching for a short time, he caught sight of someone, a man he thought, making his way to the stable. The man was limping and having difficulty moving about. Clint made a decision to watch a bit longer before coming to any conclusions that could prove to be erroneous. But, for someone to be inside the castle was most unexpected.

Word had gotten around the village about the deaths of the Cameron women, and fear began to raise its ugly head. Most of the village women were afraid to go anywhere alone, or even to go outside without someone with them. The staff at the castle were truly frightened out of their wits. Even the cook, Ethel, had left, fearing she might be next. The young girls went home to their families and had not come back again.

That only left Clint and Winston to do whatever they could. There really wasn't a whole lot to do anymore, since the Mistress had sold most of the sheep to a farmer in the upper regions of the Highlands. Clint and Winston looked after the few horses that were left, fed and watered them, and as there were still numerous chickens running about the yard, they fed them and kept water in the trays for them.

When the two mistresses were alive, they didn't require much and had enough resources to keep the castle working and paying the help was not an issue. Most of all, they kept the "family" together and would have continued to until their passing. Clint had assumed Mistress

Moira would inherit the place, and after her, then the granddaughter, Millie, in England. They had all thought that was still some time off, but all that had changed in just one evening.

Clint wondered what would happen to the place. He and Winston would continue as best they could, but someone would need to take over and see the place was cared for, and if they couldn't find Mistress Millie, then he just couldn't see how he and Winston could make it work. He lived in one of the crofter's huts, as did Winston, but that belonged to the estate and he would have no means by which to live anywhere else.

By his age, Clint had weathered many difficulties before, and would not allow himself to dwell too long on this as he had learned long ago that each day would take care of itself. You must see where it takes you before deciding whether to go along with it or whether to make your own choices, however limited they may be.

Clint continued to watch from his vantage point somewhat higher than the stable. Just a little later, he watched as a woman, a very small woman with bright red hair and wearing some kind of breeches, crossed the distance from the castle to the stable. She, too, entered and pulled the door to behind her. Now who could they be? And a woman wearing a man's clothing? Surely they must be kin of some kind, thought Clint. But, he didn't know the family nearly as well as another one did, Dorothea.

With that thought in mind, he hooked up the mare to a small cart and started out. This old girl was the one he had ridden home every evening for many years now. In fact, Clint wasn't sure who was older, himself or the mare. He trotted the old gal out of the paddock and across the little bridge that spanned the stream running next to his hut. The old horse snorted her displeasure at having to get moving on such a cold morning, but she finally accepted he wouldn't let up on that little stinging whip until she did.

"Yeah. Well, I'm not too fond of gettin' up and out here meself. So, on with ye now." And he snapped the reins once again.

***

Clint reached the cottage behind the vicarage, where Dorothea and her little boy, Garry, lived. He had visited here before and knew her cottage was small but every inch was spotless. She had such a green thumb, and flowering plants, herbs and various sorts of greenery could be found in every room. Clint knew that anything in Dorothea's care was fortunate.

"Clint? Come in." Dorothea opened the door widely and closed it quickly as it was even colder this morning than when she went to bed. Her small fireplace was more than adequate to keep the entire place warm, and she and her boy were comfortable here. When Dorothea had agreed to take the little boy, she had no idea what his name was, so she decided she would call him Garry, the name of a young man she had known long ago. And, it fit the little boy perfectly as he was a happy child. Dorothea doted on him as she had Lady Millie. The difference here was that Dorothea was the only mother this child would ever know, and Dorothea loved him as if he were her own.

"Whatever brings you out on this cold day?" she asked.

She had known Clint all her life, and knew he didn't usually make house calls. So, she was most apprehensive about this visit.

"Oh, Dorothea, I hate ta bother ye again, about the castle and all that's happened. I know ye've written Mistress, er, Lady Millie, and I guessed she didn't write ye back, eh?"

"That's right, Clint. I didn't ever hear from her, but then I didn't expect to. You just can't know what a miserable husband she has to live with. It's such a sad story, and she was such a wonderful child, and woman."

"Well, I need to ask ye to come to the castle with me. There are some folks there now, and I don't rightly know that I would even recognize Mistress, er, Lady Warwick, Millie, if I saw her. But, then, it may not be her either. This morning I saw a man go into the stables. Then a few minutes later, a small little lady, with this fiery red hair followed him, it seemed to me. And, there was smoke coming from two chimneys. So I don't know rightly what we may find, but I wondered if ye would go with me to try and find out who they could be."

"Oh, my. You think it may be Lady Millicent?" "Who else could it be?"

"Do you think we should get the parish constable to go with us?"

"Well, I dunno. I only saw a man and a woman this morning. I'm not sure, but he seemed to be limping. Or at least moving slow like."

"I see. What if we ask Winston to come too? I would feel better if there are at least as many of us as there are of them. Just a man and a woman you say?"

"Ye got a point there. Alright. We'll get Winston and go over there. That can't be too dangerous I don't believe. And we must go, because no one else will, that's fer sure! As it is, none of the castle staff will go back into the house since the murders. 'Cept me and Winston."

After stopping at the crofter's hut to pick Winston up, Clint, Dorothea, and little Garry started out in the cart on their way to the castle. They were all a bit anxious, but went on in spite of it.

Chapter 52

With the decision made for Wabi and Alex to travel back, they all put their heads together to make their plans. Wabi agreed that the ladies and child should go with Jack and he would make his way back along the trail on the east side. Maybe he would come upon Warwick. If so, he would make short work of taking care of him. Alex would take the path that led through Tate's Hell, not a path that was used often as men had been known to go in there and never come out again.

"Let's hope Warwick did go through Tate's Hell — probably where he needs to be anyway," said Alex. There were nods of agreement all around.

So, with a long hug for Caitlin and another for his new friends, Millie, Jack and Alex, Wabi was on his way. Both he and Alex needed to get moving.

***

Alex was loathe to leave Caitlin so soon after just finding her. But running from some blasted soldier just didn't sit well with him. So, he got his small pack together and readied himself to ride out with Wabi. He looked over at Caitlin, sitting in a chair with her leg resting on another. How had he ever been so lucky as to find this woman?

"Caitlin. I'm leaving now with Wabi. You're in good hands with Jack. He'll take care of all of you. I trust him totally."

"Aye. I know, Alex. He's already shown me what he's made of. Just you be careful and come back to me." A look passed between the two that they both understood.

Millie was not yet convinced this was a good plan, her going with them. She was reluctant to put them in even more danger.

"I don't think we have a lot of choice, Millie," Jack responded. "We don't know for sure who killed your family members, but they could be out for ye, too. And yer husband or his men are sure to come here looking for ye. I would do my best to protect ye, but there is only one of me and no telling how many men he may send. Our farm will give ye protection. Trust me."

"But, how are we ever going to travel with Caitlin nursing a broken leg?" asked Millie.

She was still having some difficulty getting around herself. Having a baby did leave one lacking in energy, and she could use a few more days to heal also.

Jack observed that Caitlin had sat, saying nothing, which was most unusual for her. He was sure she understood the predicament they were in and realized he was right. They must move on and quickly.

"Jack, do you think you could rig up some sort of bed, like you did for Ian, for me to travel on?"

"What kind of bed is that? A traveling bed?" asked Millie.

Jack explained what Caitlin was suggesting and before he could finish, Millie stopped him.

"You don't need to do that. There used to be a cart that we hooked to the ponies when we were children. It would be plenty large enough for Caitlin to ride in, and perhaps she could hold the babe also. Look in the back part of the stable. It was kept in a large open room with several other wagons. Maybe it's still there."

Jack liked this idea, and it would save a lot of precious time. So, he quickly went outside and found his way to the rear of the stables. There, just as Millie had described, was the pony cart. It was a little worn to be sure, but good enough for their purposes.

As he was about to enter the door at the kitchen entry, he saw a small wagon pulling up at the front. There were two men and a woman with a small child. He hurried inside and locked the door behind him.

Calling out to Millie, he ran to the great hall where both the women were warming at the fireplace.

"Millie. There's someone here. They just pulled up in the yard."

"I'll see who it is," said Millie.

"No. Let me go." Jack didn't want Millie to open the door to anyone without him being there first.

The two men and the woman came up the steps and rapped the door with the large brass knocker.

"Who's there?" asked Jack, not venturing to open the door to anyone just yet. "It's Dorothea. And Clint and Winston," said a female voice.

Before Jack could say anything, Millie had come forward and thrown the door wide open.

"Dorothea! Is it really you?" Millie towered over the older woman, and wrapped her in a hug that almost cut off her breath. Dorothea still looked the same. A few more gray hairs mixed in with the dark ones, but still wore the same loving expression Millie remembered always.

"Oh, my Lady Millicent! It is you! Oh, what a relief!"

Millie held the woman at arm's length and just stared at her.

"Dorothea. Please come in. And Clint! And Winston!" Another hug for the men also. She had never been so glad to see anyone as she was to see these people from her past.

"And who is this?" The little boy had grabbed his mother's skirt and was holding on for dear life.

Millie smiled at the little lad, with his sandy colored hair which was thick and curled about his ears. Millie knew Dorothea would have been ever so careful when she trimmed it.

"Oh, milady, this is Garry. He's my son," stated Dorothea, as proudly as if she had birthed him.

"Oh, Dorothea, how wonderful!" And she put an arm around the small boy.

Insisting they come in, she ushered them to the kitchen where Caitlin rested with her leg on a chair, holding the baby. Jack introduced himself, and old Clint remembered the young man had come with a brother and bought the sheep when the mistress decided to let them go.

Everyone started to talk at once, and Jack had great difficulty following the conversation, as did Caitlin.

But, once they got down to discussing the family situation, Millie could not believe what had transpired.

"They were just smothered in their beds?" Millie could not believe this could have happened, or that anyone could be so cruel. Tears were threatening to spill over any moment.

"Aye, milady, it is so. But, so far, we have no way of finding out who might be responsible for committing such crimes. The mistresses were greatly cared about in this region. And, of course, the estate provided employment for many villagers. Now, what is to happen to the place and the people? But, we're so glad to have ye here. The place would be yers now, wouldn't it?" Clint stated it more as a statement of fact rather than a question. He was standing in the hallway with his tam in his hand, having removed it immediately upon seeing Lady Millicent. His sparse hair was standing on end and his ears had reddened from the cold. Millicent asked them all to sit, but Clint knew better than to sit in the presence of a lady!

Millie was in shock, most certainly. But, as much as she didn't want to believe it, she knew immediately who had committed these atrocious crimes.

"Yes. Yes, he would be so cruel." She seemed to be speaking to herself as she was staring out into space.

Millie looked over at Jack. He had walked to the window, holding the baby close, looking out. Then he turned back to Millie. She searched his face, trying to find the words to say to him to make him understand her dilemma.

"Jack. Caitlin. We must go. Now! Edward would not hesitate for a moment to do the same to any of us." She was trembling and certainly struggling to keep her composure.

"Oh, milady. Do you truly think even he is that evil?" Dorothea came close and put her arms around her, just as she always had.

"Yes, Dorothea. You know he is." "Oh, aye. I would not put it past him."

Jack was worried about all of them, and now, also about the two old men, Clint and Winston and the woman, Dorothea. The best thing he could do would be to get the women as far away as possible, as quickly as possible.

"Millie. Let's get going. Now."

Jack nodded to the men, motioning for them to come outside with him.

"Take Dorothea and the child and leave immediately. Hopefully, Warwick will not come, but Millie and Dorothea seem to think he is capable of doing most anything. "

"I'll take Millie and Caitlin and the baby with me to my home in the higher region. They'll be safer there than anyplace I can think of. And I've got brothers and uncles and others that will see they stay safe."

"Aye, I think ye be reading the situation rightly, young man," Old Clint shook his head in agreement.

"I think we should all leave and try to keep out of the way of this murdering fool.

Meanwhile, we'll tell the constable what's happened. Maybe he'll find enough help to stop this madman."

∗∗∗

Millie was torn between keeping her child safe and caring for these people who had depended on her family for years. Yes, the estate would be hers now, but until Warwick was stopped, she knew she had no choice but to go with Jack. She further knew that Warwick could buy off anyone trying to stop him.

"Dorothea, you must leave at once, all of you. He could be here any moment now. We will all leave immediately also. And if there is any way I can return, I will! Just take care of yourselves. But know I will find you again!"

Chapter 53

Alex and Wabi walked to the stable together. They both were torn between wanting to stay with Caitlin and keep her safe and knowing they must leave and try to find Warwick. Alex had never cared much for running from a problem. In his opinion, facing a problem head on was a quicker and more satisfying way of doing most anything.

Alex saddled his favorite horse, Zeus, and Wabi had opted to go on foot. Looking around, Alex frowned.

"What is it, Alex?" asked Wabi.

"Don't see Campbell's body."

"Well. Clint probably sent the farm boys over early and took care of it. Never been so glad to see the last of anyone. He was indeed a most evil man." Wabi replied.

Wabi looked at Alex as they reached the fork where they would part ways.

"Alex. Take care now. I'm sure you can handle any situation with Warwick, but he's bound to have a few tricks up his sleeve. Be careful. If I find him, rest assured he will no longer give us any trouble. But if I don't run across him, I'll be on my way home to Skye. I'm quite sure Caitlin is in good hands. You and Jack have shown me that much. But, if you ever need me, Caitlin knows how to get in touch with me. We'll see each other again — of that I'm sure."

"Aye. And ye be careful too, Wabi. Caitlin needs ye. We all do. See ye later."

Alex spurred his horse on. He was anxious to get this chore completed. He had watched Wabi until he was out of sight. He didn't know much about this old man, but knew enough to realize what an important part he had played in Caitlin's life and how much she cared for him. Funny, thought Alex. You never seem to realize how much the old ones mean until they are gone— and he smiled as his mind brought up a picture of Mam.

Alex was going the opposite direction from Wabi, towards the path that led through an area known as Tate's Hell. It was probably more legend than truth, but the old folk told stories of men going into the woods there and never being seen again. Alex wasn't much on legends without proof, but he knew the area was especially wooded, and hunters talked of hearing howling at night, but never were able to find any animal that made that particular sound. More legend for sure, thought Alex. He also knew there was a loch somewhere deep inside the area. He, himself, had never traveled through there before, but thought that might be the way Warwick would have come. It was actually the shortest route, but again, most folk that knew about it used one of the other paths.

When Warwick had left Alex's fire, just a couple of nights ago now, he was certainly drunk enough to have lost his way, and could have easily taken the wrong turn in the dark in his state. Yes. He most probably did get lost in Tate's Hell.

Alex made his way through some of the thickest brush and woods he had ever tried to go through. He swatted at flies, midges and some of the biggest ants he had ever seen had crawled up his legs.

"Jesus! I've seen ants before, but you bunch are twice the size of any I've ever seen!" He brushed them off, but they left some stinging in their wake.

By late afternoon, Alex was pretty sure Warwick had not come this way after all. The Highlander was a fairly decent tracker, and he had yet to find any tracks.

"Well then. I'll go back and make another stop at the castle, just in case someone there has learned anything. Maybe Clint and Winston will have some news." Zeus, his favorite steed, shook his withers and snorted briefly.

Alex had just come along the bank of the loch which was, indeed, very deep inside the woods. He stopped, dismounted, and walked to the edge. He let Zeus have a drink, and he bent down and washed his face in the cold water. His reflection showed him that he was in need of a haircut and shave. Well. They would just have to wait. He stood back up and pulled the horse away from the water, ready to ride again. But, as he pulled, Zeus shied away and let out a cry that Alex had never heard from the animal.

"Whoa boy. Whoa now! What's got ye so riled up?" Zeus was very even tempered and not a horse that spooked easily.

Alex stood very still and listened. He heard nothing for several minutes. Then, an eerie sound got his attention. A mournful howl coming from somewhere across the loch. The horse stomped and jerked back again, as if trying to get away from the sound.

"Hold on. Hold on, now." Alex tightened his hold on the reins and pulled the horse's head down so he could stroke his forehead.

"Easy boy. It's just a coyote, or wolf. Nothing to worry about. Easy now."

So. The legend was real — or some of it anyway. Howling sounds didn't bother Alex. But he did mount up and move on rather quickly.

He took a short cut, he hoped, around the loch and came out on the other side. As he got to the edge of the water, Zeus suddenly reared and before he could even think straight, Alex was surprised to find himself flying through the air and landing in some very cold water. He spouted out a string of expletives that Mam would have boxed his ears about had she been there.

"Damnation! What's got into ye?" he yelled at Zeus.

Then, once again, the howling came riding on the wind. And now it was much closer.

Alex was about waist deep in the water and began to work his way back to the shore. But, something was holding him back — his feet wouldn't budge. He struggled another moment, then realized the more he tried to lift his feet, the farther down he was being pulled. He knew continuing to struggle would only make things worse. But, by heaven, how was he going to get out of here? And the water was freezing!

"What the hell?" He had pulled many sheep from a bog, and it was a slow, tedious, process. He also had lost a few to the bog also.

"Think, Alex! Think! That's what yer good at. What's yer strategy for this situation?"

But he found he couldn't think. Not about a solution to his problem anyway. For some reason, he found himself thinking about Caitlin. He still pictured her back in the cave, serving him tea and cakes. She was smiling and telling her "story," and she kept pushing that hair back up. And her voice was etched in his brain. All this brought a smile to his face and caused an ache in his heart. He could almost feel her. And her scent seemed to blow across the water and surround him. He felt that her very spirit was here.

"Jesus, man! Now ye going to start hallucinating?" Shaking his head, he tried to focus again on his situation.

"Well, she's not here with ye old boy. So, if ye want to see her again, then ye'd better get yerself out of this bog. Just relax. Try to get Zeus to come over. Get the reins. Get Zeus to back up. BE CALM!" His internal dialogue was working overtime, and so was his anxiety.

Zeus was still standing at the edge of the loch. Alex whistled quickly. "Hey now. Zeus. Come."

Zeus snorted, but only moved a few feet closer. Still out of reach for Alex to get the reins. Meanwhile, Alex felt himself sinking deeper and deeper. Jesus! How had he gotten into this predicament?

But, this Highlander didn't give up on much of anything that was important to him. As he lay there pondering his next move, Zeus suddenly walked into the loch and waited as if Alex were just there enjoying the water.

Alex reached out, took the reins and gave them a quick jerk. Zeus began to back away, slowly pulling Alex out of the boggy loch. And, for just an instant, the scent of lavender — Caitlin's scent — was even stronger.

"Good fellow. Good fellow." Alex finally extracted himself from the water and washed as much muck off as possible. But, removing the muck didn't remove the cold that had seeped into his bones.

"Whew! Well, old man. Guess we can add another chapter to the legend of Tate's Hell. But don't bet on anyone believing us!" For a second his mind wandered off again — had it been Caitlin that he felt back there in the bog? He mounted up and gave the horse a quick slap on his neck. "Let's get out of here." And they did.

Chapter 54

When Wabi left the castle on foot, it was at his own choosing. He could have taken any horse from the stable, and actually Jack had tried to get him to do just that.

"Wabi. Here. Use one of the horses. Ye'll make a lot more time on horseback than foot.

No use walking when ye can ride."

"Ah. Well. Thanks, but I prefer going on foot. If I need to get anywhere quickly, then I'll manage to do so."

Jack had already seen enough unexplained occurrences that he knew better than to ask any more questions.

"Yessir. If that's what ye want."

Wabi had walked all day on the path that ran along the eastern side of the village, but like Alex, he had not seen any evidence that led him to believe Warwick had traveled this path either. In fact, Wabi didn't think anyone had been down this way for a long time. Grass was not matted from use, and nature had been undisturbed. He was actually glad to see that. But, having not found Warwick, he decided to head back to Skye. As he had told Alex, he felt Caitlin was in good hands with the MacKinnon brothers, so it was probably best that he went home. He knew that Owl would keep him informed about any events that may need his attention.

He sat down by the path and enjoyed one of the apples he had brought from the castle. The fruit trees at the castle orchard were still producing, but someone needed to prune them. Of course, now, Wabi wasn't sure anything was going to be taken care of at the estate.

He was looking forward to a dinner with Mrs. Favre and getting back to his own bed where he knew old Groucho, his favorite feline, would be resting at the foot. The old cat had traveled with him in many lives and would do so again. There was some comfort in knowing that old fellow was always with him.

Chapter 55

Jack made short order of getting Caitlin, Millie and the babe ready for travel. Millie had packed what food she could gather quickly, took a few clothes from her aunt's wardrobe and some blankets for the cart where Caitlin and the babe would try to stay warm. The horses were well rested and had been enjoying the warmth of the stables, as well as the very fine rations of oats and hay they'd been given.

Jack had traveled this path many times and knew every turn and twist it took to get back to the sheep farm. Going on horseback, with Alex, it was not a difficult trip. But with two women and a child, it could be trying and dangerous.

Jack was glad to have the wolf with them. He had watched in awe when Willie had come flying across the stable, leaping from the floor and, with canines flashing, attacked the soldier, and latched his jaws onto Campbell's neck. Of course, the soldier was already dead, but just seeing that magnificent animal in action had reinforced Jack's respect for him. It was easy to see why Caitlin kept him at her side.

Millie's husband could be on their heels any moment now, and he wanted to put some distance between them and this man. How had Millie ever gotten herself involved with such a man? There was much he didn't know about this woman, certainly. But, what he did know was to his liking and his instincts told him she was worth protecting. But, he had just learned that Millie wasn't just "Millie." She was Lady Millie!

"Jesus, man! Do you know what yer doing?" he muttered to Goliath as they hurriedly moved along. And he thought Alex had a difficult undertaking! Whatever might occur, however, it was not lost on him that when Millie looked at him her face softened and she obviously found something that pleased her also. And the feel of that small babe snuggling close to him was not forgotten.

At the moment, however, his mind needed to focus on getting higher up the country and getting to the sheep farm as quickly as possible. He knew they would have to stop when night came, and try to keep warm the best they could. If they could make the edge of MacKinnon land, they would stay in the crofter's hut on the edge of their property. He and Alex sometimes used it when they went down to market and were too tired to complete the journey home. There were several huts, and they were pretty basic. But the hut would shelter them, and they could have a fire there. Traveling in the dark with your brother was dangerous also, but he would never attempt it with the ladies and child. He smiled to himself. Whatever would Da say when he showed up with two women and a child in tow?

***

Caitlin had never felt so helpless. For someone who prided herself on taking care of others, here she was lying flat in a pony cart depending on someone else to get her to a place of safety. She had been independent all her life, thanks to Uncle Wabi's help and upbringing. She had fought off the mad soldier, with Willie's help, of course, and found her own dwellings, and provided for herself fairly well. But, she had to admit she needed Alex, Jack, and Millie. And she would really like to see Alex. Where was he? Had he found the commander? Something inside her refused to believe that anything had happened to him. She just believed she would feel it. She would know somehow.

At the moment, she hoped that Alex came across Warwick quickly and was able to stop the fool from causing more disasters. But, what if Warwick killed or hurt Alex? That was unthinkable.

Chapter 56

"Oh good God! Where am I? What day is this?"

Lord Edward Warwick tried to raise up from the hard ground on which he found himself.

But his head seemed to be heavier than his entire body and the throbbing inside it could be felt with every heartbeat! As soon as he was able to rouse himself enough to get on all fours, he immediately regretted it, for severe nausea set upon him at once. Retching with every movement of his body, he concluded that if he would just stay perfectly still, then he might survive, but had some doubts about it. So, he lay back again, on the cold ground.

Venturing to slowly look about, he was relieved to see his horse was tied over in the trees near where he was lying. He didn't remember much about the previous evening, but apparently there was some alcohol involved. Even he recognized this was becoming a destructive habit of late, but, he could change that whenever he wished. So he thought.

Finally, the nausea seemed to have spent itself and he attempted to sit up and order his thoughts. Yes. He had been traveling last night. And it was extremely cold with a snowstorm blowing like all blazes. He remembered seeing a fire somewhere in the distance and had ridden toward it, hoping to find some shelter and warmth. And he was driving a coach — his coach! Why was he driving? Where was the coachman? He couldn't remember everything about that particular part of the evening. He knew he had met someone, a man, who refused to drink with him, stupid man. But, he had warmed himself and then continued. And, he remembered paying someone for a horse? Why? Where was he headed? Where was his coach?

Thinking for another minute, he took a deep breath, trying to fight off another wave of nausea that was about to wash over him. But it passed. Ah, yes, he was headed to the Black Isle where he knew Millicent would have gone. She had no other place to go and, surely, she would have guessed he would follow her up here. He cared nothing about bringing her back with him, but his son would go back to Warwick Castle where he belonged.

Of course, he reasoned, Millie did not know he'd taken care of the Scotland estate business. However, by now she would have discovered both her grandmother and aunt had been murdered.

"I'd do away with you too, you miserable woman, if I could get away with it!" he muttered.

But, Sinclair would never stand for him getting rid of Millie, so he would just keep her cooped up in some keep somewhere, far away from him and his son.

Warwick was also aware that Millie was no fool. She would probably suspect he had arranged for these murders, but she wouldn't be able to prove it or do anything about it, so he wasn't greatly concerned.

Realizing he couldn't recall some events of the previous evening, he decided to stop thinking about that. He would go into the village and get a feel for what was being said about the Cameron women, then would work his way to the estate and Millie. Some food would be in order, and he needed to find another source to refill his flask. It was totally empty at the moment. Groaning with the effort, he got on his horse. This horse was certainly not what he was accustomed to. Why had he bought him? Again, he just let it go and began the last leg of his journey.

Warwick rode through the village to the east end, where the tide brought in the loose seaweed and any number of dead crustaceans, filling the air with a pungent, salty scent. Not everyone appreciated this smell, but Warwick had grown up on the coast and found it nostalgic.

Stopping at the livery, just a block from the inn, The Mermaid's Harbor, he dismounted and saw the stable boy come running over. Warwick was quite certain it wasn't every day the livery had a visitor such as he, dressed in fine clothing and the best boots. Of course, the stable lad would be hoping for a coin or two, thought Warwick. And, at times he had been known to be generous, so he would be sure to give the boy his due.

As Warwick opened the door to the inn, a young lass took his greatcoat and hung it on a peg by the door. She led him to a table close to the fireplace. This was the best thing she could have done as he felt his very bones had frozen, sleeping on the ground with his coat over him. Of course, the snow had pretty much stopped when he got off his horse last evening, but still a small sprinkling of it covered him when he awoke this morning.

"I'll take some coffee if you please, lass."

The girl curtsied, not knowing what else to do, and replied, "Of course, sir. We have the finest cook in the village working here. And Ethel's coffee is the best, if I say so meself."

"Ah. Sounds as if this establishment must have a fine cook, then." Warwick was trying to make conversation with this young girl, knowing she might be a good source of information.

"Aye, sir. Miss Ethel, the cook, was the cook at the Cameron estate 'til just recently. After her husband passed some two years ago, she had to take care of herself. But after that business at the estate, she come here to the inn, and the innkeeper is ever so glad to have her. Why, our business is much better now that she's here."

"Well, I'm sure to have a fine breakfast, then. "Oh, to be sure, sir."

"Then, I'll take some poached eggs, sausages, some grilled tomatoes, bread with butter, and some beans on toast, along with the coffee." Lord Warwick was accustomed to having the best of everything, so expected the same from this establishment. The skinny little lass flexed her knees and flew to the kitchen. She placed the order with Ethel and took a large mug of coffee out to the "gentleman." She, too, hoped for a little extra coin coming her way.

As she was pouring his second cup of coffee, the "gentleman" began asking her questions, about the village, her family name, how long had she lived here, and any local gossip she may have heard.

The lass answered as best she could and, without thinking, she all but blurted out what had occurred at the Cameron estate.

"An awful happening, sir, just an awful thing!" "What awful happening would that be, lass?"

"Oh, sir, I probably shouldn't be talking. Miss Ethel will skin me hide!" "Oh, now, surely, it's not as bad as that."

"Oh, aye, sir, it 'tis."

Dropping her voice to a lower tone, so as not to be heard by everyone, she continued. "The mistresses, both of them, was found dead in they beds!"

"What? You mean someone killed them?"

"Aye. Both of them, sir. And no one knows who did it! We all be right scared, too!"

He shook his head as if gravely concerned. "Certainly, you would be. Such a tragedy for the family I am sure. Are there other family members still living there then?"

"Oh, no, sir, but there was some activity yesterday, I believe it was. You see, there was some folk there early in the morning. The farm hands seen them, but then, they was gone before nightfall."

"Who were these folk?"

"Oh, well, I don't know for sure, but I heard it was the Lady Millicent, ye ken, the granddaughter of the old mistress. But, if it was her, then why would she leave?"

"Yes. That does seem strange," replied the gentleman. "You say she wasn't alone, huh?"

"Oh, no, sir, they was some others, but that's about all I know."

***

Watching from the kitchen, Ethel observed Miriam, the serving girl, engaging in some lengthy discussion with the gentleman.

"That girl needs to talk less and work more!" she said as she came out in to the dining area, retying her apron strings. Ethel had come up behind the girl and heard some of the tale she was telling the gentleman.

"Miriam. Get on about yer duties. Let this gentleman be on his way. Yer detaining him with such wild talk. Git on with ye now!" and she pushed the girl towards the kitchen.

The gentleman finished his breakfast, leaving some coins for the serving lass. Then he put his coat back on and went out the door, looking about for the stable boy.

Ethel watched as the gentleman shrugged into his coat, which was very fine she noticed.

Then, seeing the coins he had left for the serving lass, watched him leave.

Warwick walked back to the livery, mounted up, and handed some coins to the stable boy, who grinned his appreciation. He went toward the path that was most used by everyone, kicking his horse mercilessly. Back at the inn, Ethel wondered who the man was, and what was he doing in their village?

Going back to the kitchen, she came up behind Miriam as she was putting away a stack of clean dishes in the cupboard.

"Did he say what his name was, girl?" "No, Miss Ethel, he never did."

"Mind you, Miriam, no more discussing the Cameron's to anyone else, especially someone not from around here. There's much we don't know about that sad morning."

"Aye, Miss Ethel." Miriam scampered out of Ethel's way, glad the old cook hadn't swatted her about the ears as she sometimes threatened to do. Of course, she had never actually seen her do such a thing, but still, she didn't wish to be the first.

***

So, thought Warwick. His lovely wife had been here but had already left. Who was with her? He could have gotten more information from that serving girl if the nosy old cook hadn't interfered. He had found out enough to know Millie was somewhere close, and he would surely catch up with her now.

It was no problem finding out where the estate was. It seemed everyone knew the family, and some of them, apparently, knew Millie as well. He didn't realize she had spent so much time here in her youth. That didn't change his plans for her, however, and he would make sure she didn't come back here again. He would take over the estate and find someone who would work it and ensure he got a healthy amount of funds coming from it.

When he got to the top of the hill, looking across the moor, the castle was an imposing building, to be sure. Well, now. He had known it was an estate, but he had no idea it was so grand. This castle was very large, and built probably a hundred years before. It was constructed in the Tower House design, which was more popular in the last century. A Tower House castle was a vertical design, not so much used for defensive purposes as earlier designs had been. There was a moat as Millie had mentioned, and a gatehouse stood almost as tall as the castle itself. A narrow path took you over to another building, connected to the castle by a covered walkway. This would have been the chapel early on, but probably had not been used as such in some time. Sinclair had not exaggerated for once, it seemed. Maybe he was hoping to keep it for himself as long as he could. But, Warwick was pleased this holding was about to be his and would go a long way to creating a special place for him with the nobles. It was a shame it was located in Scotland. Had it been in England, he would have made it his permanent home.

As he walked up the cobblestone walkway to the front entrance, it was easy to see the place was deserted. There were no sounds anywhere. No birds, no dogs, none of the usual sounds that you might expect to hear around any home. But, that actually made it easier for him. He just walked up the steep steps to the front of the castle, went through the unlocked door and began walking about, looking through each and every room.

So, this was what a true gentleman's home looked like. Unlike his castle, which was rather bare with some ancient weapons and suits of armor about, this one was filled with fine pieces of furniture, large chests, breakfronts, hand-woven rugs, and pine tables that were polished with lemon oil and shone in the morning sun. And, even though it had been deserted for several weeks now, there was still the scent of dried roses in the air, a feminine scent that was missing from his castle. Of course, he had never allowed Millie to put her signature on anything, and he kept her in the upper rooms as much as possible. Or maybe, she just preferred to be up there away from him. He knew Millie was as unhappy with him as he was with her. But, she had served a purpose, and now this place was his. What was to happen to her now? He wasn't sure just yet. But he would come up with something.

Chapter 57

Making his evening trek about the moor, old Clint once again saw activity at the castle. "Now, who could that be?"

Lady Millicent had left earlier that morning with the Highlander, the healer, and the babe. Then, Clint and Winston had taken Dorothea back home with admonishment to keep every door locked and not to open them to anyone she didn't know. The two men had decided they would keep an even sharper eye out now they had reason to believe Lady Millie's husband, Lord Warwick, may be responsible for the deaths of their mistresses. Clint and Winston were no spring chickens, but both could still brandish a firearm with some accuracy, and they were both of a mind to shoot first and ask questions later.

So, when he saw a lone rider coming up the path, Clint immediately got on his old mare and took off down to the rear of the stables. Whoever it was probably didn't belong here, and Clint was tired of strangers just taking up in this place, a place he had been taking care of for most of his life. He wasn't an owner, but he had taken pride in being a part of the Cameron "family."

Clint got to the rear of the stables and tied his mare. He watched the man go into the castle through the front entrance. Clint thought it would be a better idea for him to enter through the cellar entrance, going up the stairs and coming out into the kitchen. That way he may be able to take the man by surprise and be in a position to stop him from stealing or destroying any of the Cameron belongings. With most folk around knowing about the castle being deserted, there could be many looking to take anything they could get their hands on.

As Clint was quietly coming up the stairs from the cellar, Warwick stopped at the top of the stairs leading down from the upstairs bedrooms. He thought he had heard a noise from below and went down to investigate. He saw nothing, but continued to walk softly through the great hall toward the kitchen. Just as he entered the kitchen, Clint opened the door from the cellar. It was difficult to say who was the most surprised, the lord or the farmhand. But both men were startled when they saw each other. Clint reached behind his back to pull out his pistol, but Warwick, being considerably younger, had already crossed the room and, with the butt of his pistol, struck Clint a direct blow to the temple. The blow would have been devastating for a young man, but especially so for a bloke as old as Clint. He immediately fell to the floor and lay there unmoving.

"You old fool! Now what am I going to do with you?"

Irritated beyond reason, Warwick thought briefly, then decided he would just leave the old man here, in the castle. No telling how long before anyone would find him, and he would be long gone before then. It was getting to be dusk, so the old man never really had a good look at his face, and Warwick didn't think he would be able to identify him. He hoped the old man survived as it would be better not to have another dead body, he thought, and left quickly, leaving the door ajar behind him.

***

"So. She's not traveling alone, then," Warwick spoke to himself again. So who was with her? And just where would they be going? No doubt Millie had figured out his role and was trying to hide from him. He pulled on the reins and tried to decide which way to go. She wouldn't be going back south, certainly not back to

Warwick Castle, but she wouldn't go back to her father's place either. Warwick wasn't sure which man she loathed the most. So, where else would she be headed?

Suddenly, he threw his head back and burst out in laughter! In that instant, he knew exactly where she would be headed.

"Of course! You'll be looking for that busybody old nursemaid! Ha!"

What was her name? He thought another moment. Dorothy. No. Dorothea? Yes, that was her name. He recalled he had sent her back to Scotland just as soon as he had taken Millie to his castle. That old nursemaid was forever coddling Millie, and he had acted quickly to send her back where she belonged, where Millie couldn't go to her with every complaint she had about him.

So, finding Dorothea was his next task, and one that wouldn't take too long. He just needed to find that talkative serving girl who worked at the Mermaid Harbor Inn and throw a few more coins in her direction. She was a local lass and would know where the nursemaid lived.

Chapter 58

After not finding Warwick on the trail, Alex felt that Warwick must be ahead of him already. But he had traveled the path to his home all his life and knew exactly where he would find Jack and the women. He just hoped Warwick didn't find them before he did. Alex believed Warwick was responsible for the deaths of the Cameron women. He may not have killed them personally, but apparently the fiend had no scruples about hiring it done. Alex wouldn't bet anything on trying to figure this man's actions.

It was well past dusk now, and Alex could see the Cameron place just up ahead. Having a warmer place for his horse and himself for the evening would be good. Maybe Clint or Winston would have news of Warwick. It was worth stopping a moment to check.

He walked over across the bailey yard and knocked at the rear door. No answer. Going around to the front of the castle, he climbed the steps and saw that the door was slightly open. He rapped the large brass knocker several times, hoping the open door meant maybe Clint or another worker was here. But, getting no response, he turned and started back down. Just then, he heard a voice calling, but he couldn't understand the words. So, he quickly went back up the steps and called out,

"Hello. Anyone here?" "I'm here! Help me!"

The voice was very soft, almost like a woman's voice, thought Alex. He entered the room and looked about. He half expected to find a girl or woman. But as he got to the great hall, he stopped, abruptly, as he came upon an old man lying on the floor.

Old Clint! The old gentleman was bleeding from his head, and a good amount of dried blood was on the floor.

"Hey. Easy now, old fella," said Alex, bending down to see what condition the old man was in. He immediately saw the man was in trouble.

"Can ye talk to me, tell me what has happened to ye?"

"Aye. I be able to talk all right. I just be having one helluva headache though. But, me brain still seems ta be working. As much as it ever did, I reckon."

Alex smiled. The old ones always made light of their ailments, no matter how serious the problem may be.

"Then, let's see if we can sit ye up here, then, my man." Alex was beginning to hope that maybe the injury wasn't as bad as he had first thought, but there was a good amount of blood on the floor. And, the man's voice was very scratchy, but you might expect that from an oldster such as this one.

"Just sit there a minute. Let's try to see exactly where ye hurt."

Alex wished Caitlin would appear out of the blue as she would know just what to do and be finished with it before he, Alex, could even decipher where to start. But, she wasn't, so it was up to him to help this old man.

"Looks like ye've been knocked about the head, and a good wallop it was."

"Yep. He was on me 'afore I could even get me pistol out! I didn't see him 'til the last minute and he hit me right hard, I do believe."

Alex had a moment of concern.

"Do ye think he might still be about the place?"

"Nae. I reckon he took off, but I could be wrong, too."

Alex took a quick turn about the great hall, and the kitchen, looking down into the cellar, but saw no one.

"I believe he's gone now. There's no sign of anyone."

Alex grabbed a cloth from the kitchen and began to clean up the man's head, enough to see that there was a giant goose egg on his temple, blood having dried all along his hairline. The entire side of his face was swollen, and his eye was just beginning to close slightly. It was quite a sight, and painful, surely. But there were no other wounds he could see, and the old one did seem to have his wits about himself.

Alex finished cleaning the wound and was about to ask the old man where he lived so he could take him there, when he felt his sleeve being pulled on. The old one was trying to pull Alex's face down closer so he could get a better look at him.

"But I know ye, young man. Yep. I do. Ye be the one who was here with Lady Millie, and your brother, that big fellow with the red hair. You two be them that bought the sheep from Mistress Moira, just a few year back."

The old man was beginning to get agitated, thought Alex, and he tried to calm him down. "Easy now. Ye be right. I did meet you the other day when you came out here to see Lady Millie, and had Dorothea and that other farmhand with you, Winston, wasn't it? And yes, I did buy some sheep from the Cameron family, and I did come down with Jack, my brother, to herd them back up to our place. Ah! Ye must have been one of the hands who helped us round them up."

The old one was trying to get up and was becoming even more riled by the minute. Alex had to hold him down as he was trying his best to stand up.

"It's all right, just sit back down again, now, we'll get ye up shortly."

Alex was afraid that too much movement would start the bleeding again, and he didn't want to have to deal with that.

"But I though ye was all headed to the upper regions, to yer own place. And ye was taking Lady Millie and her babe, and that other woman with the wolf."

"That's right, Clint. But we decided to let Jack take the ladies. The old man and I thought it would be better for us to try to find Warwick. I've had about enough of everybody running from that idiot."

"So, yer brother is trying to get the women back home so they'll be safe, right?" asked

Clint.

"That's right. Jack will look out for those two ladies. And that babe couldn't be in better hands. Jack particularly likes bairns ye ken."

"Aye. That was easy to see. Even for an old one like meself. He seemed right fond of our Lady Millie and that babe. Fact is, I was jest wondering if maybe he was the da?"

Alex blanched!

"Oh, no! Not Jack! He's never been close enough to any woman for anything like that to happen!" Alex was shaking his head. What was he to make of this latest information?

"Huh. Well. I agree with ye about getting the women to safety. They could be in mighty danger down here. Jest lookit what happened to me!"

"So, back to ye, have any idea who it was that hit ye?"

"Well. 'Course I can't be sure. But I suspect it may have been that Lord Warwick hisself, 'cause the man be wearing some awful fine clothes, ye see. He had on a fur hat of some kind and this long greatcoat and the finest boots I ever did see! So, it was somebody that were used to the best, ye ken."

"Warwick, you say. Well, then let's get ye back home, old timer, if you think ye can ride, that is."

"Oh, aye, I'll be all right I will."

"May be. But I'll go along with ye just to be sure."

"Then, let's git on about it. It be getting pretty dark out, and Ethel will be wondering where I am."

Ethel, the cook, had her own crofter's cottage as did Clint, but most evenings they could be found sitting together by the fire, Clint enjoying Ethel's delicious cooking. So, he knew she would be waiting for him tonight.

Going over the moor, they were at Clint's hut shortly. Alex dismounted and made sure the old man got off without falling. Going up to the cottage door, Alex found himself envious of this old man, going home to someone who cared for him and who gave reason to make another day. What a fortunate man this crofter was, and apparently, he knew it.

Ethel met them at the door. "Oh my heavens! What have you done now, you old wooly goat!" She was pulling Clint in and forcing him to sit down, making over him as if he were a child.

"Oh, Ethel, I'm fine, just a bit of a scratch, and this young fella done cleaned me up. Now stop your frettin'!"

After listening to Clint's explanation for his goose egg, Ethel began a tale of her own. "Oh, he was mighty finely dressed, I give him that. And Miriam, that serving girl at the

inn, she went on and on about the goings on at the Cameron place 'til I went in and sent her to the kitchen. Somehow I knew that visitor weren't one to be trusted; it was written all over him. From your description, what with the greatcoat and the boots, it was him for certain!"

Alex spoke then.

"Well, believe it or no, I, too, have had dealings with someone I believe to be this same man. We met out on the path a couple of nights ago. It was beginning to snow pretty heavily, and I tried to find some shelter. But, out there last night, there was nothing, so, I just tied my horse to the trees and made myself a fire to help keep me from freezing. Not long after I had settled down for the night, I heard a coach coming down the path, so I hid in the trees and had my pistol ready for whatever may come."

"This man was dressed just as you describe. Greatcoat, fine boots and hat. But the most noticeable thing about him, other than his clothes, was the fact that he was well into his brew. He offered me a taste, but I know not to mix alcohol and cold, so I thanked him, but didn't drink with him. It seemed he took offense and decided he would move on. According to him, his wife had family in the Black Isle, and he was headed there to be with her as she was due to have a child any day now. In his drunken state he said their name was 'Cameroom,' but, no doubt, he was trying to say 'Cameron.' So, he must have figured out where the keep was and happened to be just a bit too late to catch up with Lady Millicent."

Both Clint and Ethel were nodding their heads in agreement. The two of them were most fond of Lady Millie, but beyond that, they were most afraid for everyone in the village. What that man would stop at was unknown, and what would happen to them with no one in charge at the estate?

Clint sat upright, trying to ease the pounding in his head.

"But tonight, we will rest easy enough, I guess, as that man has probably gone on, having not found Lady Millie."

Yes, thought Alex, but where?

"Did anyone else know Jack was taking the women and going north?"

Ethel thought for a second

"No, well, nobody except Dorothea and Winston. But they wouldn't tell, that's for sure. Dorothea raised Lady Millie from the time she were small and stayed with her til that lord sent her back to Scotland. That was when Lady Millie married him. 'Twas a most disturbing time for Dorothea, as she was like a mother to Lady Millie. But I reckon she's doing well enough now. She has another child to care for now, ye see, so she be doing what she was put here ta do."

"Then, it seems to me I should try to catch up with Jack and the ladies. If Warwick should figure out which way they're traveling, then Jack could use another man at his back. But, meanwhile, ye two stay here in your cottage and if Warwick should return, leave him be. He's a very irrational man, and he wouldn't think twice about committing another crime. And, I feel sure he won't stop looking for his wife, which means he and I will meet again."

Alex excused himself and started out again. At least from here he could make the trip with a blindfold on. It was a ways yet, but he had friends up the way and several places to go for shelter if he needed. His greatest fear now was that Jack would be greatly slowed down traveling with two women and a child. But, Jack was pretty savvy, and Alex knew those women were rather resourceful themselves.

Tonight the stars were bright, and a full moon shone on the snow covered ground. Letting his thoughts return to Caitlin, he always pictured her sitting at the table in the cave, talking with him, having tea with him, using that tiny teapot she was so fond of. All that seemed so long ago, and much had happened since then. Trying to look out for Caitlin was reason enough to keep going, tired though he was. Jack, too, needed someone looking out for him as well, thought Alex.

Chapter 59

Warwick wasted no time getting back to the Mermaid's Harbor Inn. He left his horse at the livery, instructing the stable boy to take care of the horse, meaning to feed him, water him, and give him a good rubdown. Warwick knew he would head out immediately, and he needed his horse to be ready. The stable boy was eager to do anything for this gentleman, Warwick could see that.

Lord Warwick walked just a short block, turned the corner, and was at the inn in no time.

Opening the door, he found the serving girl mopping the floor after the evening meal.

"Hello again, my pretty lass!" hailed Warwick, taking the girl by surprise. It looked as if she was alone. At least that meddlesome cook didn't seem to be around.

"Oh, 'tis you, sir. Would ye be needin' some supper?"

Miriam was not truly pretty, and was aware of it, but it was still pleasing to hear someone call her that. She was extremely thin, and her greasy, mousey hair could use a good washing.

"No, lass. You fed me very well this morning. Actually, I'm in need of your knowledge, and I'm sure you have much." Warwick knew how to get what he wanted.

The girl blushed. "Oh, not me, sir. Miss Ethel tells me I don't know nothin'!"

"Well. I'm betting you can help me. My friends in England are looking for a nursemaid for their young one. Someone mentioned a woman, Dorothea, I believe was the name, and that she lives in your village. Do you happen to know this woman or where I could find her?"

"Oh, that be easy enough, sir. Dorothea was nursemaid to another family in England some years ago, but then she came back here to her home and still lives here. But, now she has a child of her own, so she may not be so inclined to go back jest now."

"Yes. I see what you mean. Well. I should at least make her aware her services are needed, and she would be well compensated, I assure you."

"Yessir. Well, she lives over behind the kirk, in the small cottage at the rear. She lives there with her little boy. But then, I told you that already, didn't I." It didn't take much to get Miriam confused.

"One more thing I do need — a bottle of your finest whiskey. Could you get that for me?"

Taking her hand, he placed several coins in it and nodded slightly in her direction. "I do thank you, my dear." Miriam smiled brightly. She had never had so much money in one day!

Tossing even more coins to the stable hand moments later, Warwick left the village at a fast pace, heading out to the kirk. It was easily seen from almost anywhere as the steeple spire was taller than most buildings.

In just a matter of minutes, he was at the door to Dorothea's cottage, knocking loudly. Why didn't that woman just answer the door? Warwick needed information, and he needed it now!

After rapping again with no response, he walked around the cottage to the back entrance and pounded on that door. There was a light coming from somewhere, probably a candle in the kitchen. Out of the corner of his eye he just caught movement of a curtain, then it closed again. That dratted woman was here, alright, and she would let him in!

He resorted to yelling at that point. "Dorothea. It's Lord Warwick. I must speak with you.

Open the door!"

There was still no response and by this time Warwick had lost all patience with that stupid woman.

"Dorothea, open the door or I'll break it down!" Dorothea wrung her hands. What to do, what to do!

She knew he would be true to his word and her door would be knocked off its hinges. She had seen firsthand how he behaved when in one of his rages, more times than she liked to recall. So, trying to think what to do, she called to Garry.

"Garry. Come here to Mommy." The child came to the kitchen and Dorothea took him to the larder, which was small, but large enough for her to place the wee laddie inside.

"Garry. You must stay here until I come for you. You must not make a sound! Do you understand? This is very important, my boy!"

The child nodded his head and sat down on the floor of the larder. At the last moment, Dorothea placed a small candle on the shelf so that the closet wouldn't be totally dark. Her lad was terribly afraid of the dark, as was Dorothea.

"Yes, Lord Warwick. I'm coming."

Opening the door, she stood back as far away from him as she could. Fear of this man had been instilled long before now.

Warwick walked closer and looked down to her.

"Well, Dorothea. It took you long enough. Aren't you glad to see me?" This was said with a smile that belied his threatening words and tone.

"Lord Warwick. Do come in." She indicated he was to sit on one of her two chairs.

"So, Dorothea. You seem to have landed on your feet pretty well, and have your own cottage now. Life is good then, I presume."

Dorothea sat lightly on the edge of her chair.

"Yessir. I'm happy here." She dared not respond any more than was absolutely necessary as she feared him and was certain he knew it.

"Let's get down to business, then. And don't waste my time telling me you don't know where Millicent has gone, for I know you do. She's not at the castle. That only leaves one other place she would have come to. Here. And, seeing she isn't here either, then I'll thank you to tell me where I can find her."

"Lord Warwick. I haven't seen Lady Millie since I left your castle several years ago now.

Surely, you know more about her whereabouts than I!"

Warwick saw through this charade as Dorothea knew he would. He stood up slowly and walked over to her chair. He jerked her up and lifted her completely out of it, holding her tightly about her small shoulders.

"I said don't waste my time! I know you've seen her!" "But, sir. I haven't!"

Her voice was shrill and his had become very loud. He would get the information from her somehow. A few backhands to her face would be a good starting place. Then a noise from the kitchen got his attention, and he set Dorothea down again.

A small child darted across the room and ran into his mother's, arms, crying and holding on to her."Oh, Garry. I told you to stay put!" Dorothea wrapped the child in her arms and held him tightly.

"Ah, so, a child. And who does he belong to?"

"He's mine. He belongs to me. He is MY son!"

"Then I don't suppose you would like me to take him away with me, would you?" "No! Lord Warwick! Please! He's just a child!"

"Yes, and I don't particularly like children, but I will get the information I need from you, or else I will take this child and you will never see him again!"

He started toward the child. Dorothea jumped up quickly, putting Garry behind her. "She's gone north. To the upper Highlands. That's all I know!"

"North, you say. And how is she traveling? Is she alone?" "She's going by horseback and she has two friends with her." "What friends? She has no friends!"

"I don't know them, Lord Warwick. That's all I can tell you! Please! Leave now!" "These friends. Men or women?"

"There is a man and a woman traveling with her."

"But, she can't be able to travel very well. She is carrying my son that should be born any day now!"

"Yessir. I could see that."

"When did they leave this village?"

"Early this morning, sir. I believe it was."

"Where in the upper Highlands? That's quite a large area. What was the man's name?" "MacKinnon, sir. I don't know the lady's name."

Warwick stood and started to pace back and forth. He looked at the floor, studying the pattern in the small bit of carpet lying there.

"What is that ridiculous woman thinking? Going on horseback in her condition! She could harm my son! Well, that just means they'll be moving very slowly, and I'll be able to catch up with them before long."

Without another word, he quickly fled the cottage, leaving the door standing open as he rushed to his horse. There was only one good path to the north, and thanks to the snowfall, tracking three travelers would be easy enough.

Chapter 60

Wabi had walked most of the day, reveling in the beauty that surrounded him. The snow was still on the ground, looking like a soft blanket spread upon the earth. Every once in a while he saw a sprout of greenery trying to peek out and reach for the sun. The trees, now seemingly vulnerable without their leaves, stood out in stark contrast to the evergreens and hollies that were proudly strutting their red berries of the season. He looked about and was even more sure everyone should make a "walkabout" occasionally because it did wonders to restore balance and calm.

Presently, his mind was at ease about Caitlin's discovery of her personal gifts. What she did with them would be interesting to observe. Perhaps she would bring some "magick" to the Highlands — to add to the magick already there. In one of his lives, Wabi had lived among the wee ones, the fairies, and the Highlands were still alive with them. You just had to know where to look.

Caitlin was in for many surprises, of that Wabi was confident. These gifts were given only to ones the Creator believed to have the capacity to use as they were intended, for man's betterment. Caitlin would come to that understanding in her own time as had Wabi.

As for her new relationship with Alex, Owl had expressed his opinion to Wabi recently. He trusted Alex and felt he would be open to Caitlin's unusual qualities and not stifle her when she was called on to use them.

Owl had been around for a long time, too, and was a good judge of character. All was well for the moment. Caitlin now knew how to call Wabi. But the fact that she was traveling with the Highlander, Jack, and eventually his brother Alex, made Wabi realize he wouldn't be needed anytime soon. Perhaps this chapter of his many lives was over. This thought was not a sad one, but rather, an exciting one. He would now contemplate what his next assignment might be.

Chapter 61

Jack had tried to move them along as quickly as he could. Millie had yet to complain even one time, but her face told him she was barely able to stay in the saddle. Caitlin, lying in her bed of blankets with the babe snuggled up close to her, seemed to be faring very well. But, having had several broken bones himself, he was quite sure her leg must be giving her fits. The cart was better than trying to go on a horse, however, so Caitlin had kept her discomfort to herself also. With each passing minute, they were getting closer to MacKinnon land, and he was hoping to get to the old crofter's cottage that sat near the creek at the edge of their property boundary. Other than stopping a couple of times for nature calls and for Millie to nurse the babe, they had been steadily moving upland. It had occurred to Jack he may be bringing danger to Da and the others, but Da would have done the same thing. He had no doubt about that. As he aged, it was becoming clear to Jack he was most fortunate to have been born into a family whose very bones were filled with compassion for others, even if it put them in harm's way sometimes.

The snow was not as heavy up higher as down in the lower regions. But, it was still covering the ground, and they had to make their way carefully and not stray off the path.

Little light was left in the sky, the sun already beginning to hide behind the hills. In the distance, Jack was ecstatic to see the old crofter's cottage he had been striving to get to before nightfall.

"Not much father now, Millie. We'll be there soon." That got him a quick smile from Millie and gave him more reason to continue this trek.

Pulling on his reins, he spoke to Goliath.

"Hey, old buddy. Looks like we don't have too much farther to go. We'll be at our destination soon and then we can all rest."

Within another half hour, they had arrived. Jack climbed down and walked over to assist Millie, reaching up and steadying her as she slowly climbed down. The days of travel, giving birth, and grieving over lost family had taken a toll on her, Jack thought. He took another moment then took her hand in his.

"We're almost home now. We're on MacKinnon land now. You're safe here."

Jack walked over to the pony cart to see about Caitlin. Just as he got there, Caitlin sat up and began to scream!

"Alex! Alex is in trouble! Jack! We've got to help him!"

"Easy, Caitlin. Easy." Jack looked over at Millie as she came over quickly. "Caitlin. Quiet now." Millie felt her forehead and then looked back to Jack. "She's burning up with fever."

Then she looked at Caitlin's leg. It was very swollen and had to be causing Caitlin a lot of pain.

"Her leg must be infected, Jack. I think she's delirious. It's the only thing that makes any sense."

"No! I tell you he's in trouble!" Caitlin screeched at them. She had used whatever energy she had left and collapsed back onto the cart. Jack quickly lifted her head and spoke softly to her.

"Easy, Caitlin. If he's in trouble, he's a good one to figure out how to take care of it. Don't you worry about Alex. He's come through many troubling situations before, lass. Just be calm now. He'll be all right I tell ye." Jack hadn't had much experience in dealing with distraught women, but it looked like he was going to get some on this trip.

Going inside the cottage, Jack knew what he would find. The brothers stayed here anytime they found themselves too tired to continue on to the farm, or the weather conditions prevented them from moving on. They would have left it in some order, or Hector would have their skins. And, there would be firewood or peat ready also. Looking about, it looked like it would be peat this night, and was he ever glad to see a large stack of it waiting to be used.

Getting a fire going was the first job, and then helping the ladies get settled inside would be next. Tomorrow morning they would be at the sheep farm and who knew what would happen after that!

***

Millie had seen crofter's cottages many times, but from a distance. She had never actually been inside one, and was surprised to see there were several beds, a cook stove of a fashion, peat stacked by the hearth, and several cooking utensils hanging from the wall. There was only one room, but the hut was so much better than being outside in the cold. They had blankets from the Cameron estate which would be helpful, too. She had taken a number of dishcloths from the castle, and they were serving as diapers for her new arrival.

After the fire was going strong, flames licking at the walls of the fireplace, they all had a supper from supplies Millie had packed. Ethel apparently always kept the larder in the estate well stocked, so there were edibles still there, and Millie had taken what she needed. The peat burning in the fireplace lent a comforting smell, and they devoured the food, leaving nothing.

Millie and Jack ate heartily, but Caitlin barely picked at hers.

***

Jack took the horses to the side of the cottage and let them drink their fill from the trough. In another month or so, the water in the troughs would be frozen. Farm hands would be looking for that and bring water for the sheep daily.

The horses would just have to wait for oats and hay until tomorrow, but they were used to this. Highland animals were much like the people who live up there, a hardy breed.

Jack had observed that Caitlin was very quiet, and seemed content to just lie on her bed, not insisting on doing something, which she usually did. He came over to her bed and tried to make small talk with her. But she only wanted to rest, so he let her be.

He watched with great interest as Millie took the baby and, after feeding her, let her just lie upon her breast, once again sleeping. Thank goodness new infants slept a lot, he thought.

Else, it could have been an even longer trip! He remembered how Ian had cried a lot when he was a baby, and it really bothered Jack.

Jack actually seemed to know much more about babies than Millie did. But he could see she was learning quickly that babies didn't need much, mostly a full stomach and a place to lie down. They also seemed to like shoulders to lie on, or this one did. Jack's shoulder had served this purpose many times already on this trip.

Jack, too, was feeling the stress of the past few days. He just needed to get these women to safety. That thought kept him going.

With Caitlin already sleeping, Jack and Millie sipped on their mugs of tea and talked briefly about the day's events. Jack still remembered the look on the faces of old Clint, Winston, and Ethel, all folk who had cared for Millie's grandmother and aunt. What would happen to them? Did Millie need to help them? Somehow he didn't think she would just leave them with no help. The place was hers now. What did that mean to her?

With these thoughts running through his head, he banked the fire and lay down on a cot, then watched as Millie and the babe joined Caitlin on the larger bed.

Jack was concerned about Caitlin's swollen leg, but knew the best thing he could do would be to get her to the home place. Alex would be coming along soon. Jack knew Caitlin's leg would need to be reset and didn't know if they could do it. If not, then they would have to find someone who could. But, finding a healer in the Highlands was difficult.

Everyone was abed now. They were all asleep before the owl had even found a proper resting place in the evergreen tree at the back of the cottage. None of them heard his last "hoo hoo" of the evening.

Chapter 62

Jack got up early and made a small fire in the fireplace, the one from last night having been reduced to smoldering ashes. With his peat all ready by the hearth, it was a quick task to complete. He then found himself being nudged in the back of the knee, and looked down to see Willie peering up at him.

"Hey now. You need to go out for a quick run?" Willie was ready for his early morning romp, no doubt finding his own breakfast and scouting about in the snow, which he liked to do whenever Caitlin would give him permission to run freely. Jack opened the door and off Willie went. The wolf always returned and, if he hadn't returned quickly enough, Caitlin had but to whistle once and he would be at her side in moments.

As the sun was just beginning its morning struggle to overcome the moon's dominance, Millie and the babe began to stir, coming over to warm themselves by the flames. Jack watched in amazement. This woman, holding her child and sipping her tea, was the most feminine creature he had ever laid eyes on. When she walked, she seemed to glide across the floor, and she went about it so quietly she would be behind you before you even knew she was there. With her long black hair trailing over her shoulder as she leaned over the babe, the fire was picking up reddish tones in it. He thought he would never see anything as lovely ever again.

Jack helped Caitlin to a chair, hoping a change of position would ease the pain in her leg.

She hadn't said a word to anyone, but the swelling was continuing to get worse, and from the look on her face, Jack assumed every heartbeat sent a message of pain.

"Is it bearable, Caitlin? We'll be home shortly. Hector is a fair hand at binding wounds, so he might can help."

"I'll make it, Jack. My medicines are almost gone, and I'll need some herbs to make more.

Maybe there's a healer in your local village that can help me."

"Well. There's some medicines at the house, from the time when Mam was with us. But I don't know what it is exactly. But, we'll find whatever you need."

Caitlin looked up at him. "Jack. I know you think I was out of my mind yesterday, but I know that something was happening to Alex. But, today, the feeling is gone, and I don't quite know what to think about it. It was so very real for a few minutes. He's become very special to me, Jack. I wish he were here."

"Aye. So do I. But Alex will catch up with us. Don't worry about that. He's able to take care of himself, and Wabi is probably already home by now. And I pity anyone who might try to get in his way!"

Jack saw that Caitlin was past going much farther. There was simply no way of knowing when they would see Alex. He quickly brought the horses around front where they had left the pony cart.

"We'll be at the home place in about two hours, ladies."

"Oh, my. That's the best news I've heard in a long time. Do you think there's a stream nearby where I might get a bath?" Millie asked.

"I believe we can probably manage that," Jack smiled at her.

Then he caught the reins of Caitlin's horse and hooked up the pony cart once again. That had been a lifesaver if ever there had been one! It might have slowed them down a bit, but the cart was a great help to Caitlin and the baby.

Jack approached Caitlin who was still sitting in her chair as she had to depend on him to move her. Seeing the despair in her eyes, Jack tried a bit of levity, hoping to bring a little lightness to their situation.

"Are ye ready to get back into yer very fine carriage, milady?" Jack asked Caitlin quietly, seeing she was just about done for. He bent over and picked her up. She was like a child almost. Why, Ian weighed more than she did for heaven's sake! He again wished Alex were here.

"Oh, aye, me lad. I'm ready to get this journey over with. And my carriage is most stupendous!" Jack noted that she tried to make light of their problem too, but knew she was about to expire from pain and weariness. Soon. They would be there soon.

Millie had made a pallet of blankets for Caitlin and placed it in the cart. Each woman knew the other was more than uncomfortable, but neither spoke of it. There were some things women just understood about each other. Millie got the blankets arranged and waited for Jack to bring Caitlin out. When she saw him carrying Caitlin, she went back inside to get the rest of her belongings, and the babe.

She came back out and placed the babe inside the blankets with Caitlin, who was enjoying the company of this little creature. The babe never seemed to cry, but just slept.

"You know. It's kinda nice, feeling her tiny body next to mine. I've never thought much about having children, but I could become accustomed to this." Caitlin had made this statement yesterday, but today she just pulled the child close. Conversation was just too tiring. Then she lay back, and exhaustion once again took over.

Having satisfied herself that Caitlin and the baby were as comfortable as she could make them, Millie walked over to Dillon, ready to mount up one more time. Jack stood next to her, ready to give her a leg up as Dillon was quite a tall mount. As he held the stirrup for her, he heard a "click" up next to his ear.

"I'll thank you to take your hands off my wife, sheep man!"

Jack had better sense than to argue with someone holding a pistol to his head. He released the stirrup and Millie quickly pulled her leg back down. She didn't have to look to know who it was — Edward!

Whirling around to face him, she unleashed her pent up anger and screamed. "Edward! Put that pistol away! You have no quarrel with him! It's me you want!"

Millie looked at the man she had married. How had she ever let this happen? Why hadn't she stood up to her father years ago and refused him? She loathed everything about this hideous man. And now she feared him more than ever. She had no doubt he had arranged for someone to kill her family, and now her friends were in peril because of her.

"Oh, yes, my dear. It is you I want." Warwick took one look at her and realized she was considerably thinner than she had been the last time he had seen her.

"So, my dear wife. You appear to have had my son! And, where is the little Warwick man?"

Millie glanced toward Jack then looked back to Warwick. She would do whatever she must to protect her child, even if it meant returning with Warwick. She would have to find another time and place to make her escape, again. She was frantic, trying to keep her thoughts from running away with her.

Jack still hadn't moved, not with the pistol still pointed at his head.

"Can't you see she doesn't want to go with you? Let her go and get back to your English castle where you belong!"

"Keep your thoughts to yourself, sheep man. What I do with my wife is none of your business. What is it with you heathen Scots? My wife is my property. I'll decide what I do with all my properties!"

"And, speaking of properties, my dear, it seems you are the latest mistress of the Cameron keep. And, of course, that too will be added to my holdings. But, it was such a shame about your family. Both in the same night! But, let's not cry over spilt milk. The place will need someone to look after it, so we must send someone to the place to make it worth our efforts."

"Come, Millie. Where's my son?"

"Our child is here." Walking over to the cart, she leaned over and looked down at the babe, tucking the blanket around her tightly. Then, turning to face Lord Warwick directly, she smiled when she said,

"But, Edward. You don't have a son. You have a daughter. And a very beautiful one at that!"

"What! I don't believe you! I will have a son, I tell you! You lie!" He struck her so hard she fell to the ground and cried out in pain as her head struck the cart. She slowly stood up then, trying to protect her baby from this insane man.

Warwick walked closer to the cart and jerked at the blanket, trying to take the child from Caitlin's arms.

Jack took this one moment of opportunity when Warwick was focusing on the child to make a move. He jumped in front of Millie, trying to shield her and the child. Warwick, also a large man, grabbed Jack's neck with one hand and, with the butt of his pistol, struck Jack's skull with a thud that would have brought any man down. Jack lay crumpled at the lord's feet in an instant.

Millie backed away from Warwick and bumped into the pony cart where Caitlin lay. The healer was quiet, as she had been all morning. In fact, both Millie and Jack figured Caitlin was past making conversation and decided to let her be.

"Leave us alone! You don't want me or your child! All you want is more property! Leave here! I'll never go back to England and live with you!"

"You'll do whatever I tell you, just as you always have! Stupid woman! How dare you produce a girl child! She's useless to me! But I'll take you back, and you'll get the papers for the Cameron estate. They will be mine!"

"No! I…"

Suddenly, the earth began to tremble — like a small earthquake. Then it began to quake violently, causing them to fall to their knees. Millie held tightly to her babe, fear taking hold of her mind. A whistling coming from the top of the trees was deafening and the noise became so loud it had Millie trying to cover her ears with her hands.

At this very moment, Jack tried to get up from the ground, but was just too weak. Unable to do anything but watch, he was confused for a second. Then he realized what was happening.

"Oh, Jesus!" said Jack. "I've been through this before! Heaven help us!"

He knew that whatever it was would end only when the "instigator" wished it to. He had experienced only a brief touch of this power back in the stables, but that was enough for him. And, now, apparently this man was going to get the full treatment.

Warwick dropped the gun, let go of the blanket, and held his hands to his ears also.

"What in God's name is that?" he screamed. His head ached, his eyes burned, and blood began to trickle from both his ears.

The wind swirled around him, blowing snow in every direction, then the snow wrapped about him like a cocoon. But it wasn't cold, rather, it was like liquid fire. And it scorched his body everywhere it touched him!

He leaned against the cart, trying desperately to get to his feet. Then, Caitlin raised up slightly and reached out her hand. She grabbed Lord Warwick's wrist and held on tightly. He glanced down, wondering what was happening. As Caitlin's hand touched him, a blistering bolt of lightning came streaking from the sky!

Warwick could no longer see or hear. He could only feel. And every inch of his body screamed in agony. He felt his skin begin to melt.

"Dear God! Stop this madness! Help me, Millie! Aiiiiiiiiiiiiiiiiii!!"

There was a sound of glass exploding as the flask in his coat burst with shards of glass going in a thousand directions. At once his screams stopped abruptly.

The last coherent thought Lord Warwick had was that he wished he could have a drink of the alcohol. Perhaps it might ease his pain. As it was, his pain was eased when his body, the essence of him, melted down to the gleaming snow, which was quickly covered in soot. Ashes to ashes — dust to dust.

Caitlin groaned and fell back on the blankets. Millie rushed over to the cart. "Oh, Caitlin! Have you been struck? Speak to me!"

Caitlin lifted her head slightly and whispered, "Is it done? Is he taken care of?"

Then she closed her eyes and could no longer hear Millie's voice.

Millie looked back and saw that Jack was lying, unmoving, still on the ground.

"Oh, no! It struck Jack! No!"

She didn't know what to do now. Caitlin was unconscious and Jack was perhaps close to death. What was she do? Now she was alone with an infant and her dear friends were both either dying or close to it.

Chapter 63

Alex had heard his mother speak of an ancestor who had what Mam called "second sight," which meant that person could foresee some happening in the future. Now, Alex never put much belief in anything he couldn't personally see, but at this very moment he felt as if he might crawl out of his skin. And as surely as his name was Alexander MacKinnon, he knew that Caitlin was in trouble!

There weren't any voices in his head, and no trumpets blaring, but there was such a stirring in his heart that told him he had no choice but to move quickly and get to her. It was as if he could feel her presence, or sense the spirit of her. Having never had this experience before, he stopped and looked about. Maybe he was just tired. But, no. The urge to get to Caitlin immediately was greater than ever. Something flew over, close to his head. As he looked up to the sky, a great owl soared just above him. Alex watched a moment, and the bird circled his head then headed north. Alex knew this bird was leading him, and he never hesitated as he gave his horse his head.

"Well, Mam. If this is 'second sight,' then so be it!" Alex talked to his mother often.

He asked Zeus to go as fast as he could, and that was pretty fast. It wasn't long before he spotted the crofter's hut. All along the trail, the tracks in the snow told him there were three horses traveling together, one pulling some kind of wagon. But, now, coming from a little used side road, he saw another set of prints also. A lone traveler. It didn't take much to figure out who those tracks belonged to. He knew that, as he had feared, Warwick had beaten him here.

As he came through to the wooded side of the cottage, Alex could hear voices coming from the front. But not Caitlin's voice. It was Millie's voice. But not Jack's. He might not hear Caitlin, but he could feel her and his need to get to her all but made him run around the cottage with no thought as to what he might find. But, knowing what he must do, he squatted down and peered around the edge of the small hut. His heart raced as he clearly saw Jack lying, totally still, in a heap on the ground. His first reaction was to run to him, but at that moment he watched as a man twisted Millie's arm behind her back and began to yell at her.

"Where is he? Where is my son?"

He then struck the woman so hard she lost her balance and fell to the ground, crying out in pain as she struck the edge of the cart.

Alex knew Caitlin would be in the cart, and he needed to go to her. But Warwick was brandishing a pistol in one hand and pulling at Millie with the other. His strategy was to get behind Warwick and put his own pistol to the lord's head. Alex began to slowly make his way, keeping low, crawling along when the ground began to shake, and he fell to his knees. What was happening? Then the whole world seemed to convulse! An instant later there was a great roll of thunder and a streak of lightning lighted up the sky and Alex was stunned as he saw it strike Warwick.

The Highlander watched in disbelief. He couldn't believe his eyes. Was that Caitlin's hand he had seen, reaching out of the cart and grabbing Warwick's wrist? Had she caused this unbelievable cascade of events to occur? He had not forgotten the incident at the well, but he had thought that Wabi had conjured that one.

The earth gave one last quiver, and a quiet settled over the whole area. Alex ran to the cart and looked down into Caitlin's face. She was so still. So pale.

"Oh, no! She can't be dead. No! I won't let her be dead!" Millie pulled herself up and rushed to Alex's side.

"No, Alex! She's only unconscious. Not dead. But I'm not so sure about Jack."

Alex felt Caitlin's pulse, and his heart slowed just ever so little. Yes. She was alive. He reached Jack in a second and raised his head up. Jack opened his eyes and lifted his hands upward to his head.

"Ah, Jesus! My head is coming off!" He held his head in both hands and Alex bent down to look at him.

"Well, thank God it was your head he hit. Else we might have had a real problem." Jack was in pain, but still knew what was happening.

"Alex. We need to get Caitlin home. She's not doing so well."

"Right, brother. Come. Let's get you up here in this cart too. We'll be home before you know it and get you both sorted."

"I can ride, Alex. I can ride."

"Not this day, Jack. Now, get up here and stop your whining. We need to go."

Millie held the little midge to her breast and tied the blanket as she had when she first carried her on horseback. Had that only been a few days ago? So much had happened since then.

"Alex. Do you think we can make it to your home quickly?"

"Aye, lass. Not long now."

He walked over to Warwick and just stared. The man's lifeless body, with his greatcoat and fine boots, lay on the ground — a mass of melted fabric, leather, skin and bone. Alex got down on his knees and looked more closely at the body, or what was left of it. Lord Warwick's very fingertips were charred, his ears tipped in ash, his beard burned to a crisp, and the bottoms of his boots were missing, exposing the blackened soles of his feet, still within the confines of his boots. Whatever had she done to him?! There was no blood, and no wounds that he could see. But the man was most definitely dead.

"We'll send the lads to bury him, Millie. Or whatever you wish us to do with his body." Alex stated.

"Please. Just bury him somewhere and never let me know where. He is no longer a part of my life," replied Millie.

Alex nodded and helped her to mount up. He, too, was ready to leave this place. Well, thought Alex, most things have an explanation, but he had never seen a body with these markings. Was she a witch after all?

"I don't care what she is. She belongs to me and I'll no let her go!" Maybe Mam was still listening.

As he walked back to the others, he looked about the area. It was so quiet, with the snow beginning to fall again, like a blanket of loneliness covering the entire moor. Alex couldn't leave fast enough. It was time to go home.

Overhead an owl accompanied him in his travels. Alex didn't see it, however, He was in too big a hurry.

Chapter 64

Wabi sat straight up in bed, grabbing his head with both hands. "What? What is it?"

Finally, waking enough to get his wits about himself, he calmed down and quieted his mind.

Ah. Caitlin. She was calling.

"Yes, my girl, yes. I hear you. What? Caitlin. Hear me. Listen to me carefully. Whatever power I have, you have also. But you must take possession of it and use it when you are sure there is no other choice. And, only you can make that determination."

Wabi considered going to her for a quick moment, knowing he could be there almost immediately. But if he did, then she may never trust her own abilities to make these same decisions. He could tell she was having a dilemma as to whether to try to stop this man, who was most certainly a madman, or whether she should ask Wabi to intervene as he did in the stables.

Whatever she decided, it must be now, this instant, thought Wabi.

He knew exactly what her decision was because, immediately, the mental connection was severed with a forcefulness that took him by surprise. Well. What was he expecting? She had always done everything with a certain flair, so this was in character. He just hoped she would be prepared for the physical toll she would pay for the energy required to complete this task. He would have Owl check on her. But, his mind was at ease knowing she had taken this most important of steps, and there was no turning back now. The Creator had chosen well again.

Chapter 65

Millie had not spoken as yet, and Alex did not try to engage her in any conversation.

What would he say anyway? Like most men, he felt he was expected to have an explanation for most happenings but he was as dumbfounded as anyone else. What was he to think of witnessing an earthquake, an ear splitting wind, a man being enveloped in a virtual tornado of snow, then being struck by a blinding bolt of lightning, and literally dropping to the ground as his life was taken away from him?

Was this witchcraft? No. He thought not. His understanding of witchcraft was limited, but he knew it was a wicked thing, and brought only disaster. But this had saved lives. No, not witchcraft. Was Caitlin responsible? Definitely. He saw her face when she touched Warwick and the strength he saw written in her every feature was unlike anything he had ever witnessed. Her entire body and spirit were being called on to come to the assistance of all. And, come she did!

He would think on this scene many, many times over the years. And, he decided this very minute, he would never question Caitlin about it. They all owed their lives to her.

Even though Millie had told them on more than one occasion that she "loathed" Warwick, Alex assumed there must be some sort of grieving on her part. She had been married to this man for three years, and he had fathered her child. So, with that thought in mind, he continued to ride quietly at Millie's side, looking back occasionally to see that Caitlin, Jack and the babe were safety tucked in their blankets on the cart.

Caitlin was still in the same position she was in when she collapsed following the demise of Warwick. That event had apparently taken the last vestiges of energy she had left. What could they do to help her? Alex didn't have the foggiest idea and figured no one else would either.

***

Pulling back gently on her reins, Millie came to a halt. She looked over at Alex and touched his arm briefly.

"Before we get to your home, please allow me to express my thanks for what you have done and are still doing for me and my child. Without you and Jack coming to our aide, both Caitlin and I would not be here now. You are the most generous men I have ever known."

***

Alex didn't think of himself and his brothers as being generous, rather just doing what any honorable man would do in these circumstances, or at least what any man that Mam had raised would be doing. Only now, after she was gone, were they truly beginning to understand the depth of her teachings and realize what a fine woman and mother she had been. No wonder he and his brothers had not found mates. Mam was a hard act to follow! But, his Caitlin, and this tall, gracious, beautiful woman riding next to him just might pass the test.

Unable to find any words that seemed to be a proper response, Alex smiled at her and nodded his head. "Look, just ahead there. That's our home. See? At the top of the ridge?"

"Yes, but my goodness! It's so large! I thought a sheep farm would be just a few cottages with sheep running about! But, that looks like a lodge of some kind. How many rooms does it have?"

"Oh, well, it started out as just another crofter's cottage, and then Da added a room or so each time a new babe came along. Well, there were four of us, plus Uncle Andrew who needed a room when Aunt Florence passed away. He didn't like staying in his cottage alone. Plus, him being the bard, we like having him around. At night, he keeps us entertained with stories of our ancestors. We're not sure they're all true, ye ken, or maybe we hope not! Then old Jamie, he's our cousin, he needed some space. So, it just sort of grew as the family grew. But, Mam put her hand to it, and it's fairly comfortable. Well, at least to all of us menfolk. But, there's plenty of room for ye, Caitlin and the babe. Da will be surprised."

Alex felt his body relax for the first time in many days. He was almost home.

"Do you think we could stop for just a second, Alex? I need a private moment, if you please."

"Aye, lass. Should have asked ye long before now."

Alex pulled on the reins and drove the cart over to the edge of the wooded area on the right. That way Millie could take care of her personal needs and he would get off for a moment and take a look at Caitlin and Jack.

He watched as Millie, carrying the babe with her, walked into the copse of trees. His Mam had taught him that sometimes ladies just needed a bit of privacy, whereas men just didn't seem to think much about where they were when nature called.

Before he could even reach the cart, however, Caitlin had raised up and was muttering something, but for the life of him he couldn't hear her very well. He stepped closer and she grabbed his sleeve.

"Henbane! I smell henbane! Campbell's here! He's here!" she cried.

"Hey, now. Hey, now. Easy, Caitlin. Lie down, lass. He's gone. He'll not bother you again. He's gone. Rest now."

Caitlin lay back down within moments and seemed unable to respond to Alex.

He so wished they were at the house this very moment. Then, in the next instant, he heard a scream coming from the trees.

"Millie!" Jack tried to raise up, but his head pounded so greatly that he could no longer bear to keep it up.

Alex raced toward the tree line, but as he saw Millie coming out of the forest, he also heard the crack of a pistol — actually, more than heard it — he felt it even more so! The soldier was still a good marksman and had placed the shot in Alex's right hand, and he had hit it square on.

"Ach! Jesus Christ!" Alex had made it through the entire Culloden affair with only a few grazes from a couple of bullets and a broken ankle at some point. But, Lord how this hurt!

He dropped his gun and grabbed at his bleeding hand. By then Campbell had pushed Millie in his direction, and she practically fell on top of Alex. Campbell rushed over and grabbed up Alex's pistol and tossed it into the trees beyond.

"Campbell! Ye need to think now man. I've been in battle. I know what it's like to lose someone ye care about. But, this woman didn't kill yer son. Stop now before ye regret yer actions. A soldier never kills except when he has no other choice. Ye are a fine soldier. Don't leave this stain on yer soul."

But Campbell continued to walk towards the cart.

"I told you I would kill you, witch!" Campbell had known the witch had to have been injured at the well. But he didn't know how much. But, here she was, just lying helplessly in the cart. That fiery hair spread out everywhere. Well. He would finish her off NOW! And, though he really wanted to light a fire and watch her burn, at this point he could barely even keep himself together long enough to fire another shot. His ability to think was so diminished by the henbane, and with his wounded throat, and his exhaustion from traveling, he could barely go any further.

Alex saw the soldier was trying to get to Caitlin and he felt his blood begin to boil. This man had harmed enough people already and Alex would die before he let him hurt Caitlin.

With his pistol having been thrown far into the trees, Alex reached to his waist, reaching for his dirk. Two things he never traveled without were his plaid and his dirk. In fact, those were two pieces of equipment no Highlander would be without. Long before Da had ever taught the MacKinnon lads to shoot, he had spent long hours behind the sheep barn making them learn to throw a dirk at numerous marks that he had drawn on the back wall. A pistol was a good thing, but knowing how to throw a dirk was something he knew was even more important. A gun wasn't any use if you ran out of ammunition. A dirk could always be counted on — if you knew how to use it.

Yes, Commander Campbell had been a fine marksman to hit Alex's right hand. And that suited Alex just fine if he had to be wounded. As it was, his left hand was much more useful to him, however, and that one miscalculation in the Regimental Commander's strategy was his downfall. Alex took just one second to get his aim, drew his left arm back, then let loose of his dirk. He fully expected it would pierce the commander's back and lodge square within the area where his heart, whatever small one he had, would be located.

Alex heard the solid sounding thud as the dirk found its mark. And at that very same time, a red streak of fire blistered its way from the cart and Campbell's body was immediately ablaze with flames reaching for the sky.

"Holy Jesus!" exclaimed Alex. Where did that streak of fire come from? He was almost afraid to look in the direction of the cart. But, of course, he did. Caitlin was leaning over the side of the cart as if she had expired once and for all.

Alex flew to her and thought his heart would explode. She was lifeless, but still breathing. Jack was mumbling something, but Alex's attention was all on Caitlin. He had to get her home and now! So, he eased her back down in the cart and snugged the blankets around her.

When she felt Alex's hands tucking her in, Caitlin looked up at him.

"Alex…Alex….Campbell….he's still here?"

"Nae, lass. He's gone for sure. Trust me. He's no longer in this world."

And Alex was almost relieved when she lost consciousness. Presently, Jack too seemed to be residing in some other place.

Alex himself was a bit shaky. Had his dirk done the soldier in? Or had the fire coming from the cart finished him off? Or a combination of the two? He was in uncharted territory now and knew it. For a long moment, he thought and sat still — and for another short moment he felt Mam's arm around his shoulder — just for a second.

He shook his head. "Hmm. Yer pretty far gone yeself, man," he thought to himself.

Campbell's bleeding and burned body lay at his feet. He retrieved his dirk, and returned it to his belt. This time he was sure the man was dead, but how many lives did this man have! He'd have the lads take care of this body, too. Such a waste, he thought. Such a waste.

Helping Millie to her feet and getting her and the babe settled once again, he looked at the woman. She kept her fears to herself, but Alex knew she had to be past going much farther either. Certainly she was made of some pretty strong stuff to have endured this much.

"Let's get home now, Millie."

Millie tore off a piece of her petticoat and wrapped Alex's hand. Then they started on the last few minutes of their very long journey.

***

Millie looked around as they continued up the path leading to the lodge. There was land as far as she could see, on all sides of the place. And sheep! They were as thick as flies. But the lodge was spectacular. Someone with an eye for architecture had to have had a hand in this. Jack made it sound like it was put together hosh-posh, but it was a most attractive dwelling, two storied in the central part, with single storied wings on either side. The walls were made of fieldstone of some kind, a cream colored stone, some of which had blue veins running through them. And, around the property, the same stone had been used to create a small, short wall, probably a way to keep the sheep on their side. She could readily see why Jack preferred being up here than down in the village. The sky seemed bluer up here and heather was popping up out of the light snow. There was such tranquility in the setting. Yes. This was what a true home must feel like.

As soon as they arrived at the front, Alex climbed down from a very tired Zeus. He patted the horse on the neck, and just about that time the door of the lodge flew open and Hector was taking the steps two at a time, rushing out to greet them. His long legs had him at Alex's side in moments.

"Alex! Thank heavens! We thought maybe ye and Jack had been done in for sure!" He reached his brother and embraced him with all his might.

Alex looked down to his "little" brother with a grin. "Aye. We're back, as ye can see."

Hector finally found his manners and, looking at the tall, beautiful woman, bowed slightly to Millie.

"And I see you have brought some guests for us?"

"You could say that, yes. This is Lady ..."

Millie cut him off immediately. Extending her hand she greeted Hector.

"I'm Millie Sinclair. It's a pleasure to meet you. Your brothers have spoken of you often on this trip."

Hector accepted her hand and bowed again.

"Well, just don't believe everything Alex and Jack tell ye. They're known to stretch the truth at times. But, we're glad to have ye, I'm sure."

Back in the cart, Jack began to try to get on his feet. Regaining consciousness shortly before they arrived, he was having a little trouble remembering everything.

"Hold on there, Jack. We'll help you." Alex called out.

"I'm all right. I'm all right. Just a bit of a headache."

"Yeah. Well. Don't try to move so fast."

Hector had hurried over to the cart by now and was taking a good look at his big brother.

"What happened to ye, Jack?"

"Ah. Hector. Just got on the wrong end of a pistol. Nothing serious. I'll be fine. Stop yer fussing now."

Hector's attention now moved to Caitlin. She lay very still and was still unconscious.

"What's wrong here, Alex?" Hector climbed up onto the cart and stood over the healer.

"I'll tell ye shortly. Right now let's get her into Mam's sewing room. It'll be warm there. Here, hand her down to me.

Alex took Caitlin's limp body, again marveling at how tiny she was, but he knew in her case that was not to be confused with "defenseless." The brothers rushed through the front door and down the hallway without stopping to greet anyone, and left their guest standing at the cart, all alone.

Getting to the front door, Millie stood there holding the baby, waiting for someone to tell her where to go.

Just then an older man came out, followed by a young lad who was limping around with a crutch under one arm and studying her from head to toe.

The older gentleman greeted her.

"Madam, please come in. My boys sometimes forget their manners, but they mean well." He held out his hand, and she took it in hers.

"I'm Daniel MacKinnon, and you're welcome to our home."

Millie saw immediately this gentleman was an older version of Alex. He was tall, handsome, and a bit imposing, but with those same crinkles at the corners of his dark eyes.

"I'm Millie, Millie Sinclair," she replied.

He led her to a small chair close to the fire, what one would think of as a lady's chair and probably had been his wife's seat. Of course, Millie filled the chair, but if felt so good to her. Just getting off the horse was such a relief!

The young lad came over and bowed to her, just a bit, as it was difficult to do so while holding on to his crutch.

"I'm Ian, another one of the MacKinnon brothers."

He didn't think he had ever seen such a beautiful woman. Looking at the tall woman, he asked rather sheepishly,

"Are you a friend of Alex and Jack?"

The older MacKinnon stepped in then, taking the lad by his shoulders and turning him toward the kitchen.

"Here, boy. Don't ask so many questions. See about finding a spot of tea for the lady. That's a good lad." Then he turned to Millie.

"If you'll excuse me, I'll see about Jack's head and see what else needs to be done." She nodded.

Millie watched the young lad leave the room, using his crutch, and only then did she notice that he was missing the lower part of his left leg. It certainly didn't seem to be slowing him down much. Looking about the room, Millie could see a woman had lived here, her touch was everywhere from curtains to window boxes, which surely held flowering plants in the spring. Daffodils, thought Millie, smiling at the thought. And these men were doing a pretty good job of keeping this lodge orderly as well. She could even detect a faint scent of lavender in the room. The scent of lavender was known to bring a feeling of calmness, and Millie had always liked it.

Chapter 66

Alex and Hector laid Caitlin down on the small cot in Mam's sewing room. This room was where she had spent a lot of time when not in the kitchen. At the last, she preferred lying in this room where a large window allowed the sun to come through and kept the cot warm. There was a chair next to the cot where Daniel would sit and read to her during her last days. He had no formal education, but his love of reading made up for that in many ways.

Hector looked over at Jack. "Tell me what ye know, Jack."

"Oh, Hector. It's a difficult story. But Caitlin's obviously struggling and we don't know what to do to help her." He stood looking down at his feet, shaking his head and rubbing his forehead with his hand. His head ached like the very devil.

"Hector. Ye just had to be there to believe it! Caitlin brought down the demons of hell on that man! But, he would have killed Millie and the babe, and probably me and Alex too, otherwise."

"The babe. It belongs to the tall woman?" asked Hector.

"Millie, yes. The babe's only a week or so old, but she's doing well. Millie has managed to care for her through this whole ordeal."

"And how do ye know this Millie?"

"Oh. I don't. Or didn't. She came to the castle with Caitlin and Alex. And I was sleeping on the floor, and Caitlin tripped over me. And then Millie came down the stairs and tried to take my head off."

Jack saw the look on Hector's face.

"Hector. Listen to me. I'm telling ye it happened, man!" "Jack. Let's get some food into ye, and some rest I think."

"Hector. I'm all right. I know it sounds crazy, and it is. But we've got to find a way to save Caitlin. She's pretty well gone, I'm afraid. And Alex is beside himself with worry."

The two brothers watched helplessly as Alex stood by Caitlin's bed, holding her hand. "Her breathing is very shallow, and I'm no healer, but I know that can't be good," said

Alex.

"Aye," said Jack. "I see it too."

"I'll get Millie back here, but she's no healer either. But, she may know something we don't know."

Jack brought Millie back, and he took the baby, holding it nestled up on his shoulder, as usual. Alex and Hector passed a look between themselves — what was this? Something here they didn't understand, yet.

Millie turned the blankets back, looking Caitlin over carefully.

"Oh, Alex. The only thing I can tell is that her leg is much more swollen. We must loosen the wrappings and see if that will allow the swelling to go down some. I wonder if maybe the bone has been misplaced again, maybe from the jostling in the cart. But, this is not anything I know much about. We need some help. Is there no one up here?"

"Nae, lass, not just now." Daniel had come into the room.

"Annie was our healer for the longest, but she went on too, just shortly after my Alice.

So, we've been without a healer for some time now."

"Then, we'll send to Edinburgh if need be!" shouted Alex, getting up and pacing around the room.

"We'll not let her die, I tell ye!"

He was down on his knees, taking Caitlin's hand in his. It was so very cold, so small. His fear was evident to all in the room, and fear was something that Alex didn't wear very well.

With a quick jerk of his head, Jack motioned for everyone to leave Alex with his Caitlin.

He needed to talk with her by himself.

***

Ian's tea was a very fine one. It was a most unusual one Mam had kept in the top part of her cupboard.

"Mam said this tea came from India, and she saved it for special occasions." Smiling, he continued with his pouring of the tea as best he could.

"To me, having everyone back home is a very special occasion."

Jack's head gave him an awful ache, but he took time to give a short version of what had happened since he left. Was it truly only a short time? Somehow, it seemed like ages to him. He left out a few details that were just too difficult to explain and, thankfully, no one asked for more information. He had an inkling that Da might corner him later, but not just now.

Jack took Millie back to a fairly large room, near the rear of the lodge. It was much quieter back here, and he thought Millie and the infant would appreciate some privacy. The room was actually the bedroom where Da and Mam had slept when she was alive. But when she was no longer with them, Da had taken to sleeping in the small room next to the kitchen. He just didn't like being in that large room without Alice. Anyway, this way he could always have the coffee on the stove when his boys got up and came to the kitchen. He always said the scent of brewing coffee filled the house and had them all getting up. The real reason was that it gave him a small bit of purpose, a reason to get up each day.

Millie was never so surprised. "Oh, my! I never expected such comfort on a sheep farm. The coverings on the bed are very fine. I'm sure they are handmade. Someone spent a lot of time making those crocheted edgings on the sheets. And curtains that reach the floor! And this rug is like walking on the softest wool!"

Jack smiled and left her to herself. She walked around the room which had another door across from the bed. Probably a closet. But when she opened it, she was ever so excited.

"What? Oh, I've landed in heaven!" There was a large, rectangular wooden tub for bathing sitting in the middle of the floor in the tiny closet. So, the bath she so longed for could become a reality.

***

Alex paced from one end of the room to the other, thinking, thinking. What to do. Caitlin needed help. Where could he find someone to help her?

Just then, he walked outside, looking at the sky to see if more snow was on the way. As he stood on the porch, which reached from one end of the lodge to the other, an owl came breezing by and found a resting place on a branch of the spruce tree just at the edge of the porch. Alex looked at the owl and wondered why in the world a bird would be out in this cold. Surely he had a warm nest in a barn somewhere, maybe even in their barn. But, the owl just sat there, not moving a feather. That got Alex to thinking about the falcon he had seen in the castle, sitting on the window seat. There had been an owl outside there also. They were easy to spot with their tufted spot between their ears. They were another of nature's wonders, Alex thought. He turned to go back inside and as he did, the owl took flight and with a great show of grace, sailed upward and was gone from sight within seconds.

Alex stayed by Caitlin's bedside for some time. Then, having made a decision, he came back out to the kitchen where they were all gathered. His quick, long stride revealed his state of mind.

"I'm going down to Edinburgh. There's a doctor there, one I know from my time at university. If anyone can help Caitlin, it'll be this man. Standing by her bed and watching her die is not my way. So, if ye all will care for her, then I'll be on my way. Hector, I need a fresh horse. And Ian. Make a small packet of food for me. I need to go now."

And that same determined stride carried him outside awaiting his brothers.

It was at this point that Hector saw Jack and Caitlin weren't the only wounded ones.

"Alex! What happened to yer hand, man? Git over here. Let me take a look at it."

Hector had dressed a number of wounds on the battlefield himself, and saw that this could turn out to be a very problematic one if not cleaned and bandaged properly.

"Sit down — now, brother." And he carefully cleaned the wound and wrapped it with clean cloths from Mam's closet. She was always prepared for disasters as living in the Highlands had taught her to be.

Alex said his goodbyes, except to Caitlin. He refused to say goodbye to her. That was unthinkable.

Chapter 67

Wabi was very glad to be back home in his own cottage. The walkabout had certainly been unusual and not what he usually experienced. But, he was content that Caitlin was starting her new life in the Highlands with the MacKinnon's. Alex was a good choice for her. And she would be able to use her healing skills again. Maybe she would finally have the large family she had always hoped for.

This was the first time Wabi had ever made his trek during the cold months. Usually he went in the spring when nature was waking up again after her long winter's sleep. The air was different then. New buds were beginning to open and the next generation of the various species would be bursting forth all around. But, he did admit that walking in the snow had its own appeal. Even the trees, having discarded their clothing, had their own beauty, their naked limbs exposed for all to see. Yes, he thought. Each season has its purpose, just as we all have ours.

The leaves totally covered the ground surrounding the place, and it looked like an artist had carefully painted each leaf a different color — red, ochre, and sienna. There were even some small petals that looked like faded bluebells. Sometimes a walkabout also heightened your senses, and that was always to his liking.

This morning, seeing smoke coming from her chimney, Wabi, with old Groucho tagging along beside him, had called on Mrs. Favre'. She was such a good conversationalist, but never asked questions that were too inquisitive. She had an understanding, it seemed, that Wabi had some characteristics unique to him and she accepted he was more than met the eye. She was ever so glad to see him.

"Ah, Wabi! You're back! And you are well, I see. Good. And Groucho. It's always wonderful to see you, handsome man." She reached down and rubbed the old cat along his back, which was certainly to his liking.

"Come. Let's have some tea, and you can tell me all about your walkabout!"

Mrs. Favre' invited him to return for dinner — bribed him with promise of one of her truffle soufflés — knowing he couldn't resist. Certainly not one to disappoint, Wabi accepted the invitation and was looking forward to the evening. He would bring some special wine for the occasion.

Chopping wood was the order of the day, however. Having been gone for some time now, he needed to complete a few chores to get things back in order. Stacking the logs neatly beside the shed, he started in again on his next small tree, beginning to cut it into pieces that would fit his fireplace. Just then his ears picked up a sound that only he would recognize. It was a friend coming in, and making a show of it as always. Owl slowed quickly and let his feathers ruffle in the wind as he landed on Wabi's shoulder.

"Well, my friend! To what do I owe this surprise?"

Wabi hadn't had a report from Owl since leaving the castle, but then didn't really expect to now that Caitlin was "on her own," so to speak.

"Master. I'm afraid this is not a casual visit. I come with disturbing news of Caitlin." Wabi put his axe down and looked at Owl.

"But, I just had communication with her yesterday. She was debating using her powers, but it was apparent to me that she did, in fact, use them. The communication stopped abruptly, and I'm pretty sure she acted on her impulse. So, what? Is she in trouble already? She knows how to call me."

Wabi had most definitely felt Caitlin could handle herself now and really had not worried about her for one second.

"Oh, well, yes, I suppose you might call it trouble. She made a fine show of using her powers. It was a very dire scene, Master. She called upon all her intuition and powers and destroyed a most vile man, one who would have killed all of them, no doubt. But that's not the problem. Her broken leg was causing her great pain already, and then she traveled in that ridiculous cart, which was beneath her dignity. She could have used time weaving if she wished. I think traveling in that contraption reinjured her leg. The scene with the wicked Warwick man took what was left of her energies, and she collapsed. Then that soldier showed up again! And between Caitlin and the one called Alex, he was taken care of also. But, after that, she hasn't been conscious at all. I fear she may not be able to contact you, for certainly she would have done so were she able. Master, she is in a very bad way."

"What? Campbell didn't die at the well? Oh, Caitlin. Did I let you go too soon?" Wabi pulled at his beard, as usual, and immediately made a decision. Some things can't wait, and this was one of them. He quickly penned a note to Mrs. Favre' and put it in Owl's beak.

"Owl. Take this to Aned, deposit it at her front door. Quickly, now. Then come back here. We have much to do."

Wabi knew Aned would understand; he had no worries about that. Meanwhile, he had to mentally prepare himself for traveling, and this time it would not be on foot.

Owl was back as Wabi finished his preparations. Time weaving was exhilarating, always, but my goodness, he was getting too old for this stuff!

"Owl. You must travel with me this time. I may need your services when we arrive."

"Oh, Master! You know how I hate this time and place weaving business! It makes my head spin!"

"Your head spins anyway, my friend."

"Well, yes, I suppose it does. Very well then. Let's get it over with."

Wabi would find her. He took his crooked staff and lying down on the ground, prone, with his head facing to the north, he began his chant. The same chant he had made in all his lives. Owl felt his feathers begin to flutter in the wind as it slowly began to lift them from the earth. What happened after that, Owl was never quite sure about. But a whirlwind came through, picked them up, and they entered some very dark place filled with twinkling lights — maybe stars — and moved at such speed that Owl could hardly get his breath. Wabi still chanted and now Owl could no longer see him, but knew his spirit was still there. He could sense it. Then there was a loud chorus of voices, singing in so many languages it made Owl dizzy. And Wabi still continued his chanting. Suddenly they were being sucked down, down, down, into an endless chasm it seemed to Owl.

"Oh, why did I agree to this again!" screeched Owl, drawing his wings as close to his body as he possibly could.

"Master, surely there is an easier route I must say!" Sometimes his proper, English accent was so clipped that Wabi had to laugh at him.

In another moment they both landed with a plop! Picking himself up, Wabi replied, "Come, Owl. Let's get to work."

As they got their feet firmly planted and got their bearings, Wabi looked about. Ah. Yes. They had made it to the right place. In the distance was a rather unexpected building, a lodge, he thought.

"Owl. I believe we have arrived at our destination." "Yes, Master. This is the place. Caitlin is here."

Leaning on his staff he always traveled with, they began the long walk up to the lodge. In just a moment, however, they were surprised to see a rider coming toward them at breakneck speed.

"That poor horse will never be able to go far at that pace!" said Wabi.

"Ah. That would be Alex, Master, the one that is so attached to our Caitlin."

"Yes. Of course. Alex. Good. He'll be able to tell us what has happened. We'll talk with him a moment."

Owl quickly flew up and perched on Wabi's shoulder in order to get his attention. "Master. She needs help now. We don't have time to make conversation with this man.

He's a man of few words, anyway. We must hurry, I fear."

Wabi nodded and began to run to the lodge, using his staff to help him move quickly.

Alex was almost on them now. He saw Wabi with the crooked staff supporting himself.

He pulled on the reins and stopped.

"Wabi! How did you get here?" Alex yelled.

"Oh. Whatever way I can. Tell me what's happened to Caitlin. I know she's in trouble."

"She's here, inside, and she's very ill. I'm headed to Edinburgh to find Dr. Lind."

"No, Alex. That will take too long, and Owl tells me she's critical. Take me to her. I can help her. Hurry now!"

Alex was in a quandary. Should he believe this old man? Or, should he move on as quickly as possible? Getting to Edinburgh and back in time to help Caitlin was a long shot, he knew that. But, there didn't seem to be anything else to do. He couldn't just stand by her bed and watch her die. He would not do that!

But Wabi had made that statement with such conviction — "I can help her"— that Alex found himself turning his horse and around and pulling Wabi up behind him.

"Hold on! We'll be there in a second!" and they were.

Rushing through the front door, Wabi could feel Caitlin's spirit and went directly to her room. Alex just watched and looked from Jack to Hector.

Jack nodded. "Yes. Let him go to her. He can help her if anyone can. I've seen him in action!" Jack wasn't sure whether to be thankful Wabi was here or whether to be ready for another spectacular event that would set everyone's hair on fire.

Chapter 68

Wabi and Owl entered the room, closing the door behind them. Some rituals were not for everyone's eyes and Wabi preferred to keep his interventions known only to himself, if possible. Caitlin would need his undivided attention and he wanted no distractions from others. As always, Owl was there. He was always standing by when his master needed him.

Within just a few minutes of Wabi entering Caitlin's room, a rumble could be heard coming from far away, then beginning to get closer and louder.

"Oh, good glory! Here we go again!" Jack had raised his voice and felt himself trembling. He looked over to Alex and Hector.

Grabbing his brothers' arms he yelled, "Just hold on! It will pass quickly!"

Of course, he hoped it would. But his heart was racing and his palms were sweaty. The rumble passed and there was a brief quiver felt throughout the house. Jack held his breath, wondering what was coming now. For just a brief moment, the air seemed to sizzle, making a tinkling sound like bells in a windstorm — many, many bells. Then all was quiet. Jack was not the only one who wanted this be over with. Alex and Hector looked about as if wondering what they should be doing next.

***

Inside the room, Wabi took a look at Caitlin and his heart sank.

"Oh, my dear child, why didn't you call me earlier?" He was not sure even he could bring her back from the place where she resided presently. Wabi put a hand on either side of her face and could feel her life force was so very weak. It would take every ounce of power he could muster to find her, and even then she might not choose to come back. It was always a choice the person had to make.

Letting his power flow through his fingers, he began. "Caitlin — it is not your time yet — you have much to do still — you are needed here by many people. The Creator has a plan for you — come back to us — Caitlin, hear me — come back, child."

Wabi felt himself being drawn deep into the place where Caitlin was resting. Yes, resting.

And it was so warm, so comfortable. And he, too, wanted to stay. It was so tempting. The light was so soft. It drifted throughout the place and wrapped itself around you, seeping into your very being. This enveloping sanctuary called to many, and Wabi had been here before himself and knew it to have captured others long before their time. With a force of will he hadn't called on for a very long time, Wabi snapped himself out of the clutches of this tantalizing haven. As the bonds began to slowly break away, he sensed another spirit — following him. Yes! Following him!

"Yes, just a little more, Caitlin. Follow. Follow."

And finding her own formidable will power, Caitlin followed that voice, someone calling her, someone she loved. Yes, she would follow this spirit. She recognized this entity somehow. Then there was another entity, whispering to her . . . "Go, daughter. Go with him. He'll guide you back. I'm always here, but it's not yet time for you to dwell here . . . go child." And she did.

"Oh! My head! Holy Rusepheus!" Caitlin jerked up in bed and she thought her head would explode. "What is happening?" she wailed loudly.

Wabi felt his own spirit gathering itself, and his head was pounding with a vengeance also. But, he had experienced this enough times to know it would pass. But it was an excruciating few minutes for sure.

"Oh, Caitlin. My girl. All is well. All is well."

Wabi had his arms around her, and she looked up into his face. Tears were streaming down his old cheeks, following the track they always followed, tracing the scar that ran down from his upper cheek through his upper lip, leftovers from some other life perhaps.

"Oh. Wabi. I feel like I've been sleeping for a long, long time! When I touched that odious man I could feel the blackness in his soul! But, then nothing from then on."

"Where is that man? Is he still here?" she asked. Wabi quickly took her hands in his.

"No, Cait. You took care of him. And, apparently you did a very fine job of him and the soldier, according to Owl."

Caitlin looked over at Owl. Shaking her head, she had to smile.

"My new friend. You made a believer out of me when no one else could. You are an extraordinary bird for sure."

Owl held his beak up high with a small nod in Caitlin's direction, once again reassured that he was still needed in the lives of these two friends.

"But, Wabi. I don't remember anything much about Campbell. But I do remember smelling henbane. But didn't you take care of him at the well?"

"Yes. Well. Alex will have to fill you in on that. He participated in that event as well. Better let him explain from his point of view."

"Now, my girl, there are some others who might want to see you. Then, as distasteful as it may be, we will have to rebreak and reset that leg of yours. From the looks of it, you will most certainly be crippled if we don't."

"Aye, Uncle Wabi. I knew that was coming. But Wabi, something else is wrong. I remember feeling it before I lost consciousness. But what? It's like a family member in need. I can't explain it. But I know I'm right."

"Caitlin. You'll learn how to understand these new feelings that go along with the powers. Don't be in such a rush. It will all become clear to you. Soon."

Alex and Jack were standing so close to the door it almost hit them in the face when Wabi came out.

"She's all right now. She'll be well." Said Wabi.

***

The old wizard walked back out to the sitting room. He looked about this most comfortable home. Evidence of people involved with life was everywhere. There were hats on pegs, jackets hung in the mud room, vegetables in bins in the kitchen, flowers in window boxes. Yes. This place would be good for Caitlin.

When he had run through the room earlier, in his desperate effort to get to Caitlin, he had caught a glimpse of a young lad. Somewhere he had made a mental note the lad was walking with a crutch, and his leg had been amputated just below the knee. What a waste, thought Wabi! That boy was too young to spend the rest of his life tied to a crutch that limited his every movement. Wabi decided he would give the matter some thought, and he would indeed do that.

As Ian hobbled into the room, crutch and all, Wabi called out to him.

"Young man. I wonder if I could trouble you for a cup of tea. I do believe it would do wonders for this old man who presently finds himself just a wee bit tuckered out."

"Oh, aye, sir. There be plenty more. Mam always kept a pot on the stove. She said ye could always use one when ye needed a little pick-me-up."

And with the crutch under this arm, Ian went off to fetch the tea. He actually had learned to work with his crutch under one arm and carry items in his other hand, but certainly it was difficult for him. But, of course, in true MacKinnon fashion, he never uttered a word of complaint about his situation.

***

After Jack had brought her up to date, Millie breathed a great sigh of relief. She sat on the edge of the bed looking at her little daughter. Whatever was going to happen to them? What was she to do? But, she had learned that Jack MacKinnon made many things possible she would never have believed.

At that very moment, there was a knock at her door. Opening the door quietly, she was met by a very young man carrying a large bucket of hot water.

"Oh, miss. I be Kenny. Mr. Jack said to bring some hot water up to you. If you'll let me in I'll start filling the tub."

"Oh, heavens! Do come in. The tub is here in this closet."

"Yes, miss," and Kenny poured the hot water into the tub.

"I'll be bringin' a couple more just to make sure you have enuff," and he dashed off back to the kitchen.

Millie thought she had never been so comfortable as when she laid back in that large tub and soaked herself in the warm water. And there was a bar of French soap on a ledge in the closet! Another "leftover" from Mam, no doubt. Jack MacKinnon had performed another miracle in her eyes.

Chapter 69

Alex thought he would tiptoe into Caitlin's room, not sure what he might find. But, before he could even take a step forward, she called to him.

"Alex MacKinnon. I would know that evergreen scent anywhere! What took you so long?"

Alex felt drained, his relief was so great. It had not escaped his attention that his every thought in the past days had been of this woman, and now she was here, safe at last.

"Caitlin. Like it or no, ye'll no be leaving this place. If that's imprisonment, then so be it.

But it's here that ye belong."

"Yes. I thought you might say something like that. But, as you can see, I don't think I'll be going anywhere for a while."

"Ah, Caitlin." He sat on the small chair and took her hands in his, covering them completely. His right hand was healing, but still had a bandage.

"I thought I would never see ye again, lass. Every time I thought I had maybe found ye, ye were gone again. And every time I thought I had caught up with Campbell, he was just out of my reach."

"Alex. You're here and I'm here. That's all that matters. Now, before I rest I would like to see Willie, please. He'll be wondering what has happened to me."

Alex looked at her with a blank face. "Willie?" He thought for a minute. Suddenly Caitlin sat straight up. She knew!

"That's what's wrong! I felt him! Oh Alex! I know I felt him!" Alex stood and looked down at her.

"I haven't seen him, Caitlin. Maybe he ran off. But, no. He'd never leave your side. Maybe he just strayed off the path. Wait. I'll ask Jack if he knows anything.

Of course, he didn't have to go far as Jack and Hector were both standing out in the hall, just waiting to hear what Alex had to report.

Jack spoke up right away. "Well? Is she all right then?" "Oh, aye. I think she'll be all right now."

"Alex, that's some woman ye have in there. A very fine woman."

Jack was hoping Alex wasn't looking to him for any answers about her dispensation of Warwick, nor Wabi's "healing" of Caitlin. He had just accepted it and that was an end to it.

"But, she's asking to see her wolf, Willie. But I don't remember seeing him at the crofter's hut. Was he with you all before I got there?"

Jack looked up at his brother.

"Ah, Jesus, Alex! I let him out for a run early in the morning. He came scratching to go out and I was building a fire, so I just let him go. He always comes back. But there was so much commotion going on with Warwick, I completely forgot about him. But, he must not have been close or he would have been there at Caitlin's side. He would never leave her! Something's happened to him. Glory! Caitlin will skin me alive for sure!"

"Nae. She's too tired to do any real damage to ye just now," smiled Alex. "But, we'd better try to find him before she regains her strength!"

That was Jack, not wanting to be on Caitlin's wrong side.

Alex went back in and explained to Caitlin that Willie was still out in the woods somewhere, and they were going to look for him.

Caitlin tried to sit up and Alex rushed over to help her. He put a pillow behind her back and tucked her blankets back in. She was quiet for a moment.

"Bring Wabi. Now."

Without questioning, Alex called for Wabi. "She's needing ye for a minute."

Wabi walked in, closing the door behind himself. Caitlin's color had returned somewhat, which was a good sign, but something was amiss. Her facial expression told him that.

"Ah, my girl, feeling a wee bit better, I see."

"Wabi. Willie's missing. He would never abandon me. Something's wrong." As Wabi came closer, his piercing eyes took hold of Caitlin's aqua ones. "You must call him, Caitlin. He will hear you."

"Call him? I don't know where he is!"

"Caitlin. Calm down and clear your mind. YOU can call him. Just concentrate your energies, just once more. Then we'll let you rest."

Caitlin finally understood what he was asking her to do. This was still new to her, this communication ability, but she was beginning to see that it had purpose at times. So, relaxing and clearing any distractions from her mind, she silently called.

"Willie. Willie." And nothing happened.

"Willie, hear me. Willie." Then a very faint echo came, drifting across the empty place in her mind.

"Willie. Willie." Then she heard a mournful howl. Then another.

With her face registering her fear, she looked to her uncle. "Oh, Wabi! He's hurt! I can feel it! I can hear him!"

"Caitlin, quiet, girl, listen again and look around. Try to locate him. Find something that might show where he is."

Focusing once again, she called. "Willie. Hear me. Willie."

Closing her eyes once again, getting back to that place where she was learning to go in her mind was easier this time. She heard Willie howling again, but very faintly. She could only see snow covered ground and a stream with a small tree. It looked so desolate without its leaves to give it cover. And there was an owl sitting on the branch. As she watched in her mind, the owl flew off and the picture faded.

"He's lying near a stream. There's a small tree next to it and Owl was in the tree." Wabi left her bedside and came out to tell the brothers what she had seen.

"She says Willie's lying by a stream of water and there's a small tree close by. That's all she could see. But, Alex, be careful. The wolf is hurt."

"Then that's got to be the stream behind that old shearing shed, on the west side of the lower pasture, where Mam kept everything she wouldn't let us throw away. Her empty jars she used for her jam making. You know, all the old stuff she just couldn't part with. There's a small stream behind the shed, but it's usually frozen over this time of year. It's a place to start."

Alex was pulling at straws trying to bring this picture together. Had Uncle Wabi said "that's all she could see?" What did that mean? Whatever, he nodded to Wabi and with Hector and Jack right behind him, they strode quickly out and hurried to the stables.

Wabi returned to Caitlin's room.

"Caitlin. You must rest now. We'll find Willie. No worries, child."

Now that he was back at home, Alex was giving orders as usual, and he called to Jack and Hector.

"I'll go to the stream in the lower pasture. You two take a look over at Jamie's old cottage. Seems to me it has a small stream also.

"Hold on, Alex. Ye'll not be going anywhere. That hand's not something to fool around with. Ye'll be staying here with Caitlin.

Hector can check out the east side, and I'll go to the west pasture. Caitlin needs you right now. We can handle this."

"Ah, Christ!" Throwing open the stable doors, Alex walked away, knowing his brother was right. Caitlin needed him now.

Jack's head was threatening to come right off any minute. But the responsibility he felt for not realizing Willie had not returned and was out there somewhere was just too great to ignore. He must find that wolf.

"Jesus! Why didn't I remember Willie? I'd kick my own arse if I could!" Frustration didn't help his already aching head.

"There are several streams on the place, you know that! But that wolf is important to her, and we'll find him!"

He rubbed the back of his neck.

"But we may discover something else has found him first. The coyotes in this area wouldn't welcome a newcomer to their territory. Now, let's get on about our work."

He tore off headed to the old shed, but he didn't have much confidence the wolf would be there. And, how had Caitlin been able to "see something?" Jack just shook his head and decided he would think on that later. Right now he had his hands full. And so did Alex!

Jack reached the pasture, slowing his horse to a walk. This pasture wasn't used very often, but occasionally during lambing season, they would herd the new mother ewes and their calves here where the stream was shallow. They could drink and not be overrun by the more aggressive older rams. There was a small bridge over the stream, and it needed some repair, he noted. He followed the stream which led him to the backside of the shed. At that point he got down and started walking, still following the water. In just a few moments, he stopped and listened.

Nothing. Only the crunch of his boots in the crisp snow. Walking on he looked about checking for prints. Maybe those coyotes he was worried about. Again, nothing. The snow was undisturbed. As he rounded the corner of the shed, there was a small tree, tall but not very big around. Its leaves had all dropped to the ground already and had been covered by the recent snow. As he reached the base of the tree, he came to a halt. A deep throated growl met him and he proceeded with caution. Great caution!

"Ah! No! No! I should have thought of this!" Jack ventured another foot closer and saw the huge black animal lying on his side, still growling, even if weakly. As he had said earlier, sheep and wolves don't mix. And, as most sheep farmers do, they had set out several traps to snare wolves and coyotes. Sometimes they even caught their own sheep in them. And Willie had found one of them.

Jack thought for a moment. This was a ways from the crofter's hut. Why had Willie come this far? He was surely able to find food and didn't need to come all the way up here. What else would have gotten his attention and brought him to this area?

He rubbed his neck again.

"Of course! The same thing that has my attention and Alex's at the moment — a female!" Jack said this aloud and Willie didn't offer any denial.

"They're no different than we are. Or maybe it's the other way around." "So, fella. Here ye are. Got yeself caught, did ye?"

Willie had been at ease with all the MacKinnon brothers back in the cave, and Jack had liked having him run along beside the horses on the trip. But did the wolf remember that?

The Highlander got down on one knee and continued to talk softly to the wounded animal.

"Sure looks like ye need some help, old buddy. So, maybe if ye let me get closer, we can get ye out of there."

Moving just marginally closer, he watched the hackles go down and the growl turned into a whimper, a sure sign of submission and a call for help.

"That's a boy. That's a boy."

Jack contemplated hitting the animal on the head, just lightly, and then removing the trap. A wounded wolf was nothing to mess around with. But, this poor boy didn't look like he could take much more abuse. He had been here some time now. So, with great trepidation, Jack got a bit closer. The growling continued, but the wolf made no move that indicated he would try to get up. However, his ears were sticking straight up and his hackles were trying their best to stand tall.

"Hey. Let's see about getting ye out of that trap, eh?"

Jack quickly saw Willie had been caught by his right rear paw, and it was being held firmly in the trap. A lot of blood had been spilt, too. Reaching over slowly, he rubbed the fur behind the wolf's ears, and his gesture was met with another whimper.

"Easy now, boy. Hold on."

The trap was a steel-jawed, leg-hold trap and was easily retracted by putting a foot on either side of the trap, then pressing down with both feet. You could then pull the animal's leg out. But, that meant you would have to pull the animal up and hold him close to you while you put your feet on the trap itself.

Jack thought for a moment. He sensed that Willie knew who he was and he was not going to attack him. But still — he was a wolf! So, once again rubbing the wolf's head, he gently pulled him closer to his body. The wolf was almost lifeless and offered no resistance. Jack struggled to get him to even budge. He was one heavy animal. But, he finally got him up next to his chest. He put a boot on either side of the trap and with some pressure, it sprang open immediately.

With the paw now released, Jack hoped Willie would be able to stand up and make his way back with him, back to Caitlin.

But even though the trap had been removed, Willie just lay there, immobile and looking up at Jack as if waiting for the man to give him a signal, as Caitlin always did. But, even if Jack had given him one, he would not have been able to obey the command. He was just too far gone.

"Well, my furry friend, looks like I'll have to bring the cart for you, too. I've spent some time in it myself, and it's not too bad actually. I can't carry you, that's for sure."

***

Hector had not found any prints, nor seen any other animals in the upper pasture. Coming just past the lodge, headed down to the shed, he found Jack still kneeling next to Willie and talking quietly to him.

Hector walked over, not sure what the situation was.

Is he dead?" asked Hector, frantic to know the condition of Willie.

"Na, not dead, but pretty bad off. We'll need the cart for him I think, brother."

Hector took off and was back shortly with the pony cart hooked to his mount. The two of them had several tries before they were able to lift Willie and placed him in the cart. That cart had now carried several wounded ones. The others were recovering, so maybe this wounded one would also.

As they came up on the porch, Wabi met them and without any fanfare, told them to bring the animal back to Caitlin's room.

"That may take some doing, Wabi. He's quite a load. But, we'll give it a shot," said Jack.

"Here. Place him on her bed," instructed Wabi.

Caitlin had felt him long before they got to the room with him. "Jack! You found him!"

Willie sighed deeply and rested his head next to Caitlin.

"You have all repaid any debt you ever thought you owed me. He's most important to me — as all of you are. And Alex, even without knowing the details, I know you saved my life. I am now in your debt, it would seem." Her voice held tears that threatened to spill.

Alex smiled and left the room, his mind trying its hardest to come to terms with her statement. They were all important to her. Did she group him with his brothers, or did she consider him as important as he did her?

After checking on both his patients, Wabi reported to the men.

"As much as I wish it weren't necessary, we're going to have to reset Catilin's leg. But, that will just have to wait a couple of days until she's recovered somewhat. But, she's already guessed this much."

He started to walk away, then turned back to the three brothers.

"They'll both be fine, now. Willie just needed his mistress, and she needed her companion. They have an understanding, you see. Relax. They'll recover and be better together than apart."

Chapter 70

Millie had no wish to ever go, but she knew that she could not leave the Sinclair estate untended. And, what about the oldsters, like Clint and Ethel, Winston, and others who had spent a lifetime taking care of the place and her family? She owed a debt of gratitude to them that must be paid. Mulling over it a while longer, she decided to discuss the matter with Jack before she got any further along with her plans.

She watched as Caitlin, having survived the resetting of her leg, rested in Mam's chair with a small stool to hold her leg. Willie, his leg in a splint, lay on the floor next to his mistress.

Millie knew that everyone liked to be in this room. There was always a crowd in the evening, and she loved that time. They all spoke of Uncle Andrew, the family bard, but he hadn't made an appearance just yet. She'd been told he was off to Edinburgh trying to document births and deaths of some ancestors. Alex was concerned that when Andrew was gone no one would remember anything. So, Uncle Andrew had promised to put it all "down on paper" as he called it. And, he should be returning soon. Her little Midge was constantly passed from one to the other, to her delight. Millie was unused to so many people, as she knew Caitlin was also. But this group of folks were the finest example of what family truly should be, and she had decided she wanted to be a part of it.

Just yesterday, Hector had walked into the kitchen where Millie was trying her hand at making apple pie.

"Well, now what have we here? Looks like a proper pie to me. Now, lass, if ye can manage that, then ye are better than I am." Dipping his finger into the pie filling, he causally asked, "So, do ye think ye could manage the kitchen for a couple of days? I need to get some legal papers down to the solicitor, and Alex doesn't want to leave Caitlin just now. So, I told him I'd make the trip."

"Why, yes, I suppose I could do that, with a little help from your Da maybe. He's a fair hand in the kitchen too, I notice."

"He is at that, lass. Mam made sure everybody could carry their weight around here, including Da! And don't forget Wabi. He seems to have a knack for cooking too."

So Millie was in charge of the kitchen until Hector returned. She couldn't remember ever being responsible for anything in her entire life. The thought gave her pause, but in a satisfying way.

While Millie was learning about making stews, Jack took charge of the babe that they now called "Midge," as Jack had thought she was as small as a midge when he first saw her. Millie had not decided what her name would truly be yet. But, she knew it would have Caitlin in there somewhere. The healer needed to be honored for her part in bringing this child into the world. Both Jack and little Midge were happiest when they went about the lodge, he with her resting against his shoulder, and she gurgling and drooling on his shirt collar.

As Millie busied herself in the kitchen, she couldn't help but see Wabi, Da and Ian making numerous trips in and out of the woodshed for several days now, refusing to allow anyone to enter. Millie wondered just what those fellows were up to. She didn't give it much more thought, however; her kitchen duties were keeping her busy enough.

A couple of days after Hector left, Millie got Jack's attention and they sat down at the big oak table, gleaming from her polishing. The room was filled with a fresh lemon-wax scent. She poured tea for the two of them. Jack had the ever-present Midge sleeping on his shoulder.

Unsure how to approach the subject, Millie decided to just jump in and see what happened. So, twisting a long lock of hair, as she always did when nervous, she began.

"Jack. I need your thoughts about my family's place, the estate. I have to go back down and figure out how to help the workers. They need some way to make a living, some way to finish out their lives in the place they've called home. Yes, some of them are old, but they aren't past doing their jobs, and I need to take care of them. But I don't want to leave here!"

She was close to tears, and Jack couldn't take that! "Ach! Don't be getting on so, Millie, No tears. No tears." Reaching out and taking her hand, he continued.

"I suppose I forgot to tell ye, but Hector is already down there at the estate, and knowing him, the whole place is humming with activity and everybody has found some job that needs doing. Lass, I know ye would no let them down any more than I would let ye down. 'Tis all but taken care of already. But, let's see what Hector says when he returns, and we'll both go down and make plans and changes if we need to, Millie.

"But. What if they won't listen to him or believe that I sent him?" asked Millie.

"Millie. Hector can talk a jackass into braying at the moon! Trust me. He knows how to get folks to do what they wanted to do already, and he has a great mind for remembering figures. He'll do a fine job."

"We'll do whatever needs to be done. But, Millie. Ye must know by now ye and Midge belong here. Or maybe I just know it."

His voice came to a halt and he was afraid he had said too much already. "Do you mean that, Jack?"

"Yes, Millie. I want ye and Midge to be in my life. I'm hoping you'll consider that thought."

"Oh, aye, Jack MacKinnon. I believe that can be arranged," and her smile lit up the room as it always did for Jack.

Chapter 71

Alex had spent the entire day walking over the farm seeing what needed to be done. This place, his home, had never been so precious to him. Perhaps he had always taken it for granted. After Culloden, seeing all those men die, and then Ian's leg and the desperate journey to find Caitlin, he would never be so callous again and would thank his lucky stars from this moment on. Each day he watched in amazement as Caitlin and Millie brought life back into this house. Mam had to be smiling, he thought. Her presence seemed closer than ever.

Coming back into the lodge and walking down the hallway, Alex's nose brought him to the kitchen.

"Ah, Alex! Come. Taste this," called the old wizard.

Wabi had been busy creating some sort of dessert he called Pain au Chocolat and was going to serve it after dinner tonight in celebration of something, but no one seemed to know exactly what.

Alex took the spoon and licked it clean.

"What do you think? Is it edible?" asked Wabi.

"Ummm, not sure. Let me have one more taste," teased Alex.

"Well. Then I'll take that as a yes!" Wabi replied.

Alex continued assessing the place, now from the inside. With Caitlin, Millie and little Midge joining the group, he wondered if Da would be wanting to add on more rooms. He watched as Millie placed her meal on the table. Alex knew she had been worrying there wouldn't be enough, but he assured her it was plenty. But as he looked at the table now, they were elbow to elbow. In addition to himself, there was Da, Jack, Hector, Ian, old Jamie, Uncle Wabi,

Caitlin, Millie, baby Midge, and the farm hands, Donald, Kenny and Hamish. Jack had put two tables together and now they could seat everyone. Quite a gathering!

As they finished their delicious evening meal, Alex thought it appropriate to make a toast now that all the family was back together and everyone who had been injured was on the way to recovery. He took his spoon and tapped the side of his glass, which held a tasty wine that Uncle Wabi had come up with from who knows where! Just as Alex was about to deliver his well- rehearsed speech, Da, Wabi and Ian, hobbling along with his crutch, got up from the table and made a quick exit, saying to "hold on just a minute, Alex. We'll be right back." So, he continued standing, waiting for them to return.

Da entered first, holding the door for the other two. Wabi came in next, carrying his dessert on a dish above his head in a very dramatic fashion. Lastly, Ian came through the door. He tossed his crutch over to Jack and walked across the room unaided, wearing a wooden prosthesis that Wabi had carved for him. The prosthesis was covered with a leather boot fashioned by Da, and the entire creation was a work of art. Ian grinned from ear to ear as he sauntered around the room with just the slightest limp, but nothing that would cause him any problem for anything he wanted to do.

Alex, Jack, and Hector jumped up from the table and gathered around Ian. "Whoa! Look at ye! Ye three have outdone yeselves for sure!"

All the brothers were talking at the same time, so happy for Ian they could barely keep from tearing up themselves.

"We'll have a ceilidh and invite all the neighbors! This calls for a great celebration!" said Hector, already planning what to serve.

Alex once again tapped his glass and was about to deliver his speech when the front door swung open and a very old man came in, hanging his tam on a peg with the others. Everyone stopped and turned toward the old one.

The old gentleman, weathered and wrinkled, looked at this gathering of folk, folk he thought was his family. But for the life of him he was a little confused.

Reaching up to scratch his mostly bald head, he looked about and looking from one to the other he began,

"I do say! When I left here there was just ye bunch of ugly sheep herders, and now I see two lovely ladies and a young lad with two feet! Mayhap I be at the wrong place, but I sure hope not!"

Laughter rang throughout the room. Alex reached the old man first, giving him the traditional MacKinnon hug, which was hardy.

"Uncle Andrew! It's about time!" Jack grabbed him for another hug.

"And, aye, ye be at the right place, too, Andrew." Da chimed in.

"But ye be wrong about one thing. There are actually three lovely ladies with us now!" Jack held little Midge up high in the air as if he had something to do with her being here.

Alex gave a big smile in all directions. He shook his head, lifted his glass and simply said, "Thanks be to the Creator for this gift of family." "Amen to that!" This coming from Uncle Wabi.

***

Caitlin glanced over at Wabi, and an unspoken communication flowed in both directions. How had she been so lucky as to have had this special man for an uncle, a friend, and mentor? The Creator must have had his or her reasons, and Caitlin would forever give thanks.

She was surrounded by all these unbelievable people who would make her life richer and more complete. She found herself wondering who the true healer was. Was it her? No. Not even a great healer such as she could provide the healing that this family brought to herself, Millie and Midge. Perhaps it was a contagious disease. If so, then may it spread and be filled with magick!

***

Some time later, after all had found their beds, Alex gently placed Caitlin on her bed in Mam's room still. Alex acknowledged to himself that he had much to learn about this woman. And some of it he may never understand. Then so be it. She was his.

He sat down on her bed, and without more words, he leaned down and kissed her. And this time it was a kiss that spoke of the passion he had held back for what seemed like an eternity. And Caitlin's response told him, she, too, had been waiting a long time to give in to her own passions.

***

The first indication of perhaps a thunderstorm came in a distant rumble . . . then it came closer . . . and closer still. Then lightning streaked across the sky and it seemed the entire universe came to life!

"Oh, Jesus! What now?!" asked Jack.

Dear Reader,

Healer's Magick was written at a furious pace, and I hope it stimulated you to read it in that same way. The characters, Caitlin, Uncle Wabi, Owl, and the MacKinnon clan kept me on my toes. Even I was never sure where they may lead us! Well, they are constantly in my head, and presently, Caitlin has learned much about the MacKinnons from Uncle Andrew, their bard. Of course, she knows nothing about her own family, so this interesting old bard has her curious to know more about her ancestors, and she has to find a way to learn more about them. So, you'll see Caitlin, Uncle Wabi, perhaps Flinn, and a few new characters in the next novel, which will be out very shortly. Of course, there may possibly be a magical character or two from the animal world too!

Some of my friends have offered feedback already, which is delightful. I am hoping to have some from you as well. It will be from you that I know how to take these characters on to their next magical adventure. Let me know your favorite characters and any other pertinent information you feel would be beneficial to me as an author. I would truly love to have your comments.

Reviews are difficult to get, and one from you, my reader, would be so appreciated. Through you, I will be successful in this endeavor. Your input is meaningful, and thanks so much for following my characters on their many and varied adventures. You are the reason they exist.

Thanks again,

F. L. Karsner

About the Author

F. L. Karsner is a fifth generation Floridian who grew up in a rural Panhandle village near Tallahassee. In the late 60's, she married a Navy Ensign and followed him from Florida to the South Pacific island of Guam. It was in the Navy that she first experienced different lands, peoples, and cultures all of which would forever influence her view of the world.

On returning to Florida, she and her husband raised two daughters. She received her Bachelor of Science in Nursing from Jacksonville University, became a Registered Nurse, and began to pursue her love of the art and science of medicine. The care of cardiac patients took her from the nursing floor to the cardiac catheterization laboratory to clinical research, ultimately becoming a Certified Clinical Research Professional. To maintain her interest in the arts, she painted, created pottery, and sang in the Sweet Adelines as she moved from Florida to Georgia, North Carolina, Tennessee, and finally back to the Sunshine State. At the millennium, she was President of her own consulting company which provided clinical research services to the domestic and international pharmaceutical markets.

Today, she lives with her husband on the Intracoastal Waterway in Ponte Vedra Beach surrounded by the marsh, two rivers, a resident eagle, and untold hawks, egrets, raccoons and slithery friends. Her new novel, HEALER'S MAGICK, is the first in a magical realism series set in the 18th century Scottish Highlands.

She can be reached online at flk@flkarsner.com.

Find other books by F. L. Karsner at Amazon.com and other online book sellers.